# Exiled Heart

## Jennifer Haynie

# Other Books by Jennifer Haynie

Last Chance Series

*Operation Shadow Box*
*Operation Peacemaker*


Unit 28 Series

*Orb Web (short story)*

*Panama Deception*

*Loose Ends*


The Athena Trilogy

*The Athena File*


Other Books

*Hunter Hunted*

To Steve, my beloved, for encouraging me in my writing.
You will always be my sweetheart.

And afterward, I will pour out my Spirit on all people. Your sons and daughters will prophesy, your old men will dream dreams, your young men will see visions.

—Joel 2:28 (NIV)

# Preface

I like to watch home improvement shows, especially those where the contractors take an old house, rip it down to the studs, and redo it, making the original house with its good bones even better. I see *Exiled Heart* in the same way. The first edition came out in November 2012 through a publisher. Due to a series of fortunate (or unfortunate) events, depending on your perspective, I got the rights to this novel back, which has enabled me to take a look at it in view of my current writing style. I knew the novel had good bones, and Claire and Ziad's story was too powerful to leave it as it was.

I decided to rip away the old writing, to take their story down to the studs in terms of plot and character. Like a contractor who removes walls to create a larger space, I took a hard look at the scenes within the novel and removed some to take out more than 16,000 words. The plot for *Exiled Heart* remains the same, as do the major characters. Combined with editing to fit my current writing style, this intensified the romantic and suspenseful sides of the plot.

I left the setting to take place in 2009 and 2010. Ten years ago, smartphones and iPhones were just beginning to become commonplace. Social media had yet to proliferate and become the societal force that it is to say. Some might even say that our country was kinder and gentler at that point. That doesn't mean the tensions that are out in the open weren't there. They were, most likely seething below the surface. As you read about Claire's and Ziad's struggles, you may find yourself sad, angry, maybe even outraged. I encourage you to keep reading. And may you find blessing as you do so.

# List of Characters

*Main Characters*

Ziad al-Kazim (38) – Saudi Arabian National Guard colonel, based in Jeddah, Saudi Arabia

Claire Montgomery (35) – Flight nurse in Charleston, South Carolina

Ben Evans (39) – FBI junior attaché based at the Jeddah consulate

Emma Montgomery (33) – Ben's fiancée and Claire's sister


*Minor Characters (in order of appearance)*

Sami Rafiq – Saudi Arabian National Guard major, based in Jeddah

General Tariq al-Talil – Ziad's commanding officer and Sabirah's second cousin

Prince Yasin – Minor prince in Saudi Arabia

Muhummed Amir (12), Tariq (10), Basil (8), Khalid (6) al-Kazim – Ziad and Sabirah's children

Adnan Rahman – Ziad's attorney in Jeddah

David and Allison Montgomery – Claire and Emma's parents

Elizabeth McMillan – Bible study leader and mentor

Sonja Williams – Claire's best friend and Circuit Solicitor for Charleston County

Mike Winthrop – Clerk at the port where Ben picks up his Forester

Special Agent Angie Rogers – Ben's Unit Supervisor at the FBI and Zap Task Force member

Mrs. Chitworth – Claire's elderly neighbor

Eddie Davis – Ziad's mentor at the Charleston PD

Alan Rothschild – Detective at the Charleston PD

Faith Montgomery (22) – One of Claire's identical twin sisters

Note: Claire has three other sisters beyond the two mentioned above: Allie (39), Delia (31), and Grace (22).

# Notes and Glossary

Saudi Arabia's work week varies from that of the western world. The work week begins on Saturday and ends on Wednesday. The weekend culminates on their holy day, which is Friday.

One of the biggest challenges of this novel is to convey that Ziad speaks English as a second language while Ben speaks Arabic as a second language. When Ziad speaks English with no contractions (I will run vs. I'll run), he's speaking in English to Ben. However, he'll use contractions with his point-of-view for thoughts and actions. It will be the reverse for Ben. When he's speaking Arabic, he won't use contractions. This style of language, while sounding more awkward to native English speakers, conveys the language that is a second language for the character (English for Ziad, Arabic for Ben).

I've supplied the glossary below to enable you as a reader to understand the terminology without interfering with the point of view of the characters.

Abaya – Long black robe worn by women

Ana behibek, habibti. – I love you, sweetheart (said to woman).

As-salaam 'alayka – Peace be unto you.

Gutra – Checkered headdress worn by Saudi men

Habibti – Feminine version of sweetheart

The Haj – Pilgrimage completed by all Muslims, one of the five pillars of the faith

Hasana'at – Reward for good deeds

In sha'Allah – God willing

Isa – The most common Arabic name for Jesus

Jinn – Spirits that cause mischief

Majlis – Open meetings held by Saudi royalty to listen to their subjects

Majlis hareem – Room in the house where women can receive other women as guests

Marhaba – Hello

Matawaen – Saudi Arabian religious police

Muhalliabia – Pudding dessert popular in Saudi Arabia

Sayia'at – Reward for bad deeds

Thobe – Long white robe worn by Saudi men

Wa-alaykumu as-salaam – And unto you peace

# 1

*April 2009*

Ziad al-Kazim tore through the night. He gasped in the fetid, salty air in the humid darkness of Jeddah's port. His quads burned. The metal siding of warehouses blurred as he ran.

His fleeing suspect dashed ahead of him.

The young man hung a hard right. A whump echoed when he slammed into the side of a warehouse.

Ziad followed.

The suspect raised a pistol.

Gunfire popped.

Ziad fell to a crouch, and the bullet cracked over his head. Bolting to his feet, he rounded the corner and pushed off from the warehouse. As his sides heaved, he slowed to a halt.

Shipping containers blocked the suspect's escape. He whipped around.

His Beretta raised, Ziad shouted, "Drop the gun. Now!"

The pistol clattered to the ground.

"Hands on your head and get on your knees!"

The young man complied.

Ziad kicked the pistol away. It skidded into a pile of fetid garbage stacked against a container. After holstering his gun, he approached the suspect. "Trying to escape, are we?"

The young man spat a curse at him.

"Shut up." Ziad stepped behind him and gripped his wrist.

Like a snake, the suspect grabbed his arm and flipped him over his shoulder.

Ziad crashed onto concrete. The breath whooshed from him.

The suspect reached for his pistol.

"No," Ziad mouthed. No sound came out as he tried to suck in air. He kicked at his legs.

The man hit the ground with a grunt.

Ziad pounced and banged the young man's wrist onto the hard surface. The Beretta's blast nearly deafened him as a shot went wild and pinged off the side of a container.

Pain arced up Ziad's arm. He yelped and released the suspect.

Gun still in hand, the young man scrambled to his feet—and froze.

FBI Special Agent Ben Evans stood with his Glock pointed at the man's heart. In Arabic, he said, "I would not do that if I were you. On your knees with hands on your head. Now."

The young man hissed another curse, this one about Americans.

"Just what part of that did you not understand? On your knees." Ben jerked the pistol. "Now, or you get to find out how good of a shot I am. I do not aim to injure."

The suspect's shoulders drooped. He sank to his knees.

Ziad pushed himself to his feet. "I thought I told you to stay and observe."

"Just providing assistance, my friend." Ben's aim never wavered. His lips quirked upward. "You look like you needed it."

Ziad winced as he checked his arm. Red teeth marks had already formed. "Nothing I couldn't handle."

Ben snorted. "How about cuffing the guy so we can get a move on it?"

Ziad did exactly that and hauled the young man to his feet. He gripped his arm and twisted the collar of his fatigue jacket in his hands. "You and I? We're going to have a talk."

The man squirmed. "I'll never tell you anything."

"Oh, I think you will because your friends are already in military police custody." Ziad fast-marched him toward the warehouse where the chase had begun.

Members of his Saudi Arabian National Guard military police team had set up a perimeter. Ziad shoved him through a crumpled metal pedestrian door hanging from one hinge. Inside, lights blazed. Exhilaration coursed through him when he noted the suspect's two friends on their knees, hands cuffed behind their backs, heads hung.

The young man froze.

Ziad forced him down. "Do you know how long we have tracked you? You and your two friends? We know you came to meet your supplier. And now you will tell us who he is. Major!"

"Sir!" Sami Rafiq approached and saluted.

"What have you found?"

"We're searching."

"Get these three to Headquarters. I'll interrogate them later."

"Yes, sir!" Sami barked orders to his crew. They hauled the suspects to their feet and dragged them outside.

"Where are the dogs?" Ben asked.

"On their way." Ziad glanced at his watch. "I called the contractor an hour ago."

Dogs began barking in the distance. They came closer.

The junior FBI attaché grinned. "On time. Good, Swiss, precision time."

"Hah."

"Ziad." A deep voice, one that told him his commanding officer, also his wife's second cousin, had arrived.

He whipped around and found General al-Talil striding toward him. His heart pounded. What was he doing here? This was typical business.

Then he remembered who owned the warehouse. He saluted. "Sir, it is good to see you. Why are you here?"

General al-Talil smiled. "I signed off on this raid, remember? I wanted to see your results."

"Nothing yet." Warmth began in Ziad's neck. Oh, he didn't want to come up short on this one.

"The dogs are here." Ben offered a hand. "General al-Talil, so good to see you."

"And you too, Special Agent Evans." The general greeted him with a handshake. "Let them search. In the meantime, brief me on what happened."

Ziad kept his eyes on Sami, who led the Swiss handlers into the maze of crates in the cavernous interior. "We had the warehouse surrounded. I sent the battering ram in. One of them escaped through a window. I chased and apprehended him."

Ben winked and said not a word as Ziad continued the briefing.

His radio crackled with Sami's voice. "Sir, we found something. Northeastern corner."

"On my way." Ziad broke into a jog as he hustled toward the other end.

A Belgian Malinois sat beside his handler.

Sami paced nearby.

"What are you waiting for?" Ziad grabbed a crowbar and began working at the top. "We need to get that crate open. Now."

A sergeant joined him.

With a screech of nails on wood, it popped up.

Ziad stepped back. "Get it off."

Two others shoved the lid aside. Packing straw flew through the air.

His hands met a rough weave, and he peered inside. "Rugs?"

Ben joined him. "Looks like it."

"Get one out."

Two privates heaved a roll onto the floor.

With his foot, Ziad shoved the material. It uncurled, and he grunted in satisfaction. Before him lay a cardboard tube the rug had been wrapped around. Plugs blocked the ends. Strange. Why the need? After pulling on nitrile gloves, he knelt and popped one out. He shook the tube.

Plastic bags full of white powder slid onto the rug. "Ben? What do you think?"

Ben crouched beside him. "It could be Zap. It depends on where this crate came from. If it's Afghani, it probably is."

Ziad closed his eyes as weariness filled him. He rubbed his chin. "I never thought I would say the Kingdom had a drug problem."

Ben shook his head. "Me neither."

Ziad straightened. His knees protested, and he muffled his groan. "We need confirmation. Major, I want all of the warehouse's records seized. No questions from anyone. Not even Prince Yasin."

Sami nodded and entered the order into his Blackberry.

A commotion at the front of the warehouse caught Ziad's attention. He tensed.

A man wearing a red and white checkered *gutra* and a white *thobe* marched toward him.

Ziad didn't miss the gold trim along the edges of the black robe he wore over the *thobe*. Or the aides who flitted around the warehouse's owner.

Prince Yasin. Why should he be surprised?

*Breathe. Slowly. Deeply.* Anything to dispel the anger creeping into his soul.

Prince Yasin put his hands on his hips. "How dare you come in here without my permission! What is the meaning of this?"

Ziad approached him and stared into the shorter man's eyes. "Your Highness, how dare us? When we find what is most certainly the drug Zap in one of your crates?" He brandished the package. "Perhaps I should be saying, 'How dare you?'"

The general inserted himself between them and forced him back a step. "Your Highness, we received credible evidence someone was transporting Zap into the country and stowing it in your warehouse. Some of our men were caught as dealers who were due to meet their supplier here tonight. Would you know if anyone would have access to this space without your permission?"

"Perhaps." Face reddening, Prince Yasin focused his ire on Ziad. "I love the Kingdom. Why would I endanger it by poisoning our youth? Certainly not like America does!" He switched to Ben, who shrugged. "I will gladly supply all of my records to you. Without seizure being required. I'm sure you will find that this crate," he tapped the wood with his foot, "was not among my recent arrivals."

He rubbed his chin and glanced at his aides. Then came that smirk.

Ziad's fists tightened as he battled the impulse to wipe it off the prince's face. He folded his arms across his chest. "Did it just show up? Did someone say, 'I was mistaken and left the crate at the wrong place?'"

General al-Talil almost imperceptibly shook his head as if to say, "Don't go there."

"Or perhaps, Colonel, they got the wrong warehouse." Prince Yasin stepped closer. "It happens all of the time in Jeddah. You and I both know this."

Ziad lowered his voice. "I want those records."

"You can have them." Prince Yasin narrowed his eyes. Once more, his lips twitched upward. "Are you trying to turn this into more?"

Ziad's stomach dropped. "I don't follow."

The prince closed the gap to mere centimeters. "I believe you do. You can't win. You didn't then. You won't now." He backed away a step. "You can have those records, Colonel." He wagged his finger in his face. "But I'm warning you. You are meddling with the wrong person. I would never run drugs in this country. Never!"

He whipped around. Robe billowing behind him, he stalked toward the front of the warehouse. The general followed as if to placate royalty.

The nerve of him! Pain shot through Ziad's jaw. He huffed out a hard breath.

"Down, boy. Down," Ben murmured in English.

Ziad had forgotten about him.

Ben took his arm and led him away from where Sami and his men had begun processing the scene. "What was that all about?"

He didn't want to talk about it. "Nothing."

Ben cocked his head and raised an eyebrow.

Time to focus on the here and now. "I'll have all shipments coming into the prince's warehouses checked. I guarantee we'll find the 'good prince' will claim someone is illegally using his space. Possible but doubtful. Major Rafiq, finish up here. Ben, let's go."

They passed through the shattered door and stepped outside. In the faint light of dawn, he discerned the outline of a SANG Land Rover. In the distance, the call to morning prayers filled the air. "Ben, I must pray."

His friend nodded and leaned against the hood.

Ten minutes later, Ziad joined him and rested his elbows on the cold metal. He scrubbed his hands across his face before pulling out a pack of cigarettes. He shook one out. Using a mother-of-pearl lighter, he lit it as he assessed his next move. "Ben."

"Yup?"

In Arabic, Ziad continued, "I'll prepare a sample of the drug to have your laboratory in the States analyze."

Ben muffled a yawn. "Sounds good."

"We'll also interrogate the suspects and start reviewing the paperwork. Allah willing, we'll have our answers tonight or by Saturday. Meet me after sunset prayers at our usual spot, and I'll give you a report."

"That I can do." Ben clapped him on the shoulder. "You did a good job. We will find the supplier and get those drugs off the street."

"You helped."

"Nah. Your case, your glory. I'll see you soon."

"*Insha'Allah.*" Ziad nodded. He watched as Ben climbed into a Subaru Forester. Then he nodded to his driver and slid into the passenger seat of the Land Rover.

A drug bust. Three suspects in custody. He congratulated himself.

All in a good night's work.

# 2

At the end of the day, the Wednesday evening sun poured through the windows of Ziad's office. Light almost seared his retinas. Hah. No, they burned from exhaustion. Smothering a yawn, he pored over the handwritten notes he'd made during the course of his investigation into the arrival of the drug Zap in the Kingdom.

Nothing made any sense. It wouldn't. Not when he could barely keep his eyes open. Making himself comfortable would help. With chin in hand, he closed his eyes. Just for a few seconds. Then he'd get to work again.

A door creaked open.

He jumped.

Sami grinned. "I didn't mean to disturb you, sir."

Ziad swiped at some drool seeping from the corner of his mouth. He coughed. "I… was awake. What do you have?"

"Hard copies of the photos we took during the interrogations." Sami laid them on his desk. "I've placed the digital images on the server along with the MP3 files of the interrogations."

Ziad flipped through the glossy prints, then shoved them away. "The files we requested from Prince Yasin?"

His executive officer groaned. "There's so many!"

"How many?"

"I counted a hundred file boxes. They fill our largest conference room."

Ziad's eyes narrowed. "I'm sure he intentionally mixed them up."

He studied the major. Dark shadows under his eyes. Two days of stubble on his face. Not that he looked any better, at least judging from the last time he'd glanced at himself in the mirror. "Go ahead home and get some rest. We'll deal with them on Saturday. Have a good weekend."

"I will, sir." Sami reached for the doorknob.

"And Sami."

He paused. "Sir?"

"Good work."

Another smile. "Thank you, sir."

Ziad spread the photos on his blotter. They were of the hands of the three suspects. On the left hand of each, between the ring finger and pinkie, was a tattoo, one of the Arabic word for Brother. The tail of it extended approximately a centimeter onto the top of the hand. He remembered his questions. "Who is your supplier? How often did you visit the warehouse? What is your manner of communication with him? What is that symbol on your hand?"

Not that he got answers. Hah! Hardly. Each man sat stone silent, yet he hadn't missed the fear in their eyes when he mentioned transfer to SANG headquarters in Riyadh. After they thought about it over the weekend, they had one more chance to confess.

Ziad lit a cigarette and began writing his notes on a notepad as he recalled all of the events of his forty-eight-hour day. As he added them to the case file, he glanced at the clock. Almost time for sunset prayers. Maybe he could make it to the mosque near the coffee shop where he would meet Ben. Rubbing his chin, he winced. Time to clean up. And rest. He turned to place the folder in a file drawer in his credenza.

*Stop!*

He jumped. "I'm so tired I'm hearing things now,"

The drawer scraped as he opened it.

*Take it!*

He whipped around. No one. Not Sami. Not any others on his staff. A chill shimmied down his spine. Were the *jinn* after him? He set the folder on the desk and stared at it.

*Hide it!*

Should he? Why? It wasn't like he was a criminal. The three men residing in the brig had that honor.

Grumbling, Ziad undid the clasps holding all of his notes and placed them in the scanner on his desk. It began the slow process of scanning no less than fifty pages into a PDF format. A sigh escaped him as he waited. At last! He inserted his personal jump drive, placed the PDF file on it, and copied other files related to the case, including the MP3 files of the interrogation. He looped the drive's lanyard around his neck and slid it under his shirt.

His gaze shot to the clock. Too late to go to the mosque for prayers. He completed them alone in his office. Or tried to. Yawns interfered. Such was his life at the moment. At least he had a couple of days off that included his weekly meeting with Ben.

Ziad rose and stuffed his beret onto his head. As he left, he touched his chest and felt the hard outline of the jump drive. Only then did he head into the cooling April air.

"So sorry I am late, my friend." Ziad said in English as he joined Ben at their favorite coffee shop near the edge of one of Jeddah's more fashionable shopping districts. With a steaming brew in hand, he pulled out a chair. "I had to eat supper and find parking."

Ben, who'd stretched his legs under the table while he fiddled with his phone, shrugged. "No worries on my part. I've been texting with Em. Seems she found her dress online."

"How is she?"

His friend smiled, and his eyes took on a sparkle that wasn't there when they talked work. "Wonderful. She's been at the consulate as she's worked on wedding stuff with her mom. She's using our Internet connection so she doesn't drive the *matawaen* crazy looking at wedding dresses."

Both men chuckled.

Ben yawned. "Sorry. I told her I needed tonight off. You're such a slave driver."

Ziad laughed. "I never heard you object to joining us on our raid."

"You got me there. But you're glad I'm did, right?" Ben nudged him.

"Thank you for not telling the general you were the one who made the suspect give up."

"Never, my friend. Like I said, your case, your glory. What did you find out?"

Ziad glanced around. In a low voice, he began speaking in Arabic. "Nothing. Prince Yasin sent me all of his records. A whole conference room's worth."

"Not surprising."

"Exactly. We'll get through it. As for our suspects?" Ziad shook his head. "They refuse to talk. Although I noticed something." He spread his left hand on the table and pointed to where his little finger and ring finger joined near his gold wedding band. "All three of them had a small tattoo here that extends a little onto the top. No larger than a centimeter in diameter. I made photographs of it."

"What was it?"

"The Arabic word for Brother."

"Like brother-in-arms?"

"Perhaps. Since all three of them had it, I wonder if it's a way to mark them as being part of the same network."

"Or gang," Ben turned his cup in his hands and then took a sip.

"Gang?"

Ben nodded. "You have heard of gangs."

"In America, yes."

"Right. Usually, they have tattoos that mark them as being in one particular gang. Like the Crips. Or the Bloods."

"We have no gangs here."

"I guess what I am trying to say is maybe this is a way to identify these guys. From what the DEA has told me, this Zap, this purified form of heroin, is making its way across the world through the States and Europe. Asia too." He sipped some more. "Maybe they use tattoos as a marking to identify operatives they might not know personally and who may be spread across the world. This Saudi end of things—what you busted this morning—could be one cog in a very big wheel. Could be the big boss is here."

Ziad lit a cigarette and puffed away as he considered his theory. "It's possible. Every rug in that crate we found was loaded with Zap. And another crate as well. Approximately one hundred kilos. You said how much can kill?"

"The DEA thinks just a gram. Users shoot up and get crazy highs, at least until it bioaccumulates enough. Then it is lights out."

"Yes, it's quite possible that just a part was meant for here. Prince Yasin is known as a worldwide trader."

"Or traitor." Ben steepled his fingers and rested his chin on them. His lips curled.

"Hah. Perhaps."

"But he is royalty."

"Minor royalty."

"But royalty, nonetheless."

Ziad rolled his eyes. "Who cares? The man is a fool."

"Even fools have millions, and he stands to make more if he is the supplier." Ben leaned forward and rested his elbows on the metal table. In English, he asked, "What's up between you and the prince?"

Ziad stilled, then closed his eyes and rubbed his temples to stave off the sudden tension in them. Maybe deflection would help. "Would you like to go camping in the desert before it gets too hot?"

Ben's eyes narrowed. "After the raid, you looked as if you wanted to pound him to a pulp. You were grinding your teeth."

"I was not."

"Yes, you were. I've been out to the stables with Em. I know what it sounds like when horses grind their teeth."

"I am not a horse."

"No, but you sounded like one."

Ziad folded his arms across his chest. "I really do not want to talk about it."

"I've got all night." Ben reached out and snagged Ziad's keys off the table. "And now I have your keys. So unless you want to hot-wire your Land Rover, let's hear it."

Ziad groaned and pinched the bridge of his nose. "We are in a… a feud."

"A family feud?" Ben leaned closer and in Arabic asked, "Like the Hatfields and McCoys?"

"Who?"

"Two families in the States who were bitter enemies. I guess you could say they became a metaphor for bitter feuds."

"Yes, we're like your Hatfields and McCoys." Sweat broke out on his hands as he continued in English, "I really do not want to talk about it."

"Look." Ben glanced around as if to ensure they were alone. "I'm here as a listening ear and someone who might have a different perspective."

Ziad considered his motives. A curious friend. Nothing more. "This goes no further than you?"

"Promise."

"Not to Emma or her aunt and uncle?"

"Promise. Scout's honor."

Ziad stubbed out his cigarette on the table. "In the early nineteen hundreds, the House of Saud began uniting clans to form the Kingdom. Back then, the al-Kazim clan was huge. My great-grandfather was the leader, and my grandfather had ten brothers. We were closely allied with Prince Yasin's clan since both were Hejazis and resistant to uniting with the House of Saud. My grandfather was the youngest."

Ziad lit his final cigarette of the day. "When he was about six or seven, Prince Yasin's clan betrayed the House of al-Kazim. The House of Saud offered them a royalty position through the marriage of one of their daughters—if they helped defeat the al-Kazims and other Hejazis in and around Jeddah. They agreed." His free hand gripped the edge of the table. "One night, we al-Kazims met Prince Yasin's clan at an oasis near al-Sharana for a celebration. The men all gathered in a tent on one side. On the other side, the al-Kazim women and children gathered."

Ben began shredding his cardboard cup holder. "I'm afraid to ask what happened."

Ziad's jaw tightened. "My grandfather was too young to attend with the men. He had a hiding place at that oasis, and he snuck out of the tent where he should have been sleeping. His mother sent his older sister Hanan to find him because she knew his hiding place." Metal bit into his fingers. "Just as she was about to scold him and make him return to the tent, screams began erupting from the men's tent. You see, Ben, Prince Yasin's clan brutally murdered all of the al-Kazim men. All of them. Close to twenty-five. My grandfather's nine brothers? Gone."

"Wow."

"Once they finished at the men's tent, they did the same to the al-Kazim women and children." A line of pain opened up along the fingertip of his index finger. "My great-aunt and grandfather witnessed it all. They realized the only way to survive was to remain still. By dawn, the murderers were gone. Only my grandfather and great-aunt remained. A twelve-year-old and six-year-old!" He released his grip and glanced at his finger. A line of red had formed. He pressed it against his pants leg. "They had no choice but to try to make it to Jeddah. They took a camel and made it to the outskirts before my grandfather collapsed from exhaustion and dehydration. But they had arrived at the edge of the al-Talil camp."

"Sabirah's family?"

"Right."

Ben sat back. "Well, I'll be!"

"What?"

"An expression. Go on."

In Arabic, Ziad continued, "They adopted them as if they were family. My great-aunt never let my grandfather forget what happened. She told him every chance she got. And also that he was the last al-Kazim left. He knew his duty. To produce sons to restock the clan and to take revenge for what had happened. He married into one branch of the al-Talils. My father married into another branch, and obviously, I did the same." Oh, did he remember his father's charge to him shortly before he married Sabirah. In a low voice, he added, "My four sons are the start of the rebirth of our clan."

Arms folded across his chest, Ben frowned. "If Prince Yasin's clan betrayed you by going over to the House of Saud, why are you so loyal to the crown? It does not make sense to me."

"Something happened between the House of Saud and Prince Yasin's clan. His own great-grandfather must have displeased the king somehow because he wound up where Prince Yasin is now, a small prince of a small part of the Kingdom near al-Sharana. Meanwhile, the al-Talils, being the smart merchants they were, saw no future in continuing to resist. They turned and united with the House of Saud. Since my grandfather was under their protection, he had to acquiesce and limit his feud only to Prince Yasin's clan. He vowed to protect the House of Saud." Ziad stared at the pile of scraps in front of Ben. "Did I make you nervous?"

"Nope. Bad habit, I guess." He pushed some of them around. "I take it that is why Prince Yasin insulted you like that."

"Yes."

"Ziad, my friend, you must let it go."

Ziad glared at him. "Let it go? I can't! You of all people should know that."

"Look." Ben sighed and continued in English, "The good prince is baiting you, okay? He's trying to make you lose your head on this."

"Lose my head?"

"Act on those old grudges."

"I will not."

"And, my friend, it might be good to consider ending it. Before anyone—you or them—does any more damage."

Ziad's eyes narrowed. "You know that is impossible."

Ben shrugged.

Cheeks flushing, Ziad asked, "Have you ever had someone act grossly against you?"

"Yeah, I have." Ben winced. "My biological father. He walked out on Mom and me when I was six. Left us with nothing. No money. No shelter, not even suitcases for our clothes." He leaned forward and rested his elbows on the table. "We were homeless. Mom's parents took us in until she could get her nursing degree. It took five years for us to get out on our own."

He stared at the table and took a deep breath.

Ziad tapped ashes into his empty cup. "If I have upset you—"

"No, no. I was remembering. Yeah, I had some huge resentment against my father. It hit big time after Mom married Dad. I had to work through it, let it go. And to do that, I had to forgive. If Jesus could forgive me for my sins, who was I to hang on to old grudges?"

"I do not need a religion lesson." Ziad took a drag and jabbed his cigarette out.

"I know." Ben dumped his scraps into his empty coffee cup. "Look. We're both tired. That's another conversation for another time, okay?"

Ziad tossed the butt onto the pavement. "Enough of this." In Arabic, he said, "We should probably leave."

"Yeah. Hey, I have a question for you."

Ziad cocked an eyebrow. "What is it?"

Ben's Adam's apple worked. "Em and I set our wedding date for March twenty-seventh of next year. In Charleston."

Suddenly, Ziad realized the implication of his words. His stomach dropped. "Does that mean your time with us is drawing to a close?"

"Not for another year or so, but yes." Ben shifted his cup between his hands and continued in English, "Her contract's up next March, and I can understand why she wants to live in the States. Sorry, but I have to concede to her wishes on that one."

"I understand, my friend." Ziad winced. "We will miss you. Having you here these past three years is," he struggled for the right word, "a blessing."

"I've been honored to work with you as well." Ben raised his gaze, which remained sincere in the dim light. "I do have one question for you."

"That would be?"

"In weddings in the States, we have a tradition where the bride and groom have friends who have meant much to them stand with them when they say their vows. And you, by far, have been my closest friend during these past three years. I know it takes some planning, but I would be honored if you'd be my Best Man."

"Best Man?" Ziad frowned.

"Oh." Ben chuckled. "Emma said I'd better explain it to you. The Best Man is the groom's best friend. Sometimes it's his dad. Look. You've kept me out of trouble. You've had me into your home. We've been through a lot together. I want you as my best friend to be there with me."

"I would be honored. And Sabirah would be greatly pleased for a trip to the States. We could leave the boys with Mama and Papa. Yes, that would work very well."

Ben checked his watch. "If you don't mind, I'll head out. I know it's early, but I'm exhausted."

"I will see you Thursday night." Ziad rose, and they shook hands. "Until then, Ben."

He headed to his Land Rover. Thoughts whirled through his head. Ben's impending marriage and move. Their discussion about his family feud. And visiting Charleston the following year.

None of it mattered at that point. The weekend had arrived. He planned to enjoy it.

"You knew I was going to be gone for a couple of days." Half an hour later, Ziad folded his arms across his chest and glared at his wife.

From where she stood in the doorway of their master suite, Sabirah leaned against the door frame. She closed her eyes. After a deep breath, she shook her head. "That's not my point. You snapped at Khalid when he only wanted your attention so he could show you the perfect score he got on his letters."

Ouch. She was right. All four boys had ambushed him when he'd arrived home. Twelve-year-old Muhammed Amir with the grade from his math test. Tariq, his second at age ten, babbled about the video game he'd been playing. Then eight-year-old Basil, the budding engineer of the family, pushed forward to show him a bridge he'd made. And finally, little Khalid at the tender age of five had squealed for attention of his own.

What had he done?

"I need *silence*, Khalid."

That produced tears from his youngest.

If anything he'd learned in his nearly nineteen years of marriage, it was to apologize when required. Now, he hung his head. "I'm sorry."

"I know." She stepped forward and wrapped her arms around him. "You're exhausted."

"I am." He felt the curves her caftan hid. He buried his face in her neck. Hmmm. Jasmine, the scent he defined as her, filled his nose. "Could I stay like this all night?"

She chuckled. "I wish. Change. After evening prayers we can all have some of that *muhalliabia* you like."

His stomach rumbled at the mention of dessert. "I'll be down in a few minutes. But first…" He threaded his fingers through her ebony locks that hung to mid-back. He kissed her long and deep before whispering into her ear, "Perhaps we can have a little time together this weekend."

"Maybe so." She ran her hand down his cheek. "Join us when you're ready."

Once she shut the door behind her, his smile faded as he undid the tactical belt to his uniform and shucked his fatigue jacket. He knelt at the edge of the Oriental rug in the sitting area of their suite. After rolling it up, he counted eight tiles from one wall and eight tiles from the one perpendicular to it. With his fingers, he pressed on all four corners at once. It popped up. Using his fingertips, he lifted it free. Beneath it sat a compartment he'd installed upon buying the villa to house sensitive information related to his work.

Only he knew about it.

Not the children or his parents.

Not even Sabirah.

Ziad lifted the lanyard from his neck. For a moment, he rubbed the drive with his thumb. That same chill from earlier washed over him. He shivered and placed it in the compartment. Maybe after they solved this case, he'd laugh about his paranoia. Not now. He returned the tile and rug to their places.

Once cloaked in a *thobe* and a pair of sandals, he joined his family downstairs.

Papa gazed at him with that disapproving stare that would have raised his anger if he hadn't realized the way he'd wronged his youngest son. Mama chatted with Sabirah and Rani, their housekeeper. The boys huddled around the television as they played video games.

"Khalid," Ziad softly called.

Eyes downcast, his youngest rose and approached his father.

Ziad knelt in front of him. "Son, I am sorry for the way I snapped at you. I was tired, but that's no excuse." He reached up and pushed a lock of downy hair off his son's forehead. "I love you."

Khalid threw his arms around his neck. "I love you, too, Papa."

Tears sprang to Ziad's eyes over those simple words. Out of the corner of his eye, he caught Papa nodding in approval. He pulled back. "It's time for evening prayers."

Ziad, his father, and his sons lined up and faced Mecca. Behind him, Sabirah, Rani, and Mama covered their hair. As his lips formed the words, a feeling he could only describe as serenity overtook him.

An hour and a half later, Ziad's yawns came every minute as he finally crawled into bed.

Downstairs, Sabirah laughed at something Mama said.

He closed his eyes and fell into a deep, hard sleep.

# Exiled Heart

He awoke and stared at the top of a tent. Screams erupted. He bolted to his feet and burst into the hot night air. He stood not in his suite but in an oasis. In front of him, his family lay in pools of blood.

His eyes snapped open. Sweat sheened his forehead. His breath came out in a hard gasp.

Beside him, Sabirah slept in a nightgown. She remained oblivious to his nightmare.

*It's okay. I'm fine. I'm safe. So is my family.* Ever so gently, he took her in his arms and molded his long frame to her petite one. He buried his nose in her hair as he repeated those four sentences to himself. Deep inside, he wasn't so sure he believed it.

# 3

Early Saturday afternoon, Ziad slicked back his damp hair and gazed at himself in the mirror of the master suite's bathroom. What a great way to begin the work week. Midday prayers. A meal with Sabirah. A bit of romancing afterward. Well, a lot. A grin teased his lips. His cheeks heated, and he opened the door to the bedroom.

His beloved pulled the covers up and fluffed the pillows. Now, she wore a deep blue caftan rather than the western-style dress she'd sported when he'd arrived home for lunch. She almost ran into his arms.

Blessing. That's what Ben would have said. Ziad held her close and kissed her on the top of her head as he wove his fingers through her damp tresses. "We are so perfect for each other, *habibti*. Allah be praised he brought us together!"

She pulled back. Her lips trembled, and tears pooled in her beautiful, dark eyes.

"What is it?"

Her hand shot to her face as she turned away.

He put a hand on her shoulder. "What's wrong? Did you and Emma argue last night when she visited?"

"No, no." She turned, and her taut features relaxed a little. "Not at all."

She drew in a shaky breath.

He skimmed her cheek with his fingers. "Is it Khalid? You said it's a mild fever he woke up with this morning."

"I…" She shook her head and sighed. "I'm fine. Just much on my mind."

He knew to let it rest. She would share when she was ready. And truly, he had to return to work. "I'll leave early and be back by afternoon prayers."

She nodded as she busied herself with straightening the picture of her in her wedding finery that was on his dresser.

Ziad pulled on his fatigue jacket, then buckled the tactical belt around his waist. After ensuring the strap was secure over his gun, he rubbed her shoulders. "When I get back, I'm sure Khalid will be running around, maybe even in the pool." He nuzzled her hair. "Look at it this way. You got a day off from work."

"True." Sabirah turned and coiled her arms around his neck. She kissed him until his knees trembled.

Ziad seriously considered calling in sick for the rest of the day. "I love you, *habibti*. I'll see you tonight."

He headed down the hall to the bedroom of his youngest. He peeped inside. Surrounded by toys and stuffed animals, Khalid slept on the floor with a blanket over him. He'd tucked his favorite toy, a stuffed dog Ben had given him, underneath his chin.

Ziad knelt and kissed his hair before retreating downstairs. Mama and Papa had gone for the morning, as had Rani, so he let himself out and settled behind the wheel of his Land Rover. As he passed through the villa's auto gate and turned onto the highway leading to SANG head-quarters, his mind switched to work. A light load today. A staff meeting, then going through those blasted forms Prince Yasin had sent.

Once at the office, he passed through security.

As he walked by Sami's cracked door, murmuring caught his attention. He paused and listened.

His executive officer talked in low, urgent tones. Had they received a lead on the case?

Sami would tell him when he was ready.

Once settled behind his desk, Ziad checked his e-mail. Nothing of great import. All the better since he planned to leave early.

He glanced at his chrome in-box. A single sheet of paper sat atop some files. Ah. He nodded in approval as he noted a schedule of Prince Yasin's activities for the next few days. Sami must have printed it. He picked up a couple of folders. All routine paperwork. Nothing he couldn't handle tomorrow. Right then, he needed to prepare for his weekly staff meeting.

"Sir."

Ziad glanced up from his notes. "What is it?"

Sami gazed at him. "Um, sir, we, uh, have a problem."

"A problem? Too many boxes to review? We can pull in additional staff."

Sami fidgeted with the pen he held. "It's not that."

Ziad rested his elbows on the desk. "Then what is it?"

"It, um, well…" Sami shifted from foot to foot and stared out the window next to his boss. "It has to do with our suspects."

Ziad's chest tightened. "What about them?"

"Uh, I don't know—"

"Out with it, Major."

Sami's eyes widened. He took a step back. "They're gone."

"What do you mean, they're gone?"

"They're… not there."

Ziad jumped to his feet. He pushed past his startled executive officer and blasted through the door leading to the outside. The bright sunlight nearly seared his retinas. Squinting, he raced down two buildings to the SANG brig.

Sami followed on his heels. "I went to check on them and—"

"Quiet!"

"Yes, sir." Sami nearly ran into him as he flung open the door.

Behind a ratty desk, the receptionist scrambled upright and saluted.

Ziad ignored him. He raced down the hall to the three cells holding his prisoners.

Nothing but concrete, single beds, sinks, and toilets. Could they have been transferred to Riyadh without his permission?

He dashed to the small office of the officer in charge of the brig. "Captain!"

The captain, a wiry man a good ten centimeters shorter than Ziad, met him with a salute. "Sir!"

Ziad jerked his head toward the door. "Where are the prisoners?"

"We released them."

Ziad's eyes narrowed. "By whose orders?"

The captain frowned. "G—General al-Talil's orders, sir."

Ziad leaned on his hands against the desk. "The general left this morning and is in Riyadh until tomorrow."

The captain scooted backward. "Sir, I saw him with my own eyes." He picked up a clipboard and leafed through it as if to reassure himself. "He signed for their release at 1115 hours."

"Let me see."

"What?"

Ziad held out his hand and snapped his fingers. "The forms, Captain."

He handed him the clipboard.

Ziad studied them. Messy handwriting, so unlike the neat, curving loops of his superior. Release time: 1115 hours. He checked the signature. Illegible. "What did this 'general' look like?"

The captain chewed on his lip. "Like General al-Talil."

"We'll check. I want to look at the video of this lobby."

The captain's cheeks reddened. "It… has not worked in a month."

Ziad cocked his head. "A month? Why not?"

"I hadn't placed the work order yet."

With a low growl, Ziad tossed the clipboard onto the desk. "Why didn't you contact me?"

"I didn't think it was necessary."

Ziad crowded him against the wall. "No one should have signed them out without my express permission."

The captain's eyes widened. "But the general—"

"I. Don't. Care!" Ziad whipped around. "Major!"

Sami cowered near the door.

Ziad stalked toward him. "Come with me. We're calling General al-Talil. Now."

They retreated to his office.

Sami jumped when he slammed the door. Once the dial tone filled the room, Ziad punched in the number for General al-Talil's cell phone. He messed up, then tried again.

"General al-Talil."

Ziad glanced at Sami, who hung his head. "Sir, Colonel al-Kazim and Major Rafiq here. We have an issue."

"What is it?"

Ziad paced around his desk. "The suspects were released without my approval. The captain of the brig said you signed for them."

"I did what?"

Ziad repeated himself.

"Impossible. I didn't come into the office because I took the ten o'clock shuttle to Riyadh."

Ziad quickly did the math in his head. The general would have left for the airport straight from his house. "I agree, sir. Someone impersonated you."

The line fell silent for a few moments. Then came a sigh. "What's done is done."

Ziad threw his hands in the air. "It's blown the whole case."

"Not if we catch them. Do what you need to do to find them. When you do, arrest them and take them immediately to the airport. I'll have a plane waiting to take them to Riyadh. I'll be back tomorrow evening, and I'll expect a report."

"Yes, sir." Ziad hung up and sat down on the corner of his desk. He rubbed his chin as he considered the monumental task before them. "Major."

Sami kept his gaze pinned to the concrete floor.

"Sami, look at me," Ziad softly added.

Like a whipped dog, Sami met his gaze with a sideways glance.

Ziad returned to his chair. "Send out teams to stake out our suspects' houses. Their mosques. Gyms. Unit buildings here at Headquarters. Coffee houses. Anywhere where they might go."

Sami finally met his gaze, if only for a brief second. "Already done, sir. That's what I was doing when you got back from lunch."

"Good." He clapped him on the shoulder. "Then sit tight."

His executive officer slipped from the office.

Ziad focused on the single sheet of paper he'd left on the blotter. Prince Yasin's schedule. Had he… Who else would have done such a thing? Prince Yasin had stashed the drugs in his own warehouse. He'd do anything to thwart the investigation.

Ziad grabbed his beret from the blotter and yanked his keys from his desk drawer. He bolted through the door.

Sami nearly ran into him in the hallway. "Sir, where are you going?"

"To see the prince."

"Shouldn't we—"

"I'm following a lead." Ziad stalked toward the outside door. "Isn't that what as military policemen we're supposed to do?"

"But the general said—"

"I'm doing my job," Ziad whirled on him, "and that is following all possible leads. And yours?" He jabbed him in the chest. "You get those teams reporting to you and let me know what they find out when I return."

"Yes, sir." Sami almost squeaked out those words. He scooted around him and fled.

Ziad slid behind the wheel of his Land Rover. An hour's ride up. Half an hour talking with the prince. An hour's ride back. He'd be home in time for sunset prayers.

Easily.

Sami could report to him via phone. In the meantime, he relished the opportunity to have a little chat with the prince.

# 4

Ziad shut the door to his Land Rover and stuffed his beret on his head. Even with wraparound sunglasses, the sunlight radiating off the desert floor of al-Sharana nearly blinded him. Sweat beaded on his scalp. What a horrible place.

Nearly a kilometer away, Prince Yasin's palace loomed. From there to where he stood, cars lined the edge of the road. Sleek, shiny Mercedes sedans all the way to battered pickup trucks with peeling paint. All had gathered for the prince's monthly *majlis*. Here, all men were equal, from the richest banker to the lowliest laborer.

That included SANG colonels.

By the time Ziad reached the towering portico, sweat poured down his back. Hot wind had blown dust into his face. What he'd do for a cool shower right then! He barely nodded at the two local policemen who stood guard at the entrance.

Once inside a vestibule with mahogany inner doors soaring toward several-meter-high ceilings, he paused. Two more policemen stood next to the inner doors with rifles slung over their shoulders. More window dressing than anything else.

A Yemeni man in an ill-fitting suit rose from behind a Louis XIV desk. His smile revealed two large front teeth with a gap. With beady eyes he noted the crown and two stars on Ziad's collar. "Colonel, may I help you?"

Ziad removed his beret. "I must visit with Prince Yasin."

"If you would put your name on this list, he will see you." The secretary held out an acrylic clipboard with a fresh list on it.

Ziad headed toward the doors.

The two guards blocked his path.

The secretary cleared his throat and offered the clipboard again. "Colonel, I ask that you put your name on the list."

Ziad snatched it from him and scribbled his name before shoving it back. The outer doors opened. A couple of old Bedouins hobbled up to the secretary's desk. Then the biggest banker in al-Sharana and a couple of young, poor fathers with their small sons in tow. All of them added their names to the list below his.

Ziad paced the elegant marble floor. The sooner he got inside, the sooner he could be on his way home. He checked his watch. 4:30. He'd broken his promise to Sabirah. He dug out his cell phone. "Sabirah."

"Where are you?" she asked.

"Al-Sharana." He glanced at the secretary, who conferred with an aide. "I won't be home by afternoon prayers but should be there by sunset prayers."

She sighed, and he envisioned her thoughts. Thanks to work, he'd reneged again—a constant source of friction in their marriage. "I suppose I'll see you then."

*Don't snap back.* He hung up and dialed Ben. "My friend, how are you?"

Ben chuckled. "Very good. I am headed to see Emma. She called in sick today."

"You'll have a better time than I." Ziad filled him in on the day's events.

"Be careful. The prince can be like a lion. Nice until you get between him and his food."

Ziad shrugged. He could handle him.

"Let me know what happens."

"I'll call you later." With that, he shoved his phone into an outer pocket of his pants. The doors opened, and he spun around.

The secretary called names. Ziad started when the banker stepped through the doorway.

"What is this?" He gestured to the doors. "He arrived after I did. Why does he get to go before me?"

No apologies. No nothing except for a small bow from the secretary. "I'm sorry, but the prince asked you to wait."

Heat began building in Ziad's neck. His hands tightened into fists. "I must see him. Now."

"It was his request, sir. I'm sorry."

Ziad muttered and resumed pacing. The sun set. His stomach rumbled, and hunger made him ornery.

"Sir."

He glanced up.

"Prince Yasin will see you now."

The guards opened the doors, and he strode into a huge hall twice as big as the footprint of his villa. All around him, those who had already visited with the prince sat with various aides. Several began leaving.

And Prince Yasin?

He held court on a gold chair atop a marble dais. An aide sat at a small table beside him and took notes on a laptop as one of the young fathers made his case with passionate pleas. Prince Yasin murmured something. He rose and held out his hand. The man grabbed it and feverishly kissed it, all the while jabbering his thanks. With an aide, he headed toward an empty desk.

Ziad marched toward the dais.

Another aide scooted in front of him. "Sir, you are not next. I'm sorry, but—"

"Let him approach." Prince Yasin straightened. "Colonel al-Kazim, it is good to see you."

Time to work the plan he'd formulated on the ride up. Cut to the chase first. Ziad folded his arms across his chest and raised his chin. "Where are my suspects?"

"What?"

"Where are my suspects?"

The prince cocked his head. "What are you talking about?"

Voices faded to silence as more aides approached.

Ziad continued, "They were released without my authorization."

The prince started chuckling. He shook his head.

The aides on the dais nervously joined him.

He stopped and glared at Ziad. "Colonel, you seem to have picked up some very nasty habits from your pushy American FBI friend. What was his name?" He gazed at the ceiling and tapped his chin. "Ah, yes. Special Agent Evans. Perhaps you've forgotten your manners. And to whom you speak."

"I've forgotten neither, your Highness." Ziad kept his gaze on the prince. "Nor have I forgotten what we found in your warehouse a few nights ago." He mimicked the prince's chin tap. "Of course. Rugs containing a special derivative of heroin called Zap."

Startled murmurs rippled through those closest to the dais.

A smirk curled Ziad's lips. Score. The first part of his plan had succeeded. Apply discomfort by stating his case in front of witnesses.

Prince Yasin raised his voice. "Have you found that crate on your forms, Colonel?"

"We will."

"I told you. You're wasting your time. And now, you're wasting mine." Prince Yasin resumed his seat and gestured for his aide with the clipboard to step closer. "Who is next?"

The man glanced at his sheet. "I think—"

"I'm not finished, your Highness." Ziad stepped onto the dais and pushed the aide aside. He'd expected this deflection.

"I have nothing more to add. Your suspects." The prince shook his head. "Tsk. Tsk. Tsk. Pity your men are so incompetent." He shrugged. "Your problem, not mine."

The nerve of him! Ziad clenched his jaw. "No, it's yours!"

The aide put his hand on his shoulder. "Sir."

"Take your hand off me!" Ziad shoved it away and turned back to the prince. "I'll ask one more time." He spoke slowly as if to ram home his point. "Where are those suspects?" He leaned forward until their faces were centimeters apart, a move that had always worked during interrogations. "I know you sent an imposter to pose as the general."

Prince Yasin's dark eyes narrowed. They blinked slowly like those of a lizard. He stroked his bearded chin, then chuckled. "Yes, Colonel, I would say you have a lot of gall to come here and accuse me in front of my subjects. But you have to remember one thing." He rose and forced him back a couple of steps as he picked up a sheet of paper. "I can tear your career apart like this, do you understand?" He ripped it up and let the pieces flutter to the floor. "I warned you to back off, did I not? Repeatedly. Yet you've refused!" He paused. A sneer curled his lips. "I told you before. You can't win. Not then. Not now." He wagged his head. "Poor Ziad. The house of al-Kazim. What do the Americans say? So yesterday's news. So twentieth century."

Red crept into Ziad's vision. He grabbed at the prince and came up with a handful of *thobe*. They grappled. The prince's robe fell to the floor.

Prince Yasin struggled against him. "Let me go, you fool!"

Someone yanked Ziad off the dais.

Chest heaving, he glared at the prince. Blood pounded in his ears.

An aide offered Prince Yasin the gold-trimmed black robe. He stalked toward Ziad as he drew it over his *thobe*. "I've had it with you, Colonel al-Kazim."

Ziad tried to break free of the guards. He spat a curse in the prince's direction.

The guards tightened their grip.

Pained burned across his arms where they held him.

Prince Yasin stopped mere centimeters away. His eyes almost glowed with rage. "You forget one thing. You can't touch me. Just as dusk cannot touch dawn, you cannot touch me!"

He jabbed his finger into Ziad's chest.

More pain blossomed.

"If you think you can, I will tear you apart so badly the only thing you'll be able to do is sweep floors for the rest of your life. Just like your grandfather! Adel, get me General al-Talil on the phone." Prince Yasin turned away and settled on his chair. "Guards! Remove him."

The local policemen maintained their grip on Ziad as they almost dragged him to the massive doors, through the lobby, and to the portico. They thrust him onto the marble, where he nearly fell down the steps.

Ziad caught a column and regained his balance. Behind him, the doors thumped closed, and the two policemen stepped in front of them.

On the long walk to his Land Rover, his adrenaline drained away. He began trembling.

Bad. Bad. Bad. He'd erred. Seriously so. To the point where he'd probably face discipline. He recalled Ben's warning. What had he done?

Somehow, he made it to his SUV and turned onto the highway. The shakes worsened, and he pulled off to the side of the road. Maybe hearing Sabirah's voice would calm him. When she answered, he sagged against the leather seat. "I'm so glad you answered."

"What's going on?" Worry laced her words.

"I erred badly." He pinched the bridge of his nose as a headache kicked up behind his eyes. His stomach rumbled as a reminder of the supper he'd missed. In the barest of words, he relayed what had happened.

"Oh, Ziad."

He grabbed onto her soft voice like a lifeline. "I'm sorry."

"It's not your fault."

"It is. Totally."

"We'll be fine. We have each other, right?"

His smile trembled a little. "I love you."

"Come home. Tell Sami where you'll be in case the general calls. I promise tomorrow will be better. If anything, I'll talk to my cousin. He's a reasonable man, after all."

"Oh, I'll be getting a call, for sure."

Suddenly, he knew home was where he wanted to be. His eyes shot to the gas tank needle. Almost empty. "I need to get petrol. Then I'll be on my way. I'll be there by 8:15."

She hesitated.

"Sabirah?"

"I thought I heard something downstairs. I'll see you soon."

"I love you, *habibti*."

"I love you too." The smile in her voice sent waves of relief through him.

Ziad sat there for a moment longer. A truck blew by and shook the Land Rover. Dust from the highway muted its headlights. He put the SUV into gear. Then he pulled onto the road and headed toward home and Sabirah's arms.

# 5

Weariness. To Ziad, it didn't feel like 8:15 when he pulled onto his street. More like midnight. The auto gate slowly opened to reveal darkness. Strange. Sabirah always turned on the outside lights at dusk.

Ziad remained in the Land Rover and collected his thoughts. Consequences from his actions awaited him. Papa would be embarrassed, Mama worried. Regardless, he'd report only the truth to the general.

With a deep sigh, he pushed open the door and approached the front steps. His keys slipped from his fingers and clinked on the concrete porch. Grumbling, he picked them up. The bolt slid back, and the door opened on soundless hinges.

"Sabirah?"

Nothing. That same darkness clung to the interior. Had everyone decided to go to bed early? No. His wife would have left a lamp on for him.

"Muhammed Amir?" he called.

No answer from his oldest.

A shiver worked its way up his spine. Stepping into the great room, he turned on a lamp next to the couch and faced the kitchen. After approaching the pass-through window and the archway leading into the room, he flipped on the overhead light.

His eyes widened.

Rani lay on her back, gunshot wounds in her chest and stomach. Dark red blood pooled on the tile beneath her.

"No!"

Rationality fled as panic set in. He dashed up the stairs to the residential wing. "Sabirah! Muhammed Amir! Tariq!"

Each child's name flew from his lips as he rushed upward.

He tripped on the top step.

Ziad tumbled to his knees, then staggered upright.

He caught the door frame leading to Khalid's room and slapped the light switch.

Khalid lay in the middle of the area rug, his *thobe* red going to rust with blood from multiple gunshot wounds.

"No!" Agony colored Ziad's cry. He fell to his knees beside his youngest. No pulse.

Jumping to his feet, he stumbled toward Muhammed Amir's room.

Light revealed the horror of books spilled across the floor and an overturned desk and chair. His oldest lay crumpled against the wall, bullet holes in his head and chest, blood and gore on the wall behind him. His lifeless eyes stared at his father.

The same for Basil and Tariq.

Sabirah. Where was she?

He burst into the master suite.

"No! Sabirah, no! Not you! No!"

She lay crumpled underneath the archway that separated the sitting area from the sleeping area. A knife stuck from her chest.

Agony seared his soul as he fell to his knees beside her. He gathered her limp form in his arms and rocked back and forth. "Allah! No! Please!"

The door to the bathroom squeaked.

Ziad whipped around.

A man raced toward him.

Ziad tumbled off balance as he reached for his gun. Stars sparked in his vision when his attacker's fist slammed into his face.

Two shots slammed into a wall.

Ziad rolled to his hands and knees. He thrust out his leg.

His attacker crashed into the nightstand. The lamp fell onto him.

Ziad got a knee under him.

Like a cobra, the man grabbed the lamp. It flashed downward.

Pain exploded in Ziad's head.

He sank into blackness.

Oppressive. For Ben Evans, the word perfectly described the darkness enshrouding him and Emma Montgomery as they sat on the front portico of her aunt and uncle's villa. Temperatures remained in the nineties, and the humidity so characteristic of Jeddah summers had arrived. It made it hard to breathe, almost like he was drowning. Thank goodness for a sea breeze.

Soft notes emanated from the guitar he plucked. He glanced up when Ziad's white Land Rover turned through the auto gate across the street.

"Ben?"

At Emma's soft voice, he paused. "What's up?"

"Can we talk?"

Uh, oh. She'd stayed mad when he'd blown her off Wednesday night. He paused. "Yeah?"

From where she'd lain on the rattan sofa since supper, she pushed herself upright. "I'm worried about Sabirah. You know I went over there Friday night, right?"

"Yeah. What happened?"

It took fits and starts, but gradually, she revealed their conversation. As she finished, his heart simultaneously sang with joy and pounded with worry. "Wow. I... never knew."

"I didn't either." She sighed and leaned forward as she raked her hands through those light brown curls he loved. "Oh, we'd talked about it here and there, but never in my life..."

Ben slid over and held her. Her forehead, still warm with that day's fever, rested against his cheek. Dove soap and shampoo scents tickled his nose. "You know how life-changing that is." He paused as he struggled for the right words. "She may very well go to her grave with that. If Ziad knew… He's a proud man, Em."

"I know. Ever since he got home earlier this evening, I worried he'd read it on her face."

"What?" He pulled back and stared at her. "He just got home a few minutes ago. I saw his SUV."

"I saw him arrive when I was talking with you on the phone while you were on your way over here for supper. If he just got home, maybe he ran some errands."

"That can't be." Coldness washed over him. "I talked to him literally five minutes before I called you. He was up in al-Sharana, which is an hour away from here."

"Then who—"

"I wish I knew." Ben rose and peered through the ornate latticework covering the portico. Only one streetlight a couple of houses down lit the area. Shadowy forms slipped through the pedestrian gate of the al-Kazim villa and scurried through the darkness.

In the distance, sirens began wailing

His hand went for the gun he didn't have with him. "Something's not right. Go get your aunt."

"What?"

The sirens drew closer.

"Get your aunt. Two women equal one witness here. Go!"

Emma fled inside.

Ben bolted through the sitting area of Emma's suite on the second floor. He tore down the front staircase and into the night.

In front of him, two Land Rovers and a Suburban screeched to a stop with sirens strobing red and blue. Six local policemen poured out. They banged on the pedestrian gate. No one answered, and one of the officers raised a radio to his lips.

Ben withdrew into the shadows as more backup arrived, this time in the form of a team with a battering ram. The clang of metal on metal echoed through the thick air.

The pedestrian gate crumpled inward.

Most of the team rushed inside.

Heart pounding, Ben approached the guards.

One of the soldiers noticed him. His hand shot to the rifle slung over his shoulder.

Ben raised his hands and called in Arabic, "I mean no harm."

"Who are you?"

"Ben Evans. American FBI. May I show you my ID?" Ben kept his hands visible and his movements slow. "It is in my pants pocket."

The soldier nodded.

Ben slid out his cred pack. He flipped it open. "See? I am American FBI. May you take me to your commanding officer?"

The sergeant slung his rifle back over his shoulder. "He's inside."

"What is going on?"

"We got a call about gunshots at this house." The sergeant kept his gaze focused on Ben.

"I do not understand."

From within the villa, someone shouted. Feet scuffled. Two soldiers dragged Ziad, his hands cuffed behind him, through the pedestrian gate.

Ben stared. "Ziad! What happened?"

His friend stumbled as if not balanced. Blood from a head wound covered his face and streaked his fatigue jacket. His normally slicked-back hair stood out in spikes.

Ben bolted toward him. "Ziad!"

Ziad forced his escorts to stop. "Ben!"

"What—"

"Shut up." The commanding officer shoved him back. Over his shoulder, he called, "Get him out of here."

Ben held his ground. "Why are you arresting him?"

The officer glared at him. "Murder—of his entire family."

"Let me talk to him."

"I'm taking him to the—"

"Please! Sir," Ben softly added when he remembered his precarious situation. "Sir, if I may. I humbly ask for your generosity in that regard."

The officer stared at him, then nodded. "Let him through."

Ben knew he had maybe a minute. "Ziad, what can I do?'

"Call my lawyer. Adnan Rahman."

"Get him out of here! Now!" The commanding officer shoved Ben so hard that he staggered. "Out of my way before I arrest you too."

Ben knew better than to argue and create a potential international incident. He backed toward the Montgomery villa.

A van carrying Ziad sped away. Some of the policemen left while others began milling around.

Sadness ripped through Ben. He glanced toward the upper portico. He didn't see Emma or her Aunt Janet, only their fingers as they clung to the latticework in stunned silence. He faced the al-Kazim villa again. With shaking fingers, he pulled out his cell phone and dialed the number of his administrative assistant. "Carol? Hey, I need your help. Could you find the number of an Adnan Rahman?"

"For the first time since I arrived three years ago, I don't know what to do." A week later, Ben sat in Sami Rafiq's office at SANG headquarters. He rested his elbows on his knees and stared at the painted concrete floor. Over the quiet hum of the air conditioner in the window, he said, "When I visited Ziad this morning, I never saw someone as hopeless as he was."

Sami focused on his desktop. The tendons in the tops of his hands worked as he clenched and unclenched them where they clasped together. He shook his head and in English with the barest of accents said, "This is a frame job."

"Don't I know it." Ben straightened. "I wanted to wipe the smirk from that brig captain's face."

"Ziad dressed him down last Saturday. Big time. Once the local police transferred him here since he's a SANG officer, he personally requested to be on day duty."

Ben's cheeks heated. "Scumbag."

"I'm serious about it being a frame job." Sami reached into a drawer and pulled out a thick accordion file. "The medical examiner is a friend of mine." A smile appeared, then vanished. "He's like I am, a Saudi-American who returned to take care of his ailing grandfather. And now, he has no family here save for him. Because of that, we've become friends, and he provided me with his report on the autopsies. All eight died of multiple gunshot wounds even though Sabirah had a knife in her chest."

"Any ballistics reports yet?"

Sami shook his head. "Those will take a bit, maybe even months. I can say that the number of bullet holes indicates way more bullets expended than he had in his gun. The ME placed time of death anywhere from 1800 hours to 2000 hours."

Ben jumped to his feet and peered over Sami's shoulder. "This is purely circumstantial evidence with no motive, right? I mean, Ziad loved his family."

"But the SANG captain investigating the case has no love for Ziad. Their personalities clash too much, and he's willing to formulate and believe anything, no matter how flimsy."

Ben ran his hands through his hair as he thought about that one. "Ziad said he called Sabirah when he was in al-Sharana. He called me too. Can we verify that?"

A quick smile flashed across Sami's face. "Already on it. I may live in Saudi now, but I understand the need for speed in something like this."

"Let's hope the cell companies do."

Sami scowled. "Don't count on it."

Ben stared out the window. Temps had soared to above a hundred, and the parking lot shimmered in the heat. "He also said he called Sabirah again after he headed out, around seven or so. And he stopped for petrol. Y'all need to talk with the gas station guys. See if someone saw him up there. And get a list of who was at Prince Yasin's *majlis*. If we can place Ziad there at seven, then we're golden."

Sami sighed. "Not so fast, my friend."

Ben whipped around. "What do you mean?"

"In the States, we say innocent until proven guilty. Not here."

Ben swallowed hard. "Guilty until proven innocent."

"Exactly. Courts follow *sharia* law and are very capricious. If the judge hearing his case has a bad morning, he might declare Ziad guilty despite the evidence. And this is a capital offense. He'd have three mandatory appeals that could take fifteen years. In other words, he'd be beheaded or die a pauper since the al-Talil clan has essentially disowned him."

Ben rubbed his chin as he considered the dire outlook. He faced the window again. "It can't get that far."

"How can we avoid it?"

"Weight of evidence." Ben turned and tapped the accordion folder. "We get the ballistics reports. Crime scene photos. Anything and everything. We take enough evidence to the prosecutor so he has no choice but to drop the charges. No prosecutor will go to a judge with a case full of holes."

"*Insha' Allah.*"

"Sami, it'll work." His phone began chiming. He ignored it. "We do our homework—"

"You mean I do my homework." Sami laughed without humor.

"True. I sometimes forget I'm not in the States. I'll take a look at it with you. Then you take it to Adnan. He'll know what to do."

Sami shrugged. "One can hope."

"He will." Ben's phone chimed again, and he checked the number. Work. He had to get back to the office for an afternoon meeting. "Look. I've got to go. Keep me posted?"

Sami nodded. His gaze radiated determination. "You know I will."

"We'll see what happens." Ben opened the door. "That's the best we can do right now. Talk to you later." He checked out, then headed outside. The heat nearly bowled him over. As he slid behind the wheel of his white Subaru Forester, he murmured, "Ziad, we're doing our best. Hopefully, it'll be enough."

# 6

*March 2010*

From where he lay on the bed in his prison cell, Ziad stared at the ceiling. Nothing had changed. Not in the days, weeks, and eleven months since he'd become an unwilling guest of the SANG brig. What did it matter? With Sabirah and his family gone, he had nothing left.

Footsteps approached.

He sat up.

They receded down the hall, just as they had since the interrogations had ceased shortly after his arrest. Elbows on his knees, he winced as he combed his fingers through greasy, long hair almost to his shoulders. And his beard? Heavy and thick since they'd confiscated the razors that had been part of the latest care package brought by Ben a couple of weeks before.

He reached for his Koran, which sat on a table made of concrete blocks. He thumbed through the verses. Nothing in those words comforted him. Ziad rested his head against the wall and closed his eyes. The trial loomed a week away. At least when he was beheaded, he'd join his beloved in death.

The gray of the ceiling blurred. Ziad dreamed in flashes, like bits of a movie popping through darkness. He sat in a garden where a stream emanated from the base of a tree sporting vivid green leaves and bursting with fruit.

Sabirah sat on her knees across from him. His love dressed in a white caftan while he wore a white *thobe*. Her eyes sparkled as she gestured to a set of scales made of gold between them. The base contained the letter Z etched in English. Two trays, one labeled *Hasana'at* and the other *Sayia'at*.

More darkness, then light.

Sabirah cradled a gray stone in her hand. She placed it on the *Hasana'at* tray.

Something thumped.

Ziad's eyes flew open. "Sabirah!"

She'd vanished, just like his hopes and dreams almost a year before.

He lay on his side. The hard concrete beneath the thin mattress bit into his hip and shoulder.

His Koran now lay on the floor. Chalk one more up for *Sayia'at*. With an automatic, muttered prayer for forgiveness, Ziad reached for it. His world swam before him, and he tumbled off the bed. With a groan, he pushed himself upright and set the book on the mattress. He ran his hand along his ribcage where a bruise already formed due to his thinness from barely eating during the past several months.

He cocked his head. More voices in the hallway. And footsteps. Someone was coming.

Ziad hauled himself onto the bed.

The lock rattled in the door.

He stared at the ground.

When the door swung open, the captain of the brig stood there. Not the one who hated him but a new one as of a few weeks ago. "Colonel al-Kazim, you have three visitors. Come with me, please."

Ziad rose, and his world tilted. He swayed but steadied. Almost automatically, he held out his wrists for shackling.

"No need for those," the captain said. "Your friends are here to see you."

Maybe Ben? He was due for his weekly visit.

He shuffled in front of the captain to an interrogation room.

"*As-salaam 'alayka.*" Ben stepped forward and greeted him in typical Saudi fashion with a long handshake.

Sami too.

"*Wa-alaykumu as-salaam.*" His voice fell flat as he exchanged greetings with his former executive officer. He had no energy left to greet his attorney.

Adnan Rahman only nodded, then set his briefcase on a square table and undid the clasps. "Your trial is still set for the eighth."

Ziad slouched in a chair. "I know."

"It is not going to go to trial," Ben said in Arabic. He grinned—positively grinned.

Adnan took off his glasses and polished them with the edge of his red and white *gutra*. "The three of us visited the prosecutor this morning. This time, we had the last piece of evidence to convince him to drop the charges."

Oh, why couldn't excitement greet that bit of news? Ziad tried to focus on his lawyer. "What?"

"The cell phone records." Ben took several papers from Adnan and laid them on the table. "Sami said it would take time to get these, and he was not kidding."

"Eleven months." Sami shook his head. "But worth the wait. They pinpoint your location in al-Sharana and near the petrol station when you spoke with Sabirah for the last time."

"Couple that with the number of eyewitnesses at the *majlis*, plus a negative ballistics report, and the prosecutor agreed to drop the charges," Ben added.

What? Was he serious? Ziad cocked his head. "I'm—I'm—"

"Don't get too excited." Adnan rummaged around in his briefcase and pulled out a folder. "Your release comes with conditions."

Doubt chased away anticipation. He drew in a shaky breath. "I'm afraid to ask."

"We talked about this, remember? Tomorrow, before your release, you'll be publicly flogged."

Ziad winced as if the whip had already struck him. Public humiliation and physical pain would complete his punishment for shaming the SANG and Sabirah's family. "I… I can do that."

"Following that, you'll be exiled from Saudi Arabia."

Ziad flinched. Then he remembered a conversation with Ben when his friend had visited a few weeks before. Ben had begun laying out a plan. "Ziad, my friend, we got the ballistics report back last week. Only three bullets match your gun. The rest are from an unknown weapon."

Ziad hunched forward with his elbows on the table. "That's still enough to convict me since one of those went through Sabirah and my prints were on my gun."

"I know. That is why we need those cell phone records." Ben's jaw clinched. Switching to English, he continued, "Even if we get you released, you're probably going to be exiled."

Confusion washed over Ziad's muddled brain. "Why? I do not understand. This is my home. Upholding the throne has been my life. My life! How can they—"

"Retribution." Ben laced his fingers together on top of the table. "Adnan and I have talked with General al-Talil. He brought up a salient point. He fears additional retribution. Your sister fears the same."

Ziad's head sagged. He couldn't argue, not when his brother-in-law, in his one visit to the prison shortly after Ziad's arrest, had spent two hours haranguing him for shaming the family.

"Thing is, this is permanent," Ben added.

"What?"

"Ziad!"

He snapped back to the present.

Adnan stared at him. "Did you hear me?"

"Uh, no."

Adnan shook his head. "You're to completely divest yourself of Saudi Arabia by selling your house, your rental property, anything you own, and removing your funds from the banking system."

Pain seared Ziad's heart, and he gasped. "Please!" He hated the desperation in his voice. "I'll do anything to stay here. Anything! Even—"

"It's a complete divestment," Adnan said.

Ben briefly touched his arm.

Ziad's world reeled. He closed his eyes. "But... where would I go?"

Ben shifted. "We talked about this a couple of weeks ago."

What? Time had run together for Ziad. Two weeks? Or earlier? No wonder he'd forgotten. "Forgive me. I am not remembering."

Ben leaned forward and continued in Arabic, "I have been thinking about this for a while, and I started talking to some of the guys at the consulate. Look. You have a great reputation there. The staff was more than willing to work to get you a special immigrant visa. It is one reserved for people who worked with our government and are in mortal danger if they stay in their home country. You worked with us on several occasions, especially those related to radical Islamic terrorists. Since we helped you with the Zap bust and your family was murdered, we thought you were eligible."

Now, he remembered. "But I'm not a refugee." Wrong. He had no country now. "But in Charleston, what would I do? Certainly not sweep floors for the rest of my life."

He wrinkled his nose at the thought.

Ben closed his eyes for a long moment.

Ziad fought through the haze of the past several days. Vaguely, he recalled Ben's discussion with him. "We need to talk man to man here. Sami and I paid the general a visit. We presented to him the exact same evidence as Adnan did to the prosecutor. He agreed with our assessment, but he is nobody's fool in many ways. Your career in the SANG is finished regardless of the outcome."

Even today, nausea tinged Ziad's stomach. He couldn't argue with that. A SANG colonel accused of murder—even if found innocent—had tarnished the reputation of the organization. He tuned back into the conversation.

Once more, Ben spoke Arabic. "But he also recognizes your service, twenty years this summer. With your sick leave, you could honorably retire today with full benefits, including a pension—if you will accept the conditions laid out by the prosecutor."

He had no choice. Ziad closed his eyes and took a deep breath. The queasiness remained as he contemplated his next question. "What would I do?"

"This is what we discussed last week, remember?"

"I don't. So sorry."

Ben paused, then took a deep breath. At least he didn't dress him down for words that had fallen into the gray mist of Ziad's malaise. "When I went to Charleston with Emma last summer, I interviewed with the police department in case my transfer with the FBI did not work out. I ran into the chief by chance, and he invited me to come to his office. We talked. I mentioned you, that you were a great investigator with natural skills and talent. You have deep knowledge of Arabic and Middle Eastern culture. You would make a great reserve officer."

Finally, Ziad remembered. He'd be a volunteer, like one of many to fill gaps created due to budgetary issues. But one not allowed to carry a gun or make arrests. That would come in the future. Once he obtained citizenship and the necessary educational credentials, a GED was what Ben had called it. Pity his university degree wouldn't suffice.

"Ziad!"

Irritation pushed at Ben's voice.

Ziad's mind must have wandered again.

Ben paced around the small conference room. "Look. Charleston is the fourth largest port in the States. The DHS guys plus the police department have been desperate for a native Arabic speaker who is familiar with the culture. And a good detective who operates on hunches and instinct is something that is a natural talent, not something that is learned. Just know I had to come clean with the chief."

Ziad flinched. He stood no chance now.

"Rest easy, my friend." Ben resumed his seat. "He reviewed the evidence we had, and he agreed it was a frame job. He is still willing to take a chance with you."

"Perhaps I could live off of my pension, then." Ziad nodded. He could do that. He wouldn't get paid, but at least he be a reserve officer and work on this GED.

"Actually, you would need to hold down a job."

Something they'd not discussed. And another twist in what had turned out to be a labyrinth of complications. "A job? Why?"

Ben straightened. "Because a refugee agency is resettling you, you will be expected to work. Normally, they would be the ones to get you that job, but David, Emma's father and your sponsor, has a client who owns a bunch of convenience stores in and around Charleston. He is holding a clerk position for you in one near the port."

Ziad felt the blood drain from his face. "A clerk? As in..."

No. He couldn't!

Ben bowed his head. His jaw twitched. "My friend, I know it may seem like it is beneath you, especially since the wage is not great. But it is a job, one that you do not have to do forever if you do not want to. Work for a few months until you get your GED. Then maybe you can do another job if you do not like it."

Ziad could only nod. In a low voice, he asked, "Is that all?"

"When you are released tomorrow then you will be in my custody both on and off consulate grounds until we leave the country in two weeks."

Adnan cleared his throat. "What is your decision, Ziad?"

Oh, why couldn't he get rid of the fog in his brain? "I don't know."

Adnan stared at him. "The prosecutor is on his way to the judge's office. If he leaves today without that agreement signed, the trial will go forth as planned."

Ziad drifted to the window. Outside, a merciless sun beat down on the parking lot and bleached out all color. This was his homeland. Or was it? Years ago, Sabirah had become his home. Where she was, so was home. With her gone, his anchor had vanished.

To go would mean turning his back on his homeland. But to stay meant his homeland would turn its back on *him*.

He faced them. "I will. I'll sign."

Ben rose and put his hand on his shoulder. "A difficult decision, my friend."

Ziad eased onto his chair at the table. "Where's the paper?"

"Here." Adnan placed it before him as if it were fine china.

Ziad read through the document. It outlined the conditions for his exile exactly as Adnan and Ben had explained. He signed and dated it.

The captain and another guard served as witnesses.

His lawyer tucked the paper, now worth more than all Ziad had in his bank accounts, into his portfolio. "We will see you tomorrow."

The three men rose.

Ziad bolted to his feet. "Please! Let me go with you tonight."

In his mind's eye, a sword flashed in bright sunlight. His chest tightened, and he sucked down panicked breaths.

Ben must have understood his worry. He gripped him by the shoulders. "My friend, we will be back tomorrow. I promise."

Ziad blew out a hard breath and watched them go.

"Sir, I understand your fear." That came from the captain. "*Insha' Allah* your release will come tomorrow." He tugged his arm. "Come now. Just one last night."

Ziad allowed him to escort him back to his cell. As the bolt slid shut in the door, the same sound echoed in his soul. The die had been cast. The al-Kazim clan was gone now. Never to return to Saudi Arabia. Perhaps gone from the earth. And his own life? His future remained a huge question he didn't want to answer right then. Or maybe not ever.

Pain. It kept Ziad ramrod straight in the consulate's Ford Explorer Ben drove. Each bump sent a jolt up his spine. During the week since his flogging, Ziad had remained bedridden in Ben's second bedroom at the consulate. Only that morning had he felt well enough to rise and venture to his villa.

Now, he wished he hadn't. As the auto gate swung open, his breath hitched. Maybe this hadn't been such a good idea. But he had to gather any belongings he wanted to take before Adnan began overseeing the cleaning out and sale of the villa.

"You okay, my friend?" Ben asked in English.

"It is still painful." Ziad stared at the front porch. The clink of his keys on concrete that fateful night filled his ears. He shuddered.

"I can call Adnan and have his guys start day after tomorrow."

"No." Ziad shook his head. "I—I need to move forward."

"I'll come with—"

"Give me a few minutes alone." Ziad grimaced when he realized how abrupt he sounded. Softly, he added, "Please."

"Understood." Ben cranked up the air conditioner.

Ziad opened his door. At least the humidity hadn't begun creeping into the air quite yet. He eased from the leather seat and hobbled to the front stoop. This time, his fingers remained steady, and he entered the foyer.

The door echoed as it closed behind him, a sound that reminded him of how empty his soul had become. Holding his backpack in front of him like a shield, he stepped into the great room. All nice and neat, just like Sabirah had kept it. Nothing moved, not even the gauzy curtains covering the windows. He avoided glancing at the kitchen where his ordeal had begun.

Where to start?

The wing where his parents had lived. Someone had changed the bed and removed the Oriental rug Sami had reported was stained with his father's blood. What should Ziad take? Pictures, for sure. He had precious few of those thanks to his strict Islamic beliefs. Now, they were his one connection to a life fading to gray. He selected one of his parents together, then found his father's campaign ribbons for his time in the SANG and the jewelry he'd given Mama when he'd wed Sabirah almost twenty years before.

His back protested each step down the stairs, across the house, and up the stairs to where his family had lived. He paused in Khalid's room. They'd removed the creamy carpet since blood had stained it beyond repair. Clean tile glistened in the late afternoon light. He found Khalid's stuffed dog on top of the toy chest. Ziad's back shrieked as he crouched and picked it up. He buried his nose in its soft fur. Little boy scent. His eyes filled, and he swallowed his emotion.

He hobbled to Muhammed Amir's room. They'd taken the mangled desk and chair. Ziad's chest tightened. He glanced at the floor, then upward. His oldest lay against the wall, his head and chest pitted with bullet holes and with blood and gore on the walls behind him. Panic seized Ziad. His shoulders heaved. He backed against the door frame.

Agony seared his spine. He closed his eyes against it.

When he opened them, Muhammed Amir was gone. So were the bloodstains, most likely washed away or covered over by paint of a cheery pale blue. What should he take? A picture. His son had loved going shooting with his Papa, and Ben had snapped one of them at the range together.

Ziad went through the rooms of his two other children. He got pictures of both, a boat from Tariq, and a little bridge Basil had made.

One last stop, one he didn't want to make. He limped to the master suite and stared. No more Oriental rugs. Their bed, as neatly made as it had been after that last time together they'd shared. Sabirah's bell-like laughter briefly filled the room. A lump formed in his throat.

*Breathe. Take deep breaths. Get what you must get first, then focus on her.* That steadied him. He turned his gaze to the sitting area and the tile that concealed his secret compartment. It still looked the same as the others. Hopefully, the investigators who'd gone through the villa hadn't found it. How would he kneel without tearing his healing wounds?

Very carefully.

Grasping the edge of the couch, he eased onto his knees, then crawled to the tile. Once more, the compartment's door popped up at the press of all four of his fingers. He nearly sagged to the floor as he stared at the jump drive. With shaking fingers, he withdrew it and cradled it in his hand.

Ziad fisted his fingers around it. A year ago, he'd been so focused on Prince Yasin and arresting him for running Zap in the Kingdom. Hah! What folly. It had cost him the lives of his family, his dreams, and any hope of remaining in Saudi Arabia. *I should leave it. It's cursed and has brought nothing but pain.*

*Take it.* This time, that voice came in a gentle whisper.

He lowered his head.

He stashed it in an inner compartment of his backpack. Ben didn't have to know about it. Not then. Probably not ever.

After repeating the process in reverse to get to his feet, Ziad approached his and Sabirah's dressers. Emotion tightened his chest as he gazed at the photograph she'd given him ten years ago on their wedding anniversary.

"For you, beloved," she'd whispered as they'd curled up together on their bed. At that point, she'd been almost bursting with their second son in her belly. "I had this taken a few months ago, right before I learned I was expecting Tariq."

He ran his finger across the glass as he gazed at her in her wedding finery. "You saved your dress?'

"Of course! A bride never forgets that day." She leaned over and kissed him slowly. "And that includes me."

"Oh, Sabirah!" He braced his hands against the dark wood and hung his head as his chest heaved. He raised his face. "I can't do this. How... how can I leave?"

He slid it into his backpack, then approached her dresser. In the upper drawers lay all of her jewelry. Most of it had come from the al-Talil clan. Necklaces. Bracelets. Earrings. Rings. He opened velvet jewelry boxes until he came to the one he sought. With trembling fingers, he flipped up the lid to reveal a diamond set in a circle of rubies.

His present to Sabirah on their fourth anniversary, the year he finally understood the way a healthy marriage should work.

"I love you." He uttered those words to the still air.

"I love you, too, my beloved." Sabirah.

He turned. "I can't do this."

She sat on the edge of their couch in her wedding dress, then rose and approached him. "You must. It's the only way." She ran her hand down his jaw. "You will survive. I promise."

"I'm not so sure." He closed his eyes and reached to tuck some of that ebony hair behind her ear. His hand found air. He stared at it. *A hallucination. That's all.* New agony seared him, and he wanted to bellow from the grief.

"Ziad? You up there, my friend?"

Ben. How much time had passed? If the setting sun were any indication, too much.

Ziad stepped into the hallway. He cast a glance at the bed one last time. With a deep breath, he turned to begin the next chapter of his life.

"You know, I've lived here for four years," Ben said as he and Emma stood together a week later in the Jeddah cemetery on top of a hill. "And I honestly don't feel sad or remorseful about leaving."

Emma kept her gaze on the man who knelt at each of seven graves. "What do you feel?"

Ben sighed. "Relief. It burns me that one of the Kingdom's greatest patriots gets framed for murder and jailed for nearly a year, then exiled while the murderers run free."

Nearby, Ziad shifted his prayers to Muhammed Amir's headstone, just as he had for the past fourteen days since his release from jail.

Ziad finally knelt at Sabirah's marker. He bowed his head. Grief choked his murmured words.

Ben shifted his gaze toward where the sun made its descent. His final sunset in Jeddah. He glanced at Emma. The warm wind coming off the desert whipped her *abaya* around her and pushed back her headscarf so some errant curls escaped. She sniffled and lowered her head.

He touched her hand. "Thank you for coming with us."

Her smile was watery. "I wouldn't miss this."

Her presence eased his sadness, if only a little. He approached Ziad and laid his hand on his shoulder as he said in Arabic, "I am sorry, my friend. Sorry for all that happened."

Ziad refused to look at him. "I don't know how I'm going to survive."

Ben remained silent for a few minutes. What could he say? He wasn't the one being forced to leave behind everything he knew and enter a culture that would rub him wrong at every turn. "One day at a time. One hour at a time. One minute at a time if need be, my friend. Emma's family will welcome you. I promise."

Ziad straightened. "What do they know about what happened?"

"Emma's parents? They had to know everything to sponsor you. All the rest of her family knows is your family was murdered and you are coming to the States under a special immigrant visa."

"Even her sisters?"

"She and Claire, her older sister, are very close, but this is your story to tell, not ours."

"I would like for it to remain that way." Ziad focused on him. "To be framed and spend almost a year in prison for my rash actions has greatly shamed me." He shook his head. "They do not need to know."

"Ziad, we promise," Emma said. She glanced at Ben.

"Thank you." As if someone had flipped a switch, Ziad strode toward the Explorer.

Ben followed. He opened the driver's door, then offered a last, backward glance toward the city below and the sea beyond. In a last flash of light, the sun sank below the water. Night had begun. He only hoped the sun would once more shine on his friend.

# 7

Thursday night, Brad Paisley's "Online" blasted from the speakers of Claire Montgomery's Mustang convertible as she turned into the long drive leading to her parents' house. Under-lit trees on each side of the drive slid by. Ah, the feeling of royalty they produced. Three hundred horses pounding under the hood completed the feeling. Her yellow carriage. She pulled up beside a detached garage and cut the engine.

Purse in hand, she bounded up the steps of the farmhouse and threw open the door. "Mama? Daddy?"

"In here!" Her mother's voice floated from the back of the house.

Claire hung a left through the mudroom and emerged in the den.

Beyond open French doors, Mama stood at the kitchen stove and pulled a hot kettle of water off the burner. She smiled over the rims of her reading glasses. "I got some hot water for tea all ready."

"I need it now." Claire hugged her. "Sorry I'm late. Sonja's meeting ran long, which meant we were late meeting up for supper. She promises she'll make it up to you."

"That's all right."

"Where's Daddy?"

"Speaking of meetings, he's with a client at the office. He'll be home by ten."

"Have you heard from Emma?"

"Just a quick call. Their Lufthansa flight got delayed, so they barely made their flight to here. It was a quick conversation."

"Yikes. But they're Stateside."

"Hopefully getting on their plane now."

Claire set her purse on the counter and located her favorite mug in a cabinet. "I told Daddy I'd go with him to the airport."

Mama offered her a small tea chest. "There's not going to be room for you."

Claire froze as she reached for a bag of peach tea. "What?"

"Don't you remember? Ziad's coming with them."

"Wait." Claire frowned as she tried to remember an e-mail Emma had sent her. She dug out her phone and found the message. "That's right. Something about his immigration status was unclear." She set it down. "But I was planning on going with Daddy. I mean, I haven't seen Emma in six months!"

"Neither have I." Mama settled at the kitchen table, reached into a bag, and pulled out a stack of programs for Emma's wedding. "Emma's probably going to have to sit on Ben's lap. Would you want to sit on Ziad's?"

Claire cringed. She, sit on the lap of a Muslim male, a Saudi nonetheless? No way! "Uh, no."

"That's what I thought. Now have a seat."

Claire filled her mug, then joined her on the bench where she'd sat growing up.

Mama paused from leafing through the programs. "Are you still good with Emma staying with you until the wedding?"

"Of course! I've already got tomorrow planned."

Mama set a couple of spools of narrow, navy blue satin ribbon on the table. "What are you going to do?"

"First, we'll sleep in. Then we're going to go out for lunch somewhere. Delia's meeting us. So are Faith and Grace."

"Allie isn't?"

Claire shrugged at the mention of her oldest sister. "She said she's got too much stuff going on during the day. We'll still have fun.

Manicures. Shopping for a fab dress for her to wear at the rehearsal dinner." A grin crossed her lips. "Girl stuff."

They both laughed.

"These turned out great." Claire picked up a program and studied it. "I never knew the printer could do a job like this in ink to match our dresses."

"It took some doing. We need to tie the onion skin onto the front of the program." Mama gently extracted a stack of thin sheets of paper. "Here's how the cover came out."

"Nice." Claire ran her finger gently over the fragile paper, where the theme verse for the wedding was printed. "This is really neat."

"And a lot of work. Emma finally called a few days ago and confirmed Ziad was indeed coming." Mama laid her teabag on a saucer. "I didn't want to send this until I knew who was going to be best man."

"Why was that an issue?"

"Because of his immigration status. Things were… dicey there for a bit."

"Why?"

Mama shrugged. "That's the way they can be sometimes, I suppose. Anyway, we've got a lot to do."

Claire knew better than to press for details. "How much for each ribbon?"

"Let's try six inches."

Claire picked up a pair of scissors and snipped off six inches. She tied it and held up the result. "You like?"

Mama smiled. "Let's start with that."

"Where will Ziad stay?" Claire asked as she began snipping off lengths of ribbon.

"Where we always put guests who are staying for more than a few days. Up in the suite over the garage until he can find an apartment. Goodness knows it's calling it tight. We've got some missionaries who are coming in four weeks, and we told them they could stay there."

Claire thought about Emma's comments regarding Ziad. "She's not told me a lot about Ziad. What's he like?"

Mama shrugged. "I don't know. Ben speaks very highly of him. So does your sister. Ben helped him with a drug bust, and he thinks whoever was behind that murdered Ziad's family."

Claire drew in a sharp breath. Absolute agony. First-hand experience had taught her that.

"Ben knew he was still in danger, so he secured a special immigrant visa for him to come here and start over." Mama tied her ribbon. "And we have only 188 more of these to do."

"Did Emma say anything about their flight over?" Claire asked.

"Oh, not much. Except that Ziad barely said a word. Sounds like he's exhausted."

Claire set down her scissors. "What's on tap for Saturday? Can I go to the fitting with you and Emma?"

Mama finished another program and set it aside. "To be honest, I need your help on some other things."

"Like what?"

"This whole thing with Ziad came at a bad time."

"What do you mean?"

"Normally, we'd show him around. Teach him about things like laundry and housekeeping. Help him get a driver's license and a bank account set up. Get him into an apartment." Mama snipped some ribbon. "We simply don't have time right now to help him with those things—at least not until after the wedding." She laid a sheet of onion skin over a program and laced the ribbon through the holes. "And I doubt Ziad has any idea of what being a best man entails. Or even what an American wedding is like."

"Ben and Emma haven't told him?"

"After everything that happened, I don't—" Mama sighed. "Most of that can wait. But Saturday, I need you to take Ziad. Tell him what he needs to know about weddings. Maybe show him Charleston."

Do what? Show Ziad around? Uh, uh! Claire's hand jerked, and she snipped off three inches instead of six. She tossed the length onto the table. "Why me? I'd planned on going to the fitting and then biking with Anne Marie Saturday afternoon. Why not Allie?"

Her mother gave her That Look over the rims of her reading glasses. "Why not Delia? Or Faith?"

"Delia is on call. Faith is headed out of town Saturday morning for her spring break."

"Why can't Ben do it?"

"Because I need Ben and Emma all day. Look." Mama pulled her appointment book off the notebook that had had been their lifeline while planning the wedding. "At ten is the fitting. Ben's going to meet us after that at the tux store to make sure we have the order right. Then comes a meeting with the caterer at one o'clock. Then with the photographer at 2:30. Then with the party people at four o'clock. Then Ben and Emma are going to supper with their minister."

"Why not tomorrow?"

"Because everyone will be jet-lagged." Mama took off her reading glasses and gave her That Look again. "Claire, why is this such a problem?"

Claire cringed like she always did when Mama drew her name out to two syllables. "I…" What could she say? She'd rather get rabies shots than spend the day in the company of a man who represented all she despised? Mama would never stand for it. "It's, um, not a problem. Not at all."

*Liar.*

"Look. Emma needs your help. Please. Just take him out on the town and get to know him. It might be good since he'll be your escort for the weekend."

*Oh, yeah. That's right.* Ziad was best man, partner to her as maid of honor, and essentially her date for the weekend since she had no boyfriend.

Whether she liked it or not. Whether *he* liked it or not.

But to help Emma, she'd do it, even if it meant counting the minutes until she could be rid of him. "All right."

"Good. Now tell me how Sonja's adjusting to married life."

Claire let the subject drop. They chatted about nothing in particular until heavy footsteps clomped in the mudroom.

"Allison? Claire?"

"In here, darlin'," Mama called.

"Daddy!" Claire jumped up and hugged her father.

He kissed her hair. "Good to see you, sweetie."

Claire appraised the flowers she'd nearly squashed. "Bouquets?"

"Wild flowers for Emma and yellow roses for your aunt." Daddy kissed Mama. "Honey, I need to head out."

"I'll put them in some water." Mama took the flowers.

Claire's thoughts turned to the impending arrival and what it meant. Emma, her sister, her best friend, would shift her loyalties to her new husband. An expected change but one that stung a little. Suddenly, she wanted to be alone. "Mama, do you mind if I head to the dock?"

"Not at all." Mama cast a glance at the programs. Only a few remained. "Run along. I can finish these in ten minutes."

Claire slipped onto the screened-in porch at the back, then wandered down a path between the live oaks of the back yard. Willows along the banks of Willow Wood Creek hid the dock beyond from the house.

Her boots touched wood, and she wandered to the end of and eased onto wood planks still warm from that afternoon. She leaned against a piling. Cool air washed across her face. She closed her eyes. Weariness oozed over her as a week of working nights as a flight nurse finally caught up with her. Water lapped at the pilings. Beneath her, a small splash broke the rhythm as a fish jumped out of the water. Oh, what good memories she'd made out here.

"Do you know how to find the Big Dipper?" Twelve-year-old Claire had asked ten-year-old Emma.

In the gloom, Emma's eyes widened. "How?"

"Start with the North Star." Claire pointed to the night sky. "Then go here. And here."

"Show me another one." Emma pulled out a book on constellations. Under the dim glow of a flashlight, they picked out several more. Finally, after Claire called it a night, Emma took her hand as they walked to the house. "Let's always do this."

Now, Claire swallowed the lump in her throat. A little over ten years before, things had been flipped. Claire had been the one getting married, and Emma had been her maid of honor. Claire knew she would have been part of the wedding party for Emma, but never had she planned on being single again.

*Lord, you have a plan in this. I know you do. I'm just having a hard time seeing it. Show me how to be a blessing to Emma instead of a burden.* Slowly, it came to her. *Take care of Ziad on Saturday.* She muffled her groan. *Lord, that's not what I meant, but because I love Emma, I will.*

She lay back, and her mind wandered again, this time over the years she and her sisters spent splashing in the creek and exploring nearby Sutton Hall Plantation. She dozed.

"Claire! Hey, Claire! Are you down there?"

Emma.

Claire climbed to her feet.

"Claire!" her younger sister shrieked.

Emma nearly bowled her over. Laughing, crying, they jumped up and down and hugged each other.

Claire held her at arm's length. "Oh, Emma, it's so great to see you!"

"Boy, it's good to be back! I can't wait until I can see everything in broad daylight."

"Where's the rest of the crew?"

"Up at the house. They're pooped, so I told Mama I'd come and get you so we can get going."

"Let's go, then. Where's your stuff?"

"Daddy already threw it into your car. Although my huge suitcase wouldn't fit into the trunk. It's in the backseat."

"Then all's well and good. On the way there, fill me in on your trip."

"I will." Emma grinned. "Ziad didn't want to talk about anything on the flight over, so he has no a clue about anything."

"We'll take care of it." Claire offered what she was sure was a sick smile. One could hope they'd not be a best man and a maid of honor with black eyes from fighting so much.

# 8

The next night, Claire stopped the Mustang in the driveway in front of the garage at Mama and Daddy's place. She stayed glued to her seat as she contemplated the evening ahead. Her hands remained curled around the steering wheel. She swallowed hard and glanced at her sister. "I'm sorry about earlier today. I in no way meant to smear Ziad's rep."

Emma, who'd barely said a word on the ride over, shifted. Her fingers skittered over a shiny mixing bowl full of salsa. "And I'm jet-lagged. Look. I know what happened two and a half years ago. Ziad's not like that. All I ask is that you be nice to him for one week."

Claire stared at her freshly done French manicure. Did she really believe her? *Face value. That's all Em asks, and you promised her.* "I will."

Her sister smiled. "Thanks. You ready to go?"

"I got the other bowl." Claire hopped out and extracted a smaller bowl covered in cling wrap.

She followed Emma onto the porch. Her breath hitched, and she tucked an errant strand of hair behind her ear.

Ben opened the door. "Hey, love-of-my-life." He swooped Emma into his arms and laid a kiss on her lips. He grabbed Claire and planted one on her cheek. "Hello, second-love-of-my-life."

"Are you trying to score points with your future sister-in-law?" Claire drawled as she disengaged herself.

Ben laughed. "I'm trying."

"You're doing a good job." She led the way back to the kitchen and uncovered the bowl. "Where are Mama and Daddy?"

"Out for the evening with your aunt and uncle." He peered over her shoulder. "What's that?"

"Salsa. Mama should have some chips here."

"In the cabinet. Ziad and I already discovered them. What's March Madness without chips?"

She glanced into the den. A basketball game flickered on the television. "What did you two do all day?"

"Slept until about eleven. We had some lunch. Then your daddy took me to get a rental car while Ziad crashed here. We kicked around the soccer ball some out front, watched more ballgames, and napped. I've been teaching Ziad the rules to basketball. Time well wasted if I don't say so myself."

Cellophane crinkled as Emma opened another bag of chips. She winked at Claire. "You've been busy. Here. Try some."

Claire's lips twitched in a smile.

"The Montgomery salsa? I remember that from Jeddah. I think I will." Ben grabbed a chip and spooned up a liberal portion. He popped it into his mouth. His eyes widened, and he grabbed a glass from a cabinet. He threw back some water. "Man! What did you put in that thing?"

Claire laughed. "The bride-to-be made it with hot peppers. I can't remember what kind. Here. Have some milk. That'll help."

"You stinker." Ben kissed his fiancée.

"And here's the mild salsa." Emma uncovered the larger bowl. "Where's Ziad?"

"Finishing up evening prayers. The pizza just came." He nodded toward two boxes on the stove.

Claire turned away. So far as she was concerned, it was fine if Ziad didn't show up. "I'll dish it up."

She pulled down four plates and carried them to the table.

"Hey there!"

She paused at Emma's voice, then swiveled.

Her heart raced, and heat hit her chest. Oh, my… Not what she'd expected. For starters, she found herself looking up a little to meet his gaze. A good six feet tall, just like Emma had said. At least she could wear her heels rather than going barefoot.

A victim of good manners, she crossed the kitchen.

Emma drew her closer. "Claire, meet Ziad al-Kazim. Ziad, this is my sister, Claire Montgomery, who is also my maid of honor."

Ziad hesitated.

Claire almost rolled her eyes.

*If he won't, I will, just to make him uncomfortable.* She extended her hand. "It's a pleasure to meet you. I've heard a lot about you."

He paused, then took it.

Something close to electricity shot through her. She masked her gasp with a cough.

Ziad smiled, revealing beautiful white teeth save for a small gap between the two front ones. "It is a pleasure to meet you as well."

Ben cleared his throat. "The pizza came while you were saying prayers. I hope you're hungry because I got two."

Ziad glanced at him, but his gaze flicked back to her. "I am. Thank you."

Would that blush just go away? To distract herself, Claire asked, "Drinks?"

"Tea for me, darlin'," Ben said.

"Ziad?"

"Tea as well."

She ripped her gaze from their guest and stuffed four glasses with ice as she released a measured breath. She tried to tell herself the pounding in her heart came from holding it. As she poured the tea, the hair on the back of her neck raised.

He watched her.

She knew it.

Like she was some kind of steak or something.

*I am not a piece of meat!* She whipped around, and some liquid splashed into her hand. Without a word, she retrieved the other two glasses and seated herself at the table with Ziad on her right and Ben on her left. "Let me say grace."

She bowed her head and clasped her hands on her lap. "Lord Jesus, I thank You for today. Thank You for the chance to meet new people. And thank You for the food. Amen."

She opened her eyes and glanced at Ziad.

His face remained expressionless.

*So dumb, Claire. Give him a break.* She pasted another bright smile on her face. "Who wants onions and green peppers?"

"Did Em tell you what happened when we got to Dulles from Paris?" Ben asked.

Claire shook her head as she shifted a piece of pizza onto her plate.

"She got up from her seat, and it looked like she'd had a party."

Emma scowled at him. "Not so, Ben Evans."

"Ziad, you were beside her. Say it ain't so."

Ziad smiled at Emma. "I counted a dozen straw wrappers, two candy bar wrappers, and three bags of pretzels."

Emma swatted him. "You did not!"

He chuckled and took a bite of pizza.

Emma glared at them in mock indignation. "That was all Ben."

"Hardly." Ben winked. "But let me tell you about making our connection. It almost didn't happen."

Throughout the meal, he and Ziad bantered back and forth with Emma interjecting to defend herself.

Claire laughed along with her sister.

Then she knew. Ben and Ziad had that close friendship of brothers, and Emma viewed Ziad like the brother she'd never had. If they could accept him, why couldn't she?

Emma rose and collected their plates before opening a drawer. She turned with a deck of cards in hand. "Spades, anyone?"

Ben leered at his fiancée. "Sure, hotcakes!"

Claire lightly kicked him in the ankles.

Ben turned to his friend. "Hey, don't worry about not knowing how to play. It's easy to learn. I can explain the rules really quickly."

Ben began discussing the rules of the game as Emma located some pens and a notepad. He partnered with Ziad.

After a practice round, they began a serious game.

Ben studied his cards and began speaking Arabic to Ziad.

"None of that." Emma's eyes narrowed. "Claire doesn't speak Arabic."

"Oh, have a heart, Emma."

She glowered at him.

Ben nudged her. "C'mon, sweetie, you're a diamond in the rough."

Claire muffled a laugh.

Emma rolled her eyes. "You're talking code to Ziad."

"Code?" Ben winked at his friend. "Do you hear a code, Ziad?"

"In spades." Ziad's eyes twinkled. He smiled at Claire.

More heat, once more in her cheeks.

Ziad rearranged his cards. "You are such an ace at it."

Emma groaned. "Guys! New hand!"

Everyone laughed.

Two hours later, Emma yawned as she stared at the notepad. "Ziad, for a newbie at the game, you and Ben did well. You beat us by twenty points."

Ben threw his hands in the air. "Victory!"

"Until the next time." She gathered the deck and slid it into its box.

Claire rubbed her eyes. "I'm beat. It's been a long couple of days. Em, don't feel like you need to come back with me."

Ben rose. "I'll be sure to get her home in one piece."

She mock-punched him. "Be sure you do. After all, you sleep down the hall from the father of the bride."

That earned weary chuckles all around.

Claire located her purse.

Ziad joined her. "I am tired myself and need to rest."

Claire retreated to the mudroom. Just as she reached for the doorknob, so did he.

Their fingers brushed.

She swore she saw a spark between them, and her heart raced.

Ziad opened the door and stepped aside. "Ladies first. Is that not what they say here?"

Still recovering, she blurted, "Thank you."

They paused in the breezeway.

After pulling a pack of cigarettes from his shirt pocket, he shook one out, lit it with a mother-of-pearl lighter, and took a puff.

Yuck! Why did all Arab men have to smoke? And why couldn't she just leave? She leaned against a post. "It was good to meet you."

"As was you. I am to be your escort next weekend. Ben's best man."

"Right."

"As maid of honor, are you to be my escort?"

Say what? Had he realized what he'd just said? Judging from his sincerity, no. Only cricket chirps filled the night air. She struggled with the right words to say. "Um, I know what you mean, but please don't use that phrase in public when referring to a female."

"Why not? That is what you are doing, is it not?"

"Um, it's okay to say a guy escorts a girl. But when you say a girl escorts a guy, it, well…" How could she explain this without embarrassing him? She couldn't.

"Yes?"

She pushed away from the wood and murmured into his ear, "It means that woman is a prostitute."

"Oh." The color rushed to his cheeks. "I am sorry. I did not mean to—"

"You didn't offend me." *Yeah, right.* Her nose detected the faint scent of his aftershave, a rich, spicy scent that sent quivers down her spine. Did she detect the faint crackling of the electricity she'd felt? *Sorry. Wrong guy. Remember who he is.* No more electricity. "It's all right. A simple mistake."

"But one I will not make again."

"I'll pick you up at nine tomorrow."

"Your mother said you will teach me all about weddings and Charleston."

"Hopefully. We've got a lot to cover." She smiled. "And I don't mind squiring you around town."

"Squiring?"

Before she realized it, she winked. "A tasteful way of saying I will innocently escort you around town."

"I—I see. Well, good night, Claire Montgomery." Ziad saluted her with his cigarette. "It was so good to meet you in person."

Once behind the wheel of the Mustang, she glanced at him. That gaze. One of curiosity and sincerity, almost like he wanted to be her friend. No. She'd fulfill her promise to Emma, but that was it. No more.

Then why did she get that feeling she'd be seeing a lot more of him than intended?

# 9

Ziad leaned against the post of the Montgomery's front porch. A cool breeze bearing scents from the hot pink azaleas in a front shrub bed washed over his face. Birds twittered and darted among the branches of the pecan trees lining the driveway. To thwart the nerves tingling along his spine, he lifted a cigarette, his first of the day, to his lips and took a puff. He exhaled into air rapidly warming in the sun.

Behind him, a newspaper crinkled as Claire's father, David, turned pages.

"Hey, my friend."

He shifted.

Coffee mug in hand, Ben settled his lanky frame on a rocking chair. He swung his bare feet onto the porch railing. "Something tells me you're going to be the one having all of the fun today."

Fun? Perhaps that wasn't the term Ziad would have used. Maybe only if he let down his guard, something hard to do with Claire. She intrigued him, for sure. A beauty, one only a few centimeters shorter than he and with deep green eyes matching the finest jade in Jeddah. An undercurrent of standoffishness fairly crackled beneath her mannerly exterior. Why, he didn't know, and he didn't dare ask Emma or Ben.

"Ziad?"

"So sorry. I was thinking." *About Claire,* he almost blurted. "Why do you say that?"

A lazy smile crossed Ben's face. "Claire's a nice person. And a beauty. She's—"

"Son, remember I'm here." David Montgomery gazed at his future son-in-law over the top of the paper.

Ben laughed. "Yes, sir."

"That's better" David laid the paper on his lap. "Ziad, you'll be in good hands. Claire loves Charleston history."

Ben pushed against the railing. "Remember a couple of things Don't stare at people, especially women, in shorts."

Ziad nodded as he remembered Ben's advice about firm handshakes.

"And don't use Southern terminology because you'll come across as making fun of them."

Absolutely. Especially with Claire. That delicate scent of the shampoo or perfume she'd worn the night before lingered in his nose.

He heard the music first, then the growl of the yellow Mustang's engine as Claire turned into the long drive.

David rose. "There they are."

Ziad took another puff as the car drew closer and pulled into the circular drive in front of the house. It stopped at the steps.

The two women hopped out.

"Daddy!" Emma ran up the steps, hugged her father, and kissed him on the cheek.

Interesting. Still her father's daughter even with her fiancé mere meters away.

She quickly disengaged and smiled at Ziad. "Good morning. You slept well?"

"I did. Thank you." Ziad turned and jabbed his cigarette into a saucer Allison had supplied as an ashtray.

"Good morning, Ziad."

At that slow drawl, his attention swiveled to the tall brunette in front of him.

Sweat broke out on his hands, and for a moment—a brief moment—he forgot to breathe. Ben's advice suddenly tangled in his head. Was he

staring? What should he say? The English words fled. *Say something. Now.*
"I—I like that color of shirt you are wearing."

Oh, no.

Ben snickered and turned it into a sneeze.

Claire brushed her shirt of jade green. "Thank you. It's one of my favorite colors." She coughed. "Are you ready to go? We've got a lot to see."

He nodded and followed her down the steps to the convertible.

"I'll have him back by dark." Claire winked. "Or later."

"Y'all have fun." Ben wrapped his arm around Emma's shoulders. "Remember you'll have more fun, my friend."

Emma mock-punched him on the shoulder.

He laughed.

Claire slid behind the wheel. "I hope you have comfortable shoes on."

"Ben suggested running shoes."

She started the engine.

Music blared from the speakers, and he jumped.

She quickly turned it down. "Sorry. Em and I were singing Martina McBride songs on the way over here." She put the car in gear, and they rumbled down the driveway. "Have you been away from the house yet?"

"No. It was nice to rest yesterday."

"I'm sure." They slowed, then turned left. "Do you like country music?"

He chose honesty. "I do not know."

She lowered her sunglasses and gazed over the rims at him. "You don't know?"

His hands moistened. "I did not listen to music in Saudi Arabia."

"It's sinful, right?"

Ziad stiffened at the cutting edge in her voice. *Judging already, eh?*

She focused straight ahead. "What do you know about the South?"

"Only what your aunt, uncle, Ben, and Emma told me."

"But what did you expect to see here?"

He paused and tried to collect his thoughts as he slid on his own pair of sunglasses. "I do not know. When I was a child, I heard about a series called *Gray and Blue*."

Claire glanced at him. "That's too funny."

"What do you mean?"

"*Gray and Blue* was filmed at Sutton Hall, which is right next door to Mama and Daddy's property."

"Really?"

"Yep. You'll see it on Friday." The light turned, and as they proceeded down US 17. Noise and breeze surrounded him.

"This is the main highway between Mount Pleasant and Charleston."

They paused at another light. With it quieter, he picked up on the mellow strains of the music. Strange as it was, he enjoyed the female voice. "This is your Martina?"

"The one and only." Her teeth flashed against her lips. The light turned, and they accelerated onto the bridge. "Charleston, here we come."

What a beautiful bridge with pilings jutting from the water and cabling supporting the deck. Tangy scents reminding him of the water in the port of Jeddah washed over him, and tense muscles in his shoulders began relaxing. Maybe this day would truly mark a new beginning.

Claire glanced at him. "You doing okay? Not too much wind, is it?"

"No, no. I like it. This is a beautiful bridge."

"Isn't it? It's so much better than the other ones. They were so old I was afraid they'd fall into the river." She nodded to her right. "That's the Cooper River, by the way. Welcome to Charleston. What suits your fancy?"

"My fancy?" Ben hadn't taught him that one.

"Do you want some breakfast? Or a cool drink? Or coffee? Because what you want to do will dictate where we go first."

"I ate with your parents. Coffee is good."

"Then I'll take you to my alma mater."

"Which is?"

"College of Charleston." They exited from the highway. Soon, the buildings of a college campus appeared on the right. She drove past them and parallel parked near a coffee shop. "Here we are. I sometimes meet Faith here on Saturday mornings."

"Your youngest sister, yes?"

"Almost. Second to youngest. She graduates in May. Grace is younger by ten minutes and graduates from Clemson next year since she's majoring in civil engineering. C'mon. Their coffee is to die for. What do you want? I'll be glad to get it."

"A Coffee of the Day."

"Grab a table. I'll be right back." Claire pushed her way inside.

Ziad found a table next to one of the picture windows of the storefront. Once seated, he deeply inhaled. More scents emanated from the flowering shrubs and trees across the street. He gazed around him. So different from Jeddah. Lots of trees. Laughter. And the women? He caught himself gawking at a college girl wearing pajama bottoms and a top that left her shoulders bare. And the two who strolled by in tank tops and shorts. He focused on the cigarette pack he put on the table, then a newspaper someone had left. A headline caught his attention.

2 Teens Dead from Zap Overdoses.

His gut tightened. *Here? In the States?*

"Here we go." Claire plopped onto a chair across from him and set some cream and sugar on the table. "Do you want any of this?"

"I like my coffee black."

"Suit yourself." She dumped generous portions of each into hers.

Ziad took a sip. Good, but not as good as his favorite place in Jeddah. "What does being best man entail?"

"You didn't talk about this on the flights over?"

"No." *Because I wanted to be left alone then.*

"We'll start at the beginning. As you found out last night, one of your functions is to be my date for the weekend."

How could he forget?

"You're my escort for the weekend, yes?" He winked.

"No, you're *my* escort." A smile quirked her lips. "Thursday is a party thrown by some of Mama and Daddy's friends. Friday, the festivities officially start with the rehearsal and rehearsal dinner. The rehearsal is when we meet at the church and learn about how the ceremony will go. You don't mind stepping into a church, do you?"

*Yes, but I refuse to offend Ben and Emma.* "No."

"It doesn't take long. Maybe an hour, hour and a half tops. You'll meet the rest of the wedding party and the family. Then we head to Sutton Hall for the rehearsal dinner. That's a big party. We've gotten lucky in that a lot of Mama and Daddy's friends have gone in together and planned an after-rehearsal-dinner party for out-of-town guests and the wedding party."

A nice idea, for sure.

"Also, the best man's traditionally responsible for the bachelor party."

He frowned. "What is that?"

"When the guys, usually the groomsmen, celebrate the groom's last day or night of singleness." She took a deep breath. "It can get kind of wild. Lots of drinking. Maybe a stripper."

What? Ben would never stand for that. Would he?

She leaned forward. "From what I understand, one of Ben's college buddies is taking care of it, and no worries on that end. Ben will fill you in. I think it's on Wednesday. Meanwhile, we're having the bachelorette party for Emma that same night."

She smiled, and mischief glinted in her eyes.

"What are you going to do?"

"A girls' gathering for supper. We're probably going to watch movies at my house."

Much more his speed. "Perhaps I should come to your house."

She shot him a look. "Sorry. No can do. Girls only. Back to Friday. At the rehearsal dinner, you and I have an important duty."

"What is that?"

"Normally, toasts are given at the reception, but Emma and Ben wanted them to be at the rehearsal dinner."

A toast? Was that a Southern thing? "Forgive me, but what is a toast?"

"Oh, a short speech, usually complimenting the couple." She shrugged and sipped her coffee. "It doesn't have to be long. Maybe a minute or two."

A minute or two? Of course he'd spoken publicly many times during his career. This was different. Scarier. Especially in a second language. He shuddered.

Claire must have noticed because she added, "You'll do fine. On Saturday, you've got five duties. First, you hold Emma's ring until the time in the ceremony when they exchange rings." She ticked off the next item on her finger. "Second, Daddy will give you the fee for the minister. Once the ceremony finishes, you'll give it to him. Third, you'll sign the marriage certificate with me. Fourth, you'll run interference with me during pictures because the groom isn't allowed to see the bride until the ceremony."

Another phrase he didn't understand. "Run interference?"

"Keep them separated. I'll help. Don't worry. And last and most importantly." She ticked off the last item. "You'll keep Ben from running away."

She'd lost him. He cocked his head. "I do not understand. Why would he do that?"

"Weren't you nervous when you got married?"

He bristled. "I think that is a bit personal."

"Well?"

What a pushy woman!

"Of course I was." *No, I was cocky at the age of twenty when I lifted the veil concealing Sabirah's face.*

At his silence, her eyes narrowed. Then she shrugged and took another sip. "I think Ben recognizes the magnitude of what's about to happen. To have another person completely and fully know him. And to love him despite all faults. And to care for her and future children. I think it'd make even the most confident man quake in his shoes."

Too true. "After the ceremony?"

"You escort me from the church, and we head to the reception, which will be at Mama and Daddy's. They'll introduce the wedding party, and then we'll have the bride and groom's first dance. You and I will also do that dance as best man and maid of honor. Then you'll dance with Emma, and I'll dance with Ben."

His stomach churned on the coffee. He gaped at her. How could he dance? *I can't do that. It's bad enough that I'm paired with an unmarried woman.* He began shaking his head.

"What?" Her eyes narrowed. "What's so bad about dancing?"

"I do not dance."

"But it's custom. It's not complicated. I can teach you."

"Perhaps so, but I will not."

She rolled her eyes. "Ziad!"

"I am sorry."

"You don't do any dancing?"

"The Bedouin sword dance?" His attempt at humor fell flat.

"Look. I hate to say it, but you're also going to have to dance with Emma. If you can't lower that Saudi male pride of yours, you're going to ruin a perfectly good time." Claire jumped to her feet. "If you'll excuse me, I'll be back in a moment."

She turned away, but not before he saw tears in her eyes. She yanked the door open.

*So much for the kind, compassionate woman Ben had described. Who cares? It's not going to happen.* He conveniently scooted past the fact that he'd offer her his arm for the walk down the aisle.

Such a thought started the shakes in him. He shook out his second cigarette of the day and lit it. Maybe that would soothe the nerves that had begun jangling because of their conversation.

"I only do the Bedouin sword dance." Claire mimicked Ziad's accent as she pushed open a stall door in the bathroom and stomped to the sink. *What a jerk!*

She glared at herself in the mirror. Her eyes had reddened. So much for a good day. Hah! As she continued her monologue, she scrubbed her hands so hard they heated up. "It's a silly dance." Hardly. "And I'm stuck with the most bizarre best man on the planet!" She took deep breaths and willed herself to calm down. "Lord, you're trying my patience in a big way here." She shook her head. "Thanks for nothing. And now, I'm stuck with him for the day as well."

Before shoving open the door, she took a breath. *Lord, don't let me leave him in the middle of Charleston. It's a mighty long walk back to Mount Pleasant.* Once at the counter to ask for a cup of water, she stared through the front window.

Ziad slouched on his chair with his elbows on the table. Smoke streamed from the end of a cigarette, probably something he'd done to calm his nerves. The corners of his mouth turned down as he lifted a page of the newspaper she'd seen on the table.

Suddenly, Mama's words from two days before washed over her. He'd lost his entire family only a year ago. Maybe she should go easier on him. She rejoined him. "How many of those do you smoke a day?"

He smoothed down the newsprint as his face slid into a neutral expression. "Four."

She gawked. "Four packs?"

"No. Cigarettes."

"Whew. I was worried for a second."

He chuckled, a rich sound that rested easy on her ears. "I am very— how do you say it?—health conscious."

*Uh, no you're not.* "Me too. Shall we? Charleston calls our names."

He rose and offered his arm. "We shall. Practice for next weekend?'

"Absolutely." She took his arm. As she did, that spicy aftershave hit her nostrils. She wanted to slide closer to him. What? Uh, uh. "I still have much to teach you."

The day turned upward from there as they found a parking spot downtown and spent the afternoon walking around. As she explained the city's history, she found him to be a willing student with his questions. Her guard began dropping, especially as he charmed her with that smile of his. Maybe next weekend would work out.

The sun set. Her stomach rumbled. "Do you like seafood?"

"Of course."

"Then I know of the perfect place." Before she realized it, she took his hand and led him toward an intersection. Her cheeks heated, and she dropped it. "This is some of the best casual dining in town."

Once they were seated, a waiter approached and asked for their drink order.

Nothing but water for the Saudi.

She ordered a beer.

Ever so slightly, his eyes narrowed. "Should you drink that when you are driving?"

What? No one had ever questioned her like that. "Excuse me? I know my limits, okay?"

He opened his mouth, then suddenly seemed to realize where he was. He shook his head.

"Ziad!" The nerve of him! She finished her beer as they ate in silence. No words, nothing. *Emma, I don't care what you say. Ben's best man is a total bonehead.* She began reciting in her head conversations she'd have with her sister later that week.

When she finally headed to the restroom, she glanced at her watch. Eight. She could take him home without suffering an attack of the guilties. As she approached their booth, she found him sliding his wallet into his pants pocket. "I could have paid for my part."

"No, no. My treat. Because you put up with me this afternoon."

"It's okay." *Not really.*

"Would you like to get some ice cream?"

*No! I want to take you home.*

Then he pointed to her favorite ice cream shop, and she couldn't say no. With cones in hand, they wandered toward the more residential area of Old Charleston. They wound up at a park near the Battery and strolled along palm-lined streets. She sighed in ecstasy as she finished hers with one last bite. "I love ice cream. Do they have it in Saudi Arabia?"

"Of course. I confess to a secret liking of ice cream as well."

She chuckled.

Ziad smiled, and her neck began warming.

She glanced toward the nearby water.

"Tell me about your family."

She tucked a strand of hair behind her ear. "I'm the second of six girls. Allie's the oldest and is four years older than I. She's got three kids. A nine-year-old son, six-year-old daughter, and three-year-old son. Then there's me. Emma's two years younger than I, and Delia's two years younger than she. She's a pediatrician. She and her husband are expecting their first child in July. Faith and Grace are identical twins who are thirteen years younger than I."

"It is a shame you have no brothers."

She whirled on him. "Excuse me? Why is that a problem?"

"Um…"

What nerve! Time to set him straight. "Maybe in your society, women are considered to be worthless, but—"

"Did I say that?"

"It takes two women's testimony to equal that of a man. Women can't drive. A woman gets blamed for not producing sons when—if you get down to it—it's really the man's fault. And marriages are—"

"I do not have to listen to this!" Ziad hurled his cone into the trash.

She jabbed her fists onto her hips. "Maybe you need to."

He muttered something under his breath. "I am finished with you today. Take me back. Now."

He began marching up King Street.

What? Where was he going? "Ziad!"

He ignored her and like a striker breaking through defenses on the soccer pitch, he slipped through the tourists meandering through the cool evening.

"Ziad!" She bumped into someone and mumbled an apology. "Ziad, please!"

With a white-hot look that could have melted the wrought iron railing beside her, he turned onto a side street.

Claire darted around him, and he knocked her off balance as he halted.

She staggered. "Uh, wrong street. We're on Market. Two streets up."

He gripped her arms with startling force. "What is your problem?"

As he released her, she shivered. What could she say? "Um, I—"

"I am trying my best, yes? I try to be nice to you." He turned away and raked his hands through his hair as he said something in Arabic, probably about what a, well, she knew what she'd been. "Just because I am your captive audience does not mean I am your…" He obviously struggled to find the right word. "I do not like being a target. Do you understand?"

His dark eyes bored into hers, and she felt as if he could see into her soul.

What he possibly saw scared her.

That fierce gaze rendered her speechless. She turned and fled toward the car.

*I won't do it. I can't be your best man, Ben. Not when the maid of honor despises me in her heart and treats me like dirt.* Ziad mentally rehearsed his speech. A headache, which had begun that morning when he'd seen the headline about Zap, had escalated until it pulsed in time with his heart. He wanted out. Now.

Out of the car.

Out of his role as best man.

As Claire turned into her parents' driveway, he gripped the door handle of the Mustang as if his life depended on it. The convertible stopped in front of the garage.

He wasted no time in undoing his seatbelt and grabbing the door handle. Maybe Ben was home and they could talk. He'd deal with the fallout later.

"Ziad, wait. Please!"

*What now?* He closed his eyes as nausea joined the mad dance of his headache.

He shut the door. "What?"

Silence. Then, "I'm sorry," in the smallest of voices.

He faced her. "What did you say?"

Claire kept her hands on the steering wheel, but her head drooped. "I'm sorry."

He let her suffer in silence for a few moments.

"I—I was taking potshots at you, and I'm sorry. I was being stupid."

*Will you stop with the colloquialisms already?* He wanted to scream. "And what are potshots?"

"I—I was baiting you."

He rested his head against the seat. "Should I ask why?"

More silence as if she contemplated her motives. "No."

A strange answer, for sure. One he hadn't expected. He sensed her honesty in it.

Maybe he'd come down too hard on her. "Please try to understand something. I am not from here. Perhaps my ways are not your ways. If you promise not to take these… what did you call them?"

"Potshots."

"If you promise not to take potshots at me, then I will try not to…" Why did the English words he needed fail him? "Well, to impart my culture upon you. I would like to be friends, after all."

*Huh? Why did I say that?* He knew in a flash. Those words had come from his heart.

"Okay." She lifted a hand to her cheek as if swiping a tear.

"I will see you Thursday." He opened the door and slid from the car.

"Yeah." Finally, she glanced at him. A small smile crossed her face. "If not before."

*Not if I can help it.* He leaned in, and a whiff of fragrance hit his nose. "Good night, Claire."

Once the shadows concealed him, he paused and listened. It took a few seconds, but the Mustang started, pulled away, and rumbled down the driveway.

Ziad shook his head, a motion that aggravated his headache.

"Why her?" he asked the night.

Using his key, he headed into the main house in search of some ibuprofen since he didn't have any in his suite. He found some in a cabinet. When he filled a glass with water, toenails clicked on the floor.

Sherlock and Watson, the family's two Australian Cattle Dogs, joined him. As he scratched them behind the ears, he surveyed the refrigerator door where Allison left notes. He found one for him. "Hmmm. What does this say? 'Ziad, we've taken Janet and Mark to a play in town and will return by eleven or so. Ben and Emma will be back around nine.' So it is you two and me, eh?"

He checked the clock. So much for praying today. He grimaced.

"Shall we walk the property together?" With the dogs following, he wandered onto the back porch and into the backyard. What with the new moon, the live oaks scattered throughout loomed over him like blackened sentries. He shuffled his feet along the path, lest he wander from it and trip over some roots. Spanish moss brushed his arms as he drifted toward nearby Willow Wood Creek.

Sherlock, who'd sniffed and snuffled around the edge of the path, headed toward the low, wispy branches of a tree. He slipped through and disappeared. Watson followed.

Worry tightened his gut. "Sherlock! Watson! Come back here."

Had the dogs slipped off the property? Fallen into the water? He hadn't heard a splash. He reached out, and his hand parted feathery branches. Lights caught his eye, and he noticed a linear shape extending over the water. A dock. His running shoes made no sound as he carefully made his way to the end. He eased onto his rump.

With a deep breath, he inhaled earthy smells. Bullfrogs croaked here and there. Crickets chirped on that warm night. His headache began dissipating as he breathed in and out. He pulled out a cigarette from his pack and lit it. With wrists resting on his knees, he leaned against a piling.

Claire. Her face floated before him. What drove her hostility toward him? Media influence? A run-in with someone? Did she dislike him? Or Saudi men in general? All he had were questions and no answers, something the dormant detective in him disliked. It made him want to dig deeper. His pulse picked up as he contemplated those beautiful jade green eyes and hair such a dark brown it was almost black. A beautiful woman. And one who, when she let her guard down, could be quite nice.

Suddenly, an image of her almost seemed to appear before him, one of her when she was a child. He imagined her sitting on this very dock, gazing at the stars, and dreaming. Perhaps she'd dreamed of her own wedding and those of her sisters. Maybe he'd been too harsh, made too rash a decision.

He closed his eyes as a new round of weariness took over the space left vacant by his rapidly departing headache. As he wove the fingers of his free hand through Sherlock's thick fur, he thought of all she'd told him about Southern weddings. Strange traditions, for sure, but ones from the culture in which he now lived. Why did the thought of dancing with her make him want to hide?

Because Sabirah lay in the hard Saudi soil.

He could almost hear what she would have told him about his discomfort. "Would it be such a problem if I were there with you?"

That was it.

He was single.

Claire was single.

Something about her kept him coming back. Thinking about that warmed his cheeks.

Just then, Sherlock barked once and ran off the dock. Close to the house, a car door slammed. Ben said something, and Emma giggled.

Maybe they could help. Ziad tossed his cigarette into the creek and joined them. "Ben, my friend."

"Hey." Ben approached him. "I thought you'd still be out."

Ziad couldn't tell them how awful Claire had been to him at points during the day. "We were both tired."

"Hello, best man." Emma took her fiancé's arm.

All desire to back out as Ben's best man vanished. "I have a question for you both."

Emma rested her hand on her hip. "What would that be?"

"Would you… would you teach me how to dance?"

# 10

Such a beautiful Thursday night. Green grass stretched into the deepening springtime dusk at the home of the Montgomery family friends who hosted a party for Ben and Emma. Delightful aromas from trees and shrubbery filled the air with a luscious, almost heady, scent. As he stood alone at the yard's edge, Ziad lifted his face. Velvety air on his cheeks. A pleasant feeling, one he wanted to savor before things got really busy.

Speaking of busy, he hadn't seen Claire since Saturday night. He teetered between relief and anxiety. Relief since he didn't have to worry about the acrimonious start to their relationship. Anxiety from wondering about how things would go this coming weekend.

Ben had listened to his concerns with care and provided wisdom. "Go easy on her, my friend. She'll come around. And I promise she has a compassionate heart."

Ziad could only hope so.

"Are you enjoying yourself?"

At Claire's Southern accent, he glanced to his right. "I was getting worried."

With a graceful gesture, she pushed some hair behind her ear. "Gift baskets. I promised Emma I'd deliver them to the hotel so the staff can put them in the guest rooms tomorrow. How was your week?"

So far, so good with their conversation. "Very nice. I received my driver's license." He pulled out his wallet and extracted a card. "See?"

She studied it. "Looks like you and I have the same birthdays."

"What? We do?"

"August eighteenth."

"We were meant to be together."

She laughed, a bell-like sound that reminded him of Emma. "At least for this weekend."

On the house's patio, the guitarist who plucked calming melodies paused. Their host joined him and welcomed everyone.

She pressed closer to his side. "I take it supper hasn't been served."

He inhaled. Oh, that perfume. "Not yet."

Once the guitarist resumed, people moved toward a table with a red and white tablecloth on it. Ziad joined them. "You said this was a pig picking."

She followed. "It is."

He quelled at the notion of pork. "Do they perhaps have other meat?"

"They should. Probably barbecue chicken. Not as good as pork, but still good when done right."

"I will take that as a promise."

She smiled. "You do that, kind sir."

As they edged closer to the gigantic cooker, he chatted with the new and improved Claire. Nothing seemed to remain from the hostility of last Saturday as she filled him in on her week.

They reached the cooker.

Smoke wafted his way.

So did the scent of pork.

His stomach flipped, and he winced.

"Ziad?"

He offered a sick smile. "I... Where is the other meat?"

"Oh, no." She stared at the cooker where the caterer served up generous portions of pork onto someone's plate. "I guess there's not one. Didn't Ben and Em tell them you were joining us?"

He was going to throw up.

An older gentleman in front of them turned. "I take it you're into western Carolina barbecue then."

"Uh…"

The man peered at him. "Oh, you're one of them."

"He just doesn't eat pork. No biggie, Uncle Carl." Claire took Ziad's hand and tugged him out of line. "Matter of fact, I'm don't feel like eating pork either."

She smiled at him.

The tension eased from his shoulders.

She released him. "Let's check out the sides."

"Sides?"

She gestured to a set of three tables where aluminum pans sat above small burners. "Other stuff. Hushpuppies. Vegetables. Fruit."

"Right." His stomach rumbled. At least he could get his fill of other good food.

"Uh, oh."

"What?"

She stared at the baked beans, green beans, and potato salad. "Oh, Ziad, I feel so bad!"

"What?"

"The potato salad has bacon bits in it."

No worries there. He had two other vegetables he could eat. Plus whatever she'd called hushpuppies. "I can have the beans and green beans. And fruit."

"Um, the beans have bacon in them as well. And the green beans have a bit of pork in them."

So much for eating that night. "I guess I will have fruit and those hushpuppies."

"I'm sorry. May I?" She gestured to the contaminated sides.

"Of course." He filled his plate and followed her to a table furthest away from the music.

Her Aunt Janet and Uncle Mark joined them.

"Ziad, honey, where's the rest of your food?" Janet asked.

Claire shook out her napkin and laid it across her lap. "Somehow, the hosts didn't get the message about non-pork eaters."

"Man cannot live on fruit and hushpuppy alone, son," Mark added.

"Don't worry, Uncle Mark." Claire flashed a smile at her date. "I'll make sure he eats later."

Ziad quirked an eyebrow at her.

She only asked, "Uncle Mark, have you and Aunt Janet found a house in Savannah yet?"

Ziad wolfed down his meal. Claire took her time. As she chatted, he observed her. A kind, effervescent woman when she let her guard down. He wanted to know her better. A surprise, at least for him.

Mark and Janet rose and drifted toward the guests of honor.

Claire faced him. "Here's my idea."

His stomach rumbled. "What is it?"

"You want to come back to my place? I've got some cold cuts. And we could hang out some more." She winked and touched him on the arm.

Do what? How dare she ask! He jerked back like she'd burned him. "I will not dishonor Ben and Emma."

She stared. "What?"

Didn't she see it? "We've just met!"

She shrugged. "So?"

Did he have to spell it out? "I—I am not going to go over and have…"

His English completely failed him.

"What?" She pursed her lips and narrowed her eyes. "Have sex or something?" She took a deep breath and closed her eyes as if composing herself. "Maybe in Saudi Arabia, a man being alone with a woman means one thing, but in America, it's perfectly acceptable. I'm not interested in sex. I only wanted to offer you a decent meal. Can you handle that?"

Maybe. He studied her face. Frustration. Perhaps a bit of anger, something he'd inadvertently caused. Not a good way to start the weekend. An idea hit him. "I can. But I must speak with Ben for a minute."

"And I need to find Emma." Claire rose. "Meet you at the car in five?"

"For sure." He began searching for his friend. Maybe this time alone with Claire would give him an opportunity to implement his plan.

☆ ☆ ☆

"Hey, Em, could I talk with you for a moment?" Claire approached Emma, who chatted with Ben's sister.

She turned. "Sure! Karen, I'll see you later."

Claire took her arm and led her away from the crowd. "Thanks to our Southern affinity for pork, Ziad wasn't able to eat anything except for the fruit and hushpuppies."

"I noticed." Emma winced. "I'd told Mama and Daddy to pass that on. I guess it didn't happen."

"It's no biggie. I'm taking him to my house to eat the rest of the cold cuts. Are you good with that?"

"Ben can bring me home, so he can ride back with him." Emma bit her lip. "I have a favor to ask. As my sister and not my maid of honor."

Claire cocked her head. "What is it?"

Emma swiped at the corner of her eye. "Could you keep an eye on Ziad for us?"

"What?"

"I'm worried about him." Emma shook her head. "The wedding's kept him busy, but now that it'll be over after this weekend, I'm worried that he'll go into a tailspin as he mourns losing his family."

Oh, wow. Not what she'd expected to hear. "I can understand your worries."

"Of course, Ben and I will be on our honeymoon." Emma focused on her. "I know you two didn't have the best of starts, but could you keep an eye on him for us? It's been," she hesitated as if searching for the right words, "an ordeal for him."

Claire didn't have to think too hard to imagine why. Words from her mentor at her Tuesday night Bible study washed over her.

"Go easy on him," Elizabeth McMillan had said. "He's new to the culture. He's trying to figure things out. And remember he's made in the image of God like you are."

Time to put that wisdom into practice. "I will."

"Thanks." Emma's expression cleared, and she nudged her. "You two have fun tonight."

"Em!" Claire's cheeks flushed as her sister darted away with a giggle.

Forty-five minutes later, the remains of turkey sandwiches littered two plates on Claire's breakfast nook table. Ziad set his napkin aside. "Thank you. I now feel like I have had a good meal."

"I'm glad." She gathered their plates and carried them to the kitchen. "Do you have your speech ready?"

Silence.

She set their dishes on the counter. "The rehearsal dinner is tomorrow night."

"I know. I do not know what to say."

"You don't have anything written down?"

He dipped his chin and cleared his throat. "No."

"Ziad."

He raised his hands in a helpless gesture. "What do I say?"

She knew what she'd written. Wisdom she'd learned from her all-too-short marriage to Jackson. Mindful of Emma's heads up, she asked, "What advice would you give to newlyweds? What are your wishes for them?"

His long fingers ran along the smooth surface of the island.

For a brief, insane moment, she wished the granite were her face. She released her breath and retreated to the junk drawer on one end of the island. She placed a pad of paper and a pen in front of him. "Here. Write something while I clean up."

He cast her a doubtful look before putting pen to paper.

As she put the dishes in the dishwasher and wiped down the table, Claire kept an eye on him. At first he rubbed his jaw, which showed a definitive five o'clock shadow. He squinted as if considering his words. He began scribbling.

A few minutes later, she gestured toward his work. "May I?"

He nodded.

She hopped onto the chair next to him. Such refined English handwriting, almost beautiful in her eyes. His words touched her heart. "This is really good."

"You are sure?"

She'd totally read him wrong the Saturday before. "Yeah. I am."

His dark gaze on her, he leaned forward. "None of this would offend?"

Once more he seemed to peer into her soul. Something uncurled inside of her. She fiddled with the paper. "Not at all."

"Then I will use this." Their fingers brushed as he took it from her, folded it neatly into fourths, and stuck it in his shirt pocket beside his pack of cigarettes. "And now I have a surprise for you."

He held up a CD and stepped to her stereo.

She turned on her chair.

He slid it into the tray before facing her. As the song Ben and Emma had chosen for their first dance began playing, he bowed and offered his hand. "Dance, madam?"

Huh? Wait. Wasn't this the man who'd absolutely refused to consider it? Her jaw dropped. She couldn't move.

He took her hands and drew her off the chair. "I did not want to ruin your big day."

Ouch.

Elizabeth's words from Tuesday night scored her heart. "Whose day is it, Claire?"

Suddenly, her own desires seemed so foolish, so petty. "Honestly. It's not my day. It's Ben and Emma's."

"Saturday night, they taught me to dance." He took her right hand with his left.

Automatically, she rested her left one on his shoulder. Even through the fabric of his sailcloth shirt, she felt a collarbone too prominent for someone like him. Her back began tingling where he clasped it.

For a few moments, they swayed in silence.

"This is good?"

In her bare feet, she had to lift her chin to look at him. In the dim light, his dark eyes almost glowed. She could drown herself in his gaze. "You must be a quick study."

He led her in a twirl.

As the last notes of the song faded, he released her.

Too soon. At least in her mind if not in his. She clapped. "Bravo, kind sir!"

He chuckled. "My dear maid of honor, I do think this is the start of a grand weekend."

She could only hope.

# 11

Ziad stared at himself in the mirror as he buttoned his brand-new white dress shirt, a product of a guys' day when he'd bought his first American suit. He looped his wine-colored tie around his neck. When was the last time he'd worn one? He couldn't remember. The knot looked messy to him. "Ben."

"What's up?" A model of men's fashion, Ben joined him.

"How do you do this?"

Ben studied it. "Looks good." He led the way to the sitting area, where he'd stay that night. "Some more words of wisdom, my friend."

"About?"

Ben tossed his suit jacket over his shoulder and leaned against the door frame. "You're going to see a lot of skin this weekend. Don't stare."

He'd prepared himself for that. "I know."

"And in the South, the man always opens the door for the woman."

"Understood." Ziad glanced at his watch.

Ben must have noticed. "We need to get going. See you at the church."

While his friend left in his rental, Ziad climbed into his new Toyota 4Runner. He fidgeted with the radio and air conditioning. No more delay. He had to go. Except for one thing. Claire needed a gift from him. He turned into a strip shopping mall at the intersection with US 17 and stopped at a florist shop.

Once inside, he gazed at the flowers around him. What to get her? Wildflowers like Emma preferred? No. Roses seemed more refined, more Claire.

A clerk approached him. "You're dressed up for a Friday afternoon."

"A rehearsal." His cheeks warmed. "Do you perhaps have a single yellow rose? It's for my," he caught himself before he said escort, "date this weekend."

"Of course." She turned to a vase of yellow roses, pulled one out, and wrapped the end in a mini-vase with some tissue. "Here you go."

He inhaled the fragrance. So very Claire. When he arrived at her house, he found her standing at the end of her porch and talking with an old woman watering a fern on the porch of the house next door. The woman headed inside. He stripped away the tissue and mini-vase. Grasping the single stem, he climbed the steps.

Oh, my. The expression he'd learned from Emma faded from his mind as he gazed at long, tan legs emphasized by strappy heels. The dropped back of Claire's dress revealed a generous amount of skin. His hand tightened on the stem. Heat began working its way upward from his shoulders. His tie suddenly seemed too tight.

Claire turned and smiled. "Ziad, hi!"

He had to say something. Again, the English words receded. "Claire, you are… um, you are…"

She raised an eyebrow. "I am?"

"You are beautiful."

Her eyes sparkled. "Thank you."

Relief surged over him. The rose. He brought his hand from behind his back. "I brought you this. My gift to you."

"Yellow for friends." She took it and inhaled deeply. "I love it. Let me put it in some water."

As he followed her inside, Ziad traced those curves highlighted by her dress. What was he doing? He averted his gaze—for a moment. As she filled a bud vase with water, he noted the pearls almost glowing against her skin beneath where she wore her hair in a bun. More pearls glimmered in her ears and on her wrist.

She drew a shawl of shimmery gold across her shoulders. "I'm ready. Let's go."

Once she'd locked up, she picked up a basket of bows from one of the rocking chairs on the porch.

He let her precede him down the steps. "What are those?"

"You'll see." She set the basket in the backseat.

Mindful of Ben's advice, he opened the door for her. They headed toward US 17. As they approached the intersection, he glanced downward. When she'd sat down, her dress had slid up to reveal more leg, one with definition. He couldn't rip his gaze away.

"Watch out!"

A red light. He slammed on the brakes and threw them both against their seat belts.

"Watch where you're going, why don't you?" she muttered.

"So sorry." Not really. Too bad he couldn't gaze at her and drive.

At least they got to the church with no more incidents. As they ran through the rehearsal, he understood the point of the bows. They served as mock bouquets. He certainly didn't mind Claire being on his arm as they went through their steps. Could he ask for more trips down the aisle? Probably not. Then came the rehearsal dinner. Somehow, he made it through his toast. And Claire's? Beautiful. Poignant.

"Ben, Emma, never let the sun go down on your anger," she said as she stood with her champagne flute raised. "Take time to really talk. And always, always say 'I love you' when you part ways."

He could have written those words himself.

What had inspired her? Had she been married before? His dormant detective's instincts awakened. He watched her closely throughout the rest of the dinner and the beginning of the party until he got drawn into various conversations with out-of-town guests and family.

Where was Claire? She'd danced several numbers, but now he couldn't find her. Ziad wandered toward the edge of the crowd. No Claire. He strolled around Sutton Hall's plantation home. The structure muffled the sound of the party.

There! She stood near a bench overlooking the banks of the creek. Her shoulders hunched, and she gazed across the water as if searching for her parents' house. He approached with care, lest he startle her. "I was wondering where you were."

She glanced over her shoulder, then returned her gaze to the creek. "I needed a break."

The slight tremble of her smile warned him. Best not to probe further. He gazed at her out of the corner of his eye.

She shivered slightly in the chill.

"Are you cold?"

"A little."

He slid from his suit jacket and placed it over her shoulders.

That earned another small smile. "Thanks." She turned and meandered through a garden of roses just beginning to bud. They stepped onto the main pathway. "Did I ever tell you why plantation homes have their gardens on the river side?"

"No."

"During the heyday of plantation farming, the main form of transportation was by river, so they made the best side of the house the river side." She slowed as they reached the dock. "When we were kids, Allie, Delia, Emma, and I would take the two canoes we owned and paddle across the creek to Sutton Hall to go exploring."

"Did you get caught?"

"The first time, Allie ratted on us, and we got grounded. Then Emma and I came over here a few times by ourselves. Once, the owner was here, and she caught us. She let us go after serving us milk and cookies. She told us ghosts would carry us away if we did it again. We were still young enough to believe her."

Her smile faded. She lowered her head.

He sensed a sadness within her. Why? "Do you feel like you're losing your sister?"

That earned a sharp glance. "To Ben?"

"Yes."

After a brief moment's hesitation, she nodded.

They began walking again. He clasped his hands behind his back. "Ben is… he is perhaps the closest thing I have to a brother."

"Don't you have brothers?"

"I did. And two sisters." He breathed a silent prayer for their souls. "All but one sister died years ago."

"Oh, Ziad."

"It is my youngest sister and me now." He laced his fingers behind his back. "The first time I saw them together, I could tell Ben and Emma would marry."

She glanced at him. "How so?"

"Their friendship. They have a way with each other, a gentle manner."

She folded her arms across her chest.

His breath hitched, and he rubbed the back of his neck as he struggled for words to fill the air. "You are not giving up a sister. You are gaining a true brother tomorrow. A brother and more family."

She sighed. "I know."

Ziad faced her and studied her face. She didn't meet his gaze as she fiddled with her pearls.

Before he realized what he was doing, he lifted her chin with his finger. "Shall we rejoin the party?"

He offered his arm.

As they returned to the other side of the house, she pasted a smile on her face. Emma pulled her into another dance. Ben joined him and called it the Chicken Dance.

For the rest of the night, Ziad kept Claire within sight. To most everyone, she laughed, sparkled.

And him?

He knew better. She hid something, and he'd stop at nothing until he found out what it was.

"Looks like I forgot to turn on the porch light." The next night, Claire gazed at her darkened porch from the passenger seat of the 4Runner.

"Let me walk you to the door." Ziad climbed out, opened her door, and let her precede him to the stairs.

Her cowboy boots, which she'd slipped on shortly after the ceremony, clunked on the wood steps. She fished around in the duffel bag she'd packed for the day. Makeup bag. Socks. Heels. Keys. "Ah. Here."

The bolt slid back. She stepped inside and flipped the switch for the porch light.

Her feet twinged. Time to free her toes. She bent and slid off her boots.

Ziad bumped into her. He grabbed her around the waist before she toppled onto her face. "So sorry. It is dark in here."

She turned, and his hands rested on her hips. "Wearing a midnight blue dress doesn't help."

At the rich aroma of his aftershave, her cheeks heated. He stood so close! All she had to do was— No. She couldn't. She wouldn't. She forced herself to step back. "Thanks for such a great weekend. You were the perfect escort."

"I would say the same of you, but then you would fuss at me."

That earned a weary laugh. "Hardly. How about I was a good date?"

"You were. And a good friend."

Wow. She hadn't expected that one. "Do you want to stay for a while?"

He smiled, but weariness tinged it. "May I—what do you call it?— have a nightcap?"

She stared. Had she heard right? "Maybe you mean a rain check, like to see each other later."

He cleared his throat. "Uh, yes. That."

Her disappointment confused her. "Sure. It *is* late. I—I guess I'll see you around. Good luck with getting settled."

"Until later." With that, he slipped into the cool evening air.

She released her breath, then darted into the living room. She peeked through the plantation shutters.

Ziad walked to the 4Runner. Just as he opened the driver's door, he lifted his gaze.

Her breath caught. Had he seen her?

A slow smile curved his lips upward.

He must have. She dipped her chin and plopped down on the couch. Why did it matter? Maybe sleep would help her avoid that question. Once in the master bedroom, she exchanged her bridesmaid dress for a pair of pajama pants and a cami top. She crawled onto the king-sized bed, sat there in the dark, and gazed through the French doors leading to a terrace.

What a day. What a weekend! Things had turned out much better than she'd expected the week before. What a perfect wedding day for Ben and Emma. For Emma, her groom had come as a totally unexpected answer to prayer.

"I'm never going to get married," her sister had declared three years before, shortly after she'd walked in on her then-fiancé in bed with another woman. Then she'd headed to Jeddah for a two-year physical therapist contract at the hospital Uncle Mark had managed. She'd met Ben a month later, and the rest was history.

"You're lucky, Em," Claire whispered into the dark. Her heart panged as she remembered her conversation with Ziad the night before. He'd sensed that feeling of loneliness that threatened to creep up on her and steal her joy. And his toast to the couple? Fabulous.

"To my friends. It has been an honor to watch as you two met and then became engaged," Ziad had said as he'd held a champagne flute of sparkling grape juice aloft. "Ben, you are a brother to me. A brother-in-arms, a friend. And Emma, in the two years I have known you, I have come to call you a friend as well. Honor each other. Cherish each other. For you do not know what tomorrow holds. May Allah provide his rich blessings to you."

*Oh, Ziad.* Once more, she thought about her escort for the weekend. So handsome, first in his charcoal gray suit at the rehearsal dinner and then in his tie and tails that night. She'd sought him out during the day and again as she'd preceded Emma down the aisle. A gentleman too. He'd watched over her, made her laugh, even danced that one dance together. Her guard began lowering, maybe enough to let a friendship sprout.

Until images from three years ago flashed before her eyes. Scarlet blood. Lots of it. All over her gloved hands and her smock.

"Time of death, 7:07," the cardiothoracic surgeon had said.

A wasted life, all at the hands of a man who swore allegiance and faith to Allah.

She swallowed hard. She'd promised Emma she'd look after Ziad. And she would. But that was all. She wouldn't let herself get close to someone whose loyalty lay with a faith that endorsed honor killings.

A wave of loneliness rolled over her. Claire hugged a pillow to herself and stared at the ceiling fan as it rotated above her. "I can't, God. He was a good date for the weekend. Nothing more."

Right. Like she believed that. As she turned on her side and tried to sleep, the only thing filling her mind was a gentleman from a foreign land with a gaze that could see into her soul.

# 12

Two weeks and one incredible honeymoon in the Caribbean had passed. Ben held Emma's hand as she guided her brand-new Honda Accord through the rainy streets of North Charleston. Time to get his Forester and focus on everything else required of settling into married life. He glanced at the directions on his phone. "Pier Six."

"Right." She leaned forward, then nodded. "There!" She pulled through a chain-link gate and into a parking space in front of a small building. "You want me to stay?"

"Nah. See you at home, bride of sixteen days?"

"Of course!" She accepted his kiss. "Love you."

"Back at ya." He shut the door and strode whistling toward the metal-sided building. While outside smelled of the ocean and ship fuel, the inside reeked of Pinesol. He sneezed. A young man sat behind the counter, and no one else was in the lobby. Ben approached the scarred Formica. "Hey, I'm Ben Evans, here to pick up a Subaru Forester that just came in."

"Ben Evans." The guy tapped some computer keys stained from too much use. "What was your port of origin?"

"Jeddah, Saudi Arabia."

"Oh, yeah. I remember that one. We don't get much from there. What's your address?"

Ben supplied the address of his in-laws.

"I'll need to see some ID."

Ben laid his driver's license on the counter.

The clerk nodded. "Let me get your paperwork together." He began hitting more keys. "What year is it?"

"2003."

"Wow. That's getting up there. How many miles?"

"Getting close to two hundred grand."

"And you kept it?"

Ben shrugged. "Some things are hard to let go of. Too many good memories."

"I'm sure. I've never been to Jeddah." The clerk gathered some papers off the printer. "What's it like?"

"Hot and humid during the summer. Tolerable during the winter." Ben snagged a pen from a plastic University of South Carolina cup on the counter.

The clerk laid four sheets in front of him. "Here you go. This one is your acceptance form. This is the release for us. And for the shipping company. And this one is a waiver. Before you sign, I want you to check out your Forester. It's in slot A out back."

The white SUV sat in its assigned slot. He walked around it and noted the Arabic writing on the license plates. Good memories—at least until the April before. He'd be sure to put those plates on his wall at home.

"Everything's good?" the clerk asked when he returned.

"Good to go." Ben began signing and dating the forms. As he did so, the clerk held down the sheets with his fingers spread.

Something peeked at Ben between the guy's pinkie and ring fingers on his left hand. A symbol. With the tail extending half an inch onto the top of the hand.

Suddenly, he sat with Ziad at that coffee table the year before at the edge of Jeddah's shopping district. Dressed in his SANG uniform, Ziad pointed at the exact same spot on his left ring finger, next to his wedding band. His friend's baritone echoed in his ears. "All three of them had a small tattoo here that extends a little onto the top. No larger than a centimeter in diameter."

No. It couldn't be. Not here in Charleston. He hadn't heard or seen anything about it. Of course, he'd been so wrapped up in the wedding and then away on his honeymoon that he hadn't bothered to pick up a newspaper or read a website.

Ben signed the final paper and shoved the stack toward him. "Hey, I didn't catch your name."

The clerk stapled the stack. "Oh, Mike Winthrop."

"Mike, thanks for your help." Ben flashed a wide smile that felt fake. "Have a great day."

With that, he headed into the rain and slid into the Forester. He reached for the registration, which he'd left on the front passenger seat when he'd dropped it off at the shipping company in Jeddah. He reached to open the glove compartment. A chill washed over him as he remembered the tattoo on the man's hand.

"Crap, crap, crap." He snagged a screwdriver from the glove compartment and opened the door. With one eye on the back door of the office, he popped off the side panel and checked behind it. Nothing but air. Same thing on the others. As he wormed underneath the SUV, wet soaked his shirt. Nothing there, thank goodness. Nor in the compartments in the back. Now dripping wet, he slid into the driver's seat.

So much for enjoying the afterglow of a great honeymoon. His mind began clicking into FBI mode. He was sure he'd seen a tattoo related to the Zap bust in Saudi the year before. He pulled out his phone and located the website of the local news station. Seconds later, he got his answer. Three dead from overdoses of Zap. He began shivering and started the engine.

As he pulled out of the parking lot, he dialed Ziad's number.

"*Marhaba.*" Ziad's voice filled his ear.

"Hey, my friend. Where are you?" Ben asked in English.

"On my way to Columbia for training over the next couple of weeks."

Now he remembered the required coursework in South Carolina law and federal law that Ziad needed. "Sounds like fun."

Ziad snorted. "Perhaps if sitting in a classroom can be called fun. You are back?"

"As of yesterday. Thank goodness I have until next Monday before I report to work." Ben hesitated, then continued, "But something came up that may change that. I got the Forester today, and the guy who did the paperwork for me had a tattoo in the exact same place as your suspects from last year."

Ziad drew in a sharp breath. "You are sure?"

"Not a hundred percent. I'm going to call my future boss and see what she says. Hopefully, I'm worried about nothing."

"Perhaps." Doubt rang in his friend's voice. "Will you let me know what you find?"

"Of course. Have fun, and give us a call when you get back into town." Ben made his next call to his unit supervisor in the Charleston office. "Angie, Ben Evans here."

"Aren't you still on your honeymoon?"

"Uh, well, sort of." Ben turned onto I-526. He outlined what had happened just minutes earlier.

"Meet me at the office, and we'll go over that Forester for you."

Ben made one final call. "Em? Hey. I wanted to let you know I need to go into the office."

"What?" Astonishment rang in her voice. "Ben Evans, you are still on leave until next Monday."

"I know. I know." He swallowed hard, knowing full well that if he weren't careful, they'd have many tiffs like this one. "Promise I'll be home by supper, okay?"

A sigh answered him. "All right. I'll see you then. I love you."

"Love you back." Ben focused on the task at hand.

An hour later, he stood inside a small warehouse with ASAC Angie Rogers as they watched an FBI dog team go over his Forester. He rubbed his chin. "You sure the dog would find something if it were there?"

"Positive." Her dark, tight curls bobbed as she turned and led to an office building and one of the few offices. With a sigh, she eased onto her chair. "Sorry you had to come in early, but you were right to do so. Had I been in your shoes, I'd be spooked too. And you're on to something. Teens and twenty-somethings are starting to show up dead in hospital EDs around the state. Matter of fact, I just got news of another one inbound to Roper."

Ben muttered under his breath.

"Well, we have a name now. And possibly what to look for."

Just then, someone tapped on the door frame. A Belgian Malinois, a Kong toy in his mouth, waved his tail as if in greeting. His handler said, "We didn't find anything."

Relief swept over Ben. "Thanks for checking. I can sleep tonight."

A half smile crossed Angie's face. "Good. 'Cause guess what? Your first assignment is the new Zap task force along with me. First meeting's on Monday at ten. Welcome to Charleston."

# 13

Tuesday night a month after Emma's wedding, Claire stopped in front of Mocha Joe's, the coffeehouse where her Bible study sometimes met. With study, purse, and Bible in her arms, she burst through the glass doors.

Only Elizabeth McMillan and Sonja Williams sat at a table for four. Claire set her stuff down. "Sorry I'm late. I'll be right back."

Elizabeth paused from her conversation. "Not a problem, dear. Go and get something to drink."

Claire bought a hot tea and a blueberry muffin for supper. She'd make up for that later by having some fruit before crashing into bed. With snack in hand, she plopped down with a small groan. "What a day! What a week!"

Sonja shoved her books aside. "That bad?"

"Yup. We had a briefing that ran long."

"About?" Sonja asked.

Claire dipped her teabag in the cup a few times. "You don't want to know."

Her friend raised her chin. "Sure, we do."

"You heard of Zap?"

Sonja sat back and folded her arms across her chest. "You too, huh?"

"What?" Claire frowned at her best friend. "What are you talking about?"

"We had our own little meeting about it." Sonja sipped her caramel mocha latte. "Seems it's the newest fad drug in town."

Elizabeth laid the study guide she'd been examining aside and leaned forward. "Wait. That's the drug that's killed a few teenagers, right? I read about it in the paper."

Claire winced as sadness stung her. "The one and only. A seventeen-year-old boy died a couple of weeks ago while we were airlifting him."

"Oh, dear. I'm so sorry."

"Our briefing was on what to do if we get calls."

Sonja fingered the corner of her Bible. "Tell the parents to make funeral arrangements."

"Why is it so bad?" Elizabeth asked.

Claire began breaking her muffin into pieces. "It's heroin grown in Afghanistan but juiced up with something that acts like cyanide and bioaccumulates in the body. Teenagers and twenty-somethings are using it because it creates these crazy highs. So while at hit one it may take a gram to get high, by hit four, it only takes a tenth of a gram."

"And they still think they need a gram. Zap, you're dead." Sonja shook her head. "The narc units have nailed some dealers, but no one's talking. DEA's just as clueless as we are. They and the FBI think the drug arrived on US soil in different places at the same time. I'm involved because we've set up a task force to deal with it in this area."

Claire sighed and sipped her tea. "Sorry to get us off on a morbid topic."

"That's what I get for asking." Elizabeth placed her study on top of her Bible. "Sounds like we need to talk and catch up."

"You're right." Sonja slurped the remains of her drink through a straw. She appraised Claire like a jeweler would a diamond. "You do look a bit ragged around the edges."

"I know." Claire pulled her hair band from her hair and scrubbed her hands through it. "One of the nurses got sick, so I pulled a swing shift Thursday. Then I had to turn around and go right back in on Friday to fill her position. She just came back in today."

"Whew!"

"At least I'll be off from Friday through Monday."

Sonja blew on the hot tea she'd gotten to go along with her drink. "How's Emma?"

"Fine, I think. Honestly, I haven't even had time to call her."

Sonja's chocolate-colored skin crinkled at the corners of her eyes. "You've definitely been busy then. I'd be on the phone at all hours until I got a detailed description of the honeymoon."

"That's the prosecutor in you." Claire popped some bits of muffin into her mouth. She sighed in ecstasy.

Elizabeth set her cup down. "How's Mr. Ziad doing?"

Kerplunk! Forget a good mood now. "You don't want to know."

Sonja grinned. "You know we do."

"No, you don't."

"C'mon, Claire. 'Fess up. You can't tell that to the District Nine Circuit Solicitor and expect her not to ask questions."

Her cheeks began heating. "I invited him to go to yard sales with me a couple of weeks ago. It was fine until he decided he needed to haggle for me to buy a vase."

"Why was that a big deal?" Sonja asked.

"Because I knew it was expensive, like four hundred bucks expensive, but they were letting it go for one fifty."

Elizabeth nodded. "A steal."

"Exactly. Except Ziad stepped in. He offered twenty-five for it."

Sonja began chuckling.

Claire rolled her eyes. "Then the husband got involved. I was afraid he was going to punch Ziad's lights out. I told Ziad to wait in the truck."

Elizabeth set her cup on the table. "Did you get the vase?"

"No!" Claire threw her hands in the air. "The husband told me that if I can't ask for it myself and instead let a jerk like Ziad do my dirty work, I couldn't have it."

Both women began laughing.

She glowered at them in mock indignation. "I don't think it's funny."

"You're right. It's hilarious!" Sonja guffawed and shook her head. "Poor Ziad. You can't help but feel for him. I mean, he tries to do right by his culture and gets hammered in ours."

"Oh, it got better." She really didn't want to confess the events that followed.

Elizabeth leaned back and looped an arm over the back of her chair. "How so?"

"Uh…" Why had she opened her big mouth?

"You're among friends, darlin'." Elizabeth gave her That Look over the rims of her reading glasses.

"I, uh, I made him swear not to make grown women cry." Her cheeks heated as she remembered that pleasant tingle that had rippled up her arm when she'd grabbed Ziad's hand. Figured she had to be attracted to the one man who drove her crazy. "Then he lit up in front of me for what seemed to be the umpteenth time. I guess… I guess I got frustrated with that because I began hounding him about it. And I exasperated him because he grabbed my chin and told me to knock it off."

She shivered.

Sonja straightened. "He what?"

"Grabbed my chin. He was firm but not cruel. I… It was the temper in his voice that scared me."

"How so?" Elizabeth asked.

"I got him mad to the boiling point." Hastily, she added, "I think he realized it because when I got home from work the Monday after it happened, I found this in my screened door."

She pulled out the letter she'd stuffed in her purse.

Sonja quirked a smile. "You've carried that around for fifteen days? I'm impressed." Before Claire could react, she snatched it from her fingers and opened it. As Elizabeth swung her chair around to look at it, she said, "Wow. He's got the most awesome handwriting."

"And it's from a guy, not a girl!" Elizabeth winked.

Claire shrugged in silent acknowledgment of her own messy handwriting.

Sonja cleared her throat began reading aloud as if in a theater. "'Dear Claire, I hope this letter finds you well. I know that when I deliver this, you will be at work. I am sorry I could not deliver this in person (I am on my way to Columbia), but I wanted to apologize from the bottom of my heart if I scared you Saturday morning. You see, I have been trying my best to fit in. Perhaps even to please you because I value you as a friend.'" Sonja's dark eyes sparkled as she grinned. "Hey, that's good, Claire." Her gaze returned to the paper. "'But when you criticized me for another cultural blunder and then about my smoking habit, I got frustrated. I reacted without thinking. I saw the fear in your eyes when I grabbed your chin, and I deeply regret that. Please know I have never struck a woman. Not my mother. Not my sister. Not Sabirah.'" She raised her gaze to meet Claire's. "Who's Sabirah?"

"His wife who died last year."

"Oh. I didn't know." Sonja lifted the paper once more. "'And not the hired help. I never, ever would hit you, though I am sure Saturday you did not know that. Please accept my apology. I know you may not want to be my friend, but please understand I value our friendship. Sincerely, Ziad.'" She set the paper on the table. "That's pretty big of him."

Claire wanted to crawl into a hole and die. She settled for putting her head in her arms. They muffled her voice as she said, "I know. Oh, what is wrong with me? It's like we get along great. Then he makes a mistake, and I jump all over him like stink on a dog about it. *Then* it goes downhill from there."

"Do you know why?" Elizabeth asked.

Claire lifted her face. Yes. No! Admitting it would mean acknowledging she had a part of herself she severely disliked. "I have no idea."

Bless her, Sonja didn't call her on it. Instead, she folded the letter neatly in half and slid it to her. Her fingers skittered across the shiny surface of the table. Then she lifted her gaze to meet Claire's. "Could it be because you're a bit prejudiced due to what happened two and a half years ago?"

It stung, just as Claire had expected. She couldn't say a thing.

Arms now resting on the table, Sonja glanced around before softly speaking. "Look. I personally prosecuted that case. I saw what you saw, right? Sure, I didn't live it, but I saw the evidence. I can understand why you feel the way you do."

At least she agreed with her. "Good."

"But you've got to let it go. It's done. Off into the sunset. Don't punish Ziad just because he's Muslim."

"Easy to say. Hard to apply." Claire slouched in her chair and crossed her arms. She didn't want to talk about it anymore.

"I know." Sonja nodded. "Trust me, as an African-American who's seen her share of racism, it's hard not to bite back."

Elizabeth opened her journal. "Sounds like we need to add Ziad to our prayer list. And you too, Claire, darlin'." She made a notation. "How are you doing this week?"

Claire smiled, but it faded. On Friday, it would be five years since her husband and son perished in a fireball that had taken their lives. "I don't know."

"Do you need anyone to go with you to their graves?"

"Emma's going with me."

"You know you can call any of us at any time, right?" Sonja said. "Matter of fact, I'll call you Friday night."

"Thanks."

Elizabeth jotted that down. "We'll pray for you. I know this isn't easy. And it never will be."

"Yeah." Claire swallowed hard. No, it'd never get any easier. Not five years down the road. Probably not even ten. She just prayed she wouldn't come apart at the seams—again.

# 14

Thursday afternoon, on the heels of Eddie Davis, his mentor, Ziad burst through the sliding glass doors of Potter Hospital's Emergency Department.

The cop skidded to a stop at a counter in the lobby. "Minnie, hey."

"Well, Eddie Davis." A woman, one side of her head shaved and the other flopping over her ear, leaned a hip against the counter. "What brings you here?"

"We're looking for the OD case that just came in. Clem Joyner."

Her eyes widened. "Trauma bay four. He's in bad shape. His parents—"

"I'll be back." Eddie bolted down a short hall behind the counter. He whipped around a corner and peered into a trauma room. "Is this…"

A cardiograph hummed an ominous monotone. Before them, a doctor in scrubs shook his head. "Time of death, 5:26."

Ziad's stomach tightened.

The doctor drew a sheet over his patient, then glanced at them. "Too late, gentlemen. He coded out."

"Your thoughts?" Eddie asked.

The doctor held up a finger as the nurses disconnected a cardiograph and IV line. Once they'd gone, he hit a switch, and the sliding door that transformed the bay into an emergency operating room slid closed. "Sorry, but I didn't want to discuss this with everyone around." He scrubbed his face with his hands. "I'm thinking we saw another case of Zap."

Ziad stared. "You are sure?"

"Not officially, no. The ME's exam will tell us. But he had the same symptoms. We came close on this one."

"How so?" Eddie asked.

"The kid made it to the ED in his car. You see it out front?"

Ziad shook his head. While in prison, he'd lost those observational skills he'd honed over the years.

Eddie cast him a glance, which added to his shame. "Kind of hard to miss seeing it's half on the sidewalk. That was fifteen minutes ago. We were the first cops here."

Meaning, they now had a crime scene outside.

Eddie's radio crackled, and he murmured into it before saying, "I'll go secure it right now. Backup is on the way."

The doctor continued as if he hadn't heard him. "Just as he hit the lobby, the kid collapsed and started convulsing. We got him back here—we've been treating these cases like traumas—and within ten minutes he coded."

Suddenly realizing Eddie had left, Ziad began scribbling notes. He nodded toward the body. "May I?"

"Of course." The doctor eased onto a stool and began making his own notations.

Ziad lifted the sheet. He grimaced.

A young man, probably in his twenties. A head full of dark, thick hair. So peaceful now. Maybe normal except for the streaks of foam coming from one corner of his mouth.

Mindful of his need to avoid contaminating the body, Ziad drew the sheet further down and glanced at his arms. He easily spotted the IV's mark. Then more bruising further up. "Did he have any personal effects?"

"Over there." The doctor gestured to a counter.

Ziad found a messenger bag. After pulling on gloves, he undid the clasp and began sorting through it. Cell phone. Wallet. Papers. All sorts of small trash. A vial.

He lifted it from the satchel and studied it. Clear. Maybe. He set one of the sheets of white paper on the counter, then placed the vial on top. A faint, almost fluorescent green tint to it.

Zap. Once suspended in water, it adapted that eerie hue. Ziad swore under his breath.

The surgeon raised his head.

Eddie joined them. "Backup's secured the scene outside. Detective Rothschild's on his way. Whatcha got?"

Ziad gestured to his find. "For sure it is Zap."

Eddie cocked his head. "How so?"

"This vial." Ziad held it up. "It has the same tint as Zap."

The doctor crammed in for a look. "How do you know that?"

"I am from Jeddah. I worked this case while there."

"Dang." Eddie began shaking his head. "Crap's going down in my town, and I don't like it." He sighed. "We're on hold for now. Evidence techs will be in here shortly. Next of kin have been notified, and they're an hour out. I'll secure the scene here if you don't mind grabbing me a coffee or something."

"Where is the café?"

Eddie rattled off the directions, half of which Ziad missed.

He headed out. Oh, did he yearn for a smoke! But he'd quit when he'd left for Columbia.

It took a couple of wrong turns with friendly nurses providing the right directions before he found his destination. It fairly hummed with activity, which meant no place to sit unless he wanted to cozy up to a family of a patient in the middle, sit next to a doctor who read a journal and drank a cup of coffee at a small table in the corner, or sit with a woman in a flight suit who had her back to him. She had dark hair caught up in a braid. Wait. Her straight posture gave her away.

Claire.

Case suddenly forgotten, his pulse quickened. His focus sharpened. Was she still angry with him? Would she make a scene if he greeted her?

Gathering his courage, he approached the table. "Claire?"

She glanced up. No anger in her eyes, only weariness rimmed with something he couldn't define. "Ziad, hi."

"How are you?"

"Fair to middlin'."

He raised an eyebrow.

"I'm okay."

Time to seize the moment before he lost all courage. He blurted, "May I join you?"

She smiled. "Please. I'm on my break right now. Just a couple of more hours, and then it's home to bed for me."

He snagged a cup of coffee and brought it to the table. "Has it been a long week?"

"Try two weeks. If I remember correctly, it's been a long couple of weeks for you too."

"Exactly." He popped off the lid and sipped the dark liquid. Not the best, but it would do. "I returned Friday night and have spent the past few days at my clerk job in the morning and working with a mentor at the police department in the afternoon."

He didn't care to go into why he was at the hospital.

Beside her on the table, a radio crackled softly. Her gaze shot to it, then returned to him. "Sorry. I'm a flight nurse, so I'm having to keep an ear on the radio in case I get called."

"What does a flight nurse do?"

"I go out on the helicopters that pick up critically ill patients."

"I see." Ziad sized her up in a second. Not a speck of anger seemed to remain in her. It intrigued him. Why? "Did you receive my letter?"

"I did." She lowered her gaze, then raised it. "Thank you. I appreciate your apology."

He moved his cup in little circles. "I realized I must have scared you. I did not mean to do that. You forgive me?"

"I do. Your apology meant a lot to me."

His shoulders relaxed. "I am glad."

She sipped her drink. "How are you settling in?"

"What does your mother say? It is a process?"

She smiled. "That's right. What's the process?"

"Buying furniture. Buying clothing." He left out the way his jaw had dropped when he'd received quotes for someone to do his cleaning and laundry. Too expensive, even with his SANG pension and convenience store salary. "A lot to remember."

"I'm sure." She muffled a yawn. "Sorry. I'm wiped out."

An idea popped into his head. "May I make amore with you?"

She stared.

Oh, no. Not another blunder! As her lips began twitching upward, the heat rose in his neck.

She began laughing softly. "Make amends, maybe?"

That was the word. "Uh, yes. Make amends. May I visit you tomorrow?"

"Sure." Her answer came instantly. "I'm actually off all day. What time do you get off?"

"Five in the afternoon from my reserve officer job."

"Come by when you—" Her radio beeped a long signal. She held up a finger and listened to the message coming across the speaker. A frown marred her face. "I'm sorry, but I've got to go. There's been a bad traffic accident at the I-95 and I-26 interchange."

"Be safe, yes?"

"I will be." She rose and collected the radio, then paused. "I'll see you tomorrow."

Ziad watched her leave and headed to the counter for Eddie's coffee. Suddenly, he realized they hadn't set a time. Oh, well. He'd see her soon. Then maybe he could get to the bottom of whatever sadness had tinged her gaze.

"Emma, I'll be fine." Claire stood on the screened-in porch of her house.

Her sister cocked her head, and her brow knit. "You're sure?"

"Promise. Thanks for going with me this morning." Emma's presence had saved her as she'd wept at Jackson's and Little Jack's graves. "And for keeping my mind off things by dragging me around downtown."

Emma's eyes sparkled with more unshed tears. "Oh, I don't think I dragged you."

Claire grabbed her in at hug.

Emma sniffled. "I could hang out with you."

She pulled back. "All I'm going to do is draw. And Ziad's coming over later."

"Oh?" Delight briefly lit her sister's eyes. "When?"

"Tonight. He said something about making amends after The Yard Sale Incident. Except he called it amore by accident."

That got a giggle. "I'm glad. Call me if you need me to come over."

"I will. Promise." Claire hugged her sister again, then watched as she headed down the back steps. A moment later, her Honda hummed to life. The sound faded as it headed down the road.

Once inside, Claire kicked off her sandals and wandered into her studio. Drawing. Good therapy because it required every bit of her concentration. She slid onto her chair and for a moment stared out the window. On the water of the harbor, a sailboat slid by underneath cloudless skies. Such a perfect day, so much like that day five years before.

*No. I'm not going to think about it anymore.* She selected a picture of three-year-old Randy, her youngest nephew, at the beach. A perfect present for Allie's birthday.

Three hours later, no sleep, stress, and crying for an hour straight that morning had combined into a migraine. She set down her drawing pencil and winced as she rubbed her temples and stared over the bay. Ugh. Only ibuprofen and sleep would take care of this baddie.

She reached for the folder where she kept pictures used for past drawings. Her fingers snagged one side.

"Oh, no!"

The whole thing fell to the floor. Like playing cards, the photos scattered across the tile. She groaned, knelt, and began gathering them to her. Emma and an Arabian mare a sheik had given to her. Rainbow Row at sunset. Faith and Grace in period costume when they'd worked at Sutton Hall one summer.

She gazed at the last one. Her oldest nephew, Tripp, at age two. Unlike Randy, who had sandy hair and fair skin, Tripp had inherited the Catawba genes of the Montgomery line and sported the same dark hair and tan as Claire. In this picture, Claire held him on her lap as he grinned big and wide for the camera.

So much like Little Jack.

The photo fell from her suddenly numb fingers and fluttered downward.

Grief attacked her from all angles. Her headache worsened. Her chest tightened, and a lump built in her throat. "No!"

She fled diagonally across the house to double doors she only opened once a year. Chest heaving, she burst inside and collapsed onto a barrister chair. Yanking three scrapbooks off the lowest shelf of a bookcase, she dropped them on the desk. Dust rose in an evil plume.

Her chest heaved with sobs as she flipped to the back. There, Mama had placed the articles and obituaries about the accident.

The one that had taken the lives of her husband and only child.

And her future.

Resting her elbows on the desk, she clamped her head between her hands and wagged it back and forth.

"Why, God? Why? Why did you take them?" Her shouted words bounced off the twelve-foot ceiling.

The sobs came in a torrent.

"And why did I have to lose the last vestige of Jackson? I don't understand. I don't. I don't. I don't!" Claire bolted to her feet. She stumbled down the short hall to the kitchen. Tears pouring down her cheeks, she ripped open the freezer door. A couple of packs of frozen vegetables fell to the floor as she fumbled for the cans of piña colada mix left over from when Emma had stayed with her.

She grabbed some rum from the shelf of a high cabinet.

It took a moment to mix herself a pitcher. She poured a generous amount into a tall glass and drained it almost in one long pull. She poured herself another.

"God, it's not fair. It's not! Why me? Why them?" She croaked those words and straightened. A puffball of warmth unfolded in her stomach. That light-headed feeling hit. She wandered to the couch on the screened-in porch and worked on her second glass. Head resting against the cushions, her world began spinning. Maybe now the pain would go away.

# 15

Early Friday evening, Ziad bounded up Claire's front porch steps.

Time to make amends. Perhaps the bouquet of yellow roses he held would cheer her up. An invitation to supper would help. Then maybe he could get to the bottom of what had ailed her the day before.

He rapped on the screened door frame. "Claire?"

No answer.

Strange, especially with her Mustang beneath the house. Sure, they hadn't set a time, but she'd said she'd be home all day and evening. It would be hard to cheer her up if she weren't there.

"Claire?"

Still no answer.

Moisture suddenly sheened his hands. His heart sped up as he slipped inside and locked the screened door behind him. No lights on in the family room and kitchen. He tried to quash his rising fear. "Where are you?"

"Ziad, hi."

Claire stood in the doorway of the open French doors leading to the screened-in porch. "What are you doing here?"

Relief fought with confusion. She was alive and well, but... "I thought you invited me to come over."

"Did I?" She shrugged. "Guess I forgot."

She wobbled inside.

Something didn't seem right. He nodded at her half-empty glass. "What are you drinking?"

"Oh, piña colada."

Whatever that was.

She moved toward the kitchen and staggered when she bumped into a couch. "Oops! Guess there's a couch there." She steadied herself before squeezing between him and the island. "I'm glad you came by."

He instantly recognized the odor emanating from her breath.

Alcohol.

"Have you been drinking?"

She stopped. "Huh? Oh, uh, yeah. Piña colada, right? I told you."

"How many have you had?"

"I dunno." She smiled broadly at him, then nodded toward the bouquet he'd clutched to his chest. "Whatcha got?"

He held it out. "A gift for you."

She took it and tossed it on the bar like it was garbage.

His eyes narrowed. "Why are you drinking?"

"'Cause I want to." She poured some more into her glass and sloshed half of it onto the counter. "You wan' some?"

"I have already had my drink for the night. Of coffee, that is."

She guffawed, then snorted. "Sorry! You're funny."

She wiped her hand across her mouth and drained half the glass before grabbing his hand.

He tensed and tried to pull back.

She tugged him toward the den. "Oh, don't be so scared of me. C'mon! Tell me how your day was." She drew him closer to her. "You sure you don' wan' one? Come to the couch."

She lost her balance and staggered into him.

Coldness hit his chest as most of the liquid sloshed onto his shirt. He flinched. "Claire!"

"Sorry!"

Ziad pried himself loose and stumbled against the island. "You need to go to bed."

She pouted. "No, I don't."

Before she could react, he snatched her glass from her fingers. "Yes, you do."

"No!" She sat down on the floor and crossed her arms like an angry child.

"Why are you so difficult?"

"I'm not dif… diffi…" She started giggling. "Can't talk straight."

That did it! Before she could react, he grabbed her under the arms and hauled her to her feet.

She squirmed. "No!"

Could things get any worse? He almost forcibly escorted her up the stairs to the second floor. Double doors caught his attention. He guided her through them. Good. The master suite.

Claire shook loose and swayed. "You're no fun!"

Between her and the bed, he folded his arms across his chest. "Maybe not, but neither are you at this moment."

"Party pooper."

He ignored her. "You need rest."

Lightning fast, she grabbed him.

Ziad yanked away.

Her fingers caught his shirt. Several buttons popped.

Off balance, he tumbled onto the mattress. The hard outline of a book bit into his back.

She tried to kiss him.

Things had just gotten worse.

He struggled and shoved her onto her back. "Claire, no. Stop!"

She thrashed. "C'mon. You know you want to!"

He grabbed her wrists and held them down. "To what?"

"Kiss me, you idiot! You're such a—"

"Claire!" He took a deep breath. Now what? He wouldn't have a repeat of a couple of weeks ago when he'd scared her. "I will not. I think—"

A snore answered him.

"Claire?"

No answer.

Shaking, Ziad slid off the mattress. He braced his hands on his knees and hung his head. What had just happened? She'd almost jumped him. He touched his gaping shirt as his gaze returned to the bed.

Claire lay as still as death.

For a brief second, terror seized him. He held his hand above her mouth. Breath whispered across his skin. He turned her onto her side so if she threw up, she wouldn't drown in her own vomit. He found an afghan and draped it over her.

Outside, the light began dimming, and thunder rumbled through the windows. He turned on a bedside lamp and gazed around the room.

Several frames on a dresser a meter and a half tall caught his attention. He reached for one. Emma and Ben the weekend Ben had proposed to his bride. He remembered a copy of that one from Ben's apartment. One of her with her parents. Another of her twin sisters. He set that one on the mattress with the others.

A few more were crammed at the back. Curious, he drew one to him. Claire with a handsome man and a child.

His blood chilled. His fingers tightened on the frame to the point where he worried he'd break it. Claire had a husband. And she hadn't told him!

Forget it. He couldn't be friends with a liar.

He almost ran down the stairs and fumbled with the lock of the screened door.

*Stop!*

Ziad froze.

Time to go. Except something wasn't right. What? Like his feet had a mind of their own, he returned to the bedroom.

Claire lay still.

As if preparing for a round of shots, he steeled himself and reached for the remaining frames on the dresser. Claire with the same man on their wedding day. One of them at a dinner party. Her with a little boy and a wide smile.

As if handling fine china, he replaced each frame where he'd found it. What had happened? He rubbed his chin and paced. She didn't wear a ring. Her last name was Montgomery, like her parents', not some married name.

Ziad began nodding. Maybe she and her husband were separated. If so, then surely the husband had something in the closet. He crossed the room and found the walk-in closet. He flipped on the light and searched. Nothing. No pants. No shirts. No shoes. Not even a man's belt. Not one bit of evidence that showed a man had lived there.

Of course. They were divorced. Perhaps the father had custody of their son. That was what they did in Saudi Arabia, after all. Her shame must have been so great she'd taken her maiden name. It also explained her reticence about her drinking problem.

He wandered onto the landing. All of the other doors were open save for one. He stepped inside, flipped on the light, and stared. A child's bedroom. Someone had painted on cheery pale blue walls a boat with animals in it and a rainbow over it. A wooden stork leaning next to a window proclaimed the news.

Jackson Rayford Middleton, Junior. Born March 18, 2003, 9:48 AM. 8 pounds, 1 ounce, 21 inches long.

His gaze roamed toward a dresser. He ran his finger along the top. Dusty, as if it hadn't been dusted in months, if not years. A thick layer cloaked two stacks of clothing on a table. Three stuffed animals lay scattered on a bedspread sporting little elephants.

"Strange," he whispered. Time had frozen in place here, for sure.

Why?

Ziad returned downstairs. The artificial dusk of the approaching storm almost completely darkened the foyer as he pondered his discovery.

He shook his head. Claire was obviously an alcoholic to the point where the father had gained total custody. She'd kept her son's room the same to preserve more idyllic times. He shrugged. So sorry, but he'd not involve himself with someone who had such a problem.

He stepped onto the porch and began pulling the main door closed.

*Stop!*

This time, he jumped as if the *jinn* had kicked him.

He shivered, and his mind flashed to when he'd copied all of the information related to the Zap case to his jump drive. Now, that coldness remained just as it had then.

Like it or not, he should stay.

Once in the foyer, he shut the door behind him and locked it.

A dim glow from his right caught his attention.

He pushed one of the double doors open.

"Interesting." He studied the room. Masculine semicircular desk with a credenza. Deep blue paint on the wall. Dark wood furniture. Barrister's chair. The father's study? It had to be.

Three books lay open in a golden pool of light emanating from a library lamp.

Ziad eased onto a chair in front of the desk and turned the lamp so he could gaze at them. Yellowed news articles about…

*No. Claire, not you!*

His jaw dropped as he read the obituary for Jackson Middleton, husband of Claire, father of Jackson Junior, also killed in an automobile accident on this very same day five years before, April 30, 2005.

His stomach twinged as the grief he thought he'd stowed away flooded to the surface, this time for the woman who lay upstairs. He took a deep breath to calm his nerves.

Curiosity got the better of him. He turned to the beginning. It started with a much younger Claire, who radiated happiness on her wedding day. She was so beautiful, much like she'd been just a few weeks ago at Emma's wedding. Only the Claire in the pictures had innocence about her. Life hadn't etched its marks around the corners of her eyes or created the solemnity he'd sensed within her.

Then came pictures of her with Jackson at various places. And some pictures of her pregnant. She glowed. Then came one of a tiny baby in Claire's arms, the proud father looking on. The smile on her face said it all. She'd loved being a mother.

Ziad pulled the doors closed and retreated to the family room. He paced as he thought about his options. He didn't want Claire to wake up in the middle of the night, disoriented, terrified, and in anguish.

He'd stay, be there for her.

First things first. His shirt stuck to him and stank. He'd wash it. He thought he remembered the directions Allison Montgomery had given him. After tossing it into the washer, he headed downstairs and dumped the remains of the offending drink down the sink. He placed the pitcher in the dishwasher. Once he'd wiped the counter clean of all of the sticky mess, he scrubbed his hands like a surgeon preparing for an operation.

What about the roses? She had to keep vases somewhere. He opened several cabinet doors. Nothing. Another pitcher, one he found in a glass-fronted cabinet, would have to suffice. Those, he set on the island.

Lightning lit the harbor for a second. Thunder followed, then rain. A strong breeze blew through the windows. He shivered and watched it for a few minutes. The wall next to her art studio caught his eye. Recessed lighting lit a series of eight photographs, all framed in black with white matting. In calligraphy he easily recognized as Claire's touch, she'd written the place, month, and year on the mats. All were after 2006, as if she'd checked out of life for a year.

*Not that I blame you.*

He swallowed hard and turned away as his own grief reasserted itself.

He approached the studio and peered at the paper clipped on the table. A picture of a little boy. So impressive, so lifelike yet with her own stamp on it. A folder laying on the floor caught his eyes. He leafed through it and smiled at the picture of Emma with her mare, which Ben had told him she'd receive in a few weeks. He set the folder on the table.

There!

Another picture lay face down on the tile. He stooped and picked it up. A boy in Claire's arms, just like he'd seen upstairs. Wait. He recalled the picture of Claire and Jackson, Junior. Was her son in this picture? He held it up and gazed at it in better light.

No. Another child, maybe a nephew, who bore a striking resemblance to her deceased toddler. Maybe seeing this picture had led to agony only alcohol could assuage. *I wish I could do something to ease your pain.*

At the very least, he could check on her. Upstairs, the washer chimed. He threw his shirt into the dryer before pushing open the bedroom door.

She lay on her side, her eyes tightly closed, her hand near her face where it rested on the pillow. He swallowed hard as he remembered her grabbing him. Something had been on the bed. A book. Her Bible.

Picking it up, he slipped inside her walk-in closet so his reading wouldn't disturb her. He flipped to where she'd placed a bookmark and stared at an underlined verse. *"For I know the plans I have for you," declares the Lord, "plans to prosper you and not to harm you, plans to give you a hope and future. Then you will call upon me and come and pray to me, and I will listen to you. You will seek me and find me when you seek me with all your heart."* He shook his head. Then he noticed another tabbed page. He flipped over. *And we know that in all things God works for the good of those who love him, who have been called according to his purpose.* He stared those words. Why had they caught her attention?

Nothing came to him.

He placed the Bible on her nightstand before tiptoeing from the room and heading downstairs for his sunset prayers. Weariness swept over him. Though he wanted to lie down, he began them in the den. Other thoughts—or words—intruded into his mind. *Plans to prosper you and not to harm you. To give you a hope and a future. You will seek me and find me. In all things. For the good of those who love him.*

He flopped onto the couch in the den and found a soccer match, which he watched until the last prayers. Anything to take his mind off what now stalked him. Just as he rose to spread a towel on the floor for evening prayers, the phone rang.

He let the answering machine pick it up.

Claire's voice filled the room. "You have reached the Montgomery residence. So sorry we can't take your call, but leave a message, and we'll get back to you."

The machine beeped.

A woman spoke. "Claire, this is Sonja. I'm worried that you didn't pick up. If you don't answer within five seconds, I'm coming over there."

Ziad scrambled for the extension on an end table. "Hello?"

"Who is this?" Suspicion dripped from her voice.

His heart hammered. "This is Ziad al-Kazim."

"Ziad?" Warmth replaced the suspicion. "This is Sonja Williams. I'm one of Claire's friends. Is she okay?"

"She… did not feel well." Better not to besmirch her reputation with her friend. "She went to bed early."

"Will you tell her I called?"

He sagged onto the couch. "Of course."

Finally, it was time to rest. With his shirt now dry, he turned off all of the lights downstairs, kicked off his sandals, and placed his silver watch on the end table. With a weary sigh, he stretched his long frame out and pulled a blanket he found over himself. He laced his hands behind his head. Surprisingly, he drifted to sleep almost instantly.

Dreams assaulted him. Fragments. Flashes. Sabirah in a white caftan kneeling in a garden. Golden scales in front of her. Muhammed Amir, his oldest, joining her. Ziad knelt across from them in a spotless white *thobe*.

Muhammed Amir upended a black velvet bag full of polished gray stones. He placed one on the *Hasana'at* tray.

"For caring for Claire," he said. He added another one. "And for your compassion with her."

Ziad stared. "How do you know her?"

Sabirah held up a stone and placed it on the *Sayia'at* tray. "You judged her."

"I didn't know!"

She held up still another stone. "You thought she was an alcoholic."

"It was a mistake."

A third stone wound up on the *Sayia'at* tray. "And you wanted to leave her alone and helpless."

With a jagged breath, his eyes snapped open. His mind ventured toward those words in Claire's Bible.

Did God really prosper those who had suffered great loss? He thought about Claire's situation. Absolutely. She had a close family, as shown by a portrait of the sisters he'd noticed leaning against the wall next to the fireplace. All six of them, dressed in jeans and white shirts and taken at a Wal-Mart studio. A lark during Emma's bachelorette party, she'd told him at the wedding.

What about him? No. He now lived in exile with no family save for his sister who had all but disowned him. No doubt about it, his pride had been his downfall. Allah's plans had been to harm him, not prosper him.

*You will seek and find me.* Claire sought God. She went to church and read Scripture, at least if the marks he'd noticed throughout the pages meant anything.

He'd done the works required by his faith. The *Haj.* Prayers five times a day. Alms to the poor. And still Allah had turned his back on him.

*To give you a hope and a future.* No common ground there, either. Claire had moved past her tragedy, even if she'd stumbled today.

Had he? Could he? Could he really have a hope and a future? Hah. A far-fetched concept for him since he now lived in exile.

Ziad swallowed hard. His eyes filled as he thought about Sabirah. She'd been his life, his sons the future of the al-Kazim clan. With their deaths, he'd lost his own hope and future.

He shifted and screwed his eyes shut. It was better to not think of those things. At least not then. Maybe not at all.

# 16

"What do you say, my friend? You have got to be kidding me?" Early Saturday afternoon, Ziad stared at the pile of laundry stacked knee high on his living room floor.

"Nope. Time to sort." Ben stuffed his hands into his jeans pockets. "Put everything in those great baskets we just bought at Wal-Mart."

Ziad lifted the plastic bags of items from the baskets, just a small part of his eight-hundred-dollar shopping extravaganza to his first big-box store. "How to do it?"

"Whites, darks, and khakis plus reds. So three piles." Ben smirked. "Unless you have delicate items."

Ziad scowled at him.

As he began sorting, Ben's phone rang. "Hey, babe."

Emma must have been calling.

Jeans and dark T-shirts in one basket. Undershirts in another. The same with the twenty-one pairs of underwear he now owned. He shook his head. After Ben left, he'd need to finish cleaning, then unpack the boxes that contained his personal effects from Jeddah. Ben had brought those over that morning. His ears perked up as he caught his side of the conversation.

"Yeah, I'm at Ziad's… I got the boxes… I'll tell you later… Okay. Promise I'll take care of that when I get back… Have fun. Love you. 'Bye." Ben shoved his phone into his pocket. "Em says hi."

"Does she cook and clean at your house?"

"We split it," Ben grabbed a broom and began sweeping the kitchen and dining area. He herded the dust bunnies into a dustpan and dumped them in the trash.

"Really?" Huh? In Saudi Arabia, cleaning and cooking were strictly women's work. Even a cleaning lady had paid Ben regular visits. "Even though you work more than fifty hours a week?"

"Yeah. Neither of us are neat people, but we've also learned that if we don't clean, we'll live in a pig sty. Since we both work, we switch off."

"You do not ask her to do that?"

"Nah." Ben joined the fun and tossed some clothing onto the darks pile. "I knew she was going to be working, and like you, we found out how expensive hired help is. Besides, right now it's just us in the apartment. Not too much to take care of. You done?"

Ziad gazed at the baskets. "Finished."

"Start a load and follow me upstairs." Ben sorted through the bags and dumped some bottles, a pack of sponges, and a pair of rubber gloves into a bucket.

Ziad followed.

When he stood in the spacious master bath, Ben handed him the gloves. "Time to clean the bathroom. Put these on."

Ziad took them and held them by two fingers as if they were a snake.

"Promise it won't offend your manhood. Then take the Lysol," Ben set the bottle on the counter, "and spray the inside of the bowl and outside of the toilet." He opened a pack of sponges. "Then wipe it down with a wet sponge."

For the twentieth time, Ziad wished he could have afforded hired help. Still, he followed Ben's directions.

"Congratulations, my friend, you've cleaned your first toilet. Now do the same with the counter using this." Ben pointed to a bottle of 409.

As Ziad began cleaning, his friend leaned against the wall. "I heard about your Zap case a few days ago."

Ziad whipped around so fast that a spray of the cleaner shot from the bottle's nozzle.

Ben darted out of the way. "Whoa! Treat cleaners like a gun. Keep the nozzle pointed downrange."

Ziad scrubbed the counter as if his life depended on it. "How did you find out?"

"Work." Ben scrubbed a hand through his dirty blond curls. "I'm on Charleston Metro's Zap task force, and we met yesterday. Okay. Rinse the counter."

"What do you know?"

Ben sighed and folded his arms across his chest. "A lot I can't tell you. Except it's showing up in places all over the state now. Eight here, the one at the ED being the eighth. Some in Columbia. Aiken. Spartanburg/Greenville area. Florence. Myrtle Beach too."

"Do you have a timeline for its spread?"

A smile tipped Ben's lips upward. "Maybe."

"Ben!" Frustration nipped at Ziad for being shut out.

"I'm sorry, Ziad. But yes, we do. And trust me when we say your find was helpful. We got a whole vial of the stuff from that case. All I can do is say thank you. Nothing else."

He might as well have added, "And don't ask about it anymore."

"How's Claire? Sounds like you spent a lot of time with her last night."

Ziad knew when to back off. "It was... a long night."

"Em said the thirtieth of April is always hard on her. I'm glad you could be there for her." Ben stuffed his hands into the back pockets of his jeans. "You're one of the best people I could think of to support her."

That assuaged some of Ziad's frustration. "Thank you. I am planning on visiting her tonight."

A sly grin crossed his friend's face. "Supper?"

"Perhaps."

The grin turned to another smirk. "Have fun. Shower time, my friend. Get that cleaner."

Ziad groaned. At least learning how to clean his apartment, which took the rest of the afternoon, kept his mind from spinning in all directions. Finally, after he bid Ben goodbye and headed upstairs to clean up, his mind latched on to the Zap case. Not his. No, the FBI's. And that of the task force. Well, he'd help. One way or the other. Until then, he had plans with one very beautiful woman.

# 17

By the afternoon, Claire felt human again. Along with some aspirin, a nap had chased away her hangover. A hot shower had cleansed her. If only she could repair her relationship with Ziad.

She cringed. As she stood in a pair of jeans shorts and a red T-shirt, she stared at the afghan in a wad on her bed. And her Bible on the nightstand. She closed her eyes. *What do I say to someone who I called an idiot and a party pooper? To someone I practically assaulted?*

No words came.

Maybe cleaning up completely would help. She found the piña colada pitcher in the dishwasher. The counters were spotless, not one sign of the wicked mix she'd spilled the night before.

She carried the Oriental rugs outside and hung them over the walkway rails leading to the dock. With a broom in hand to beat them, she headed back down the steps.

"Claire, dear!"

Claire smiled at her elderly neighbor, who lived next to her on the den side of the house. "Mrs. Chitworth! Good afternoon!"

"I hope you're doing well, dear." The old woman carefully made her way down the stairs and stopped on her walkway so she stood across from Claire. "I saw you had someone over last night."

Ziad. She'd probably seen his 4Runner in the carport. "I did."

"I was watering my violets in my den when I noticed that young man of yours sitting in your den without his shirt on."

Claire's stomach dropped. Her cheeks flamed. "I'm sorry?"

In a dramatic whisper, Mrs. Chitworth said, "He didn't have his shirt on. My, my, he's a handsome fellow! You should keep that one around."

Oh, dear. What could she say to that? "Um—"

"He's quite a looker. Reminds me of my Henry when we were young." Mrs. Chitworth winked. "Well, it's getting too warm out here for this old woman. Take care, all right? And if you want, bring your fellow over for tea. I'd love to meet him sometime."

She shuffled toward her porch.

Once her screened door banged shut, Claire wielded the broom like a baseball bat. What on earth? Ziad hadn't been wearing his shirt? Why? *Whap! Whap!* Dust flew into the air as she beat the rugs with more force than needed. *Wham! Slap!* What had her neighbor thought? Moreover, why did she even care? Mrs. Chitworth had certainly gotten an eyeful. A smile pushed its way loose as she thought about her neighbor's "eavesdropping."

Just as she spread the rugs on the dark hardwood, the phone rang.

"I've been worried sick about you!" Sonja's voice blasted in her ear before she even said hello. "I was so worried that if you hadn't answered, I was going to come over there. Didn't Ziad tell you to call me?"

"I remember now. He told me this morning. I'm sorry I forgot."

"Wait. He told you when?"

"Uh, this morning." Claire winced and rubbed her forehead. "He stayed over last night."

"Claire, you know how that—"

"Don't worry. Nothing funky happened." Talk about embarrassing. She drifted to the island and lightly fingered the petals of the yellow roses she'd found after he'd left.

"Actually, I'm glad he stayed over. I know the thirtieth is rough for you. Let's catch up on Tuesday, okay?"

"Will do." Claire sighed and placed the phone on its cradle in the family room. A folded towel from her half bath sat on the end table. Ziad must have used it for prayers. A blanket lay crumpled on one side of the couch.

Guilt hit her. *He was too scared to leave me alone. That's how drunk I was.* She shuddered. After folding the blanket and putting it on the bottom shelf of one of the end tables, she plumped the pillows and rearranged them. She set a stack of magazines and a picture of Ben and Emma on the couch so she could dust. A gleam caught her eye.

"A watch?" Pure silver, it seemed, with its face of rich onyx and some sort of emblem created by tiny emeralds, topazes, and diamonds. A palm tree and two crossed daggers. She smiled and rubbed her thumb across the smooth crystal. "Ziad."

She'd take it to him when she ran out to do some errands.

Now for her bedroom. She folded the afghan and draped it on a chair by the French doors before bending so she could lift the comforter to change the sheets. Wait. What were those black spots? She bent closer and studied the pale blue and yellow fabric. A button. More like three of them.

Oh, dear. She eased onto the bed as her cheeks heated. Had she tried to kiss him? Maybe. She'd noticed his gaping shirt when he'd sat down beside her on the porch early this morning. Her hand must have caught the fabric. What had she done?

She flopped backward onto the bed and stared at the rotating ceiling fan. "Lord, can this get any worse?" She held up her hand. "No, don't answer that."

She found a fourth on the carpet. She'd return those along with the watch. Maybe she'd offer to mend his shirt as penance for her stupidity the night before.

What else could she do? Prepare to have him walk out of her life. He probably thought she was promiscuous. After her behavior the night before, she wouldn't blame him for that conclusion. Regardless of his reaction, she should at least apologize, and it wouldn't hurt to dress up when she did it.

Claire chose a deep blue sleeveless top and a broomstick skirt of cool Caribbean colors shot through with gold. She took her time with her makeup and dried her hair until it fell in soft waves past her shoulders. With purse in hand, she collected the baggie containing the watch and buttons and headed downstairs.

Just as she opened the door to her Mustang, Ziad's 4Runner pulled into the driveway.

Her heart pounded. Sweat broke out on her palms, and the shakes began. Time to face him, and she didn't even have her apology framed in her mind.

Expression neutral, he climbed from the SUV and approached her.

*Oh, my…* The thought stayed stuck in her head as she surveyed his trim build cloaked in white shirt and blue jeans. "Uh, hi. Um, do you want some iced tea?"

How dumb could she get? She turned and almost fled up the steps.

Ziad followed. "Please. Your aunt and uncle always shared with me when I visited with them."

"I thought Saudi was more of a coffee place." Her hands shook as she poured two tall glasses of tea. Would they stop already?

"We drink tea as well." He took his glass. Once more, that dark gaze of his cut right into her soul.

Escape seemed to be the better option. "Do you want to go to the dock? It's too nice to sit inside."

"Of course." With a small bow, he stepped aside. "After you, madam."

As if facing her executioner, she trudged down the wood to the covered end, where two kayaks sat on a rack. A grill was in the open, and she settled on a bench across from it. What could she say? Oh, to have had more time to prepare!

She squared her shoulders and bowed her head. "I—I'm sorry about last night."

"Forgiven." That word came out almost instantaneously.

Had she heard him right? "What?"

"I forgive you." His gaze remained focused on her. No anger behind it. No judgment. Just sincerity. He seated himself and focused on his tea.

The silence turned awkward. She rushed ahead. "You've got to understand. I very rarely drink that much anymore."

"You had reason."

Huh? How did he know that? Had Emma tipped him off? She hadn't said anything to her about it. "What do you mean?"

"I confess I did a bit of snooping after you passed out. I knew something was not right. I am very sorry. I had no idea."

For a moment, Claire stared at the water. A stiff wind had come up, and clouds had begun building over the land. Storms were coming and not just over Charleston. She swallowed hard. "The day Sabirah and your family died, did you ever expect it would happen?"

A pause as if he carefully considered her words. "No. Not at all."

"Same here." She closed her eyes as she remembered that fateful day. Little Jack hugged her good morning, and they cuddled on his toddler bed for a moment. "Jackson had clinic, so he went to work at seven instead of 5:30. He liked to get some time in to catch up on charts. I got Little Jack to preschool. While he was there, I did some errands. I was exhausted by the time I picked him up."

She clamped her jaw shut. Before she realized it, she wrapped her arms around her belly, almost the same way she had exactly five years before. It twinged as if to sympathize with her sadness. "By that point, I was about two months pregnant with our second child."

"What?"

She kept her focus on the water, lest she turn her head and see pity in his eyes. "That didn't make the papers. It's funny. I called Little Jack my dream child. Hardly any morning sickness. He barely fussed. He was sleeping through the night at four weeks. But this one?" She shook her head. "I had major morning sickness. I was exhausted all of the time. It was almost like some sort of wicked, strange payback."

"Did your families know?"

"We'd told them that Sunday before." She swallowed hard and picked up her glass. It trembled, this time from nerves rather than adrenaline. "Mama and Daddy had invited us for supper that night."

Ziad leaned forward, his elbows on his knees. "But you did not go."

"No. That day, Little Jack had really gotten on my nerves. He hadn't wanted to take his nap. He was whiny. By the time Jackson got home, I told him I was going to stay home and sleep while they went."

Images from that afternoon flashed before her. Jackson kissing her goodbye and telling her he loved her. Little Jack hugging her.

She lowered her head and bit her lip.

"How did it happen?"

Oh, she really didn't want to talk about it. She closed her eyes and shook her head.

Warm hands covered hers.

She opened her eyes.

Ziad knelt in front of her. His grip remained firm, but in an assuring kind of way. As if he wouldn't judge her. "Ziad…"

"You have nothing to fear regarding last night. No one in your family knows. Not Ben. Not Emma. Not your parents."

No, but her neighbor and best friend knew.

He straightened. "I may not have an answer, but I listen well."

Did she trust him? He hadn't taken advantage of her. Hadn't hurt her at all. No, he'd protected her, not just her body but her honor.

She took a deep breath. "It was a drunk driver. Going a hundred down that road where Mama and Daddy live. Jackson didn't see him because it was racing under a full moon without lights." She covered a sob with her hand. "They never stood a chance even though the Lexus is supposed to be one of the safest cars out there. They died at the scene."

Now tears poured down her face.

Like he'd done with her almost a month before, Ziad didn't say anything, only settled beside her again and placed a handkerchief in her hands.

"It's so hard." Her voice broke.

"I know."

She took a deep breath to steady herself. "The funerals were a week later. The night after the services, I… I miscarried." No need to go into the gory details. "It… it was bad, no, worse than bad. I… I had to have a hysterectomy."

She yearned for him to put his arms around her, not in a romantic sense but in one that comforted her when she so badly needed it. She wanted to hear him say she'd see them one day again, that physical death was not the end.

Hah. Wrong guy for that.

He didn't say anything. Instead, he remained where he was on the bench, the three feet between them seeming like the Grand Canyon.

After a moment, he spoke. "Please know I am sorry."

"I do."

"And I am sorry I so misjudged you last night. I thought you were—"

"Promiscuous?" She winced. No surprise there when she recollected her behavior.

"Yes. Now, I know better."

What could she say? Nothing. She stared at the harbor, much like she'd done from her French doors during her year of mourning. This time, the water comforted her.

Ziad rose. He held out his hand. "May I?"

She offered her tea glass, but he smiled and shook his head. Still the gentleman, something she truly appreciated.

She took his hand and rose.

He released her as soon as she was on her feet, then turned to her as they began walking toward the house. "I would like to take you to supper. I was going to yesterday because I could tell Thursday that you were sad. I think it would do you some good to breathe in life."

He was right on that count. "I'd love to."

"Then let's go."

They wandered toward the house. Claire thought she heard the back door to Mrs. Chitworth's house shut. A little smile forced its way loose before fading. Ziad hadn't judged. Maybe, just maybe, they could salvage the evening.

# 18

"May I ask you something?" Three hours later, Ziad shared a booth with Claire at the same open-air restaurant where they'd dined a few weeks earlier.

She cocked an eyebrow. "About?"

How should he phrase this without upsetting her in public? "What happened after the funerals? And your miscarriage?"

Her expression, which had been open, slid into neutral.

A blunder again, but this time not cultural. Hastily, he added, "Only if you want to."

She sipped her iced tea and shifted on her bench. "It was a hard year."

"How so?"

She lowered her gaze. "I didn't leave the house." She raised it. "Literally."

He stared. "How was that possible?"

"Okay. I take that back. I went to see my doctor for my post-op appointment. But beyond that, I didn't leave. My family made sure I ate. So did Mrs. Chitworth, my neighbor. They kept me company when almost everyone else abandoned me."

"Why?"

"I don't think they knew how to deal with a woman who lost a husband and child all at once. I guess it was beyond awkward."

He could relate. Only Ben and Sami had been regular visitors during his stay in prison. "What happened? You obviously left the house at some point."

That got a smile, though those jade green eyes remained serious. "Oh, I did. I still remember that day. It was mid-May. I was staring at myself in my full-length mirror. Suddenly, I realized how skinny I was since I'd lost about twenty pounds. I hadn't had a haircut in a year, and because I'd barely been eating, my hair was coarse, dull, and plain ugly. I was pale with dark circles under my eyes. Suddenly, I hated the way I looked." She took a sip of tea. "That's when it clicked. I wanted out of my prison."

This time, Ziad let her continue when she was ready.

"Delia was visiting us while on vacation from her residency. When she came over, I told her I was going to get a haircut. I called Janie, my hairdresser, and she was so excited she came into the salon even though it was her day off." Claire ran her hands down those locks, which now shone under the overhead lights.

For a split second, he imagined himself doing the same thing. *I need to focus on her story, not what I want to do.* "What else did you do?"

"Traded my minivan for the Mustang. What?" she asked when he started chuckling.

"I could never envision you driving a minivan."

"I know it seems strange. We headed to the mall, and the makeup lady at Belk did me up nicely. I think I nearly blew Delia's mind, but it was almost like God had said it was time to dance rather than mourn. I felt as if life was suddenly thrumming through me again."

"When did you go back to work?"

"Fortunately, I'd kept up my continuing ed credits through online courses, so I got a job in the ED at Potter that summer before becoming a flight nurse in 2008." Her expression closed a bit, but it passed so quickly that he wondered if he'd imagined it.

Ziad called for the check. As they left, he turned to her. "Ice cream?"

"I'll not turn you down. Where we went last time is perfect."

150

So was the company. He took great pleasure in watching her sigh with ecstasy as she licked her cone. "Women here must like chocolate ice cream as much as women in Saudi Arabia do."

"Absolutely. I guess it's universal." She glanced at him as they strolled among the tourists on the sidewalk. "Thanks for listening. It means a lot to me. And to know you still want to be friends, even after last night." She cut her eyes toward him. "Now it's my turn. May I ask you a question?"

"Of course." He savored his strawberry cone as they crossed South Battery Boulevard and headed into White Point Garden.

A few more minutes passed as if she gathered her thoughts.

"Claire?"

"Oh, sorry. Just thinking about how to phrase this."

"Phrase what? I am your friend, yes? I promise you will not offend me."

She stopped so her back was perpendicular to the harbor. "Last night when you stayed over, did you, um, happen to wander around the house without a shirt on?"

How had she found out? And what could he say? "Uh… well…"

She began chuckling. "Did I ever catch you off guard!"

This was bad. Truly humiliating. "How did you find out?"

"A little birdie told me." She guffawed. "Actually, it was my neighbor, Mrs. Chitworth."

Oh, no. What conclusions had the woman drawn? "I… you spilled piña colada all over me. I needed to wash it."

"She told me I should hold on to you."

"What?"

"I think she thinks we're dating." Her laughter simmered just beneath the surface. "She's harmless. Really. And she's one of the most caring people I know. I mean, she kept an eagle eye on me that first year after Jackson died." More mirth burbled forth. "I can see her now. She's got these opera glasses in her den, so she probably sat on her bench and stared at you through them. She said you were good-looking."

He wanted to slink away and hide. "I am so embarrassed."

"She's right." Claire cast him a sideways glance. "You *are* handsome." She nudged him.

The wind caught her skirt and pressed it against her, revealing the outline of her figure. Heat built inside of him, and for a brief, insane second, he envisioned pulling her close. No. He couldn't. "Tell me what Faith and Grace are doing this summer."

As they returned to the 4Runner, she obliged him. Fifteen minutes later, he pulled into her driveway. He opened her door for her. "Let me walk you to the door."

"Ben must have taught you well," she said as she slid from the SUV.

A subtle scent hit his nose. Soap or body wash, he didn't know. He wanted to take her hand. "He did. He schooled me quite well."

Her lips quirked upward. "Like not staring?"

"What?"

She nudged him again. "I haven't forgotten the way you stared when you picked me up for the rehearsal dinner."

He laughed. "I was nervous."

*Just as I am now.* The soft sway of her hips, emphasized by the skirt she wore, drew his eyes toward her. What was going on?

"Would you like to come in?" Claire asked once she'd opened the front door.

He would, except he suddenly needed to get away from her before he embarrassed himself once more. "I am quite tired. I truly enjoyed our evening."

She leaned against the door frame and lifted her chin. "I did as well."

Suddenly, he feared he wouldn't see her again. "May I call you some-time?"

"To continue to make amore?" She winked at him.

He groaned. "You will never let me forget that."

"Nope. And yes. I'd absolutely like you to call. Let me get you my number."

He released the breath he hadn't realized he'd been holding.

She pulled a Post-It note from a drawer and scribbled her number on it. "House and cell numbers, just for you."

Their fingers brushed as he took it, folded it into a neat square, and tucked it in his shirt pocket. "Have a good week."

Ziad fled to the 4Runner.

Claire turned on the porch light before shutting the door.

He slid behind the wheel. Automatically, his gaze drifted to Mrs. Chitworth's house. He could have sworn the curtain in her front window twitched. He grinned.

Lightning flashed. Time to get home before the building storm hit. He arrived just as rain began pouring down. More lightning created a strobe pattern through the live oaks and Spanish moss.

He was wide awake. Unpacking was an option. No. That held no appeal, not when thinking about his evening with Claire consumed him. After dropping his wallet and keys on his dresser, he returned downstairs and settled on the freshly delivered soft leather couch.

Earlier that evening, Claire had almost begged him, if not in words, to hold her. He should have, as a friend. She spoke by touch, as did he. A nudge. A hug. A hand on the arm. He'd seen her do such with her family. Why hadn't he reciprocated? His culture. That's why. Most likely frustrating for her. And somewhat so for him as well. He was in a new place. Why couldn't he shake old ways?

Once sitting on the edge of his bed, he picked up the slip of paper that held her number. Such messy handwriting. And so Claire. Like that dark hair of hers. And her figure. And that scent of soap. He warmed.

That wasn't right. Ziad jumped up and paced as he ran his hands through his hair. "It's too soon! Sabirah has been gone only a year."

His words echoed off the high ceiling. He braced himself against the door frame of the French doors as he thought about it. Strange how he and Claire had been locked up for a year after great loss. Only his had been involuntary and a true prison while hers had been voluntary and in a gilded cage of sorts. They both had waded through their grief, lived it week by week, day by day, even hour by hour. Sure, he'd never thought he'd be happy again, but gradually, he'd felt himself ready to make a life in this new country.

Did that include Claire?

No. He shook his head. Sure, he may have found his way back to the land of the living, but he would respect Sabirah. Never could he imagine being with someone else. Never.

And that was the end of it.

# 19

Two weeks after what she called her make-up meal with Ziad, Claire sang in a sultry alto along with Norah Jones on the stereo. Candles glimmered on the fireplace mantel, and lamps provided dim illumination save for where she worked.

Bright light from the recessed lighting in the kitchen flashed on her knife as she cut up some strawberries, oranges, and apples. She tossed the fruit into a serving bowl she'd set out later along with the sides the others were bringing. The guys could grill the steaks.

She pulled out a serving plate and small bowl for the French onion dip. The dip went into the bowl, and she grabbed the carrots. Those, celery, and cucumbers would make the perfect appetizer.

As she reached for a vegetable peeler, a shadow crossed the French doors leading to her screened-in porch. "Hey! You remembered."

Ziad grinned. "Official friends use the back door, yes?"

"Absolutely. Come on in." *My, my.* Clothes definitely made the man, especially his sailcloth shirt and jeans. His silver watch gleamed on his wrist.

He joined her in the kitchen. "They did come out in the shower."

"What?"

"The speckles."

She laughed as she recalled the *papier-mâché* spider she'd been making the night before with her niece. The balloon they were using had popped, spattering them both. "Yes, they did."

She picked up the knife and began slicing the carrots lengthwise. "How was work?"

"Tiring. But something happened." His dark eyes gleamed. He leaned on one elbow against the island.

Oh, that scent, that delectable combination of peppermint from candy and spice from his aftershave. She tried to focus on spreading out the carrots and chopping the ends off the celery. "What?"

She began slicing the celery lengthwise.

"A naked guy came into the store this morning."

"Huh?" She stared at him. Sharp pain burned across her finger. She'd cut herself—and it was deep. Automatically, her gaze flicked downward.

A thick trickle of scarlet beaded and slid down her skin.

Oh, no.

Her pulse thudded in her ears.

Dizziness assailed her.

Her knees grew weak.

"Claire?"

"I'm… I'm…" She began sliding to the floor.

Warm arms encircled her. "I have you." He eased her onto the tile so she leaned against the cabinets. "What happened?" He pressed something over the cut and kept pressure on it. Warm fingers touched her pulse, then brushed across her cheek. "Claire?"

She forced her eyes open.

Ziad knelt in front of her. Concern radiated in his gaze.

"I—I'm fine." She glanced down at her finger, which he'd wrapped in his handkerchief. Bright red blood stained the cloth, and waves of dizziness crashed over her again. She moaned and leaned her head against the cabinet with a thump.

"Where is your first aid kit?"

"The half-bath." She took a deep breath, then another. *Stay upright. Don't faint. You can do this.* She drew her knees to her chest and cradled her hand against her shoulder so her finger was above her heart. She kept her eyes closed.

Fabric whispered, and he grunted as he settled in front of her. Gentle hands grasped hers. "Let me see it."

Claire risked a peek as he pulled the handkerchief away and examined the cut.

"It is not too deep, so no stitches required."

She barely heard him as her eyes remained locked on the scarlet staining the handkerchief. She felt the blood draining from her face. A moan escaped her.

"What is wrong? It may look like it, but you have not lost a lot of blood." More pressure. "Here. Place your hand here."

He now knew her most embarrassing weakness. "I—I can't stomach the sight of my own blood. So I'm sorry if I'm not opening my eyes."

His amusement clearly echoed as he said, "You, a nurse, who deals with everyone else's blood every day, cannot handle the sight of your own blood?"

"Nope. Go ahead. Laugh."

"What does Ben say? I laugh close to you but not at you."

"Hah." Despite herself, her lips twitched upward.

Water ran into a bowl.

Then came that delightful, delectable scent of his. As if he handled fine china, he took her hand and removed the cloth. "It seems as if it has stopped bleeding. Let me bandage it."

He washed not only her cut but also her hand. Where his fingers pressed, heat rose. Her heart sped up. Was it her imagination, or did he linger? *Keep it up!* her mind cried. Huh? Where had that come from?

To distract herself, she opened her eyes and immediately wished she hadn't when another thin line of red appeared.

"Just rest." He layered on some ointment. "Yes, this morning was very interesting. I was ringing up a customer who had bought some gas and a couple of candy bars. I looked up as a naked man wandered into the store."

"Oh?" She kept her eyes closed as he pressed some gauze over it and began wrapping it.

"Yes. It did not take Mira and me long to figure out he was drunk, especially when he staggered to the counter with his next pack of beer under his arm. I called the police. At least they put a raincoat on him before arresting him."

She chuckled.

"Finished."

Claire stared at her finger, which was now ensconced in a thick white bandage. "I guess I won't be cutting."

"I will do that. Can you stand?"

"I think so."

He rose, took her left hand, and pulled her to her feet.

One last round of dizziness swooped over her, and she toppled into him.

He caught her with his hands on her waist.

She rested her chin against his sailcloth shirt so they were almost cheek to cheek.

Oh, dear. Her nose quivered, and if she just—

"Are you all right?"

Moment broken. Thankfully. She forced herself to pull back. "I— I'm fine."

"Sit, and let me do the rest." He guided her to one of the bar chairs before picking up the knife.

She rested her elbows on the granite and her chin in her hands.

A smile crossed his lips.

"Ziad?"

Oh, that dark, dark gaze once more cut into her soul. "Who would have known?"

Yes, who would have known? Who would have known that just Ziad's touch made her come so alive? And that's what scared her.

"Where should I put this?" Ziad rinsed a serving plate and dried it.

Claire gestured toward a pull-out drawer in the island. "In the cabinet over here."

Once he'd done so, he turned to wiping down the counter. "Your attorney friend is especially interesting."

"Sonja's wonderful. When I was in my year of mourning, my Bible study leader, who was too stubborn to let me quit on her, introduced us and said we'd hit it off. We did." She gazed at someplace only she could see. "Do you want some hot tea or coffee? That's the least I can do."

"Hot tea, please."

As she filled the shiny kettle with water, her shoulder brushed his. Intentional or not? He couldn't decide. Halfway focusing on his task, he watched her. That white T-shirt, those jeans. Modest by American terms, but they would have earned her jail time in Jeddah. He immediately knew why since he couldn't take his eyes off her.

"You're staring." Amusement echoed in her voice.

Busted. "No, I was not."

A knowing smile crossed her face. "Do you want to sit on the porch for a bit?"

And have more time with her? "Of course."

"Go ahead out. I'll be there as soon as this is ready."

Ziad hung the towel on a rack and wandered onto the screened-in porch. A nice night, for sure, though a little cool with a breeze blowing from the harbor. He eased onto a glider. He inhaled. Marsh scents, organic and salty at the same time, reminded him of Jeddah. From nowhere, a lump spring up in his throat. *Can I not get past this?*

"Here you go." Claire handed him a steaming mug. She settled with a sigh on the end of the couch closest to him.

He peered at the running lights of a couple of ships, one large and steaming toward Fort Sumter and the freedom of the Atlantic beyond and the other smaller, faster, probably an evening sailing venture. He focused on the silkiness of the breeze and the soothing motion of the glider. "This is nice."

Claire tucked her feet underneath her and leaned against the cushions. "I love coming out here. This is where I spend most of my time when it's warm enough."

He sipped the hot brew. Once more, he compared the closeness of Claire and her friends with his almost solitary existence. Though he'd begun making friends, it was like a wall existed between him and them, one created by his reticence about his past. If only he could get peace about it! "How did you do it?"

"Do what?"

"Find that peace I feel emanating from you."

Silence, as if she expected a better explanation.

How to put words he could barely phrase in Arabic into English? He carefully considered them. "I have been thinking about… last year." He couldn't tell her about being framed for eight murders or the imprisonment that had followed. She'd never understand. "I still do not feel a… a peace about it."

"It takes time." She fell silent for a moment. "Time and God."

His head snapped up. "What?"

"During my year of mourning, I'd come out here and stare at the harbor, just like you're doing now. And yes, many times with a mug of tea in my hands." In the lamplight, her gaze grew sad. "At first, I felt as if a wall existed between God and me."

Too familiar. Allah didn't care about the problems of mere humans.

"Then Sonja challenged me." A brief smile crossed her face. "A week after Elizabeth introduced us, the doorbell rang. It was Sonja on my front porch with two Chick Fil A milkshakes in hand. I told her she'd taken a risk coming by without calling. She only laughed and said she knew I'd be home."

"A brazen statement from her."

"That's one way of putting it. She stayed for three hours that afternoon. We talked about a lot of things, and I told her exactly what I just said about God. She asked if I'd talked to him about it."

"To God?"

"Yeah." Claire leaned against the couch's arm. "She said it's okay to ask tough questions, to talk to God as if he were my father. Why not? He *is* my heavenly father."

Her statement startled him since he didn't see Allah as his father at all.

"She challenged me to get personal with him, to get real. He's the creator of this world. He could take it. Over the next month or so, that's what I did. I asked him those tough questions, like why did he let Jackson and Little Jack die? And why did he allow me to miscarry so badly that now I can't have children?"

Her words were strange to him, almost too difficult to take in. "What did he tell you?"

"He's sovereign." She sipped her tea. "I'm his daughter. Nothing happens that surprises him, and nothing happens without his permission."

"He told you that?"

"Not like you and I are talking, no. But as I prayed, I came to see that." She raised her mug to her lips. Steady, as if she were sure of her statements.

Impossible! He leaned forward with his elbows on his knees. "And you accepted that nothing happens without his permission?"

"Not right away. But yes. As I grieved that year, I felt Holy Spirit surround me and comfort me. God was with me, as he still is. Then that day when Delia came over, it's like my chains of grief fell off. I was ready to live again."

Too much to think about, to accept. He clenched his jaw as his breath shortened. He set his mug on a side table with a clunk, then rose. "I am sorry. I—I need to go."

Almost instantly, she stood at his side. "Did I... did I somehow offend you? Because if I did—"

"No, no. I... need to think." There. Where had those words come from?

With that, he stumbled inside and located his keys. He grabbed them and faced her.

Claire's brow knitted as if she doubted his words.

Ziad took a deep breath. "I am sorry if I have been abrupt. I am still having a difficult time with… everything."

"I understand."

Somehow, he knew she wasn't simply placating him.

She followed him onto the back porch. "Thanks for coming tonight. And thanks for rescuing me."

"From?"

She grinned and held up her bandaged finger. "Myself. I had to laugh when the first words out of Emma's mouth tonight to you were 'Did she pass out?' I guess I'm famous for that now."

Before he lost his nerve, he blurted, "May I ask you something?"

"Sure!"

"I would like to spend more time with you. To get to know you better," he added before he lost his nerve. "Would you, perhaps, like to synchronize our schedules so we share some days off?"

"It might be too late for June, but I can certainly try for July." She smiled, and his heart pounded.

"And I will see what I can do."

With that, he fled. Once back at his apartment, Ziad opened the French doors leading to the living room balcony so air flowed through the high-ceilinged room. Rather than turn on any lights, he stared through the darkness at the creek beyond.

So much to think about.

Too much.

Claire spoke of God as if he were personal. So had Ben and Emma when they had lived in Jeddah. All three of them viewed him as their Father. And they'd spoken of Holy Spirit. So strange. Allah was Allah, not three persons, and certainly not personal. To him, prayer was a ritual, something he did as part of his religion while they viewed prayer as a conversation with God.

He raked his hands through his hair and rubbed his chin. *This is too much to take in. How can she speak of God lovingly as a father if he let such a tragedy happen?* His fingers tightened, and his chest heaved. He flopped onto the couch and stared at the ceiling.

Outside, the breeze puffed, and it skittered across the exposed skin of his arms, just like Sabirah's silky tresses had once done.

That infernal lump returned to his throat. His yearning for her morphed into an almost physical desire. Then Claire's face appeared before him, not Sabirah's. *No! Sabirah will always be my love. My one love.*

He fled upstairs and snatched the photo of her he'd brought with him from Saudi Arabia. That smile of hers captivated him once more.

For a minute or two.

Claire's face reappeared. His fingers almost tingled as he remembered holding her hand that night as he'd cleaned and bandaged her cut. *I didn't want to let her go. Am I going crazy?*

He dropped the frame onto the mattress and paced to the other side of the room, then back to the doorway. Into the still air, he whispered in Arabic, "Face it, Ziad. You're attracted to her."

No. Yes! He was. But that was all. Once more, he picked up the picture of Sabirah. She had his heart and would always have it.

Then why did he see Claire each time he closed his eyes?

He preferred not to answer that question.

# 20

Ziad couldn't avoid it. He lived within fifteen minutes of the beach. Time to pay it a visit, at least according to Claire, Ben, and Emma.

"Oh, c'mon, Ziad," Ben had said when he'd stopped by the Quick Fill late the night before after finishing a stakeout. "Em's dying to go, and so is Claire. Take one for the team, will you? I promise Claire will have you home by noon."

He caved. Now, Ziad scrubbed his hands through his hair as he paced around the downstairs. He didn't mind the beach. Not at all. What came with going there worried him.

Too much skin.

*I'll be fine.* He retreated to his study and stuffed several magazines and his English-to-Arabic dictionary into a backpack. Then came a beach towel he'd bought the day before. He resumed his pacing since he had nothing else to distract himself.

Or maybe he did. The week before, Ben had told him more about Southern women while they'd shared coffees and spoke Arabic to keep up Ben's language skills. Ben slouched on his chair at Mocha Joe's covered patio. "My friend, you must play a joke on Claire."

Ziad sipped his brew and leaned forward on his elbows as he replied in the same language, "What's that?"

"You know how in Saudi, if someone compliments you on something, you give it to them?"

"That's how Emma gets her mare in a couple of weeks."

Ben chuckled. "No one had told her about that before she said something. At least she knows how to ride horses. Anyway," he cleared his throat, "in the South, if a woman is asked how something looks, she is duty-bound to say she likes it. So go get something completely hideous, then ask her if she likes it. When she says she does, give it to her."

"Will she say she likes it if she truly doesn't?"

Ben winked. "Trust me on this one."

Now, Ziad paused at a console table behind his couch. Despite his reservations about the day, he smiled. The lamp. His first yard sale find. So perfect for Ben's suggested trick.

"You found that where?" Ben had asked a few days ago when he'd come over for the evening.

"For five dollars at a yard sale." Ziad lifted his chin and grinned. "My first purchase."

Ben started laughing as he studied the three chintzy monkeys painted in gold that formed the post. "Those are See No Evil, Hear No Evil, Speak No Evil."

Ziad cocked his head. "What?"

"The monkeys." He fingered the red satin shade with its black tassels with rhinestones on them. "Man, this is going to be great."

Now, maybe Ziad could distract Claire, make her forget about going to the beach.

The doorbell rang.

With a deep breath, he greeted her. "Welcome to my house."

He tried to ignore her shorts, tank top, and flip-flops that revealed toenails painted a deep red.

She smiled. "Good morning."

With a small bow, he stepped aside. "Come in."

She did. "How was your first overnight shift at the store?"

Ziad grimaced. "I am staying awake until two. Then I will sleep. Let me show you around."

He led her upstairs to the landing and his bedroom. He flung open the door to reveal a bedroom suite of black furniture with sleek, clean lines. "My room."

"I can see your sense of style." Claire smiled at him. She tapped her chin as if hard in thought. "Hmmm. Za man likes za contemporary styles."

He chuckled. "Come downstairs." He showed her his study at the foot of the stairs, then the living room. "I just bought a corner cabinet for the television."

She avoided gazing at the fireplace, where he'd hung the Saudi flag.

Why? He filed that observation away for later.

"And what do you think about this?" He gestured to the lamp. "Do you like it?"

Her eyes widened. Her jaw dropped, and she blanched. "It's, uh, it's nice. Where'd you find it?"

"A yard sale. You were right." The corners of his lips turned upward. "You can find treasures among the trash."

"What?"

"You said you like it, yes?"

"Um…" She paused. "I do, but—"

"Take it." He picked it up.

"Ziad, I—I'm—"

"Please." He picked it up. "Consider it a gift."

"Um…"

"You like it." He held it out. "It is yours."

She started shaking her head. "I—I couldn't. It's your first yard sale find. How could I do that to you?"

"Please, take it."

As if Emma had told her about compliments in Saudi Arabia, she sighed. "Thanks. Uh, we need to go. Em and Ben have been there since eight."

She turned and left without another look at her gift. She was probably hoping he'd forget about it.

Wouldn't happen. He shouldered his pack and picked it up. With its rhinestones flashing in the sun, he triumphantly bore it to the Mustang, which had its top down.

She popped the trunk, and he laid it inside. As he settled on the front passenger seat, he noticed the beach chairs tucked behind the front seats. "You have been looking forward to this."

Claire started the engine. "A lot. I don't make it to the beach but three or four times each summer. Isle of Palms, here we come!" After turning onto the Isle of Palms Connector, she glanced at him. "Are you all right?"

"Tired."

"You're sure?"

She'd seen through his white lie. This time, he didn't say anything.

"It'll be fun. Isle of Palms is really nice. Lots of sand. Nice water."

Maybe for her. His stomach knotted on the fruit bar he'd choked down upon arriving home at 7:15. "I have not been to the beach in a long time."

"Didn't you go while in Jeddah?"

"I did, but…" He clamped his jaw shut, lest he have to explain spending the last year in jail.

"Anyway, Ben and Emma have all of the beach toys. Frisbee. Baseball. A football."

He settled for listening to her chatter as they found a parking spot in a public lot.

He took a beach chair, shouldered his pack, and followed her down a path of white sand to the strand. His stomach tightened as he gazed at all of the people in swimsuits.

Two twenty-something women in string bikinis strolled along the water. One of them smiled at him.

He gawked, then ripped his gaze away.

Ahead of them, a figure stood up and waved.

Emma. In a one-piece swimsuit of navy.

Ziad focused on the sand.

"Hey, you two!" Emma hugged her sister, stood on tiptoes, and kissed him on the cheek.

He jumped.

"What a perfect day! Just the right temperature. Just the right amount of breeze." She sighed blissfully. "Come on over."

Claire unfurled a blanket, which Emma helped her spread. She unrolled her towel on one side. "Ziad, feel free to use the other side. It'll keep sand off your towel."

He did. After kicking off his sandals, he eased onto it with a small sigh.

Beside him, Claire tossed a wide-brimmed straw hat she'd brought onto her towel. She began sliding from her shorts.

Panic seized Ziad. She was undressing!

To reveal a one-piece swimsuit of oranges, reds, and yellows.

His jaw dropped. Had he started salivating? And forget good manners. He stared at her figure.

Ben snickered, and he sent him a dirty look.

Ben grinned and mouthed, "Told you so."

Ziad scowled at him. He forced his gaze to the ocean.

Claire's chair creaked. She put on her hat, shoved her sunglasses over her eyes, and picked up a magazine. "Are you okay?"

"It is hot."

Another soft snort from Ben.

Would his friend ever let up?

Beside him, Claire chuckled at something she read.

Emma jumped up. "Hey, do y'all want to throw the Frisbee?"

"I do." Claire climbed to her feet and dropped her hat.

Ben joined them.

Emma turned to Ziad. "C'mon, Ziad."

"I think I will watch."

Emma tossed the disk to her sister. They threw it back and forth as they spread out until they had about eight meters between them.

Ziad watched all of them, but Claire held his attention. So beautiful in more ways than he'd expected. Never, ever in his life had he seen a woman so exposed in public! If she'd done that in Jeddah…

Forget being jailed.

With superhuman effort, he ripped his attention away from her and pulled a magazine from his pack. Reading *Newsweek* immensely beat watching Claire.

Only if he were blind.

Though he tried to focus on finding the Arabic meaning of English words he didn't understand, his gaze drifted to her. At least his dark sunglasses hid his eyes.

She had a grace about her. She snapped a hard throw that sailed toward Ben, who caught it with ease.

He lobbed it toward her in one smooth motion.

It was a high throw, and she jumped up to tip it with her finger. It sailed upward. With another easy jump, she caught it.

Hmmm. Athletic. Something he'd never seen in a woman.

Once more, he returned his attention to his magazine. An article about Zap making its way across the world. Very interesting. As he looked up words he didn't understand, he realized one thing. No one except him, Ben, and now the task force had a clue about the tattoos he'd seen on the hands of his suspects.

He took a deep breath and reread the entire feature piece, this time only in English. Progress, it seemed, since he didn't pick up the dictionary once.

A drop of water hit his foot. Claire stood over him, her wet hair slicked back and her hands wringing water from it. How much time had passed?

She cocked an eyebrow. "You don't want to swim?"

He shrugged.

She lowered her voice. "Do you know how to swim?"

"Of course." What could he do to stall? "I am not hot enough yet."

Sweat trickled down his temple.

She lay down on her stomach with her magazine in front of her. She flipped through the pages. On the other side of Claire, Emma worked a Sudoku puzzle while Ben engrossed himself in a novel.

He switched his attention to Claire.

Now she slept, her face turned toward him, her sunglasses clutched in her hand on the towel. The lines at the corners of her eyes had disappeared. Her lashes were dark against her cheekbone. Forget reading. He had eyes only for her.

Ben rose. His friend pointed at Emma and made the walking sign with his fingers.

Ziad nodded and returned his attention to his magazine. Nothing else about Zap in that one or the next. He began rummaging around in his pack for another.

"I fell asleep." Claire sat up and stretched.

Once more, he gaped. A flush that had nothing to do with the heat began.

She shoved her sunglasses onto her face. "Where are Em and Ben?"

"On a walk."

"Do you want to go for a swim?"

"Uh—"

"C'mon. The water's perfect, and I'm hot now."

No more avoidance. He'd answer her questions about swimming in an old pair of SANG fatigue pants. He pulled off his T-shirt and turned to put his sunglasses on the blanket beside his towel.

"What on earth?"

"What?"

"These!" Like a blowtorch, her fingers almost burned his back.

He whipped around. "These what?"

Claire sat on her knees, her hand still upraised. "Those scars. They look like whip marks."

His heart pounded from her touch. He swallowed hard. What could he say? Only the truth. "They are."

"When did that happen? When you were a kid? They look too fresh—"

"A long time ago." He didn't want to say anything else. Not in public. Not when one question would lead to another.

"How long ago? These look—"

"I told you, a long time ago" He took a deep breath. "Why is it so important to you?"

"Why can't you tell me?" She leaned away. "It's not like I'm going to blab it to everyone. What are you hiding?"

An out at last. He glared at her. "Maybe it's *you* who should be hiding something."

Claire's jaw dropped. "I—I don't understand. What's going on?"

On his knees, he loomed over her and wagged a finger in her face. "You and your lack of modesty! Do you not see that every man out here is staring at you?"

Her gaze flicked around the various groups around them. "Ziad!"

A couple of guys walked by, and their gazes lingered.

"See!" He gestured to them. "You are causing them to think of only one thing."

She faced him. "No, they were staring because *you're* raising your voice. Keep it down, will you?" Her lip began trembling. She shoved her sunglasses over her eyes. "It's not like I'm wearing a bikini or something."

He sneered. "You should be more modest."

"Well, *you're* staring, aren't you?"

What truth.

Not that he'd admit it.

He rose. "That is one of the things wrong with this country. The lack of control by you women! You want men to respect you for your minds, yet then you go and you dress like a pros—"

"Stop it. Just stop it!" Claire jumped to her feet and backed away. "I can't believe you. I just can't! I was curious, and what do you do?" A tear slid from under her sunglasses. "You start preaching to me about what a bad person I am simply by the way I *always* dress when I come to the beach." She crammed everything on the blanket into her bag. "If you're so concerned I'm leading you astray when it's really about your own lack of self-control and lust, then I'll leave!"

She snatched up her beach bag, slid into her flip-flops, and fled without another word.

Just as fast as his anger had come, it faded.

He glanced around him.

People stared.

The guys he'd noticed had stopped as if concerned for Claire.

His knees shook, and he plopped onto the blanket. What would he say to Ben and Emma?

Or to Claire?

*Why did you do it, Ziad? You just upbraided the one person to whom you're closest.* What could he do? Nothing at the moment. He'd have to wait until Ben and Emma took him home.

After that, he didn't know how he would repair the damage he'd done.

# 21

Much later that night, now dressed in a pair of khakis and a golf shirt with the Quick Fill logo on it, Ziad leaned against the counter of the convenience store near the Charleston harbor. Brrrr. He shivered at the cold temperature of the air conditioner. Canned music from a satellite radio station played over the speakers. Wait. A Brad Paisley tune. What was it? Something like "The Fishing Song." Claire would have been proud of him.

Automatically, he winced as he remembered her expression from earlier that day. She'd haunted his dreams as he'd tried to sleep upon his return home. He couldn't think about her, not when he needed to use his down time that night to begin studying the math he'd need for the GED.

After ringing up a customer's gas and soda, he rubbed his arms and contemplated a walk around the building to warm up.

Thoughts of Claire could do that.

Or not.

After pouring a hot, steaming cup of coffee from a dispenser into his travel mug, he returned to the counter and picked up a printout of mathematical terms he'd brought with him. Definitions of parallel and perpendicular fought with his realizations about Claire. He couldn't deny it. He wanted to get to know her better, even if Sabirah still had a hold on his heart. What did they call it in America? Dating?

Camel bells on the door jingled.

Eddie Davis, his mentor from the police department, strolled inside.

Ziad straightened and shoved his papers aside. "Hello, my friend."

"Ziad." Eddie grasped his hand in a brief handshake and leaned in for what he called a bro hug. "You too, huh?"

"Me too what?"

"Third shift."

Ziad sipped his coffee. "Yes. Why are you here?"

"Late night snack. Kind of like you." Eddie leaned against the counter. "I guess you heard I'm moving out to District Five Monday. They like to change things up occasionally."

Ziad nodded.

"Good news is, you're coming with me."

Ziad grinned. "I am?"

"You bet. You'll have your own ride, but I'll be your first line of defense." Eddie nodded toward his mug. "What are you drinking?"

"Arabian coffee. Yassir keeps some hot at all times."

He shuddered. "Man, I don't see how you drink that stuff."

Ziad set it on the counter. "It is an acquired taste, I presume."

"When did you start drinking it?"

"When I was a child."

His friend chuckled, a deep, rich laugh that always brought a smile to Ziad's face.

Maybe Eddie could help. "May I ask you something?"

He nodded. "What's up?"

"How do you… how do you date someone?"

"What?" Eddie's teeth flashed whitely against his dark skin. "Wait a minute. You, Ziad, want to date?" He began shaking his head, then stopped. "You're serious."

Ziad smiled.

"Who's the lucky woman?"

"Um…"

"Wait a minute. You keep talking about Claire." Eddie planted his fingers on the counter. "Her?"

"I cannot deny it."

"My, my. The Lady Claire."

"Why do you call her that?"

"'Cause she's classy to the core."

Ziad stared at him. "How do you know her?"

"We went to high school together, and I sometimes chat with her at the hospital. Class of 1992 at Wando High. Sad about what happened five years ago."

Ziad didn't say a word.

That smile returned to Eddie's face. "Dating her, huh? Do you realize she's turned down every guy who's asked her out but two?"

Ziad cocked his head. "What? Why?"

"You're asking me?" Eddie placed his elbows on the counter. "So back to dating. You're already doing it."

Ziad frowned. "I am confused."

"Look, man, if you think dating is flowers, movies, and an expensive dinner, then you have high school definitions of dating. The grown-up version is what you're doing. Getting to know her."

*Except now she won't speak to me.*

"But don't beat around the bush either."

Another term he didn't understand. "What?"

"If you like her, be intentional. Just don't string her along. You know."

"No, I do not know."

Eddie laughed. "Man, you're a tough case. So you like her. Convey that. Tell her."

The bells jingled again.

Ziad instantly recognized Claire's sister, one of the twins.

"Faith?"

Her eyes lit up. "Right. I just got off work at the Purple Oyster. How's it going?"

"I am tired."

"You and me both." She stuck out her hand. "Hi, I'm Faith Montgomery."

His friend shook. "Eddie Davis. You related to Claire?"

"My big sis. Well, y'all, I hate to run, but I'm pooped, and I need to get some milk and cereal before I had home."

"And I need to get my coffee." With a wink in Ziad's direction, Eddie added, "Not that stuff you call coffee. I'll be back."

"Get to work, Ziad," Yassir, the night manager, called from his office. A newspaper rattled.

Like he worked hard.

Ziad returned to his math terms while Eddie wandered toward the coffee urns at the back.

The bells clanked once more.

From dead to busy in the span of ten minutes.

Two men dressed in cargo pants and dirty T-shirts wandered inside. Almost instantly, their East African features reminded Ziad of Jeddah and the sailors who would visit. Most likely, they'd come from the cargo ship he'd noticed docking a couple of hours earlier in the adjacent port. Ziad's nose twitched at the scent of tobacco. They wandered toward the beer cooler, not too far from where Faith pulled open a door for the milk cooler.

With a box of Cocoa Krispies and a gallon of milk, she approached the counter with the two sailors right behind her.

Ziad rang up her purchase. "Six forty-eight."

She handed over a five and two ones, and he made her change. "Would you like me to walk you to your car?"

"I'll be fine." Faith offered a weary smile. "It's not too far back to the Purple Oyster."

*It might be further than you think.* Ziad watched as she paused to say goodbye to Eddie before pushing through the doors. He rang up the case of beer for the sailors, who followed close behind.

"I do not like the looks of them," he muttered to Eddie, who set a cup of coffee on the counter.

A female scream shattered the still air.

Coffee forgotten, Ziad charged outside with Eddie hot on his heels.

Ziad skidded to a stop.

On the pavement near the edge of the convenience store, a young man dressed in a pair of shorts, a button-down shirt, and deck shoes convulsed with foam seeping from the corners of his mouth. Two others ran into the night.

Faith, her skin sallow in the yellow glow of a streetlight, had her hands over her mouth and stared at the scene. Her milk puddled at her feet and soaked the cereal box. With wide eyes and slack jaws, the sailors had begun backing away.

"No one move," Eddie ordered. He radioed for paramedics

Ziad fell to his knees beside the victim.

With one final, violent jerk, he lay still.

Ziad felt for a pulse. Nothing. As sirens began wailing in the distance, he began CPR.

"I—We need to go," one of the sailors stated in heavily accented English. "Our ship—"

"Will stay in port until we get this sorted out." Eddie caught them all in his glare. "When backup gets here, all three of you are coming to the station to give statements. I've got guys after the two jokers who ran away."

"But—" Faith began.

"We need—" the sailor protested at the same time.

Eddie put his hands on his hips. "No. All of you."

Footsteps rushed toward them.

"We got this," a paramedic said.

Ziad, his hands and arms now aching, straightened. His lower back protested.

"He's gone," a paramedic said a moment later.

Ziad muttered under his breath and turned away as he raked his hands through his hair. Zap. Number nine in two months, more than one a week.

"Let's go," Eddie said. "Detective Rothschild is inbound right now."

Ziad stared at the convenience store. Silhouetted in the bright interior lights of the store, Yassir waited for his employee with arms folded across his chest. "Ziad, get back here. Now."

"Sir, he's a reserve officer, and I need his services at the station," Eddie called.

"But—"

"This is police business. Understand? He'll be back after we're finished." Eddie faced his friend. "Ziad, take Faith." He turned his attention to the sailors. "You two, come with me. Now."

Ziad guided Faith to his 4Runner. He helped her into the front seat and followed Eddie to headquarters. "You will need to make a statement."

She hesitated.

He walked her across the lobby to an elevator. "It will take only a few minutes. Do you want me to call your parents?"

Her eyes widened. "No! Please don't. If they find out what happened, they'll flip and want me to quit my job."

He sighed. What about the other sisters? "Is Grace around?"

"Out of town with her boyfriend's family." Faith fiddled with the strap of her purse.

Not Allie, since during the few times he'd met her, he'd realized she redefined judgmental. Emma? No, Ben had mentioned special plans with her that must have included some romancing. Delia? Not when she was a month away from giving birth. That left Claire.

Not his first choice at the moment, but she was his only choice. After introducing Faith to Detective Rothschild, he got a cup of coffee from a vending machine and settled at the desk he shared with Eddie. His fingers trembled slightly as he dialed Claire's home number.

It took a few rings, but her sleepy voice answered, "Hello?"

"Claire, it is Ziad."

"It's two in the morning." The edge in her words told him everything he needed to know. She hadn't forgiven him. Not that he blamed her. "If you're calling to apologize, how about waiting until dawn?"

"I am not calling to apologize. I would like to but later. Faith is with me at the police station."

"What?" Anger melted to concern. "Is she okay? Did you arrest her for something?"

"No, I did not. She witnessed someone dying from a drug overdose." *From Zap,* he almost added but caught himself. "She told me to call you instead of your parents to come and pick her up."

Nothing but dial tone.

He peeked into a conference room. Her head bowed, Faith waited.

Where was the detective?

"Ziad, this way," Eddie softly called. He gestured to another conference room. "I've got one of the dudes in here. The other's down the hall. Separate statements, you know."

A tried and true tactic he'd deployed in his former life.

Detective Rothschild arrived and turned to Eddie. "Officer Davis, do you mind interviewing Ms. Montgomery?"

"Not at all." The policeman headed down the hall.

Ziad had to know. Was his hunch correct? "Sir, would you mind if I stayed here?"

The lighter skinned one stared at his name tag, then sneered in Arabic with an Egyptian accent, "You, a clerk? In here? What are you doing? Playing policeman?"

"No, I'm—"

"English only." Detective Rothschild cast a baleful glance at the sailor. "Ziad, you may stay."

Ziad folded his arms across his chest and leaned against the wall next to the door. The detective's questions were all that he'd expected, and all delivered in a friendly, almost folksy way to put his subject at ease.

"What is your name and occupation?"

"Yousif Ali, sailor on the *Lady Beatrice.*"

"Had you seen the victim before?"

"No."

"Did you know Faith Montgomery?"

"Who? That girl? I saw her at the Purple Oyster. A waitress, I believe."

"Did you see anything suspicious in the club?"

"Nothing."

The detective approached his questioning from different angles, all yielding the same result. And no mention of Zap. He was simply taking a statement.

Oh, did Ziad want to say more! He couldn't. Not without decisive proof. As they talked, he examined the sailor's body language and expression. The consistent gaze, somewhat tense features, and upright posture indicated a young man who'd purely witnessed a death who had nothing to do with it. Except for one thing. He kept his elbows on the table, his hands together as if praying with his chin resting on his fingertips.

Ziad tried not to stare at the small black line that snaked its way from between the ring and pinkie fingers of his left hand onto the top. His breath caught. Could it be? The urge to break into the questioning nearly overwhelmed him.

Detective Rothschild finally rose. "Thank you, Mr. Ali. I appreciate your time. Let me interview your friend, and then you'll both be free to leave."

Ziad watched the sailor go. He stepped into the hall. "Sir, a word, if you would."

Detective Rothschild cocked his head.

Ziad hesitated. "I noticed something on the Egyptian's hand."

"How do you know he's Egyptian?"

"His Arabic has the accent. He had something on his hand. Here." Ziad gestured to the spot. "Could we get pictures of his hands?"

The detective hesitated. He sighed. "Not without good reason."

Ziad wanted to scream.

"But," he continued, "We did have video cameras running." He nodded toward a camera high up in a corner and facing where Yousif Ali had sat. "Let me see if we got something on his hands. Will that do?"

It had to suffice. Ziad nodded.

Seeming to understand the sense of urgency rising in Ziad's gut, Detective Rothschild caught his arm. "I'll leave whatever I find in your box. I heard you and Eddie are moving to District Five on Tuesday. Congratulations."

Ziad could do nothing more.

"There you are!" a female voice cried.

Claire rushed across the room from the elevator.

She ignored them and hugged Faith.

"I'm fine." Faith pulled back. "Just shaken up."

"Well, you scared me!" Claire released her and turned her attention to Ziad. All too easily, he noted the exhaustion in her eyes. "You were right to call me." She shook her head. "If you'd called Mama and Daddy, they'd have flipped."

"That is what Faith said."

She picked up her purse from where she'd dropped it on a table. "Thank you."

"You are welcome." He glanced at Faith, who had once more slouched on the couch. "You need to take her home."

"Yeah."

This time, he seized the moment before it passed. "Claire."

She glanced up.

"May I come by tomorrow? I mean, in the afternoon. After I have slept off tonight."

"You hate third shift."

"With a passion. At least it is my last night. I am on days from now on."

She nodded. "I'll be around."

He hoped she wasn't lying. As he watched her return to her sister and leave, he began planning his apology.

And how to continue to date her or whatever he was doing.

# 22

Sunday Sabbath. Time to rest. Claire muffled a yawn as she pulled to a stop under her house. She'd gotten Faith to her apartment and then fallen into bed by five. Her alarm had aroused her at nine for church. Then came lunch at her parents' house before some errands. After a short nap, she'd have a light supper before once more tucking herself into bed.

She popped the Mustang's trunk and peered inside. Despite her present opinion of Ziad, a smile curled her unwilling lips upward as she stared at that infernal lamp.

All because she'd forgotten a Saudi custom Emma had warned her about.

"I'll get you back, Ziad," she murmured as she carried it inside. She peered around the family room. Where to put it? Maybe in the den. Or the dining room. Better yet, in a closet upstairs. No, he'd not get the best of her. She placed it on one of the nightstands in her bedroom. Only until she figured out how to return it to him.

Where was her stuff? Oh, yeah. Downstairs on a table in the carport. Time to sleep before she did so standing up.

As she reached the bottom of the stairs, Ziad's 4Runner pulled into the driveway.

She clasped her Bible and bags to her chest. Maybe she could flee upstairs and lock the door.

Why did he have to wear that black T-shirt and jeans? They revealed a long, lean frame filling in with muscle, as if he'd spent dedicated time in the gym these past few weeks.

Her heart pounded. She pressed her lips together. He'd have to work for her forgiveness.

His expression neutral, he stopped a few feet away. "It is good to see you. I would like to take you to supper. It is almost six, after all."

Emma's words when she'd visited the afternoon before played in her head. "I know it was awful, and I'm sorry. I know he hurt you, but I think he's doing the best he can under the circumstances he's got. At least listen to him before making up your mind, okay?"

*I'll try, Em, but don't expect any grand surprises.*

She caved. "Let me go and lock up."

The smile on his face told it all. Sheer relief. Within minutes, they headed toward the Ravenel Bridge. Ziad sat erect as he drove, both hands on the wheel, his gaze hidden behind his sunglasses as they rode in silence toward whatever destination he'd chosen.

Claire twisted her hands on her lap.

At last, they pulled into the parking lot of a Middle Eastern deli. Judging by the amount of cars, it must have been good.

Ziad didn't open her door for her.

Not that she would have expected it.

He did open the door to the deli and let her precede him.

Oh, wow. She didn't try to speak over the chatter of voices. Her stomach rumbled at the luscious scents of lamb, rosemary, and other spices she couldn't place. Sparkling brass and beaded curtains leading to different dining alcoves winked at her. She stepped very close to Ziad as they pressed into a line several people deep.

"This is… What's good here?" She had to raise her voice to make herself heard above the chatter in the lobby. "I've never eaten Middle Eastern before."

"Anything." His response came from very near her. "Especially the lamb dishes." He nudged her. "You like lamb, yes?"

"You know I do. But remember I'm a cornbread and fried chicken Southern girl."

"Shall I order for you?"

She nodded because the sudden scent of his spicy aftershave choked off her reply.

He approached the counter. He and the man behind the register, who seemed to be the owner or at least a manager, chatted in Arabic.

The man scribbled something onto a pad and rang up their order. Once Ziad paid, the man clipped the ticket onto a rotating wheel that went to a kitchen.

"Have a seat." Ziad gestured toward some chairs along the wall of where they stood.

"We aren't eating here?"

Ziad shook his head as he handed her a cup. "Not tonight."

Claire filled it and settled on the hard wood with Ziad beside her.

He stretched his arm across the back of her chair.

What with her straight back, legs pressed together, and purse on her lap, she felt like some sort of a snotty schoolgirl. Why couldn't she just relax? Lean back? No, too risky at the moment.

Someone at the pickup counter called his name.

Ziad nodded toward Claire. "Refill your drink. We are ready."

"Where are we going?" she asked as he held the door for her.

This time, a ghost of a smile crossed his lips. "To a special place."

His special place turned out to be the Isle of Palms, the very scene of the crime. Claire winced as they pulled to a stop in the parking lot, almost in the same place where she'd parked yesterday. Only a few cars were there since it was evening.

"Can you carry this?" Ziad proffered the bag of their food.

"Uh, sure." What? Why was she the pack horse?

He pulled two beach chairs, a blanket, and his backpack from the backseat and led her down the path.

*Lord, I shouldn't be here. Really. I should be at home scarfing down a bowl of cereal before heading to bed.* Except suddenly, that idea seemed very lonely.

Ziad spread the blanket and settled the two chairs along the edge. "Please sit."

Oh, no. They sat at the exact same spot where they'd been yesterday morning. What was he trying to do? Torture her? Her knees went weak, and she sank onto a chair.

"Ziad—"

"Claire." He eased onto his knees in front of her.

She couldn't look at him. If she did, she might start crying.

Not in front of him.

Not this time.

"Claire, please. Look at me."

She took the risk.

The sadness in his dark gaze shook her to the core. His lips had pressed together and turned down a little, almost lengthening his face. He took a deep breath. "I owe you an apology for yesterday. The second you left, I knew I did. I lashed out at you when I had no reason to do so."

Emma's words once more echoed in her ears. "Some things are best left for him to tell when he's ready."

She clenched her jaw to avoid asking why he'd thought his harsh words had been necessary.

"I did not stop when I could have. Please forgive me."

Could she? Claire swallowed hard. She turned her head and stared at the pier in the distance. Tears filled her eyes.

Gentle fingers touched her hair, brushed her cheek.

*No, don't. I want to stay angry at you. Don't do that.* She swallowed hard and returned her gaze to him.

Ziad dropped his hand. He remained kneeling in front of her. "I care about you, and I realize how foolish I was."

"You hurt me."

The barest of sighs escaped him. "I know. And that is why I need your forgiveness."

Oh, it'd be so easy to take the low road—at least until she remembered the way she'd treated him a few weeks ago. Maybe she should call it even. "I—I do."

"Truly?"

Her shoulders relaxed as her burden of angst slid from them. "I do."

"Then we are still friends?" From behind his back, he produced a yellow rose.

Her heart skipped a beat. "Oh, Ziad. How did you smuggle that out here?"

"I have my ways." Another mysterious smile followed. "Shall we eat?"

The evening improved from there. They munched on their meal in comfortable silence. When he invited her for a sunset walk, she readily agreed. The golden rays reflected off his dark hair and glistened against skin left bare by his T-shirt. She wanted to record this suddenly special evening in her mind. Why had she left her purse and phone in the 4Runner?

As they returned to her house in comfortable silence, she didn't want their time together to end. "Would you like to come upstairs for a bit?"

"Of course." This time, he opened the door for her.

Claire turned toward the steps just as Mrs. Chitworth's elderly Mercedes pulled into the driveway of her house.

Oh, no. Could she get Ziad inside? Not a chance since he rummaged for something in the backseat of the SUV.

"Claire, dear! Hello."

Claire froze at those words.

Mrs. Chitworth hustled toward them as quickly as her legs could carry her.

Claire forced a smile to her face. "Hi, Mrs. Chitworth."

"Who is your friend?" That knowing look meant one thing. Her neighbor remembered Ziad without his shirt on.

Southern manners won out. "This is Ziad al-Kazim. Ziad, this is Mrs. Chitworth."

Almost daintily, he took Mrs. Chitworth's hand before handing her the rose. "For you, for being such a good neighbor to Claire."

"Oh, how sweet! It's a pleasure to meet you. Well, I won't keep you children for long. Take care!" She shuffled toward her house.

Claire groaned and smacked her head with her hand. "Oh, dear."

"What?" A slow, sexy smile crossed his face.

She blushed. "Uh, nothing."

"You are not angry for me giving the rose to her?"

Zing! That electricity hit her heart. "No, no. That was sweet."

He touched her on the arm. "I need to say my sunset prayers. May I have a bowl of water and a towel I can use?"

"Of course." Claire got a glass mixing bowl and led the way upstairs. She showed him one of the guest rooms. "For more privacy."

He smiled at her. "Thank you."

"And a towel." She did him one better and retrieved a hand towel as well as a bath towel from under the sink.

He'd already kicked off his sandals.

For a brief, insane moment, she wanted to step into his arms. Uh, uh. Couldn't happen. "I'll, um, well, I'll be downstairs."

Claire wound up lying on a bench on the dock and stared at an evening sky quickly going from deep blue and purple to black. One by one, the stars revealed themselves. Her innards still jangled from being so near to Ziad. Softly, her voice barely audible over the bugs and frogs in the marsh, she murmured, "Lord, I'm confused. No, I'm not. At least in some ways. I get to thinking he's like me until things like prayer times come up. That's what worries me. He's not a believer. I shouldn't be dating him."

Of course, no audible answer. Still, God had heard her.

She scrubbed her hands across her face. She could almost feel his gentle touch from earlier that evening.

It hit her.

She was attracted to him. Big time.

Her more liberated friends would have told her it was okay. No, not okay. As Sonja would have said, they weren't equally yoked.

"Lord, I'm nuts. Truly nuts!"

She took a deep breath, then released it. Gradually, she dozed to the lullaby of the bugs and frogs.

Gentle fingers brushed some hair out of her face. Total blackness with Ziad in shadow. He smoothed a lock of hair from her cheek. "You were sound asleep."

"I was?"

"You were snoring."

"What?" She sat up and crossed her arms. "I don't snore."

He shrugged. "I hear what I hear, my Lady Claire." He sat down beside her and swung his feet onto the wooden table built into the deck. "Why did you come out here?"

Not wanting to reveal the mental debate she'd had with herself, she shrugged. "It's too pretty a night to be inside."

"With the exception of mosquitoes." He slapped at one on his arm.

"True." She stretched her legs and stared up at the sky as she recited the Mother Goose rhyme about starlight.

"What?"

"You never heard that before?"

"No."

"What?" She playfully nudged him in the shoulder. "No Mother Goose for you?"

"Mother Goose? You are truly mystifying me."

She smiled. "I guess not. It's a nursery rhyme Mama taught us when we went stargazing."

"I see. Do you have more of these nursery rhymes?"

"Not off the top of my head. But I do remember Dr. Seuss."

"Doctor who?"

"Boy, you've got a lot to learn." She recited *Green Eggs and Ham* from memory, then *Fox in Socks*. By that point, they were both laughing. Then they settled into comfortable silence.

The breeze puffed, carrying with it the potential of the evening in the form of spicy aftershave. Before she realized what she was doing, Claire leaned ever so slightly into him.

He slid away a couple of inches.

She swallowed hard. Maybe she'd misread his signals. He'd probably stayed just to be nice to her. Suddenly feeling like the rejected kid from junior high, she folded her arms across her chest and stared at the harbor. Maybe later, she'd get over her disappointment.

*You're not equally yoked, remember? Friends is as far as it should go.*

Yeah, right. She chalked the evening up to a net loss.

# 23

Tuesday afternoon, Ziad checked his in-box on the desk used by District Five's reserve officers. Two interoffice envelopes rested in it. The first held his letter officially transferring him to his new posting. The second contained a glossy eight-by-ten with a sticky note from Detective Rothschild attached to it.

Ziad studied the note. He stared at the photo. A frame from the video surveillance when the detective had interviewed the Egyptian sailor. A sick feeling started in his stomach.

It showed the tail of the Arabic character for Brother on the man's left hand.

Exactly like what he'd seen on his three suspects.

Why did a sailor in Charleston have the same tattoo in the same location as the three suspects in Jeddah? He drummed his fingers on the desk. Not good. Not good at all because it meant Prince Yasin's reach extended far beyond Saudi Arabia. He considered the article he'd read on Saturday, plus Ben's new job on the Zap task force.

Maybe his friend could help. He picked up his cell phone and dialed.

"Ben Evans."

"Ben, it's Ziad."

"Hey! How's it going?"

Ziad endured the small talk before asking, "Do you have a few minutes to meet me this afternoon?"

"What's up? You and Claire patched things up, right?"

"We did." Not that they'd had any time together since then. "It is about what happened Saturday night. Claire told you, yes?"

"Yeah. Faith's lucky she wasn't alone."

Ziad outlined what he'd found.

Suddenly, Ben was all business. "We do need to meet. Say, four o'clock at the Starbucks on King Street?"

Ziad did a quick calculation in his head. He had to be at the Quick Fill by six to work until ten, but he could do that. "Yes. I will be there."

Ziad spent the rest of his shift drafting reports before he changed into his Quick Fill golf shirt and a pair of khakis and headed downtown.

Ben was on time.

Once at a table on the second floor where they couldn't be overheard, Ziad slid the photograph to him.

Brow furrowing and hand rubbing his chin, Ben studied it. He shook his head. "This is nuts."

"Nuts?"

"Incredible. Like Prince Yasin's establishing a distribution network here in Charleston. What else do you have?"

"His name. Yousif Ali. He sails with the *Lady Beatrice*."

"Bad stuff. Bad, bad stuff. But this is a great lead."

"What can I do to help?"

"Nothing."

That stung. Really, it did. But then again, Ziad was now a mere reserve officer and a convenience store clerk, not a member of the elite FBI.

Ben focused on him. "I don't want to bark up the wrong tree."

"What?"

"Get this wrong. But then again…" He cleared his throat and straightened. "I'll pass this on to the task force, okay?"

What else could he do? Frustration balled in Ziad's stomach.

"I'll keep you posted." Ben checked his watch. "Look. I hate to say it, but I need to go. I'm picking Em up since my Forester's in the shop for an oil change."

He rose and took both the photo and the note with Yousif Ali's stats with him.

Ziad remained where he was. Outside, the sky began darkening as the clouds he'd noticed on the way in blotted out the sunlight. He toyed with his phone. Once more, his questions during that final interrogation filled his mind. So did the suspects' tattoos in the exact same position as the one he'd seen on Yousif Ali.

What could he do? He thought about the jump drive sitting in a small safe he'd bought. It held everything about the case. He could translate it, provide it to Ben and his comrades.

No, he couldn't. Ben didn't know he had it. His friend would most likely make a request to SANG staff. Perhaps they would send the file. If not...

Suddenly, his need for a smoke roared to the surface. He wouldn't, not when he'd finally made it through withdrawal.

With a sigh, he rose and headed into the oppressive humidity.

Like it or not, the past had paid him a visit. And if he were lucky, it wouldn't ensnare either his present or future.

Two weeks later, Ziad sat at the same Starbucks, a steaming cup of Arabian coffee before him. Where was Ben? In a voice mail, his friend had requested another meeting. He glanced around him. A mother and a little boy sat at one table where they shared a snack and a cold drink. At another table near the windows, a college kid with earbuds in his ears worked on something on his laptop.

Footsteps sounded on the old wood of the steps.

Ziad tensed, and his reawakened detective's mind searched for a way out in case he needed it.

"Ziad, my friend." Ben said in Arabic. They exchanged a Guy Hug.

Ziad resumed his seat and continued in English, "Do not beat around the tree, Ben."

"What?" His friend grinned. "You mean beat around the bush?"

Ziad rolled his eyes. "That." In Arabic, he continued, "What did you find?"

"Lots. First off, in the two weeks since you and I talked about this, two teen-aged boys showed up DOA from Zap in Potter's ED."

Ziad froze. That made eleven dead.

"Detective Rothschild is on the task force, and he passed along what Charleston PD knows about the incident you witnessed, which unfortunately, is not a lot. The cops caught the vic's buddies, who said they just got scared when he started convulsing and ran off. Your sailor, Yousif Ali, was only a witness to an overdose. I ran his name through our databases. Nothing exceptionally criminal turned up. ICE says he comes to Charleston about every six to ten weeks depending on when the *Lady Beatrice* is in port. He has been with that ship ever since he started with the Merchant Marines. That is what I can share. It is all in here for your perusal." Ben placed a manila envelope on the table.

"Nothing else?" Ziad's hopes plummeted. For the first time since his release from prison, he'd trusted his instincts, and it had led to nothing. In English, he asked, "I was barking up the wrong bush?"

"Tree, Ziad. Tree." Ben leaned forward and in Arabic continued, "I did not say that. I talked to my bosses. They said to see if I could get the Saudi file on the case. I called Sami. No luck because he sent me to General al-Talil."

Ziad winced. He knew the response without even asking.

"No dice," Ben said in English, before adding in Arabic, "As a matter of fact, General al-Talil was not thrilled that I called. He finally said he would check with his commanding officer. It came down from the top he was not under any circumstances to give me that file."

"To save face." Ziad shook his head. "We Saudis are famous for that. They don't want to admit there's a drug problem in the Kingdom."

"That is what I figured."

Ziad's mind flew to the file. He couldn't keep it a secret any longer. Resting his elbows on the table, he leaned forward. "Perhaps I can help."

Ben mirrored him. "How?"

"Right after we busted our three suspects and interrogated them, something—probably instinct—told me to make a copy of the file. I hid it in the villa. While I sat in jail, I worried they'd found it. But no one said anything, and gradually, I realized it was still safe. Do you remember when we went through the house so I could collect keepsakes?"

"Yes."

"I smuggled it out in my backpack. It's in my safe at the apartment."

"Well, I'll be!" Ben exclaimed in English

"What does that mean?" Ziad asked in the same language. He glanced at the young mother. Her gaze, which had focused on them, dropped to the table.

"You know? I don't know." Ben chuckled. He finished his drink and set it on the table. In Arabic, he asked, "What are you proposing?"

"It has everything on it. The MP3 file of the interrogation. The photos. My notes, which I scanned. They're in Arabic."

"And my written Arabic is much worse than my spoken. I see." Ben began nodding. "You want to translate it."

"I can get it to you tomorrow." Ziad caught the little boy staring at him.

"You are sure?"

Why had the mother's eyes widened? "Of course."

"I will see what I can do with it. It will not be admissible, but maybe it can help us know where to look and what questions to ask."

"I'll start on it as soon as I get home tonight." Ziad again caught the young mother's gaze. She had her phone to her ear as she watched him.

Like he was some sort of terrorist or something.

"Ziad, thank you, my friend." Ben drained the rest of his coffee. They stood and did the Guy Hug again before turning to head downstairs. Once in the oppressive humidity, they paused on the sidewalk. "Hey, Em wants to have you and Claire over for supper sometime soon."

With effort, Ziad forced his mind to more pleasant things. "I would like that. I am sure she would as well. We are having supper together at her house tomorrow night, so I will ask."

"She'll probably talk to Claire too."

Ziad's pulse began hammering as two uniformed officers approached. He didn't know them, and his heart nearly seized when neither smiled. One of them even put his hand on his gun as if expecting trouble.

Ben straightened.

"Is there an issue here, Officer?" he asked as he stepped away from the entrance.

"We got a report of suspicious activity here," the taller one replied. "Like some information was being exchanged."

Ben slowly pulled out his cred pack. "FBI Special Agent Ben Evans. And this is my friend, Ziad al-Kazim, who, by the way, is a reserve officer with you guys. He's helping me keep my Arabic up. And he's helping me on a case."

Ziad also pulled out his ID that showed his status with the police department. "If you have a question, Eddie Davis is my mentor."

Both officers finally smiled. The taller said, "That's all we needed to know. Ziad, glad to have you onboard." As if to assuage their concerns, he added, "Just doing our due diligence. See something, say something, right?"

"Understood. Have a great day." Ben watched them go.

The mother had come out with her son. Her cheeks reddened before she hustled the child away.

"Our informant," Ben muttered. He sighed. "Let's meet back here tomorrow. Same bat time, same bat station."

Ziad managed a nod. As he retreated to his 4Runner and settled behind the wheel, he glanced at his hands. They trembled a little, the only indication of the way his encounter with the officers had rattled him. *As if I'm the enemy simply because I speak Arabic with a friend in public.*

He put the 4Runner into gear and headed home. On the way, he stopped for gas. No receipt. He headed inside. As he waited in line, his gaze slid to the racks of cigarettes behind the clerk. He bought a pack. Once inside the SUV, he ripped off the cellophane, shook one out, and lit it. So what? The case had brought back old memories, and with old memories came old habits.

# Exiled Heart

Tuesday night Bible study. Normally one of Claire's favorite times of the week. Not tonight. For some reason, she hadn't slept well, and now all she wanted to do was crawl into bed. As she curled up on the couch in her den, she muffled her yawn.

"I saw that," Elizabeth said as she smiled at her. "Rough week already?"

"Somewhat." Claire sighed. "We lost another kid to Zap yesterday. We couldn't get him airlifted to the ED in time. DOA when we arrived. The second one in two weeks, which Ziad said makes thirteen since March."

"Oh, darlin', I'm sorry." Elizabeth sighed. She gazed around at the other four ladies present. "You and Sonja need to give updates. How's Mr. Ziad?"

Despite her best efforts to keep it in check, a small smile crossed her face. She ducked her chin. "He's good. It's his third week on his own as a reserve officer. Right now, he's in your neck of the woods, Sonja."

Her friend perked up. "Off Clements Ferry?"

"Yep."

"Guess I'll have to watch myself. Although it won't be for much longer since I'm closing on my old townhouse on Monday."

"Sounds like we need to pray for your sanity."

At least they'd deflected to Sonja.

Elizabeth focused on her notepad. "Okay, Miss Claire. Back to you."

Rats. No avoiding the topic of Ziad anymore.

"We'll keep praying Ziad comes to know the love of Christ. Things between you two are better?"

"Finally—after the Skin Incident." Her pride still smarted from their argument a couple of weeks before.

Everyone started giggling. "The Skin Incident." Elizabeth peered over her reading glasses. "I must have missed something by going to the mountains. Fill me in."

Claire relayed the events of that day. Did she dare say anything about the following evening? No. Not when she wouldn't let anything happen between them. But who was she fooling? And why had he snapped that Saturday like that? "I feel like he's hiding something."

"Leave it be, darling." Elizabeth scribbled something down. "We'll pray he feel comfortable enough to share that with you. How's his other job?"

"I think he's bored with it. He's determined to take the GED in December."

Elizabeth smiled at her. "I'm sure he'll pass. Anything else?"

Time to confess. "I care about him."

Sonja peered at her. "As in?"

Claire sighed. Not willing to admit anything else, she shrugged.

Her friend's dark eyes narrowed. "Be careful, Claire."

That was all she said.

Point well taken.

Elizabeth frowned. "Sonja's right. Guard your heart, sweetie."

"But how to do that and stay friends?"

"I wish I had an answer for that," her mentor said. "You've been good for him, and that's what makes it hard. Take one day at a time."

Claire nodded. She would. Really, she would. "I'm done with me." She offered a weak smile. "Sonja?"

Elizabeth seemed to catch the hint. "Okay, Miss Sonja. What about you?"

Her friend sighed, and the levity left her pretty face. She toyed with her pen. "Pray for my friend, Annette Mubarak. I might have told you about her a few times."

"She's the one who married that Egyptian, right?" one of the others asked.

"Yeah. She and I were roommates at UGA. She got a job in Dallas after graduation, and that's where she met Kamil. They got married eight years ago."

Claire nodded. "Oh, yeah. I remember her."

"They had a son and then another a couple of years later. Annette quit work to take care of them."

One of the others asked, "What happened?"

Sonja fingered her necklace. "She said things started heading south in their marriage, like all of the sudden, he got snippy with her and very demanding. Far from the sweet, respectful, kind guy he'd been when they'd dated and first married. And he suddenly 'got religion,'" she jabbed her fingers in the air in the form of quotes, "and began taking the boys to the mosque. At first he insisted she go, but she refused."

"Why do I see where this is headed?" Elizabeth asked.

"Because it's way too common." Sonja sighed. "To make a really long, convoluted story a little shorter, a few months ago, Kamil stayed with the boys while Annette came to my wedding. I got back from my honeymoon to find a voice mail from her. She got home Sunday evening, and they were gone—along with their suitcases."

Claire's pen, which she'd been tapping on her notepad, stilled. "He took their sons to Egypt?"

"You got it." Sonja's eyes filled. "It's so sad! I mean, she called me up frantic, as if I knew how she could legally bring them back."

"What'd you tell her?"

"That it probably wouldn't be viewed as kidnapping, to be honest." One of Sonja's shoulders rose and fell. "And if it were, it's not likely she could get them back under Egyptian law. But I'm no international lawyer or custody lawyer, so not my area of expertise." She lowered her gaze and swiped at the corner of her eye. "It's been three months now, and she's had almost no contact with them. It makes me so sad."

Claire stared down at the Bible, which sat open on her lap. *Love your neighbor as yourself. Love your enemies.* How could she? That man had taken his children away from their mother. Most likely, he'd say, "I divorce you" three times and be done with it. And Islamic custom dictated that the children stay with the father. How cruel was that? Her jaw clenched.

Ziad's face flashed across her conscience. Would he have ever done something like that? Would he have divorced his wife and taken his sons away from her?

*How dare Muslim men think they can tear a home apart like that!* She shook her head.

"Claire?"

"Huh?" Uh, oh. She'd completely missed everyone else's requests.

"Will you close for us?" Elizabeth asked.

"Uh, sure. Thanks. I, um, will." As they bowed their heads to pray, she shut down that line of thought. She had to avoid it. Before anyone realized she could harbor such ugly things.

Pitch black surrounded Ziad save for a cone of light blasting from the halogen desk lamp in his study. His eyes burned as his pen moved across a yellow notepad. He stared at those scribbles of cursive English. Only thirty of fifty-plus pages translated. So much information, more than he remembered collecting during those few short months he'd worked the case for the SANG.

His watch beeped. Eleven passed. He'd completely forgotten his last prayer of the day. He flipped the page. Loud, almost like he ripped the sheet apart. He came to yet another word he couldn't translate and located it in his Arabic-to-English dictionary.

Ziad yawned. He needed something to wake him up. Without looking, he reached for his cigarette pack and lit one. Smoke hung in a blue haze above him. Who cared if he coughed from it?

Finally. He ripped the last sheet from his notepad and clipped everything together. Those, along with a data stick containing copies of everything he had, went into a manila envelope.

Once he crashed into bed, he thought he'd immediately fall asleep.

Not to be.

"Sami, take photographs of those tattoos," he'd ordered in what seemed to be another lifetime.

"Guards, remove him!" Prince Yasin shouted.

Sabirah's tender words couldn't soothe his soul. "It's not your fault."

So wrong. So very wrong.

Ziad's eyes flew open. He lay on his back, whispered air from the ceiling fan cooling the sheen of sweat coating his chest and arms.

Wide awake at two in the morning. Not good when he had to be at district headquarters at seven for his shift as a reserve officer.

With a groan, he rose and headed downstairs. He eased onto the couch and picked up the remote. Nothing on television, not too surprising seeing how late it was. He needed to find something to make him sleepy. He began flipping through channels.

Animal Planet—Claire's favorite but not his.

The Learning Channel. Nothing there.

News wouldn't work.

Sports didn't interest him at this hour.

Finally, he landed on The Reality Channel. What was this? He moved to turn it off, then stopped.

On the screen, young men and women cavorted on some sort of resort patio. Ziad stared at the women, who were practically naked in their thongs and string bikinis. And how the men pursued them! Caressed them. Fondled them.

*What filth! I can't believe people here encourage this!* He conveniently scooted past conversations he'd had with Ben about modesty and what it meant in different cultures. Or the way Claire had challenged him a couple of weeks before. No. Women asked for what happened to them by what they wore.

Before he realized it, he sneered. Reality television. What trash. More like pornography in his book. Not something he'd ever tolerated, not even when many of his relatives had watched it while abroad.

Now, he couldn't rip his eyes from it.

With superhuman effort, he turned off the television.

Forget sleep. The case and that had stolen any vestiges of it. He wound up brooding by staring out the French doors at the creek. Finally, the first vestiges of sunlight began lightening the sky.

Pride filled him as he did his first prayers. He'd do those good works required by Islam.

So what if he'd forgotten his last prayers the night before?

He pulled on his uniform and attached his badge.
Like it or not, rested or not, he faced the day.

# 24

Oh, did she ever want to go home. She couldn't. Not for a bit. Claire glanced at the time at her computer screen in the nurse's station for the outpatient clinic. Almost lunchtime, meaning no rest for another eight hours or so. With a sigh, she focused on inputting the information related to the latest case she'd seen in the clinic.

One of the nurses tapped lightly on the counter. "Claire, hey, you got a second?"

She straightened and winced. Oooh. Tight back. "Sure, Mandi. What's up?"

"A guy came in with a cut on his hand, and we need someone to get it cleaned up and ready for the doc. Can you do that for me?"

"Sure." Claire's gaze shot to her radio, which sat beside the computer. Thankfully, it had been a quiet day so far. "Hopefully, I won't get a call."

Mandi smiled at her. "Thanks, girl. If you do, let me know. He's in room ten."

She turned on her heel and bustled down the hall to another room.

Claire clipped her radio to her belt, followed, and paused outside an exam room. A folder sat in the slot on the door. She flipped it open and skimmed the information scribbled by an intake specialist. Daoud al-Rashid. Age twenty-two. Truck driver for a local shipping company. Deep cut on the palm of his left hand from a metal truck frame. He needed stitches, maybe surgery. At least a tetanus shot since she didn't see evidence of one on the chart.

She gazed through the glass.

A young man sat on an exam table. His feet swung back and forth a little. Gauze enshrouded one hand, and he rubbed his good one back and forth on a pair of dirty fatigue pants. A wispy beard coated his jaw.

She pushed through the door.

He glanced up with eyes reflecting pain.

"Hi, Mr. al-Rashid. I'm Claire Montgomery. I'll be helping Doctor Fairmont today."

He stared at her flight suit. "Are you a nurse?"

"Flight nurse. We also work in the clinic." She perused the chart again. "It says here you have a pretty nasty cut."

He nodded.

"What happened?"

"I was delivering a load of steel rebar to a job site." His voice had a faint accent to it as if he'd immigrated to the States when he was a child. "They were getting ready to start unloading it when someone released the wrong strap. I jumped out of the way before it crushed me."

"Quick thinking." She leaned against a nearby counter. "Except you got cut."

He nodded. "On the truck frame." He winced as if remembering. "Is it bad? It feels like it."

"I'll let the doctor make that call. Right now, I'll take your vitals and get it cleaned up. It says here you don't remember the last tetanus shot you had."

"I don't."

"Then I'll take care of that as well. Are you allergic to any medication?"

He shook his head.

"Noted. Let me take your temperature."

That took a moment, though she noticed an elevated respiration rate. She made a note and pulled the blood pressure cuff off its holder. "Now for blood pressure."

He tensed.

"Just a squeeze, I promise." She wrapped the cuff around his arm and pressed her stethoscope to the bend in his elbow. Blood pressure normal, despite his recent scare. She lowered the earpieces of her stethoscope and pulled on some nitrile gloves. "Good blood pressure. Let me take a look at your hand."

He hesitated.

"Promise I won't hurt you."

Wordlessly, he held it out.

Claire carefully cut the knot someone had tied in the gauze. It fell away to reveal a dirty hand with a definitively deep cut. This one would take some time to ensure the wound was clean. She gently touched the skin near the cut.

Daoud drew in a sharp breath.

"Does that hurt?"

"No."

She cocked her head. "You're sure?"

He nodded but wouldn't meet her gaze.

She turned his hand over. Nothing there but smeared blood. The same thing between his fingers. She noted a tattoo between the ring finger and pinkie finger. Interesting. "Are you able to move your fingers without pain?"

Another nod.

"I'm going to get the blood off your hand with some water. Then the doctor will—"

"No!"

"It's fine. I promise I won't hurt—"

"Don't touch me!"

At his vehemence, she drew in a sharp breath. "Mr. al-Rashid, I've already—"

"Don't touch me." That came out almost like a hiss.

Her eyes narrowed. *Don't bite back. It's not worth it.* "Is there a problem?"

His gaze fixated on her neck. Suddenly, she realized what he stared at.

Her cross. The one she always wore. She'd unzipped the neck of her flight suit, which had revealed it.

"All right," she drawled. "May I ask why?"

"I don't want you touching me! You're a—"

"Woman? Infidel? What?" She jabbed her fists onto her hips. "I'm a nurse, all right? First and foremost my—"

"No!"

"Fine." She opened a cabinet and slapped a roll of gauze onto the table. "Wrap this around your hand. Dr. Fairmont will take care of you."

She stomped into the hallway and leaned against the wall. Her mind ran back through the conversation. Had she been rude? No. Hurt him? No. He, in his Islamic maleness, couldn't even stand the idea of a Christian woman touching him, even if that woman desired to help him.

Whatever.

"Claire?" Dr. Fairmont, his blue eyes full of concern, studied her face. "Is everything okay?"

"Uh, yeah."

*Liar.*

"You look like you're ready to hit something."

"Sorry. Bad morning. By the way, the patient doesn't want me touching him."

He frowned. "What?"

"He's Muslim," she said as if that explained it. Her radio beeped the long signal for a call. "I'm sorry, Eric, but I've got to get going."

"I'll take care of it. Thanks."

She waved and tried to shove the unpleasant run-in to the back of her mind.

Ziad sat in his patrol car in the hide he'd established along Clements Ferry Road. He waited for speeders. Routine work, but at least he gained experience.

Almost three. Soon, he could head downtown and hand Ben the information he'd prepared, then hopefully put it out of his mind while he had supper with Claire.

A Cadillac Escalade whizzed past him.

He checked the speed on the radar. Seventy in a forty-five? "What the…"

He pulled into traffic and switched on both lights and sirens. Into the microphone he said, "Unit Eight-Two-R in pursuit of a white Cadillac Escalade southbound on Clements Ferry Road. Request assistance from Unit Eight-Two."

"Unit Eight-Two responding." Eddie's calmness reassured him.

The Escalade maintained its speed and swerved back and forth in its lane.

It dipped into oncoming traffic.

Ziad cringed and muttered under his breath.

Horns blared.

He got right behind it.

Only then did the driver seem to notice he was there. The vehicle slowed and pulled into the parking lot of a shopping center. It almost hit the center's sign in the process. Ziad stopped with about four meters between his car and it. The driver's door popped open.

He jumped out. "Stay in the SUV!"

Eddie's patrol car, lights flashing blue and red, pulled in behind Ziad's.

His mentor joined him. "What do we have?"

"Potential drunk driver. He tried to climb from the SUV."

"Go for it. I'll wait here."

Ziad approached the Escalade. He tapped on the window.

It hummed downward.

The him turned out to be a woman with light blonde hair pulled up in a ponytail and tied with a navy blue bow. A navy blue T-shirt stretched across her chest, and a tennis skirt of the same color barely covered her thighs.

"Yes, Officer?" Slurred words.

"License and registration, please, ma'am."

She reached for her glove compartment.

Adrenaline began pumping. "Do it slowly, ma'am."

Eddie approached and stood close enough to lend support if needed. She handed Ziad the information.

"Stay in the SUV." Once in his car, Ziad entered the woman's driver's license number into a laptop. Interesting. Shannon Radcliffe. Two previous arrests for drunk driving, both now expunged from her record yet still noted.

He approached her window. "Ma'am, have you been drinking to-day?"

"Why do you say that, Officer?" Her face remained expressionless.

Ziad winced as the smell of alcohol washed over him. "Because I clocked you doing seventy in a forty-five, you were swerving, and I smell alcohol on your breath."

"Just a mimosa. Well, just two. Hmmmm." She stroked her neck as her brow knitted. "But I'm not drunk."

And he was a Saudi prince. Just what was a mimosa? Whatever it was, it had alcohol in it. "Please step out of the car."

"What?"

"Step out of the car, ma'am."

"I'm not drunk!" Her voice rose to match the noise of the traffic.

"Ma'am, I am asking one more time. Please step out of the car." Out of the corner of his eye, he noticed Eddie edging closer.

She flung her door open.

Ziad grabbed it before it clocked him on the nose.

She squared her shoulders and glared at him. "Okay, I'm out of the car, Officer," she peered at his name tag, "Al-Kazim. What kind of a name is that?"

"Arabic. Ma'am, if you would, please close your eyes and touch your finger to the end of your nose."

"I am *not* drunk." She nearly spat those words.

Every sense came on alert. He took a deep breath. "I'm asking you to please close your eyes and touch your finger to the end of your nose."

She rolled her eyes but complied—and missed with a good couple of centimeters to spare.

"Stand on one foot for thirty seconds."

"What? I told you—"

"Now, Ms. Radcliffe." *She's trying to provoke you. Keep calm.*

"Whatever." She blew out a sigh and raised her right foot.

Ziad glanced at his watch.

She barely made it five seconds before swaying and toppling into the side of the Escalade.

"Ma'am, I am taking you to the station."

"For what?"

"For driving while under the influence." Gently, he grasped her upper left arm.

"Let go of me, you rag head!"

Adrenaline electrified him. "What did you call me?"

She yanked away. "You have no right to touch me. Now take your hands off me!"

She tried to climb back inside the SUV.

Ziad blocked her. "Listen to me, Ms. Radcliffe. We are going to go back to my squad car, and like it or not, you will come to the station with me for a—"

"You don't know who you're talking to! Do you know who my husband is? Do you?"

"I know you are drunk."

"You shut up!" She began screaming obscenities at him, things he'd never spoken or even heard before. "Take your filthy gaze off me, you camel jockey! And don't touch me. If you do again, my husband will—"

"I—"

Pain flashed across his cheek! Automatically, Ziad's hand shot to his mouth. He flinched.

Eddie shoved her into the side of the Escalade. "Ma'am, I'm arresting you for DUI and assaulting a law officer."

Ziad barely heard him Mirandize her as he backed off. His lip throbbed. Ow. That really hurt. He stared at the red sheen on his fingers.

Once he'd handcuffed her, Eddie half-walked, half-dragged the woman toward his patrol car.

"I'll have your badge for this!" she hollered. "You and that camel jockey boyfriend of yours! How dare you arrest me. You have no idea who you're messing with."

The closing patrol car door muffled her insults.

More wetness dribbled down Ziad's chin as he retreated to his car.

"Here." Eddie shoved a roll of paper towels into his hands. "Sorry, but it's the best I could come up with." He rubbed his hand over his bald head. "You handled that well. Shannon Radcliffe's a tough nut to crack."

"She… Can she really have me fired? Us fired?" Real fear filled Ziad. The last thing he wanted to do was endanger a potential career with the police department.

"Naw. She's a lot of bluster. Her husband's some high-falootin' attorney, so she thinks she can get off because of him. Problem is, she's already been arrested twice for DUI."

"I saw that."

"Sonja Williams tried both cases. Boy, she's gonna hit the fan when she hears about this latest one."

"But what she said—"

"Ziad, man, don't worry about it. We did it by the book. And thank goodness for those cams in our rides. She tries to dispute it, we have it covered. Got it?"

He nodded, but his breath came out in hard gasps.

"Listen to me." Eddie glanced around and in a low voice continued, "I know being on the receiving end of bigotry isn't cool. I've lived that, okay?"

"How do you get past it?"

"By not letting it get to me." Eddie held up a hand. "I know. Easy to say and harder to do. Trust me on that one. We both know not everyone who's different than us acts that way. Keep that in mind."

Swallowing hard, Ziad nodded.

"Let me take this—well, you know what—to the station. I'll meet you back up here, and we can debrief Stan. In the meantime, head back and get something cold on that cut."

No problem there. He could feel his lip swelling.

Ziad climbed into his car. His headache, which had never quite receded, returned with a vengeance. The cut didn't help.

As he turned his lights off and pulled into traffic, his mood, already low, sank to new depths when he thought of the insults that woman had hurled his way. All just for doing his job by getting one more drunk person off the road. Maybe one of these days he'd get used to the hatred and prejudice toward him simply because of his nationality and religion. Today wasn't that day.

Last ride of the day. And a tough one. Claire tensed as the helicopter transporting a premature baby to Potter Hospital landed on the helipad. As the rotor blades kept spinning, she popped the rear doors open and shoved them aside.

*Lord, let this child live!* That prayer rested on her heart as she released the latches for the gurney with the enclosed bassinet holding the premature baby. She checked vitals one last time. Still in the green. *Praise God!* Two pounds. So small he could fit in her hands. She wheeled the gurney to the elevator. Moments later, the doors swished open.

A neonatal nurse greeted them at the NICU. "What do we have?"

Claire spouted off the stats of the baby, then watched as the neonatal team sprang into action.

She lingered as she whispered one last prayer. *Lord, let him live. Please. His mama's so scared he won't. Be with his parents as they make the drive up.* She pulled her helmet off and brushed back some wisps of hair that had fallen from her braid.

Time to go. She had to set work aside now that her shift had ended.

No such luck. The elevator doors slid open to reveal one of the neonatologists and another doctor she didn't recognize. This one had the olive features of a hot climate along with Arabic writing stitched above his name in English.

She took a step back to allow them to exit. "Dr. Metcalf, it's good to see you."

"You brought the preemie in?" he asked.

"I did. We just arrived."

"Thank you. We'll take it from here." The doctor smiled. "I'd like you to meet Dr. Ismail Khatib. He's on a yearlong fellowship here from King Fahd Royal Hospital in Riyadh, Saudi Arabia. Ismail, Claire Montgomery, one of our best flight nurses."

Claire extended her hand. "It's a pleasure to meet you, Dr. Khatib."

The man clasped his hands behind his back and lifted his chin so he stared at her over the rims of his reading glasses. "It is a pleasure, Miss Montgomery."

*Oh, you so lie like a rug, you jerk.* She forced a tight-lipped smile to her face. "Have a good evening."

She rushed into the elevator and leaned against the wall. What an a-hole. Looking down his nose at her like she was a piece of rubbish! What was it with these Muslim men? She wanted to kick the wall.

No, better to leave. She stashed her helmet in her locker and grabbed her purse and keys. She had exactly forty-five minutes to get home, change, and get supper prepared before Ziad arrived.

As she practically ran to her Mustang, she inhaled humid air full of gas fumes and the organic smells of the Ashley and Cooper Rivers. Time to escape. Only to do it all over again the next day. Maybe then she could put the events of this week behind her.

# 25

Claire hated being late. As she crept along the Ravenel Bridge behind a panel truck, she stared at the clock on her stereo. Gads. All because of a wreck on US 17—after the split with Coleman Boulevard. 7:30. Ziad would show up starving, and she'd still be getting supper ready. Her stomach rumbled.

Finally! Traffic broke free, and she arrived at her house within ten minutes. Forget changing first. She prepared the chicken for their salad and threw it into the oven to bake.

A ten-minute shower got rid of the grime. And what to wear? Not that it was a special night, but she'd found herself much more conscious of what she wore around him. White jeans and a black T-shirt. Perfect. She yanked those on and dried her hair as fast as possible. 8:10. She rushed downstairs, pulled out the chicken, and made sure he hadn't arrived.

While she put on her makeup, she kept one ear listening downstairs. She'd told him to come to the back doors, which were open. No sound. Nothing.

Where was he?

After a spray of perfume, she rushed down the steps and prepared the salad.

As her hands worked, her mind fumed over the events of the past day or so. Annette Mubarak's plight. Daoud al-Rashid's rush to judgment. Ismail Khatib's rudeness. What was it with Muslim men? Her negative thoughts kept going round and round.

She glanced at the microwave clock. 8:30. What? Where *was* he? Her stomach growled again.

She punched in his number, but it rolled to voice mail.

*You knew we had this date.* She paced to the door and stepped onto the porch. No 4Runner pulling under the house.

"Ziad, where are you? C'mon! I'm hungry."

She threw the chicken back into the oven.

Nine o'clock. Great. She'd not be in bed until way past ten, which didn't bode well for working the next day.

Just as she picked up her phone to dial him again, she heard the SUV pull to a stop under the house.

She met him on the screened-in porch. "Where have you been? Don't you know what time it is?"

He offered a smile, one that under normal circumstances would have produced the same from her. "I am sorry I am late."

"Late! It's nine o'clock. Why didn't you answer your phone when I called?"

"So sorry. It was off." Ziad crossed the family room to the island. "What are we having for supper? I am hungry."

"That's all you can think about? Your stomach?" She put her hands on her hips. "We'll be lucky if the chicken isn't dried out."

He slapped his keys and wallet onto the granite. For a moment, he stood there as if collecting himself. "I was helping Ben with something, and I lost track of time."

"Like what?"

"Work-related." He met her at the console table and took her hands. "Truly, I lost track of time, and I am sorry."

Something teased her nose, a sharp scent she hadn't smelled on him in quite a while. "Have you started smoking again?"

"So what if I have?"

She shook loose. "I thought you gave that up."

"It is a long story." Ziad frowned and tossed his watch onto the table. "What are we having? I am starving."

"Chicken Caesar salad, though I'm sure the chicken's now dried out."

"I understand you are cross with me, yes? And I apologized. Like I said, Ben needed my help related to his work. I was happy to oblige."

Whatever. Claire retreated to the kitchen and cut up the chicken. "Can you set the table and get the drinks ready?"

"Of course. Tea, I presume?"

She nodded.

With the chicken on the salad, she added the dressing and tossed it before dumping it into a glass bowl. She pulled some slices of bread from the oven.

What a nice night. The silky air slid along her skin with bits of laughter riding on the currents. On the side closest to their table, her other next-door neighbors chatted with friends, most likely over a bottle of wine. A candle glowed on their porch. Too bad she had to rush off to bed when Ziad left.

Ziad had turned the lights to low and set out plates and silverware. Tall glasses of tea sat in their proper place. He rose when she set the bowl on the table. "Please, have a seat."

She did so and ran through the blessing in her head.

As they began eating, he studied her face. "You seem tired."

"I am." How much should she say? "I didn't sleep well."

"Neither did I."

"Maybe it's going around." Her thoughts returned to the unpleasant valley of the past several hours. "I didn't sleep well because I heard some sad news last night. One of Sonja's friends' husbands left her and took their sons to Egypt."

"That is sad. I am sorry to hear that."

"That's it?"

"Pardon?"

"That's all you have to say?" She hated the edge in her voice.

He paused from cutting up the salad. "What else should I say?"

"Like maybe her husband is totally in the wrong for practically kid-napping his children."

"You do not know that. Maybe they—"

"He left without a word to her." She opened the dressing bottle and poured some onto her salad. "I don't understand why you Arab men think you have total dominion over your wives and children. I mean, to break up a family like that."

He froze, and his brow knitted. "Perhaps there was more going on than you realize."

"But it's not fair!"

"Welcome to life." He took a bite.

What? Like he agreed? "Excuse me?"

"You do not think that is fair?" Ziad speared a chicken strip and cut it into pieces. "Do you think it was fair I was hit today?"

Huh? He hadn't mentioned that at all. "What?"

"Oh, yes. This afternoon I pulled a woman who was drunk. She failed the sobriety tests. Eddie and I were trying to arrest her. She called me a no-good rag head and then slapped me." He pointed to his lip.

For the first time, she noticed it was a little swollen.

"I got this simply because of my name and accent, like *I* am the one who's a suspect."

"I hope you arrested her."

"Eddie did. I knew better."

She barely heard him as she tore off a chunk of bread and buttered it. "Then today, I was working in the outpatient clinic when this Muslim guy came in with a cut to his left hand." She took a bite and swallowed. "He yelled at me because I was touching him while trying to help him. Just because I'm a Christian. What's your take on that?"

"You know I do not understand some—"

"Do you have an *opinion* about that?" She rolled her eyes. "He's your religion, after all."

He put his elbows on the table and leaned forward. "My religion? Is that the way you see it?"

Her pulse skidded upward. "You're Saudi."

"You want my opinion?" With his fork, he pointed at her. "You should have asked permission first."

The jerk! "What?"

"He was probably not used to having an unrelated woman not of his religion touch him."

"So? I'm a nurse. It's my job—"

"And he was not comfortable with you. Why is this so difficult for you to understand?"

Of all things! He preached her to like she was an errant pupil. "I don't believe you."

"What?"

She tossed her bread onto her plate. "How can you say that?"

"It is the culture. Your sister understood that well with her work."

The nerve, the absolute nerve of him. "Don't you dare bring her into it."

She tried to ignore the way her voice had risen.

He threw his fork onto the glass table with a clatter. "Why are you so angry all of the sudden?"

Calm, as if trying to talk her down.

Instead, he poured fuel onto her smoldering anger.

"Do you know what it's like to have an Arab man, a Saudi man, refuse to shake your hand and look down his nose at you simply because you're female?"

"Claire—"

"Do you?" That nearly came across as a shout. "It's horrible. And it happened to me today."

"I—"

"You Saudi men are all alike!"

He slammed his fist onto the table. "Claire!"

She started.

"You do not know what you are saying." He sprang to his feet and loomed over her with his fingertips on the glass.

No way would she give in. She jumped up. "Sure as the dawn I do!"

"You Americans think you are so high and mighty. But you are not. You are decadent." He nearly shouted that. "You tolerate filth. Pornography." He pointed at her. "You put women in practically nothing and do not call it pornography. You think all people who speak Arabic hate you."

"You don't respect your women." She matched him in volume now. "You take their children. Father rules, right? They want to be normal, to have a life, and you repress that. You beat your wife simply for wanting to have a job. Something more than just sitting at home and staring at four walls. And if she doesn't walk that line exactly as you want her to, you kill her and get away—"

"Claire!" A roar, a raging storm.

Oh, no. Had she really spewed that hatred? The blood drained from her face.

Ziad threw his napkin to the ground. "Shut up and listen to your foolishness. I do not have to sit here and take this garbage from you tonight or any other night. You are a foolish woman speaking foolish things. You and your pride."

He tore into the house and swiped his keys and wallet from the island.

Stunned, she stood there. Her neighbors had fallen silent. Then came nervous murmurs.

Claire bolted inside. The dishes in the glass-fronted cabinets trembled as she rushed toward the foyer. "Ziad, wait."

He yanked open the door and whipped around.

Claire skidded to a stop.

"You think you are so good, that you do not hate." That nearly came out as a hiss. "You do! I want nothing to do with you."

He slammed the front door so hard the house shook. The mirror on the stairwell wall above the foyer console table fell and shattered on the wooden floor.

The 4Runner's engine roared.

"Ziad!" She ran down the porch stairs. A splinter bit into her foot.

"Ziad, please. Wait!" She stared as he blasted in reverse down the driveway.

With a chirp of tires, he sped into the night.

Tears filled her eyes. "What have I done?"

She knew exactly what she'd done.

Grossly wounded the one man who'd become one of her closest friends.

She hobbled up the steps as fast as she could and snatched up her phone. She staggered to the couch in the family room. "Ziad, pick up. Please!'

It rang. And rang. It shifted to voice mail. His finely accented English, then Arabic, told her to leave a message.

A tear trickled down her cheek. "Ziad, please, please call me when you get this. I—I'm sorry. Please! I—I lost my head. Please call me."

She lowered the phone. With a grimace, she pulled out the splinter and tossed it onto the coffee table. She limped toward the foyer.

The mirror now lay in what seemed to be thousands of shards on the floor. She picked up a piece and stared at it. Shattered. Just like how she felt now. She clasped it to her chest. "Oh, Ziad, I'm sorry! Please come back."

With that, she bent her head and cried.

Ziad stomped on the accelerator as he sped across the Ravenel Bridge into Charleston.

Claire wanted him to be among his own kind?

He'd do exactly that.

His phone rang. Her name popped up on the caller ID.

Forget it. He'd not answer now or ever again.

He sped into the parking lot of the local mosque and turned off his phone.

The final prayers of the day were beginning. He whipped through his ablutions and found his place on the last row of men. The women lined up behind him.

Their presence mocked him.

In the row ahead of him, a man in scrubs settled on his knees.

To his right, a young man sported a thick bandage on his left hand. Maybe Claire's patient?

Did he care? No.

Like he believed that.

He bowed toward the ground and began prayers in earnest.

An hour later, after coffee with some friends, Ziad powered on his phone as he unlocked his apartment. No less than a dozen texts from Claire. Voice mails. Three of them.

"Ziad, this is Claire." Her voice sounded hoarse, as if she'd been crying. "I know you're either ignoring my call or have the phone turned off. I'm sorry. I cannot say that enough. My mouth got ahead of my mind. Please… please call me."

His fingers tightened on the phone. He hurled it onto the bed.

He'd do no such thing.

Claire had messed up. Not him.

He turned the shower on as hot as he could stand it. Maybe that would burn off the anger still streaming in his system.

Just as he returned to the bedroom with a towel around his waist, his phone began pinging again.

More texts.

From Claire.

*Please forgive me.*

His lip curled.

*Please call me. I want to talk.*

He didn't.

*I care about you.*

He didn't believe that. Not for one second.

*Please call.*

He turned it off before easing onto the edge of the mattress and hanging his head.

"You must forget her," one of his friends had said earlier that evening. "She hates you simply for who you are. Such a woman is not worthy of your time or affection."

No, he couldn't forget her. That was as likely as the sun setting in the east.

*Where did we go wrong tonight?*

He flopped back and stared at the ceiling.

*We were both wrong.*

His pride still smarted at the words she'd said and the humiliation of arguing in front of her neighbors.

He closed his eyes and shook his head. No. She'd have to be the one to apologize.

In person.

On her knees.

Until then, he wanted nothing to do with her.

The air washing across his face from the ceiling fan gradually cooled his temper. He drifted.

That dream came again, one he hadn't had since the night Claire had gotten drunk.

He wandered among roses of many colors, some white, some red, some yellow. Even yellow ones with red tips.

Sweet scents, with the scarlet ones yielding the most pleasant of all.

A woman laughed, a sound he instantly recognized.

Sabirah sat on an ornate prayer rug and hugged Tariq close.

Then came the golden scales with an English Z on them.

Dread filled him.

His life sat before him.

Tariq undid the drawstrings of a black velvet bag.

Gray stones that were his works poured onto the rug.

Ziad closed his eyes. "I can explain."

Grief filled Sabirah's dark eyes as she placed several on the *Sayia'at* side of the scale. It tipped. "Claire cares about you, and you hurt her."

"She hurt me as well!"

Another one went on the *Sayia'at* side. "You have so much pride. She had a point, even if she phrased it poorly." Yet another stone made it sag even further. "And that woman today. You judged her for her drunkenness and the way she treated you."

"I—"

"She has a miserable home life."

Tariq piled on more. "Claire struggles with her bigotry. She hates that it's within her."

"No!" Ziad's eyes flew open. His lower back ached from lying in that position for so long. With a groan, he sat up and mopped his face with a sheet. "What have I done?"

No stones in his dream had gone on the *hasana'at* side. Not one.

So much for thinking he stood in the right on this one. He had his own issues.

No chance of sleeping now. Or maybe ever again.

With a glass of water in front of him, he settled down on the couch and stared at the dark television. He reached for the remote.

No. He needed to think this through.

His own family, moreover, his beloved, had accused him. He had pride. He knew it. Too much of it. Hadn't he wound up where he was because of pride? Yes. If he'd listened to those around him, Sabirah and his family would still be alive.

*But would I know Claire as I do now?*

The thought startled him.

*Go see her.*

That voice, once again like when he'd nearly walked out of her life weeks before.

Ziad whipped around. No one stood there.

He knew what he had to do. He'd call her the next evening after he finished his shift.

Now he had to get some rest. It didn't happen. He either paced the floor or stared at the creek.

Somehow, he stumbled through his eight-hour shift at the Quick Fill the next day. When he finally dragged himself to his apartment, he needed a nap before doing anything.

When he woke up, the clock told him the bad news. He'd slept clear through the night from five in the afternoon to five in the morning. And now he had to work another eight-hour shift, this time as a reserve officer.

*Tonight. Tonight I will apologize.*

If his pride-turned-to-shame didn't get in the way.

# 26

By Friday, Claire wrote off Ziad.

She'd tried to call him three times. And did he answer? No.

And texting? Forget it.

Technology made it easy to hide.

Muttering, she pulled her Mustang to a stop behind Sonja's Mercedes sports car. Her husband's Ford Explorer sat in the other slot.

Since she didn't feel like idle chitchat, Claire settled for stretching out for her run on the small front lawn of the townhouse.

"There you are." Sonja stood over her, a hat shading her eyes from the summer sun. "Why didn't you ring the doorbell or something?"

Claire shrugged. "I needed to stretch out. I'm sorry about being late. I didn't sleep well last night."

*Because I was waiting on the stupid phone to ring.*

"No problem. Dom told me to go ahead and run before he put me to work."

A small smile crossed Claire's features. "What a way to start the day."

"You got it. Packing up the last little bit. Then cleaning so there's no excuse not to close on Monday." Her best friend sighed. "We'll be here all weekend, thank you very much."

Claire didn't laugh as she climbed to her feet with her water bottle in hand.

"Boy, something serious is going on," Sonja said as they began trotting down the road.

"I need a vacation," Claire muttered between huffs. Oh, this was a hard one, made harder by the story that wanted to burst from the pit of her stomach.

"You want to talk about it?"

"No." Sweat began pouring down her face. Her legs tightened. That dreaded stitch in her side showed up.

Gradually, the events of Wednesday came out between pants.

They turned onto Sonja's street. Claire slowed to a walk and hung her head. So much better. Except the stitch hadn't faded. Neither had her angst.

Sonja stretched her arms above her head. "I'm sorry."

"Yeah, well, I'm sorry I ever got to know him, so if you were worried about us dating, no need." That was sweat stinging her eyes, not tears.

Sonja stopped. "Claire!"

"Well, I am."

*Liar.* She winced as the stitch flared one last time. "Ever since I got to know him, it's been like I've been off balance or something."

"Maybe that's why God put him into your life."

"He put him into my life to make me miserable." Claire kicked the street as they came to a stop in front of the townhouse.

"Aren't you being just a little hard on him? He's tried so hard to adjust."

"Well, he didn't try hard enough."

"Claire."

She folded her arms across her chest and leaned over to stretch her calves. "It's true."

"Is it?" Sonja put her hands on her hips. "Is it really? Emma's told me how hard he's tried to fit in. To be a friend to you. And what do you do? You let your prejudice get in the way."

Of all things. "I do not!"

Her friend threw up her hands. "Yes, you do."

"Just whose side are you on?" Had she just yelled at her best friend?

Sonja, the Circuit Solicitor who never showed emotion in court, flinched. She closed her eyes and sighed. Quietly, she said, "I'm on no one's side. Not yours. Not his." She glanced away. "I get so frustrated with you sometimes. You're letting what happened two and a half years ago get in the way of good sense."

"With good cause."

"Was Ziad involved? Or is he guilty simply by association? I'll talk to you later." With that, Sonja fled toward the townhouse. The front door slammed.

What did Sonja know? She hadn't seen Yana hanging onto life by a thread, hadn't stared at scarlet all over her hands, her front. She hadn't heard the girl's story directly from her. Claire conveniently scooted past the fact that Sonja had prosecuted the case. She lifted her chin. What did she know about Saudi men? They were domineering, quick to condemn, to kill, even, if someone, especially a woman, dared deviate from the path chosen for her by Allah.

Ziad was just like those she'd met. No way would she apologize any more. She was done. Finished.

Time to get on with her life.

With a chirp of tires, she sped from the subdivision. Her whole body rebelled against the hot morning run. She needed more fluids. And a shower. And definitely a nap. After she got that shower, she'd—

Noise finally broke into her cesspool of thoughts. Lights too. She glanced in the rearview mirror. Oh, no!

The lights and noise came from a patrol car.

Her gaze shot to the speedometer.

Sixty-one in a forty-five!

Her heart lurched.

Immediately, she slowed and pulled to the side of the road.

The patrol car stopped behind her. Another one joined it.

Resting her elbow on the armrest of the door, she leaned her head against her hand. Could the day get any worse?

It could.

The patrol car's driver's door opened. A tall, lean man in the navy blue uniform of the Charleston Police Department strode toward her.

Claire knew that gait. Ziad.

She drew in a sharp breath and slid down in her seat.

He tapped on her window.

Almost unwillingly, she rolled it down.

"Driver's license and registration, please." Ziad leaned down so he peered into the interior.

"May I open the glove compartment?" That came out as a squeak.

"You may."

She handed him her registration and fumbled in her purse for her license. "Ziad—"

"Do you realize you were going sixty-one in a forty-five, ma'am?" All business. What did she expect?

Her cheeks flamed. "Uh, no."

"Stay here." He took her paperwork with him.

Claire slid so far down in her seat that she almost lay flat. She squeezed her eyes closed, then opened them and stared in her side view mirror.

The patrol car behind Ziad's pulled into traffic and passed her with a light tap on the horn and a wave from the driver.

Eddie had now officially witnessed her humiliation.

Ziad began walking toward her car.

She pushed herself upright.

He proffered a clipboard. "Miss Montgomery, I am writing you a ticket for fifty-nine miles per hour in a forty-five-mile-an-hour zone. If you so desire to contest this ticket, your court date will be August twelfth. Please sign this for me."

She scribbled her name, then raised her gaze to his face.

His sunglasses concealed any expression.

She handed him the clipboard. "Ziad, please, I—"

"Have a good afternoon, Miss Montgomery." He ripped off her copy of the ticket and handed it to her along with her license and registration before walking away.

That was it. Professional to the core without a word about their argument.

It devastated her.

She folded it and tossed it onto the seat beside her water bottle. With shaking hands, Claire pulled into traffic. She puttered along and cast another glance in the rearview mirror.

Ziad turned off his lights, then made a U-turn.

Right out of her life.

This time, maybe for good.

Her heart ached. She cried all the way to Mount Pleasant.

Once at home, she shut off the engine and sat there for a moment to compose herself. Now, she truly did have to adjust to life without Ziad. What an empty life. So surprising that he'd become a big part of it in just a few short weeks.

And her angst? Dumb. Sonja was right. She'd let it rob her of the friendship that now meant more to her than she'd been willing to admit. What could she do to get it back?

Nothing, if his reaction when pulling her for speeding had signaled anything.

He was done with her.

Now she had to pick up the pieces of her life and start over—this time without him in it.

First things first. That shower. She picked up the pink copy of the ticket he'd given her to search for the court date. What on earth?

Her heart hammered as she stared at the yellow sticky note attached to it and Ziad's elegant script. She whispered as she read it aloud. "'Claire, I would like to make amends with you. Please call me. I will be home at four. Z.'"

He'd signed the Z with a flourish.

Relief left her shaking so much she couldn't move. "Oh, Ziad!"

What to do?

It came to her in a flash.

First, apologize to Sonja. With shaking fingers, she called her friend. "Sonja? It's Claire. Listen, I'm sorry. Please forgive me for yelling at you."

Her friend didn't hesitate. "You know I do, Claire."

"You wouldn't believe what happened. Ziad pulled me for speeding!"

"Uh—"

"Don't worry." Claire smiled for the first time since Tuesday morning. "It's not a bad thing. It's a good thing. Really good! He wants to talk. Pray for me."

"That I can do. Keep me—"

"Thanks!" With renewed vigor, Claire jumped from the Mustang.

Now for step two. Apologize in person. And dressed up when she did it. She charged up the stairs.

She could only hope he'd accept it.

At 4:15 that afternoon Claire pulled into a slot beside Ziad's 4Runner. He was home. Thank goodness. She raced up the steps and rang his doorbell. No answer.

Had she misread the note?

It wasn't like she'd looked at it a hundred times or something.

She tried knocking.

Still no answer.

Maybe he was upstairs. She combined the doorbell with a knock. "Ziad?"

Nothing.

She *had* misunderstood. He'd probably heard her and wanted nothing to do with her.

Despair nearly bowled her over. Head hung, she shuffled toward the steps. She'd go home. Maybe use the rest of that piña colada mix to drown her sorrows.

She put one foot on the steps.

A lock scraped back. "Claire?"

She whipped around. "Hey! I... I was afraid you were ignoring the door."

"I was in the shower and thought I heard something." A brief smile flickered across his face as he buttoned his deep green shirt. "So sorry if I am still dressing."

A nervous laugh escaped her. "It's all right."

"Please." He stepped aside. "Come inside."

As she passed him, the spicy scent of his aftershave mingled with the fresh scent of shampoo. A drop of water slid from his sideburns. "I definitely pulled you from the shower."

"My towel is still on the floor of the bedroom." He turned toward the kitchen. "Would you like something to drink? Water? Tea?"

She wrapped her arms around herself and paced into the living room. "Water is fine."

She forced herself to stare at the Saudi Arabian flag hanging over the fireplace. *Lord, I repent. Truly. I do. Thank you for showing me what a bigot I've been these past two and a half years.*

Ice clinked on glass.

She turned.

Ziad stood there, his gaze solemn. An undercurrent of tension laced his manners. "Why are you here?"

Suddenly, her carefully planned words fled her mind. She opened her mouth.

He didn't say a word, only seated himself on the couch and leaned back as if expecting her to cough out an apology.

"Ziad..."

He cocked an eyebrow.

Her knees began quaking. As if God pushed her, she slowly knelt in front of him. Oh, this was hard. She kept her gaze on him.

His eyes remained dark pools of sadness.

More guilt washed over her. She swallowed against the lump in her throat. "I've always liked to think I treat everyone with respect, that I don't have a dark side. Wednesday night, God showed me the depth of my foolishness, just like you said. I do. I let it get the best of me."

233

Nothing. No words at all.

"It took the Holy Spirit through my best friend and today's events to wake me up to that. God and I had a long talk this afternoon." She'd shed copious amounts of tears after lunch as she'd read Scripture and repented. Rather than feeling a burden, lightness had touched her soul— until now. "I—I realized the way I'd let an incident two and a half years ago inform my life about others who had nothing to do with the crime of one. I didn't deal with it, and it turned into hatred. Please forgive me."

She closed her eyes against the tears and rushed on, "You have every right to order me out of your life, and I—"

A finger over her lips stopped her.

Ziad knelt in front of her. He brushed back some of her hair. "I do, Claire. I forgive you."

Something akin to weakness swept over her.

He drew her close, and she collapsed in his arms. "I do forgive you. As I spent all night awake after we argued, I realized something must have happened in your past."

Oh, he was so astute. "Two and a half years ago, I witnessed an honor killing."

His arms tightened around her. "What? Here in America?"

She swallowed hard as tears began trickling down her cheeks. Who cared? It was like once he'd accepted her apology, any control over her emotions had crumbled. "It was awful. A girl named Yana. Yana al-Hakim. Her father is—was—a rug merchant on King Street. His shop was where that antique shop is just south of Market Street."

"I know the place."

"Yana was eighteen and a teenager in every way. She was outgoing, and none of her friends cared that she wore a headscarf. She had a group of girls she ran around with. Boys too. Her mama didn't seem to mind, but her daddy?" She shook her head.

"How do you know all of this?" Ziad asked.

"She told me." She sniffled. "One night in early December 2007, I was working in the ED. She came in with a black eye and split lip, just banged up in general. Turns out lots of her friends were in a youth group at a church near where she lived. She'd started going to youth group with them while claiming to be going to a friend's house to study."

"And it is never a good idea to lie."

"I know. I guess one night, the night of the youth group Christmas party at the church, one of her brothers followed and tattled on her. Her daddy came to get her. Sure, he was polite to her friends when he asked to speak to her alone." Claire pulled back, drew her knees to her chest, and made sure her long skirt covered them. "He started hitting her. She got away only by begging to go to the bathroom and getting out a window. She made it to a local fire station, and some firefighters brought her in."

She kept her gaze focused on her skirt and picked at a loose thread.

Ziad stopped her nervous tic. "You sent her home?"

"Oh, no, no. You see, she was eighteen, so legally an adult. We called Social Services, and they were in a bind since she was still in high school. Since we needed the cubicle, I volunteered to take her to the nurse's lounge while Social Services sorted things out. She and I started talking."

"Obviously, things did not end well."

She sighed. "No. They didn't. She told me it was more. She gave her life to Jesus about a month before that. She knew what would happen because her daddy had told her when he beat her up. He was going to ship her back to Saudi Arabia for marriage. Honestly, she worried he'd kill her."

Ziad curled his fingers around hers. "A valid concern if she converted."

She clung to him as images swarmed over her from that fateful night. "Social Services took her to a battered women's shelter and got her away just in time because he showed up in a rage. He first threatened to kill us. Then as security escorted him out, he threatened to sue us."

"Unsettling."

"Oh, yeah." She shuddered. "About a week later, right before Christmas, we got word of a stabbing. It was Yana." That trembling began again. "Ten stab wounds. One nicked her aorta, and she bled out on the table. She didn't stand a chance, Ziad. She didn't! Her daddy had tracked her down and attacked her."

Once more, Ziad drew her close and let her cry. His arms remained around her, and his lips moved against her hair.

If he said anything, she didn't hear him. Her breath came in jagged gasps. "They… they arrested him for Murder One. Though Sonja was Circuit Solicitor, she tried the case herself. I had to testify, which was awful. I watched the rest of the trial. He got life in prison. No chance of parole. It's on appeal now."

"Meaning you will have to testify again?"

"Maybe. Sonja says it's airtight. I can only hope." She sniffled. "What would you have done?"

"Me?" Ziad pulled back and ran his hand down her hair. "I do not understand."

"As a father."

He took a deep breath. "Claire—"

"I want to know."

He hesitated as if considering how she would react. "I would be grieved. Would you not feel the same if a child of yours left the faith?"

She nodded.

"But an honor killing?" He shook his head. "No. I would never, though in Saudi Arabia, they never went to trial."

"Why?"

"They were seen as restoring honor to a family." His thumb skimmed her cheek and lifted away a tear. "But as a police officer? I would arrest the perpetrator with pleasure. I did when I was in the SANG, and I would here."

Some of her tension dissipated. "It angered me so much. And scared me."

"Why?"

"Emma had accepted going to Jeddah at that point. I was so scared that something would happen and she'd die and—" She put her hand over her mouth to stop a sob trying to burst forth.

Once more, he drew her close. "I am so very sorry you witnessed what I consider to be a very dark side of Islam."

She took a deep breath, then another. Gradually, her emotions calmed, leaving in their wake a feeling of deep exhaustion.

"I imagine you need some tissues or something."

A weak smile forced its way loose. "Or something."

"Stay here." He rose and headed upstairs. A moment later, he returned and knelt in front of her. He brought a white rose from behind his back.

Her heart swelled with emotion as finally, her lips turned up in a real smile. "Ziad, how beautiful!"

"The florist said this is the best color to represent making out."

She chuckled. "Do you mean, making up?"

"Umm…"

"Making out is, well, getting crazy with kissing and such."

Oh, that blush. So adorable on him as it crept up his neck to his face. And that smile.

She'd missed it.

"Yes, making up." He handed her a handkerchief. "My apologies. It was either this or toilet paper."

"This is fine." She blew her nose.

"So now that we have made out," he winked, "perhaps I could interest you in some supper? I had planned to come to your house to see if you would like to go out."

"Supper would be wonderful."

He held out his hands. Without hesitation, he drew her to her feet and into his arms.

Resting her forehead against his jaw, she didn't mind the stubble on his face or that delicious scent floating her way. She felt at home. Completely at home. And suddenly, she didn't want to let him go.

# 27

"Did I ever tell you about the first time I ever cooked a meal?" Ziad asked from the kitchen where he placed chicken breasts marinated in an olive oil and garlic mix to bake.

Ice clinked in her glass. "No. Tell me."

"It was a few months before Sabirah got pregnant with Muhammed Amir. Our housekeeper and her husband were visiting their families in Pakistan, and Mama and Papa were not at home that night. It was just the two of us." Sadness tempered his mood, but he pushed it away. "She had miscarried, and the doctor ordered bed rest for her. I arrived home late from work, and she asked me to make supper since she could not stand for long periods of time."

"What happened?"

"I asked her what to do. She told me about a lamb recipe and where to find it. Then I asked again. I think she became exasperated with me because she said to follow the instructions. That was it."

"How did it turn out?"

"Surprisingly well, and neither of us died from food poisoning."

From her place on the couch, Claire laughed.

What a welcome sound, one he worried he'd never hear again.

He slid some pita into the oven to warm. "That night I discovered I enjoyed cooking."

"Mama said you're a fast learner."

239

"Sabirah helped me start." This time, when he thought of her, no stab of pain followed. He hesitated. Why?

"Ziad?"

"So sorry. I was thinking. I would have cooked more in Jeddah, but household chores were so divided among men and women."

She didn't answer that one. Instead, a show on Animal Planet played.

Contentment washed over him, almost like her apology had erased their angst from the past week. For now, he treasured the time he had alone with her, time in which he'd been free to take her hands, hold her close, and feel her silky hair against his chin.

He cut up some vegetables and tossed them into a wok for steaming. "What is your work schedule like for the next few days?"

No answer.

"Claire?"

Still no answer.

He wiped his hands on a towel and stepped around the counter.

She lay on the couch, her eyes tightly closed, her lashes brushing her cheek much like they'd done a few weeks ago at the beach. Her chest moved in the even pattern of sleep.

For a moment, he simply drank in the gentle curve of her hips and waist that was subtly highlighted by the top and skirt she wore. With effort, he ripped his gaze away and gently placed a fleece over her.

Ziad's mind churned as he checked on the vegetables and dumped them into a serving bowl. With the storm past, he tried to empathize with Claire, to walk in her shoes that terrible night when she'd witnessed the death of an innocent teenager. Would he have reacted the same way? Perhaps. He shook his head as he pulled the pita from the oven and slid it onto a plate. Yes, he probably would have.

He tried to think of anything that had happened in the Kingdom with similar results for him. Of course. His oftentimes erroneous assumptions about Westerners.

*Prove to me you are worthy.*

That had been his mantra rather than accepting them as they struggled to adapt to his culture. *Thank you, Claire, for coming to see me. For being desirous enough to restore our friendship.*

Once he had everything on the table, he knelt beside her. He wove his fingers through her hair. "Time to wake up."

Nuzzling the pillow, she sighed and opened her eyes. Once more, he found himself nearly drowning in the deep green of those jade depths. "I'm sorry. I fell asleep."

"You must be exhausted."

She yawned and stretched.

Ziad warmed as he drank in her figure. He averted his gaze. "Supper is ready. Chicken, a recipe taught by your mother."

"Mama's chicken? Yum."

He helped her to her feet. Without dropping her hand, he led her to the table and pulled out a chair. "M'Lady Claire, please, have a seat."

She smiled at him.

Ziad settled at his place. "Tell me something."

"Anything."

"Why did you change your name back to Montgomery?"

"How long do you have?"

"How long do you need?" he asked with a wink.

"Oh, I don't know. Maybe all night?"

He chuckled. "I do not have to wake early tomorrow."

"The short story is that it came down to Jackson's mama, Margaret. She was a strange bird." Claire sipped her tea. "She never did like me. I think she saw anyone marrying her son as stealing her little boy. It was very clear that she favored Jackson over his younger sister, Lydia."

So ironic. "How?"

"Jackson could carry on the family name. Not that we'd planned any differently, but when we found out we were expecting a boy, she really pushed us to name him after Jackson, even to the point where it made him uncomfortable. She was obsessed with it."

"Is that Southern or simply American?"

"More Southern than American. I had no problem with it." She shook her head. "When he and Little Jack died, what would you have expected her reaction to be?"

Ziad thought about that one. "Supportive."

"Hah. You'd think. So wrong. The night of the funeral, not four hours before I miscarried, she pointed at my belly and said something like, 'Take care of my grandson.' Then she left without another word. No, 'I love you' or even 'I'm sorry' or anything like that."

The nerve! Ziad stared at her.

Claire nodded. "It's true. When I needed her the most, she wasn't there. Jackson's sister was. Lydia, who by that point had married with two little ones of her own, visited as much as she could. That meant the world to me. But her mama? Nope."

He took her hand. "I cannot fathom someone who would be so… unsupportive."

"I mean, I know people can act weird when someone dies. Goodness knows most of my 'friends' faded from my life during my year of mourning, but she was family." Her shoulders rose and fell in a shrug. "After that year, I knew what I had to do. I took myself down to the courthouse and changed my name back to Montgomery. Then I boxed up a lot of Jackson's keepsakes like his football trophies from high school and college. I called her up and said they were there for her. She told me to leave them on the porch, and she'd get them. And she did—while I was working." She shook her head. "No thank you note or anything. I haven't talked to her since then."

"Interesting." Ziad leaned back and toyed with his spoon as he gazed at her. Such a beautiful, vibrant woman treated so poorly by someone who'd claimed to love her like family. Yes, Montgomery fit her better than Middleton. "It would have been too strange to…"

She cocked her head. "To what?"

*To refer to you using your married name.*

He released her hand before he kissed it. "To not know you as a Montgomery."

Lame. He could hear Ben laughing at him.

A slow smile crossed her face, and they finished the meal in comfortable silence.

Later, Claire curled up beside him on the couch. They didn't need words. Only touch. He reveled in her nearness. As they watched a soccer match together, she laid her head against his knee. He ran his fingers across her hair.

Once more, she slept. Truly, the past week must have exhausted her.

He didn't care. Being with her was enough. For several minutes, he emptied his mind of everything. Then it happened. Rather than focus on the game, he thought about his lack of pain the last time he'd thought about Sabirah. *Why did I not feel great sadness like I had in the past? It doesn't make sense to me.*

In a flash, it did.

Claire.

No denying it, he wanted to have more of a relationship with her than a simple friendship.

The thought jolted him so much that he shifted.

Claire stirred. "I must have fallen asleep."

Why did he have to move? "You did."

She sat up as she smothered a yawn. "What time is it?"

He grinned. "Do you have my watch?"

"Of course." She cut her eyes toward him. "I think you have a subconscious desire to visit me."

She rose and retrieved her purse from the bar.

Ziad followed her with his gaze. "Oh? What makes you say that?"

She handed him the watch. "Because it seems like every time you come over, you leave this."

"Maybe I do, m'Lady Claire." He checked the time. "And it appears as if it is almost midnight."

She grimaced. "Which means I'll be turning into a pumpkin."

"What?"

"You've never heard of that?"

"No."

"That's right. You're not from these parts." She nudged him. "It's an expression from a fairy tale."

This time, he wrapped her in his arms. "Will you tell it to me?"

"Maybe. If you're good." She winked, then pulled back. "I do need to get going."

Oh, why did this evening have to end? "May I see you tomorrow night?"

Her face fell as she paused at the door. "I wish I could, but I'm working the next eight nights."

Eight nights seemed like an eternity to him. Suddenly, he worried. Hopefully, that wasn't an excuse. "Then may I call you?"

Why did he sound like a little boy all of the sudden?

Her smile reassured him. "I'd love that. May I offer a rain check?"

"A what?"

"An alternative plan?"

He nodded.

"Are you busy on the Fourth?"

Him and every other reserve officer. "Working crowd control for the Fourth of July celebration."

"Are you off from the convenience store on the fifth?"

"I am."

"Then come over in the morning, and we'll go sea kayaking. Then we can grill and hang out. I'll even rent a movie or something."

Relief surged through him. "I like that idea."

"Good." She squeezed his hands. "Take care."

With that, she slipped out the door before hugging her crossed his mind.

Ziad shut the door and leaned his head against it with a thump. Arrggghh. He hadn't moved fast enough. Now eight long days stretched before him. After turning off the lights, he trudged up the stairs to his bedroom.

From its place on the nightstand, Sabirah's photograph beckoned to him. He picked it up and gazed at it. Suddenly, she seemed more distant, more ethereal to him, almost like the almost nineteen years he'd been married to her had ended years, not months, earlier.

Why?

Again, he didn't have to look further than Claire. Her scent still lingered in his nose, as did the silkiness of her hair on his fingers.

Even a week ago, he would have hesitated, would have said it was too soon.

No more.

"Would you mind, Sabirah?"

He eased onto the edge of his bed as he thought about that one. What if the tables had been turned? What if he were the one cold in the ground and her alive? He would have had no claim to her anymore.

Therein lay his answer.

Once more, he gazed at the photo. It was almost as if Sabirah spoke in his heart. "You have my blessing."

He took a deep breath and lifted his face to the ceiling. His eyes filled, but the emotion quickly receded. A calm settled over him, as if he were walking squarely in Allah's will.

Without another second's hesitation, he carried the frame downstairs to his study and set it on the desk.

In eight days, well, seven days, twenty-three hours, and several minutes, he'd make his intentions crystal clear to Claire.

# 28

Such a beautiful time. The day after the Fourth of July, the early afternoon sun warmed Claire as she lay on the dock behind her house. A breeze puffed and tickled her face. Her shoulder and arm muscles ached, a sign of a good workout.

The company didn't hurt either.

Beside her on the blanket, Ziad sprawled on his back.

Oh, so perfect.

"Did I ever tell you about my cathartic moment?" she asked as she examined the back of her eyelids.

"Cathartic?" Rich laziness deepened his voice. "I have not heard that word before."

"Oh, I guess it means life-changing. Or at least, that's what I take it to mean."

"No. You have not told me."

She opened her eyes and shifted onto her side so she rested her head on her elbow.

He mirrored her.

Oh, my. Thanks to the sun's rays, his skin had turned a deep olive. He'd filled out too. Hmmm. Hmmm. She could so get used to those pecs, biceps, and delts. Not an ounce of fat on him, even though he'd turn forty in a few weeks. *Wait! What was I going to talk about? Oh! That's right. My cathartic moment.*

"Claire?"

"Uh, sorry." Her excuse of staring would never suffice. "I lost my train of thought."

A lazy smile crossed his face. "What is your story?"

"Summer of 2006, I realized I needed a change."

"Why?"

"Most of my previous friendships had faded away because they didn't know how to handle what happened to me. Sure, I had Sonja and Elizabeth, but otherwise, I didn't have any real friends. Both of them were out of town that Fourth of July. So were Em and Delia. The twins were just out of high school and doing their own thing. And Allie never was good company. Up until that day, I hated going out to eat by myself, or, heaven forbid, to a movie alone."

He nodded. "I can understand. I would feel that same way."

"I decided to be brazen on that day and do the sea kayaking trip we did this morning by myself."

He quirked an eyebrow. "Go to Fort Sumter, then to Sullivan's Island, and back here? Alone? What would have happened if you had capsized or worse?"

"I know. It was crazy stupid, but once I got that idea into my head, I couldn't resist. Problem was, I hadn't kayaked since before Little Jack was born. I was way out of shape." She smiled at the memories. "You would have laughed at me as I got the kayak into the water."

"I do not even want to think about it."

"Hah. The trip to Fort Sumter and Sullivan's Island was great. It was like today. Lots of energy in the air. Storms in the forecast. But I did it." She smiled as she remembered the freedom she'd felt that day. "I wound up at that very same restaurant where we ate, pretty close to where we sat today. I'd brought a book with me, so I sat at the table for two hours and read."

He traced the outline of a palm tree on his towel. "You did not mind?"

"No. I was content. At least until a waiter approached me and asked if I was the one with the kayak." She shook her head. "At first I thought someone had stolen it, but he said I might want to get a move on it because the weather was building."

"Wait." He closed his eyes as if trying to envision the event. "You kayaked back to the house in a storm?"

"Uh, yeah." Her cheeks heated. "Dumb, I know, but I was so determined to prove to myself I could do it. The storm caught me. I mean, the wind was howling, it was thundering and lightning all over the place, and when the rain came, I had no visibility."

"Claire," he shuddered, "this could have ended—how do you say it?—very badly."

"Oh, I know. Later, I realized I could have been blown into the shipping lanes or out to sea. But right then, I was so focused on getting to safety. I finally got the dock in sight. And it was still blowing. I tied up, crawled up here, and just lay on my back laughing and laughing while the storm raged around me."

"People would have thought you to be crazy."

"Oh, I'm sure. But it was like surviving that terrifying experience released something inside of me. The laughter came from joy bubbling up from within. I couldn't stop it. Didn't want to." A soft smile crossed her face. "Later that evening, once the storm had passed and I got cleaned up, I brought my supper out here and watched the fireworks. And then?" She nodded. "I could go different places by myself without feeling so alone."

He lifted his hand and tousled some strands of hair that had fallen from her ponytail. His fingers skimmed her cheek. "You, Claire Montgomery, are a brave, if not at times crazy, woman."

She warmed at his compliment. "It taught me a valuable lesson."

"Oh?" His fingers skittered along her neck to her shoulder, then her arm.

A shiver coursed its way down her spine, followed by tingles where his fingers had brushed. "Yeah." Better get this out before any logical thought completely scattered. "It taught me that before I could be wholly with someone, I had to first learn to be content to be by myself."

"A worthy lesson." He nodded and slid a couple of inches closer. "One all of us need to learn."

Sweat. Aftershave. Sunscreen. Salt water. All smells she now associated with him. Her breath caught as he cupped her cheek with his hand. Heat radiated off his bronzed skin.

He was going to kiss her.

Nerves suddenly assailed her. She sat up. "It's um, getting late. And I know we're going to get storms. We'd—I'd better get cleaned up."

Ziad didn't say anything, didn't sigh or shake his head. A slow smile crossed his face. With surprising grace, he rose to his feet and extended his hand. "Then I will head home and collect the food for our meal."

Once she stood, he helped her fold the blanket and towels they'd used. Before she could react, he took her hand and led her toward the house.

In the kitchen, he set his bag on the floor next to the island and faced her. "Shall I see you at six, then?"

*Don't go. Kiss me instead.* Those words remained stuck in her throat. *What? Am I crazy?* Maybe being in the sun for so long caused sudden dizziness to wash over her. "Uh, yeah. Six." So much for sounding smart. "Sounds like a plan."

Did he chuckle?

She couldn't be sure.

"I will see you then." After tipping an imaginary hat, he slipped through the back doors.

Oh, dear. She rushed upstairs and turned on the water to the bathtub. She sat on the edge and rested her head in her hands. "What is going on here? Claire, he's not a believer. What are you thinking? I'm wanting him to kiss me, but it's wrong, and…"

She groaned.

She couldn't cancel on him. Not now. And did she want to?

As she slid into a bubble bath, she left that question unanswered.

Today. Do or die. Ziad wouldn't leave without kissing the woman who captivated more and more of his attention with each passing day. With a cooler and backpack containing their food slung over his shoulder, he climbed the steps to her porch.

Claire met him at the door. "Hey! Come on in. You brought food?"

He laughed. "Someone is hungry."

"That's one way of putting it." She gestured to the granite. "Here. What are we having?"

"Lamb. Mixed vegetables. Bread. Salad."

"Oooh. My favorite." She reached into a cabinet and pulled out a dish. "We can put the vegetables in this. Do you need me to get the grill going?"

"Not yet. I will cook the vegetables alongside the lamb." He laid out squash, broccoli, and onions.

"Dessert's in the oven." She pulled a knife from the wood block and joined him.

They worked shoulder to shoulder.

Oh, that perfume.

She seemed on edge as the blade flashed in the overhead lights. Something had changed in her. Her nerves remained, but he sensed something else, something like anticipation.

"Do not cut your finger."

She laughed. "No worries there. I've been extra careful since that night. Do you need to do anything with the lamb?"

"No. It has been marinating since last night."

She cut her eyes toward him. "Marinating. My, we're getting sophisticated."

He lifted it from the cooler. "Thank the owner of the deli where we went a few weeks ago. He has been gracious enough to share many recipes with me. Shall we head outside?"

"Of course." With bowl in hand, she strolled with him to the grill.

"Why is the grill so far away?"

She slowed. "Jackson had this fear about fire. When we had the house built, he insisted on putting it here. I guess he figured if it caught fire, it'd burn and fall into the marsh." She smiled. "I let him have his eccentricities because goodness knows, I have mine."

"Which are?"

With a camp lighter, she lit the burners. "Let me think on that. I'll get us some tea."

Ziad settled on a bench and stretched his arms along the top. The breeze, intermittent during the morning, had risen to a good wind. The reeds in the marsh swayed in time with its puffs. Energy filled the air and his heart.

Something would happen tonight.

A slow smile crossed his lips.

Perhaps in more than one way.

He closed his eyes and lifted his face to let the wind kiss it. A perfect day, hopefully with a perfect evening and a kiss of another kind to follow.

The screened door banged shut a few minutes later. He rose and checked the grill. Ready to go. He glanced toward the house.

Holding a tray in her hands, Claire strolled toward him. Oh, she'd taken time with herself tonight. White pants she called Capri pants emphasized the sway of her hips. Her red T-shirt highlighted her figure in subtle ways. Her hair streamed behind her, a flag of brown verging on black.

*The meat. Put the meat on.*

With effort, he ripped his attention away from her and ladled the lamb onto one side. The dish holding the vegetables went on the other.

"Have some." Claire set a tall, icy glass of tea in front of him. "Bread's in the oven."

His love affair with sweet tea continued as he drained half the glass in one pull.

Claire grinned. "More, kind sir?"

"Of course." He accepted a refill.

"I faint at the sight of my own blood."

"Huh?"

She grinned. "You wanted to know a quirk of mine."

"Quirk?"

"Oh, eccentricity."

"I know about that one. Perhaps another?"

"I love, love, love piña coladas."

He groaned. "Do I ever know that!"

"No worries." She leaned into him. "Mainly, I drink them virgin."

He sighed in mock consternation. "I am from a foreign land, remember? I do not understand your terms at times."

She chuckled. "Virgin drinks don't have alcohol in them. If you like, I could fix one for you."

"Perhaps later."

"Here's a question for you."

"Oh?"

A mysterious smile crossed her face. "Why do you call me Lady Claire?"

Caught in so many ways. She had him enthralled.

With great effort, he rose. "Ah, but that is a secret, only to be revealed later."

"Hmmm." She stood and stopped all too near him, then ran her finger down his chest.

A line of warmth followed, almost like a burning brand.

This time, she wore a Mona Lisa smile. "I see how this works. I'll be inside getting the table set. How long?"

Oh, no. How long had it been? "Another ten minutes."

With an enigmatic smile, she turned and walked away. Was it his imagination, or did she sashay a little?

Ziad turned back to the grill and pretended like the heat from it had warmed his face. He checked the lamb. Surely ready in a few minutes. He pulled the vegetables off their burner. As he waited for the meat to finish, he located his phone. Out of habit, he checked the local news station's website.

Two Teens Found Dead From Zap in Pawley's Island Boathouse on Fourth of July.

Crash!

There went his mood. Fifteen now dead. Zap had continued its spread across the Charleston Metro area, and no one seemed able to stop it. He muttered under his breath as he read the story before shoving the phone into his pocket. He couldn't focus on that. Not now.

Finally, with the lamb on a fresh plate, he returned to the house.

Claire met him at the door. "That smells wonderful. Go ahead and put it on the table."

He did and followed her into the kitchen.

She dumped the vegetables into a serving bowl. "Why don't you take these out? I've got the bread."

He stopped short when he stepped onto the porch. How had he missed this? Claire had pulled out all the stops. Navy blue table cloth. Fine china. Silver. And candlelight glowing in the increasing gloom of the storm clouds. Tea sat in crystal for him. Wine for her, it seemed. It pulled his mind off what he'd read, if only slightly.

She set a bread basket and butter on the table. "Here we go."

"M'lady?" Ziad pulled out her chair.

"Thanks." She seated herself, and he settled perpendicular to her.

"This is very beautiful."

"It's a special occasion."

He took her hand and kissed her fingers. He took great pleasure in her smile. "It is indeed."

"May I say grace?"

"Of course."

She bowed her head. "Lord, thank you for tonight, for this special time with Ziad. Thank you for this food, and bless our time together."

"And thank you for Claire," he added before releasing her hand.

For a few minutes, they ate in comfortable silence. His mind swung around to the Zap article.

Claire nudged him with her foot. "What's going on?"

He cocked his head.

"I was watching your face, and you went from sunny to cloudy in an instant."

She was a nurse. Maybe she knew something. "What do you know about Zap?"

She fell silent a moment. "It's bad stuff. No survivors yet. Something about the way they altered the heroin's properties with synthetics makes it more than deadly."

"Do you remember the night you and I argued?"

"I'd rather forget."

He took her hand. "Do you remember when I said I was with Ben?"

"Yeah." She nodded as she cut up her meat. "You said you were helping him with a case."

"The night Faith witnessed someone dying from a Zap overdose at the convenience store, there were two others who were witnesses, both sailors. I noticed one of them had a tattoo between his ring and pinkie finger. Here." Ziad pointed to his hand.

"Wait." Her pretty face clouded. "You can't be serious."

"I am not understanding. You do not seem surprised."

"No, it's not that. You remember I told you about that truck driver?"

He cut some meat. "I do."

"He had a tattoo in the same place."

He stared. "You are serious?"

"Yeah. I remember thinking it was interesting." She sipped her wine. In the candlelight, her deep green eyes almost glowed as she gazed at him.

Ziad's grip on his fork tightened. "Do you remember his name?"

Claire sighed and shook her head. "No. I'm sorry. I wish I did. Let me think on it, though. If I remember, I'll definitely tell you."

Defeat slammed into him. So much for his lead. Then reality righted his world. He sat next to one very beautiful woman, the very object of his wooing that evening. And what was he doing? Ruining it by discussing a case. The barest of sighs escaped him as he savored his meal.

After a few minutes, Claire set her silverware down. "Are you jealous?"

"Pardon?"

"From what you said, Ben must be working a case involving Zap."

Oh, she could read him so well. Who was he kidding? "I must admit I am. In Jeddah, it was my case. I had a staff of five working on it and no less than fifty handwritten pages of notes. But here?" How he hated the envy in his voice! "I pull speeders. I ring up people's candy bars and sodas while Ben is with the FBI and on a task force about Zap. I feel… insignificant."

She touched his hand. "Oh, Ziad, no. I promise you're not. Anna Kate adores you. Tripp things you're the awesomest soccer player around."

A small smile fought against his envy.

"His word, not mine. And honestly, I can't imagine my life without you in it now."

His heart filled. He took her hand again and kissed her fingers. "Thank you."

Another smile crossed her face. "You're very welcome. Now pass the bread, young man."

The conversation turned to nothing in particular until only silverware remained on their plates. With his bare toes, he stroked her ankle. "Tell me. What are some of your other quirks?"

She stilled. "Who says I have any more?"

"Oh, I believe you do."

"Um, do you want some hot tea?" Without waiting for an answer, she sprang to her feet with their plates in hand and practically fled into the house.

*Patience. She's nervous. Don't scare her off.* His heart sped up at the challenge ahead of him. Without a word, he cleared the rest of the dishes.

"I'll cut the cobbler." She took a deep breath as she placed two generous slices on dessert plates before pouring hot water over teabags in mugs. A breath eased from her. "What about you?"

"Me?" He smiled and picked up a fork and plate before following her onto the screened-in porch. Lightning lit the sky over the harbor. "What about me?"

"Your quirks?" Claire settled on the couch across from the table.

He joined her. "Oh? Hmmm. When I smoked, I only smoked four cigarettes a day."

She smiled. All relaxed now. A good sign. "That's not a quirk."

"Hmmm." He took a few bites as he considered her question. "Perhaps this. As a soccer player at University, I had a certain order when preparing for a game. From bottom up. Socks and shoes first. Then shorts. Then shirt."

She chuckled. "Like baseball."

"Oh?"

"Yep. Baseball players are very superstitious. Another one?" She nudged his leg with her foot.

"I have more?"

"Ziad!" She was laughing as she set her plate down.

"Hmmm." He inched closer. "When I lived in Jeddah, I secretly enjoyed western fiction books. Ben kept me well supplied. I learned a lot of written English that way."

He rubbed his thumb across the top of her hand.

Claire tensed. "Let me go get our tea."

This time as thunder rumbled closer, he blocked her escape and caught her up in his arms. "Another quirk of mine?"

She trembled slightly underneath his fingertips. "You must have many."

With his left arm, he drew her closer. He almost felt her breath coming in short gasps. He ran his right hand down her hair before sliding it under those silky strands and caressing the back of her neck. "I enjoy wooing the beautiful woman before me."

With that, he kissed her.

Wham!

Ziad jumped about a mile.

So did Claire. She whipped around.

Her elderly neighbor stood on her walkway, a watering can at her feet but no flowers in sight. "Oh! I'm so sorry! I was watering my flowers. I didn't mean to disturb you."

Claire pasted a bright smile on her face. "No worries, Mrs. Chitworth."

"Carry on, children." She scurried toward her house.

Claire fled to the kitchen. "Busted, huh?"

"Perhaps." Without hesitation, Ziad backed her against a floor-to-ceiling cabinet. He placed his hands on either side of her head to keep her from fleeing. "I do not care."

He kissed her again, this time savoring her scent and taste. Flowers. Sweetness. He nuzzled her hair and kissed her neck.

She wrapped her arms around him and drew him closer. A shuddering sigh escaped her. "Keep going."

With great effort, he pulled back. Oh, did that attraction glow in her eyes. His too, for sure. "I have the feeling, m'Lady Claire, this is the start of something beautiful."

# 29

"Score!" Three weeks later, Ziad lifted his arms in victory as the soccer ball he'd just kicked sailed past the opposing team's goalkeeper and into the net.

Ben hooted, and the rest of the recreation league's soccer team jumped on Ziad. "Way to go, my friend!"

Ziad grinned as the teams lined up to slap hands on the field at one of Mount Pleasant's parks.

He collapsed on a nearby bench where he'd stashed his water bottle in a cooler. Cold water trickled down his throat, and he ripped off his sopping wet uniform shirt. He poured the rest over his head and cracked open another. "I never thought I would say the heat and humidity here is as bad as Jeddah."

Ben laughed as he joined him with three balls at his feet like small children. "Think 114 degrees and 95 percent humidity. Then I'll bet you'd reconsider."

"You have all of them?" Ziad gestured to the ground.

"Three, right?"

"Yes." Ziad stuffed them into a net bag. "I take it lunch is on order?"

"In order. And yeah, I'm starving. Let's go." Ben led the way to his Forester.

Ziad slid into a fresh T-shirt and settled on the front passenger seat. "I cannot believe you still have this."

"Ole Bessie and I were together for too many years for me to let go of her."

"Bessie?"

"I name my cars. Don't ask." Ben added when Ziad snorted. They headed toward their favorite local burger joint. On the way, he called Emma, who was at work. "Hey, babe… Yeah, we're fine… We won. Ziad got the winning goal." He grinned and stage-whispered, "Em says congrats." Then he continued, "Yeah, we're headed to lunch. Then I'll be at home… Okay. I'll take care of the laundry for you… I'll call you later. Love you."

As they placed their orders and got their food, Ziad remembered a time when he'd shared supper with Ben and Emma at their apartment. Ben's bride had looked ready to fall over.

"Em, are you okay?" Ben asked.

"Just tired. It was an exhausting day." She shook her head as her eyes filled. "I had to work with a couple of teen-aged girls coming back from ACL reconstruction just as I did all those years ago. PT's really painful when starting, and I made both of them cry."

Ben took her hand. "I'm sorry, babe."

She suddenly pushed her plate back. "I'm not hungry. Do you mind doing the dishes?"

Her husband's reply came instantly. "Not at all. Take a hot shower and head to bed. We'll hang out."

"I'm sorry, Ziad. Good night, you two." With that, Emma headed to their bedroom.

"Yo, Ziad. You there?"

Ziad came back to the present. He sat under an umbrella with a burger on its wrapper and his friend across from him. "So sorry."

"You seemed a million miles away."

"I have a question for you."

"What's that?" Ben opened his mouth wide and took a bite.

"I have noticed the way you treat Emma."

His friend cocked an eyebrow.

Oh, that hadn't sounded right. He added, "I mean, you treat her like an equal."

Ben polished off his burger and picked up a fry. "She's very much my equal."

"I do not understand why."

"God made her. Oh, she's different. Women are way different." Both men chuckled. "That doesn't mean she's inferior. Not at all. I used to scoff at the notion of marriage making the two become one flesh. You know. From the second chapter of Genesis, right? You've read that at some point, I assume."

Ziad nodded. "The first five books of the Bible are also part of Islamic teaching."

"So anyway, I did. Until I married Em. She balances me. She thinks things through, sees things from different angles when I can get tunnel vision on something. And she's wise. I've learned that when it comes to big decisions, it's best to consult with her."

"Oh?"

"Remember when she and I were engaged and I'd suggested buying a house before we got married?"

"I do."

"She wanted to hold off and said that coming back to America, plus getting married, plus finding a new church and starting a new job was enough. And you know something? She was right. Boy, if we'd tried to do the house thing..." Ben shook his head. "We were talking about marriage in Sunday School, and one of the guys said that he'd learned to always listen to his wife when making big decisions. And he's right on that one. Sure, she submits to me, but that's totally voluntary because she knows I love her and respect her. What about you and Claire?" Ben shot him a sly grin. "I have to say you both surprised us. Em couldn't believe you'd been dating for two weeks before you got busted."

Ziad thought about that one. Claire's reticence to reveal their new relationship mystified him. "It is so very strange."

"Why do you say that?"

"She is concerned," he struggled for the right words, "about everyone accepting us as a couple."

Ben opened his mouth as if about to say something. He closed it and shook his head.

He frowned. "What?"

"I… guess it's understandable."

He frowned. "Why do you say that?"

"First off, no problems with anyone in her family. Okay, almost anyone. Allie's a bit of a hard nut to crack."

Ziad let that phrase pass. "She does not accept us?"

"Probably not. But you know the rest of us do. And I understand Claire's worries about other people, unfortunately many of them Christian, who would judge her for dating you."

Suddenly, a weight dropped onto Ziad's shoulders. "You are saying we should not date?"

Again came that hesitation, as if Ben struggled within himself. Finally, he stirred the ketchup on his wrapper with a french fry. "I guess the way to look at it is that those who mean the most to the two of you accept your relationship. Period."

Then why did his words seem a bit flat? Ziad considered it. He had to take what he said at face value. Ben had expressed concern, not judgment. Slowly, that weight vanished. Tense shoulders relaxed. If Ben, Emma, Allison, David, and the rest of Claire's family accepted them, then what did it matter? "Thank you, my friend. Those words mean so much."

A careless grin crossed Ben's face. "No problem." His phone began chiming. He frowned as he checked the number. "That's work. Hold on just a second."

He lifted the cell phone to his ear and said in English, "Yeah. Hey, Angie… You got what? You're kidding me! Nope, that's good news… Yeah, I've got a camera in the car. I'll be there in about ten or so… Thanks... Yep. Talk to ya Monday." He set the phone on the table, his blue eyes suddenly intent. "You want some adventure?"

Ziad frowned. "What do you mean?"

"The sailor who witnessed that overdose is coming to town. Angie, my boss at the FBI, called to let me know the *Lady Beatrice* will be arriving shortly for an overnight stay."

Ziad rose and grabbed his drink. "Let's go!"

An hour later, he paced inside an observation room at ICE headquarters that overlooked the port. With a pair of binoculars, Ziad examined the flow of sailors trickling through customs. He murmured, "I do not see him."

Beside him, the camera clicked as Ben photographed each person's face. "Patience, my friend."

They were too late. Or they had missed him somehow.

One last sailor trailed his pals. Like the others, this one had a duffel on his shoulder. And a backpack. Ziad focused on him. A shiver ran down his spine. "Ben. There."

"Our man?"

"I believe so."

The camera whirred. "Bingo. Let's follow him."

They raced down the stairs and to the Forester. Hopefully, Yousif Ali didn't spot them dashing from the building.

He hadn't.

Ziad leaned forward. "There. He is getting into a taxi."

"I'm on it." Ben put the SUV into gear.

They followed at a discreet distance, but once in downtown Charleston, they barely managed to stay back.

The taxi's taillights flashed.

Ben pulled over and blocked a fire hydrant.

The sailor climbed from the taxi with his bags in hand. Without another look, he headed into a shop.

Ben recorded his steps before putting the camera down. "Pullman's Antiques and Rugs. Hmmm. Not a motel like you'd expect. You think that bag will be a little less heavy when he leaves?"

Oh, it felt so good to get back in action. "We should stay and watch."

Ben peered around them. "We can't. We're blocking a hydrant and traffic, and in these parts, your brothers-in-uniform will be down here in a heartbeat."

Ziad muttered under his breath as he scrubbed his hands through his damp hair. "You are right. We do not want that to happen."

"Let me check with Angie. If she says yes, then come along if you like."

Hope ballooned inside of Ziad. "Of course."

"Absolutely not." Angie Rogers, Ben's supervisor, shook her head fifteen minutes later when they met at a public parking lot in sight of the antique shop. "This is official business."

Ziad ground his teeth as he gazed at the brunette with curly dark hair bobbing in a tight ponytail. "Why not?"

"You've seen the guy. He knows your face since you talked with him. What would happen if he saw you? You'd blow months of work. Not on my watch, understand?"

What could he say? No? He got it. Not that it hurt any less to be excluded.

She sighed and shook her head. "Look. There's a coffee shop across the street from the antique store. Wait there for our call."

He could do nothing but concede.

He wound up on a stool in the window, a baseball cap from Ben's Forester pulled low over his eyes, a half-finished newspaper Sudoku puzzle in front of him. Thanks to sitting on an infernal bar stool for the past hour, his rear had gone numb. He sipped his coffee and winced. Cold. Beneath his breath, he muttered an Arabic cuss word.

A barista puttered at the other end of the bar as she cleaned up some drips and threw away empty cups and newspapers. "Another Arabian coffee black?"

Ziad forced a smile as his phone began ringing. "If you would. Thank you." Maybe Ben. Several minutes earlier, his friend and Angie had approached the store like they were a couple shopping for antiques. No, Claire called. "Hello, m'lady."

Her smile radiated across the airwaves. "I hope I caught you at a good time. How was the game?"

"Good." Ziad doodled in the newspaper's margins. "Where are you?"

"Headed to Mama and Daddy's to check on Daddy since Mama's out of town. Then to the paint store."

"Good." He straightened as another young man approached the shop, this one slouched and wearing camouflage fatigue pants, a T-shirt, and a backpack over his shoulders. He seemed as likely to go to an antique shop as Ziad was to go to a bar.

"Ziad?"

Oh, no. He'd tuned her out. "So sorry. What were you saying?"

"Uh, I'll be back at six. Allie's dropping Anna Kate off at 6:30. Want to come over at seven for supper?"

"Of course."

"And I remembered something about that truck driver I treated a few weeks ago. I was catching up at work and pulled his file. Daoud al-Rashid."

"His name?"

"Uh, yeah," she drawled.

"Thank you. I will see you soon." Ziad hung up and set his phone on the counter in front of him so the lens of the camera pointed toward the shop's entrance.

A few minutes later, Daoud al-Rashid strolled from Pullman's Antiques and Rugs.

Ziad clicked away—until the young man headed straight toward the coffee shop.

He set the phone down, then ducked his head as the bells over the door clanked. Pretending to work his puzzle, he kept a discreet eye on him. Yes, the very same man from the mosque stood not twenty feet away.

Daoud ordered a drink. He didn't stay, and when he left, Ziad didn't catch sight of his left hand.

But he did remember his face.

Across the street, Ben and Angie stepped outside. A text summoned him to meet them at the Starbucks on King Street. This time, Ziad couldn't bear the thought of coffee and instead ordered a sweet iced tea. He found them upstairs at their usual table.

Once Ziad had seated himself, he leaned forward with his elbows on the table. "What did you discover?"

"Lots." Angie glanced at Ben. "Tell him."

Ben nodded. "Mr. Pullman was out this afternoon. Seems two clerks were working since it was pretty busy, a girl named Prissy behind the register and another girl floating around the floor. Yousif Ali was nowhere to be found."

"Where was he?"

Angie shoved her drink aside. "We think in a room because another young man who looked like he had no business at an antique shop came inside."

"Daoud al-Rashid," Ziad blurted. He showed him the pictures from his phone.

Ben stared at them. "How do you know?"

"Claire called. When we had supper after the Fourth of July she mentioned treating a truck driver for a cut on his left hand. She noticed a tattoo between his left ring and pinkie finger."

Ben and Angie traded looks. He said, "That fits with what we saw. And he was talking quietly on his phone in Arabic. Sounded like he was confirming that he was where he should be. And I saw the tail of that tattoo on his left hand."

Angie leaned forward. "The clerk behind the register greeted him by name and took him behind the counter. We almost overstayed our welcome, but finally, he came from the back with that pack on his shoulders."

"It looked the same as when he arrived." Ben stared at some notes he'd made on a pad. "My theory is he brought something to the shop that weighed the same as the product he was taking out."

Something cold settled in Ziad's heart. "Zap."

"We'll see." Angie skimmed a finger down her own set of notes. "Goodness knows, Prissy warrants checking out. So does this Daoud al-Rashid guy. Ben, your tasks."

"Yes, ma'am."

"His left palm will have a scar," Ziad added. "Can I do anything to help?"

"Sit tight," she said.

Ziad glanced at Ben, who ever so slightly shook his head.

Best not to push it. But if he could do anything in his power to prevent the spread of Zap, he would.

"Sonja? What are you doing here?" Saturday afternoon, Claire approached her friend, who stood next to a rack full of paint chips.

Sonja's eyes lit up. "I live in your neck of the woods now, remember? Seems we'll be doing our fair share of running into each other."

"I'll say." Claire nudged her friend. "Painting already?"

"Dom said I could redo whatever I want."

"A new husband error."

Both women laughed.

"Seriously." Sonja removed a card with paint chips in a mellow shade of gray. "What do you think? Gray mist or storm cloud?"

"Gotta love the names." Claire grinned. "For what room?"

"The den. It's kind of dark."

Claire pointed to the lighter color. "Gray mist. It'll keep the room light."

"Ah. So what about you? What brings you here?"

A bit of sadness tinged Claire's heart as she thought about her reasons for visiting the paint store. "I'm redoing Little Jack's room."

Sonja's eyebrows shot up. "Whoa. What? Since when?"

Not wanting to get into the real reason behind her decision, Claire shrugged. "I felt like it was time. Why not turn it into a guest room? And make it dramatic, like with reds and blacks? So Samurai red it is."

"Oooh, I like it. Elegant as all get out too. Say. Want to have coffee? I've got a bit."

Claire agreed. After they bought their purchases, they wound up strolling down the walkway of the shopping center to Mocha Joe's. Claire chose a table by the window. "Sorry. It's on the hot side today."

"You'll get no argument from me." Sonja took a sip of her iced coffee and sighed. "This is going to get dangerous. Mocha Joe's is all too close now." She set her drink down. "So really. Why are you redoing Little Jack's room after five years of not touching it?"

What could she do? Lie? Claire couldn't. Not to her best friend who had an amazing gift of perception. "I guess with dating Ziad now, I feel like a new season in my life has begun."

"You're doing well?"

Where should she start? Ziad was rapidly becoming her best friend, one to whom she bared her heart. Maybe it was their shared experience with grief. Or that when she was with him, he treated her like a queen. Her cheeks heated just by thinking about his touch, the way she came alive when he held her close. "Very. For our birthdays, he's taking me to supper at the Grille and then to see *A Midsummer Night's Dream* at the Charleston Playhouse."

"Whoa. Getting fancy, are we?" A smile crossed Sonja's face, then faded just as quickly. She took a deep breath. "May I speak candidly with you?"

Claire's breath caught, and her guard went up. "You're going to say we shouldn't date because we're not equally yoked."

"I'm speaking as a friend who loves you and will love you no matter what, okay? I'd be a fool if I didn't say I was concerned."

Her and everyone else. Claire folded her arms across her chest. "We just started seeing each other. It's not like we're serious or anything."

"I know." Sonja fell silent as if carefully considering her words. "But I also know how emotions, including those that come with new relationships, can cloud reason. Why do you think Dom and I dated for four years before he even proposed? I knew he came from a messy divorce. I knew his ex hated my guts. But boy, those first days were heady. My emotions were screaming to marry him and the sooner, the better."

A dreamy smile flickered across her face.

"But Sonja, I've finally found someone who gets me. I never thought I'd get that chance again, and I did, okay?" Hot tears sprang to Claire's eyes. "We see eye to eye on so many things. We have the same values. He likes many things I like. And he's such a gentleman."

"I know."

"Sonja."

"I do."

"How old were you when you met Dom?"

"You know. Thirty-seven."

Claire carefully began pushing her point as she toyed with her cup. "And hadn't you thought you'd missed your chance?"

"You know I did. We talked about it a lot at Bible study. But don't you also remember that I begged for prayer for wisdom?"

Thwarted again. What could Claire say? No? All too well she recalled many nights when Sonja had shed tears regarding following her head rather than her heart. "I get that."

Her friend took her hands. "Listen." She stared at the table for a few seconds. "I'm not here to approve or disapprove or judge. You know me better than that. I'm here as a friend who loves you and cares about you."

"I get that. And I've got this," Claire added as she ignored a small twinge of worry that had appeared in her soul. "I appreciate your concern, but I promise I'm going to take things really slowly with him."

Doubt remained in Sonja's eyes, but she nodded. "Understood. If you need to talk, I'm here for you, okay?"

Claire nodded.

"Well, let me get back. Dom's probably wondering if I'm planning on repainting his entire house since I promised him I'd only be gone for an hour. Say. Let's double date sometime."

A small bit of relief eased the tension in Claire's shoulders. "I'd like that." Once outside, she grabbed her friend in a brief hug. "Thanks."

"For what?"

"For loving me where I am, not where you think I should be."

"You know I do, sister. Take care."

Claire watched her drive away. As she headed toward her house, she pushed that worry she'd felt earlier aside. Truly, she'd be sure to take things slowly with Ziad. They had time, and she fully intended to get to know him very well before taking things to the next level.

# 30

"This has been a great day." Two and a half weeks later, Claire sighed in contentment and licked her chocolate cone. Her heels clicked on concrete as they strolled along the sidewalks of historic Charleston. She glanced at Ziad. Oh, ever so handsome in his suit and white shirt with his jacket slung over his shoulder. "Thanks for being there for me today as we repainted Little Jack's room."

"My honor and pleasure, m'Lady Claire." He popped the remainder of his cone into his mouth.

"I know it seemed strange to do it on our birthdays, but it's the first chance we've been off together." She briefly closed her eyes as her tears echoed in her mind.

Ziad had known what to do. He held her.

"And my apologies for getting paint on your cheek."

She smiled as they entered the gardens near the Battery. "No worries. It came out. And that play tonight was great. I hope you were okay with Shakespeare."

"It was... difficult to understand at times."

She chuckled. "I'm sure. *A Midsummer Night's Dream.* Perfect for to-night."

"And a wonderful comedy."

She settled on a bench and patted the seat. "Let's enjoy the night for a moment. I have something for you."

He cocked an eyebrow and joined her. "Oh?"

She grinned. "A clue."

"Ah, the lady knows I like mysteries."

She handed him a small, elongated package she pulled from her purse.

Carefully, he unwrapped it. "Hmmm. This is a… set of spoons. Claire?"

"Not just any spoons. Very nice, elegant, antique spoons. Read the note."

He held it up in the faint glow of the streetlight. "'To sample and enjoy life. With a bit of elegance.' Hmmm. I can only imagine."

She raised a finger. "Patience, my darling. Your next clue is at the 4Runner."

They rose and began walking toward the SUV. Ziad took her hand. "It is a good thing I am a—what does Ben call it?—a fitness freak. Ice cream is all too accessible."

She laughed, then tucked her arm through his. "Me too. How does it feel to be forty? It's a big milestone, after all."

He playfully groaned. "No different." The barest of sighs escaped him. "For sure, I never expected to be here. It is a different birthday from… last year."

Something lurked behind his statement. No way would she pry. They arrived at the 4Runner and climbed inside.

She reached under the seat and pulled out another wrapped gift.

He cut the tape with his pocket knife. "Arabian coffee. From Mocha Joe's, nonetheless. And another clue." He glanced at her. " 'To someone who always knows the finer things in life.' You are truly mystifying me."

She chuckled. "I have to keep you guessing."

"Then back to your place so I can get to the bottom of this mystery." He cranked the engine. They snaked their way through the streets of old Charleston. Once they'd made the turn onto the Ravenel Bridge, he took her hand. "Ben mentioned a trip to the mountains."

"His folks have a cabin there." She smiled as she remembered when she and Emma had hatched the plan over lunch a couple of days ago. "Are you interested? I'm sure you're ready for a vacation."

"Absolutely. I…" He frowned and braked hard.

The motion threw her against her seatbelt. "Ziad!"

He yanked the wheel to the right and pulled onto the sidewalk as he turned on the hazard lights. "Call Nine-One-One."

"What?" Her anger evaporated. She followed his gaze, and her heart nearly seized. About fifty yards away, someone had pulled back the chain link fence on the railing of the bridge.

Ziad threw open the door. "Do it now. Tell them a jumper is on the bridge at marker eight. Now!"

Before she could say another word, he dashed toward the railing.

Fingers shaking from adrenaline, Claire grabbed her cell phone and dialed.

☆ ☆ ☆

One wrong move would spell disaster. Or one word. Sweat built on Ziad's palms as he approached the tear in the fence where a young man had squirmed through. Softly, he called, "Hello there."

From where he sat on the rail, the young man whirled. He tensed. "Don't come any closer, or I'll jump!"

Ziad glanced toward the 4Runner.

Claire stood outside with her phone to her ear.

He focused on the young man as his mind scrambled for a solution. "What is your name?"

"Thomas."

"May I join you, Thomas?"

He shrugged.

Ziad knelt and undid the laces on his dress shoes, then removed his socks so he'd have better contact with the railing. He wormed his way through the chain link. Below, the water of the Cooper River coursed silent and deep. And deadly since hitting it from over thirty meters up would be like slamming into concrete. *You are sitting on a fence at the stables where Emma keeps her mare,* he tried to tell himself. With both hands on the railing, he eased to a sitting position. After a moment, he asked, "What brings you here tonight?"

Thomas didn't answer, only maintained his slouch.

"It is a long way down, is it not?"

Even in the dim glow of nearby streetlights, tears pooled in Thomas's eyes. "Leave me alone. Let me jump!"

"Why?"

"Why not? Look, man. You don't know what I've been through."

"No, I do not." Frantic thoughts whirled through Ziad's mind—all of them in Arabic. He took a deep breath to slow them, to let the words form in English. What he said would either get the young man to swing his legs over the railing to safety—or send him plunging into the water. His hearing sharpened to the point where he even picked up Thomas's ragged breaths over the noise of the traffic behind them. "It is beautiful, is it not?"

"Why should I care?"

"Just an observation, my friend." Ziad glanced to his right and left. From Charleston and Mount Pleasant, police cars and emergency crews streamed toward the bridge, their lights glittering in flashes of ruby and sapphire. "It reminds me it is good to be alive."

"You don't know what you're talking about." Thomas slid closer to the edge.

Oh, no. Ziad stilled. This young man wanted to die. Wrong words would ensure he did. "Sometimes, life gets really hard. We want to give up, to let it all go."

"What do you know? You haven't lost your girl. Your job. Your parents aren't getting divorced." Thomas nearly spat that in his direction.

"How old are you, Thomas?"

"Seventeen. Just go away!"

"I cannot do that." Ziad scrambled for what would talk him down. "At seventeen, it is not easy to take a long view of life."

Thomas snorted.

"Truly. And sometimes even when older, it is easy to lose perspective."

Stony silence.

"Just over a year ago, I lost my family. My wife. My four sons. My parents. Someone murdered them. Then I lost my career and standing in society."

Thomas stared. At least his sneer had vanished. "Did you want to kill yourself?"

"Sometimes, yes. But I could not find the courage." *Careful, Ziad. Don't give him any extra reason to kill himself.* "And now, I am glad I did not. Even in the span of a year, things are so much better."

"How so?"

"I have a new country. New friends who care about me. A new job. A new love." Ziad shut down thoughts of Claire for the moment. "I learned it is possible to start life afresh."

"I don't believe you."

Ziad took a deep breath. A peace settled over him, as if he were saying the words needed to draw the teenager into life again. "If you jump, Thomas, you may think you have won because all of your pain will be over. I urge you to broaden those thoughts. This is now, but years down the road, things will be very different. I guarantee it. If you short-circuit that by jumping, you will leave behind unspeakable pain in those who love you. Would you want them to suffer like that?"

No answer.

"Perhaps, if you give this life of yours a chance, you will see what I mean."

"I don't know." This time, uncertainty rang in Thomas's voice.

Hope rose inside of Ziad. Could it be? Maybe he was changing his mind. A few more minutes slid by as the clamor behind them increased. "I know this is hard to see, but you truly do have your whole life ahead of you. This girl of yours. Perhaps she is not the right one for you. And your parents? No matter what their differences, they love you. School can be hard, but there are people to help you. The same with your job.

You will find places where you belong. Can you not see that, Thomas? Can you not see a good future for yourself? A hope?"

His words stung his own soul. Why hadn't he preached the same thing to himself the year before?

Beside him, just on the other side of the rip in the fence, Thomas softly wept. "I just don't see it, man. I don't!"

"You will not in that water. But you will if you come with me." Carefully, Ziad shifted to the opening and swung his feet around to safety, then braced them behind the railing below.

He gawked at the crowd that had gathered. Plenty of firemen, paramedics, and policemen, but also the media and passerby. And Claire? Nowhere to be seen.

He reached out and wrapped his arms around Thomas's chest. "Come with me."

Before the teenager could react, he drew him off the railing, through the fence, and onto the deck.

Cheering erupted.

With his arms firmly around Thomas's shoulders, he led him to a waiting ambulance.

Only then did the shakes begin as the rumble of the crowd grew to a roar. The questions came fast and furious.

"How did you notice the jumper?"

"Where were you headed when you saw him?"

"What did you say to bring him down?"

Trembling now, he rested against the bumper of another ambulance and searched for Claire.

"Ziad!" Her cry shot straight to his heart.

She stood near a patrol car next to Eddie and another officer. She ran to him.

Ziad grabbed her in a tight hug and held on as the shakes escalated. *Thank you. Thank you I am safe, that Thomas is safe.* He buried his face in her neck. Tonight, knowing that, and having her near, was what he needed the most.

# Exiled Heart

Two and a half hours later with Claire's keys in hand, Ziad raced up the back steps of her house. He fumbled with the lock. The door popped open, and he burst inside as he clawed at his tie. He jerked at it, only tightening it in the process. Finally, he ripped it off. It sailed to parts unknown.

His silver watch felt as if it burned his wrist. He slapped it onto a pile of *Southern Living* magazines on the coffee table. He plopped down on the couch and ran his hands through his hair as he tried to sort through all that had happened that night.

The media hailed him as a hero, someone who saved another person's life. Helper of the helpless is what one of the reporters had called him.

*If only they knew. If only they knew what a failure I am.*

Then it struck him. If things hadn't happened the year before, in no way would he be sitting on the couch in the house of the woman he loved.

He gasped as that realization caught him up short.

Claire's warm arms encircled him, and her perfume wafted to his nose. She kissed his hair and murmured, "I'm proud of you, Ziad. You saved someone's life tonight."

Those shakes returned. "But I sentenced others to die last year!"

"What are you talking about?"

He started shaking his head.

"Please, please don't shut me out about this." She eased back, then gently pried his hands away. Still in her black sheath, she sat on the coffee table in front of him, her eyes dark in the dim glow of a lamp. They pooled with questions. Several strands of hair had come loose from her chignon. Mascara stained her cheeks.

He clung to her hand and kissed her fingers. "How much do you know about last year?"

"About what brought you to Charleston?"

He nodded.

"Your family was murdered because of the Zap case you were working."

For a moment, he held onto her hands and ran his thumbs across their tops. "Exactly."

She drew in a sharp breath.

"Ben assisted me on a raid where we netted three suspects. They had tattoos here." He pointed to that spot on his hand.

"Which is why you were so curious about that a few weeks ago."

"Yes. We linked them to a minor prince named Prince Yasin. Thinking we had everything we needed, we took a break over the weekend. When I returned from lunch Saturday afternoon, our suspects were gone."

She frowned. "Why?"

"I suspected the prince had sent someone to impersonate my commanding officer." He lowered his head as regret slammed into him. "I thought I knew what I was doing. Sami, my executive officer, told me to wait on General al-Talil, my CO. I ignored him and went to al-Sharana where the prince was."

Shards of his confrontation with the prince and finding his family dead stabbed his memory. He flinched. "I confronted Prince Yasin. It went badly. They threw me out. That is when... when I called Sabirah and spoke with her for the last time. I found her an hour later. And then..." He swallowed hard and rubbed the scar at his hairline. "I was ambushed. Framed. And thrown into jail because they accused me of eight murders."

"Oh, Ziad."

He jumped up and began pacing between the island and the couch. "I rotted there for almost a year. I had plenty of time to think about what had happened, what caused their deaths."

"The murderers, who obviously wanted to frame you."

"But do you not see the role I played in it?"

"Ziad—"

"I was arrogant. Foolish. Impatient. I let my sometimes-hotheaded nature get the best of me. I set myself up to be framed. They ambushed me. Though everyone but Sabirah died of gunshot wounds from guns that were not mine, it was enough. Guilt over innocence. Had I been convicted, I would have been beheaded."

He stopped and gazed at her.

Claire remained hunched on the coffee table, her arms now wrapped around her middle. She peered at the floor, then raised her gaze. "Ben wouldn't let that happen."

"Nor would Sami. They knew I was innocent. Together, they worked to," he scrambled for the right English words, "show that the evidence proved my innocence. The judge agreed, but it came at a price."

"Coming here."

He nodded and leaned his back against the island. "I had to retire from the SANG to restore their honor. I had to divest myself financially of my homeland to restore the honor of my sister and remove her from danger. I could not return to Saudi Arabia. I cannot go back. Never. Do you know what that is like?"

She flinched.

He'd accidentally hurt her. "I am sorry." He sighed and returned to the couch. In a low, gravelly voice, he continued, "When I stayed in solitary confinement in that jail cell those next eleven months, I had nothing to do but think. I despaired. Like Thomas tonight, there were times when I wanted to kill myself. If it were not for Ben's weekly visits, I probably would have. He encouraged me, tried to say there was a hope and future for me."

"But you're obviously here."

"Because of Ben and Sami. They worked to show the holes in the evidence. My lawyer took it to the judge. And finally, he believed them. But a price had to be paid." His back itched as if the scars on it mocked him. "I was whipped."

Claire winced. "What I saw at the beach, right?"

He nodded. "That was painful. I stayed in bed for a week after that. The shame I felt in leaving… I lost all hope. Like Thomas, I wanted to die during that time."

"Yet you found hope."

He swallowed hard and took several deep, calming breaths. "I have."

She reached up and ran her hand down his cheek. "I'm praying Thomas will find the same."

He cupped her hand in his. "When people hailed me as a hero, I felt like a fraud because no one knows how low I had to be brought to get to that point."

"But you *are* a hero." She paused as if collecting her thoughts. "I believe God is sovereign—and that we live in a broken world. It's hard to deny we're broken."

He couldn't argue with her there.

"And I believe as well that nothing is wasted in his economy. He makes no mistakes, even though we question him and struggle against him at times." Those words came not as someone speaking meaningless platitudes but with empathy that came only from experience. "God brought you to this moment for such a time as this."

He took her hand and kissed her palm.

"That night when we first kissed, you said you worried you wouldn't make a difference." She slid onto his lap and wrapped her arms around his shoulders. "You will. You already have."

He closed his eyes as the last of his emotions welled. "I love you."

"I love you too," she whispered, then kissed his hair. For a few moments, they sat in silence. She finally shifted. "Let me change, and then we can do birthday presents."

The remaining tension released in his shoulders. He rose and followed her with his gaze. Oh, so lovely. So beautiful, in mind, body, and soul. His heart filled as he pulled off his socks and shoes and rolled up his sleeves. A match, for sure, and an evening he didn't want to end.

He turned off the lamp and headed onto the screened-in porch with her gifts in hand, one large, the other very small. A smile tipped his lips upwards. For now, he settled on feeling the balmy, silky breeze wafting through the screens.

"Here. A gift for you." Dim light filled the area as Claire turned on one of the lamps beside the couch and set a gaily wrapped box on the coffee table. She'd changed from her dress into a pair of shorts and a T-shirt.

He grinned. "Do tell."

"Oh, no. You've got to open it."

He eased the tape off the paper and frowned at the Arabic writing on the cardboard box. "What is this?"

"Open it."

He popped the tape and raised the lid. He shoved aside the paper shreds. As he lifted one of the four heavy mugs, he stared. The white ceramic was emblazoned with the SANG coat of arms. "Where did you get these?"

She snuggled close. "I had some help. Ben called Sami. And Sami sent them. Just call it happy birthday from everyone and an inter-continental effort. So the coffee goes into the mugs, and the spoons stir it and hopefully stir good memories as well." She leaned forward and pecked him on the lips. "Happy birthday, beloved."

"Thank you." He forced down his emotion. "And for you."

He lifted the larger package.

She ripped off the paper without hesitation. "Ooooh." She grinned as she ran her finger down a box of drawing pencils. "And totally new ones at that."

"I noticed you were running low."

"You noticed right. Thank you."

"And one more for you."

"Ziad…" She stared at the smaller box he produced. "What…"

"Open it."

She took her time with this one and opened the black velvet box. A little gasp escaped her as she stared at the diamond pendant. "Oh, Ziad."

Carefully, she freed the delicate silver chain and held it up.

Pleasure filled Ziad as it sparkled in the lamplight. He'd spent a couple of hours selecting the right diamond. It had cost him dearly, but Claire was more than worth it. "Shall I put it on you?"

She nodded and slid to the edge of the couch with her back to him as she raised her hair to reveal the nape of her neck. He hooked it, then kissed that beautiful skin. "I love you."

She stilled. "I love you as well."

He reached past her and turned out the light. In the sudden darkness, he felt her shift—right into his arms. Smoothing back her hair, he kissed her again, then deepened it. Tonight, right then, despite the horrific events that had led him to Charleston, he truly felt at home in his new country for the first time.

# 31

Knocking reached Ziad. *What...* He grumbled and turned onto his stomach as he burrowed further under the covers. He closed his eyes. More sleep. He really needed it at that point.

The banging resumed. "Ziad? Hey, Ziad!"

The doorbell rang.

Ziad finally propped one eye open as he swiped at the drool at the corner of his mouth. "Huh?"

"Ziad, my friend. You in there?"

Ziad glanced at the clock. Noon! Oh, no. He popped upright and stumbled around like a stunned puppy. Somehow, he snagged his undershirt off the foot of the bed where he'd dropped it when he'd staggered upstairs in the wee hours of the morning. He thumped down the steps and flung open the door.

Resplendent in dress pants and dress shirt with his gun and badge on his belt, Ben grinned. "Looks like someone needs his beauty sleep."

Ziad grunted and retreated to the kitchen.

"Not a morning person—or afternoon person—I should say."

Ziad scooped some coffee grounds into the coffeemaker. "I did not get to sleep until after three."

Ben's eyebrow quirked upward. "Oh?"

Unwilling to say anything further, Ziad rested his elbows on the counter and put his face in his hands.

"You're a hero, my friend."

Something skidded into his arms.

Ziad stared at the newspaper. There, front and center and above the fold, sat a picture of him from the night before as he hugged Claire. His eyes widened as he stared at the caption.

Charleston Police Department rookie reserve officer Ziad al-Kazim hugs Claire Montgomery after he rescues a teen-aged boy from a suicide attempt at Ravenel Bridge.

He studied the picture. Tendons showed in his hands where he gripped Claire. He swallowed hard as he realized again how easily things could have gone the other way.

"You even made the national news."

"What?"

"It's all over the networks. Fox. CNN. You name it. It's there. Even al-Jazeera."

Ziad yanked his laptop, which he'd left on the bar, to himself. He located the al-Jazeera site. Sure enough, not front and center but a little further down, was the article. It seemed to be something standard the Associated Press had run. Al-Jazeera must have picked up the story off the wire. "Ben, this is—"

"Incredible?" Ben asked in Arabic with a wink.

Ziad lifted his gaze. "No. Worrisome."

Ben's smile faded. "Are you concerned Prince Yasin will see you?"

"Perhaps," Ziad replied in the same language. "You're investigating a Zap outbreak. He may be concerned I'm helping."

"If they know who is on the task force. Look." Ben leaned against the bar. "I would not worry, my friend. This is going to be back-page news here locally tomorrow. And judging by the way the news cycle runs, it will not be anywhere on the networks in about three or four hours. Say, you still want to have lunch together?"

Ziad groaned as he poured himself a stout mug of coffee. "If you don't mind a long one."

"Hey, no worries on my end." He chuckled and continued in English, "This will be a working lunch for me. Go get cleaned up. I'll just get my own mug of coffee if you don't mind."

As the caffeine began awakening him, Ziad scrambled upward. He whizzed through his shower in a record five minutes. Once dressed in a pair of khakis and a Charleston Police Department golf shirt, he headed back downstairs.

"Well, don't you clean up nicely." Ben grinned. "Official business today?"

"Press conference at three."

"I can take you there if one of your pals can drop you back here. I saw them guarding the parking lot."

"The PIO told the press to leave me alone, that I would be at the press conference."

"Hmmm. Well, if that doesn't work, maybe my badge and gun will. C'mon. Lunch awaits us."

Once at a Tex-Mex fast food joint, they found a secluded table in the shade outside. Ben pulled out a small notepad. In Arabic, he said, "I have good news, and I have bad news. The good news is that, because of your involvement with the Zap case in Saudi, Angie and Sonja Williams convinced the task force members to read you in on where we are. But if you say a word about this to anyone, then it's my badge on the line. Bad news is, you cannot officially be a member of the task force since you are not a sworn member of law enforcement."

Good enough. Ziad nodded. "I appreciate your effort. What do you know?"

"We have hit pay dirt."

"How so?"

"First off, we checked out Arthur Pullman, the owner of Pullman's Antiques. Nothing there. He is pretty clueless, we believe. He has a clerk who goes by the name of Prissy Parker. No kidding on the name," Ben added in English before continuing in Arabic, "She was the one who was working that day we visited the shop. She knew Daoud al-Rashid because of the way they interacted. We are pretty sure she let Yousif Ali into a back room. Not that we can verify a deal went down, except for one thing."

"Oh?"

"We have more DOAs turning up at local hospitals. Four people, three of them teens, have turned up dead. So sixteen in five months. And it is about three or so weeks after we think we saw a deal."

Ziad nodded.

"We also did some digging on Daoud al-Rashid. He knows Prissy, and he also knows Mike Winthrop, the guy who helped me with the Forester. Seems they lift weights together at the same gym. We put them under surveillance a couple of weeks ago."

"And?"

"They are pals. And they also hang out with Prissy."

"Does she have a tattoo as well?"

"Not that we have seen. Believe me, I have had our guys focus on her hands." Ben shifted in his chair and snagged some chips and salsa. "It makes me wonder if she is a go-between and nothing more, like maybe she does not know what is going on."

Ziad thought about that one. "In those months I worked the case in the Kingdom, I saw no woman."

Ben took a bite of burrito. "Right now, I am not sure how relevant she is. Anyway, what with the timing of the Zap deaths on three occasions, tattoos, etcetera, we had enough probable cause to get warrants for wiretaps." He shrugged. "It is a treasure trove of information."

Ziad, who'd dug into his own burrito, swallowed. "How so?"

"We caught Daoud and Mike on a phone call. Seems there is going to be a huge deal going down in November. Thanksgiving night. Something like it will change the landscape in the Southeast. They seem pretty confident."

"You're not going to question them?"

Ben shook his head. "We question them, we scare them off and blow the whole thing. We want to net as many dealers as possible. We will listen in, see if we can collect more names of potential dealers beyond Daoud and maybe Prissy. We will see what happens."

Ziad noticed a small motion.

A woman stood nearby. She fidgeted with her phone, glanced their way, and stared at her purse. For sure, she'd been watching them. Finally, she edged closer. "I'm so sorry to interrupt your conversation."

Ben smiled politely at her and in English said, "No worries, ma'am. How can we help you?"

"Are you Ziad al-Kazim?" she asked Ziad.

He froze and braced for an outburst about his kind going back to their homeland. Or another call that would bring the police for a suspected terrorist planning session in public.

He nodded. "I am."

"Thank you for what you did last night. I know you'll say you were just doing your job, but you're a hero to me." Tears filled her eyes. "If someone had stepped up out of the crowd and tried to stop my daughter from throwing herself off the roof of her dorm building last year, maybe she'd be alive today."

Stunned, Ziad couldn't say a word.

"I'm sure Thomas's mother and father are so grateful. And I am too. Thank you." With that, she turned and scurried away without another word.

Ziad stared after her, then turned back to Ben.

His friend rested his chin on his hand and smiled. "You're a hero, my friend. And it's okay to acknowledge that even if you're modest."

Slowly, Ziad nodded.

"So, you got home at what time?"

"A little after three."

"And you left the scene shortly after midnight?" Ben cocked an eyebrow. "My, my. Shall I ask what you two did?"

"Ben!" Ziad laughed to cover over the way his neck heated. "We exchanged presents."

*And did a little more than that.* He smiled as he thought about the way they'd romanced until he declared he absolutely had to get home, lest he damage her honor.

"Huh."

"I love her," Ziad softly admitted. "She is a good woman. Compassionate. Beautiful. Smart."

"I'll not argue there. She's Em's sister, after all."

Ziad leaned forward. "May I ask you something?"

"What's up?"

"When did you…" He couldn't believe he was asking this. "When did you know Emma was the right one for you?"

Ben fell silent for a moment. Slowly, he replied, "It honestly didn't take me long to figure it out. Maybe just a month or so of seeing her almost every day. Of course, it took her a lot longer. She had a lot more to work through since she'd already suffered one broken engagement." He straightened. "Wait. You're not thinking of proposing, are you?"

"Not right away, but perhaps soon."

Ben's brow knit. He shoved his cup around and stared at the metal table as if struggling internally with something.

"Ben, what is it?"

His friend finally shook his head. "I guess I'm a bit concerned."

Ben's hesitance a few weeks before came rushing back. "About what?"

"Faith differences."

Ziad shrugged. "It is of no worry. She is a woman of the book. That is acceptable to me."

"It's not that." Ben heaved a sigh. "May I be frank with you?"

"Of course." Sweat broke out on Ziad's hands. "We are friends after all, yes?"

"We are." Ben leaned back and pressed his hands against the table as he stretched his neck. "I'm concerned because you two are not equally yoked."

Huh? "I do not know what that means."

"Think about oxen. They—"

"We are not draft animals."

"It's an analogy, my friend. When they work together in a yoke, they are side by side. Not that I'm an expert farmer or anything, but I imagine you wouldn't put two unequal animals together. It would make it much more difficult."

Ziad bit his tongue.

"A good marriage is hard work. You know that."

"I do."

"Having a marriage of two different faiths adds a whole extra layer of difficulty."

"So you do not approve of—"

"I didn't say that." Ben rested his elbows on the table and raised a finger. "I'm not here to approve or disapprove."

"Then why are you saying it?"

"Because I love you both. You, my friend, are like my brother in so many ways. And Claire's my sister-in-law. Regardless of what happens, that won't change, okay?"

Ziad shrugged. "To me, it is not a big problem. And it is not like I plan to propose tomorrow."

The smallest of sighs escaped Ben. "Understood." He straightened. "So. Let's get you to the press conference before your PIO goes nuts."

Ziad followed him to the Forester. Claire's face floated across his mind. He smiled. Then it dimmed as he thought about the stories. Hopefully, the good prince hadn't seen the bit of news that had shot across the world in record time.

# 32

"How much further?"

"Almost there."

"You said that the last time."

"Did I?" Ziad led Claire down a trail he'd discovered outside of Asheville months before. Now, the week after Labor Day, they had the place to themselves.

Hopefully.

Claire sighed. "We've been hiking for four hours. I'm hot, sweaty, and hungry."

"Not to worry, m'Lady." He paused as the trail made one final turn. "Close your eyes."

She stopped. "What? Ziad—"

"I will guide you."

She heaved a sigh and drawled, "Okay."

He laughed and took her hand. "A root here. Rock there. I will not let you fall."

She didn't even stumble.

The trail widened to reveal a large pool. A waterfall, nearly twenty meters high, cascaded into another, smaller pool. No roar of sheer power here, only the delightful sound of tinkling.

Ziad took her hand. "Open your eyes."

"Wow!" She gasped as she gazed at the water. "This is beautiful. When did you find it?"

"When I came here between trainings last spring, one of the locals recommended it as a good solo hike."

"I can see why."

He cupped her face in his hands and kissed her. "I am glad we decided to split up for the day so Emma could drag Ben to go shopping. That meant I could be alone with you." He pulled back. "Shall we have lunch?"

"Seeing that we have a long hike back, yes." Claire settled on a bare patch of rock and unzipped her pack.

Ziad gazed at the pool. Serene. Like it had been months before. Except the last time when he'd gazed at it, he'd wondered if he'd ever make it in his new homeland. Now he knew. He would.

"Hey, look over there." Claire nodded to the other side of the pool. "I think some other folks had the same idea."

"I knew it would be popular." Ziad munched on his peanut butter sandwich and watched as two adults and three children emerged from the thick green foliage. One of the children jumped into the water, and he squealed.

Claire chuckled. "It may be hot, but any mountain water is freezing."

As he drank his Gatorade, a memory flew into his head, that of a waterfall. And of Sabirah. "It looks like the one in my dreams."

She faced him. "What dreams?"

He set his sandwich on his knee. How much should he reveal? Everything. Her support when he'd confessed his stint in prison had assured him she wouldn't judge, criticize, or try to fix things. "They started when I was in jail, then have popped up here and there."

"What's in them?"

"Sabirah in a white caftan. A garden with a waterfall much like this. Scales with the letter Z in English."

"Huh?"

"Like the… those scales of justice I see here in this country. They have two trays. *Hasana'at*, Reward for Good Deeds, and *Sayia'at*, Reward for Bad Deeds." He shuddered as he thought about what came next. "Each time, she or one of the boys has these stones with them. They place them on the trays."

She eased over so their shoulders touched. "What do you think they mean?"

He shivered. "My life. The stones are the works of my life. She sees how they stack up."

For a moment, she didn't say anything as she opened a baggie of M&Ms and tossed a handful in her mouth.

"Claire?"

"Sorry. I'm thinking." She added another handful. "Your culture places high value on dreams, right?"

He nodded. "Very high value."

"I'm wondering if God is trying to speak to you."

"Why?"

She shrugged. "I'm no soothsayer. Honestly, I'm not. Maybe he's trying to tell you something."

"But why Sabirah?" He emptied a baggie of chips and stuffed it into his backpack.

"Dreams can be funky."

He sighed. "Funky?"

"Strange. They cobble together so many different parts of our lives."

"That sounds somewhat scientific."

She took his hand. "I know. But I also believe they can be divinely inspired."

He kissed her temple. "You sound more Saudi than you realize."

She rested her head against his shoulder. The silky wisps of her ponytail brushed his arm.

Ziad closed his eyes. Across the way, the children called to each other as they splashed around in the pool. Someone jumped into the water. They all giggled, the very sound of contentment. Oh, to stay this way forever. Could it happen? He wrapped his arm around her shoulder and caressed skin left bare by her tank top. He imagined what it would be like to be married to her, to share the deepest parts of himself with her, to be skin to skin in more than just the physical sense. "What do you think about us?"

*Why did I say that? Am I crazy?*

A smile crossed Claire's face. "I think we're good together."

"Do you think we could make it?"

"As a couple?"

"As in marriage?" he blurted. He clamped his jaw shut. *Ziad, Ziad, Ziad, can you not stop while you're ahead?*

Claire stilled. She pulled back a little and stared at him, her eyes wide, her gaze searching his face. "We've barely begun dating."

"I know." How did he get himself out of this corner he'd backed himself into? "I was... curious."

She smiled, but the hand gripping her knee had tightened. "Honestly, I hadn't thought that much about it. We—I need to pray about it."

"I know. And I understand the need to wait." He turned her head and kissed her.

They stayed at their lunch spot for a few more minutes, but something had changed in her, something so subtle the average friend would have missed it. Worry? No. Concern? No. He couldn't define what he felt emanating from her.

Finally, he glanced at his watch. "Much as I hate to say it, we must leave if we are to make it back in time for supper."

She sighed and gathered her lunch baggies. "You're right. Back to reality, huh?"

"Something like that." He helped her to her feet, and they began the long trek back to the trailhead. For sure, something had shifted in her. For better or worse, he didn't know. All he could do was wait.

# 33

On a muggy Monday evening nearly two weeks later, Claire's stomach roiled as she stared at her mostly uneaten plate of leftover chicken and vegetables. The clock on the microwave said it all.

Ziad would arrive in five minutes. She placed her elbows on the granite. Her whispered words came out so low she barely heard them. "Lord, I don't want to do this. But this is what you want. I'm so scared. I don't know what to say, even now."

As she'd prayed these past two weeks, God's direction had become clear to her.

She hated it.

*You need to come out from him. To stand on your own. You are my child. I have greater plans for you. Plans to prosper you and plans to give you hope and a future. And I have plans for Ziad as well. But for me to work in his life, I need him to be alone.*

The 4Runner pulled into the driveway and parked in the empty stall under the house.

No time to prepare now.

She dumped her uneaten meal into the trash and stashed her dishes in the dishwasher.

"Claire." Ziad smiled at her from the doorway.

She slipped around the island and met him halfway. "Hey."

He kissed her slowly, lingeringly, something that would have left her weak in the knees even three weeks ago.

Not now.

Dread knotted her stomach even further.

He tucked a strand of hair behind her ear. "You seem tired."

"I am." Claire disengaged and drifted toward the island. "I haven't been sleeping well since we got back."

"How so?"

"I've been dreaming." She closed her Bible and placed her study guide on top.

He came up behind her and put his hands under her elbows. "In what ways?"

"You and Sabirah are together, and it's like I'm in the room but I'm not really." She closed her eyes. "You and I are talking, but you're speaking in Arabic and me in English, and neither of us understands the other." She shook her head as she recalled what came next. "It got to the point where I fasted last week because I didn't understand those dreams. I still don't."

*Sort of.*

"Why does that have you concerned?"

Here went nothing. She swallowed against the bile in her throat. "Ziad, I… we, well… I can't see you anymore."

There. She'd said it.

Her statement hung in the room like a putrid mist.

His warmth, so comforting, left her. "What did you say?"

"I can't see you anymore," she croaked to the granite. She faced him.

His brow knitted as he stared at her. "I—I do not understand. Why?"

Trembling started deep within her. "Ever since we talked a couple of weeks ago, I've prayed about this. About marriage. And I—I can't do it."

He flinched as if she'd punched him good and hard. "You cannot marry me? Claire, I… why?"

At the hurt flashing across his face, her carefully planned speech disintegrated like a burning piece of paper. "I… I prayed."

His dark gaze, so open and warm, flashed to opaque. "I *know* you prayed. Oh, I get it. Because I am Muslim, yes? And you are Christian?"

*I'm going to throw up.* She put her fingers over her mouth and hung her head.

"Why now? Why not earlier?"

"I thought we could make it work. Honestly, I did. I ignored those little, concerning signs. I thought taking it slow… when marriage came up, I…" She raised her gaze, and his image shimmered through her veil of tears. "I love you, Ziad. I love you so much! But I love my King more."

"What?" He paced and rubbed his chin as if trying to figure out a complicated problem. He stopped and whirled on her as he roared, "You *used* me!"

At the anger building in his eyes, she took a step back, stumbled against one of the bar chairs, and sat down hard. "Ziad—"

"Do not tell me you did not." He muttered something in Arabic, surely a cuss word, under his breath. "I see now." He took a step toward her. "Poor Ziad. Fresh off the boat, eh? You are his only friend. He is nice. Handsome." Another step. "He does not know anybody. Or much about anything." And another. "You take advantage of him. Lead him on. Make him feel like he is loved and worth something, all the while to fulfill your own purposes." He stopped not a foot away. "And then discard him like so much rubbish. You are so selfish!"

Her hand shot to the diamond pendant she'd worn almost every day. "I never used you."

"I do not believe that." He grabbed her chin. "You think I am that foolish? You want to break up? Fine!"

He thumped toward the front door.

"Ziad!" Claire jumped off the bar chair and ran after him. She grabbed his arm.

He shook loose. "Leave me alone!" Tears shimmered in his eyes. "Now."

That came out as a hiss.

He slammed the front door so hard the house shook.

The replacement mirror she'd hung above the foyer table fell from its hook. It shattered.

Pain raged in her heart, almost as badly as it had when Jackson died. "Oh, God!"

Somehow, she stumbled to the kitchen and leaned against the counter. "I'm sorry, Ziad. I'm sorry, I'm sorry!"

She slid to the floor so she rested against the wood. His face floated before her eyes. New agony opened in a line along her soul. She laid her head on her knees and wept.

Five days later, Ziad sat in a corner of Mocha Joe's. With narrowed eyes, he stared out the plate glass windows and barely noticed the rain from a tropical storm offshore pattering on the asphalt parking lot.

Claire had called him, asked him to meet her here. Saturday evening. Six o'clock. A grim smile curled his lips upward. He knew what she wanted. She wanted to get back together because she'd realized the foolishness of her remarks. Her remorse when he'd gotten her message the night before at the Quick Fill had been all too clear.

He almost snorted as he turned his attention to the newspaper in front of him. Five more teens and two adults had died from Zap, bringing the total to a very scary twenty-three people in the Charleston metro area since March. His frustrations at being sidelined on the case mounted.

His mind returned to Claire. What would he do? Easy. He'd make her grovel, then she'd have to work hard to regain his trust. And then? Maybe he'd take her back—but only on his terms would they date.

A yellow Mustang caught his eye. He shoved his coffee aside and followed the car with his gaze as it pulled into a parking spot. Claire popped out and opened that black-and-white-striped umbrella he'd told her looked like a zebra. She dashed through the downpour to the front doors.

A few moments later, she slid onto a chair across from him and put her cup of water on the table. "Thanks for meeting me."

He didn't say a word, only waited until the silence grew so awkward that she'd say something. It'd always worked on suspects. It would with her as well.

She cleared her throat. "I wanted to meet with you because I owe you more of an explanation. I've done a lot of thinking. A whole lot. You're right."

He began smiling.

"You accused me of using you, and you called me selfish. You were right. I did both. And I'm sorry."

Wait. This wasn't how it should go. "Claire—"

She raised a hand to silence him. "Just hear me out, all right? When we started dating—no, before that—when we finally became friends—it reminded me a lot of how things were with Jackson. I felt special around you. Like when you were talking with me, even if there were others in the room, I was the only one with you. When we started being romantic with each other," a brief, dreamy smile crossed her face, "I never felt so loved. So respected. So cared for. Since Jackson had passed, I'd prayed for that kind of relationship again."

They'd gone way off his script. Why wasn't she crying? Begging? "Then what went wrong?"

Her hand shook as she raised her cup to her lips. "I ignored the differences in our faiths. Oh, Sonja and Elizabeth brought it up. Big time. I ignored little warning signs I should have seen early on, like when I was reticent to reveal our relationship. And then by that point, I didn't want to break it off. Selfishly, I didn't want to face the fact I'd be alone again."

"Claire—"

"I knew after you said you loved me on our birthdays that we'd crossed a line." She shoved the cup around in little circles on the table. "We couldn't go back to being friends. I pretended to—no, ignored—our faith differences. I selfishly didn't want to acknowledge that because we are so different in terms of faith, we could never have the true intimacy we both want and need in a marriage."

What could he—

"And selfishly, I wanted that companionship, those warm, fuzzy feelings that come with kissing. And yes, I used you so I wouldn't feel so lonely." She closed her eyes for a moment. When she opened them, they glistened with tears. "Problem is, I fell in love with you somewhere along the way."

Not what he'd expected. What could he say? They could talk, really talk. Figure out a way through this. No. His tattered pride raised its head. He folded his arms across his chest and lifted his chin. "I wasn't good enough for you, eh?"

"That's not what I…"

His voice rose. "You, a high and mighty Christian woman, can't lower yourself to marry me."

At a table next to them, a couple sharing coffee and a danish stared.

"Keep it down, will you?" She glanced around. "Please!"

"I do not care." He leaned forward. "Who told you we should not marry? Ben? Emma? Perhaps your mother?"

"Try God."

"Oh, I see. Trying to deny blame." His laugh came out as a sarcastic bark. "That is a good one."

More heads turned. People murmured as they tuned into their unfolding drama.

"It's true! I don't care what anyone thinks. I prayed. I fasted. And I *begged*." Her fingers tightened around her cup. "I love you. I want to marry you so badly! But I love my King more."

"And that is your answer? How foolish."

The rest of the noise faded away.

"It is."

He stood, leaned forward with his hands on the table, and got right in her face like he had when interrogating suspects. "Let me tell you something, Claire Montgomery. You and I, we are finished. Do you understand? Finished!" He slammed his fist onto the table. "If you cannot accept me for who I am, then I want nothing to do with you. And that pendant? I would like it back. I will give it to a woman who is more deserving of my love than you."

His voice echoed off the windows of the shop.

Cold water splashed across his face.

Huh?

He stared.

Claire jumped up. Her face crumpled as she threw down her empty cup and ran toward the doors. They banged as she fled into the rainy evening.

His gaze flicked across the shop. Those closest to him gawked with wide eyes. At the counter, the barista glared at him with white hot fury that would have made the average man cringe.

It did him.

Then came the murmurings.

That broke him from his trance. Regret slammed into him.

He'd hurt her.

Big time.

All to assuage his own pride.

He bolted into the pouring rain.

The Mustang backed out of its spot. She slammed it into gear, and with a screech of tires, hurtled forward.

"Claire, wait!" he called.

Like she could hear him.

He jumped out of the way as she sped past.

Her brake lights flashed, and water rooster-tailed as she hung a hard right and disappeared into the gloom.

The cold and wet finally penetrated his angst. He shivered. Slowly, he swiveled and faced the coffee house.

Some people still gazed at him.

Oh, did he ever want to crawl into a hole and die. He couldn't go back inside. Not then. Not ever.

He trudged toward the 4Runner. What had he done?

# 34

After eight days of rain, the world rejoiced in a day of sunshine that glorious Sunday afternoon. And after eight days of hard work, tears, and grief, Claire forced herself to go for a run.

She didn't go far, but it nearly did her in. Nausea swelled within her as she slowed to a trot, then a walk. Oh, did she ever feel like she was going to throw up. She returned to the house, braced her hands on her knees, and hung her head. Sweat dripped from her nose.

Gradually, her stomach settled.

She needed fluids. Fast.

"Claire, dear!"

She raised her face to find Mrs. Chitworth climbing from her Mercedes. "Uh, hi, Mrs. Chitworth."

"How are you doing? I haven't seen you in quite a while. How is that fellow of yours?"

Claire burst into tears—again. She stood in the driveway and sobbed like an abandoned child.

"Oh, dear. I'm so sorry. Give me your key. Let's get you inside before we both burn up. I can't believe it's almost October and still hot and muggy. But I heard cool temperatures are on the way tonight." Claire barely heard her neighbor or noticed her arms around her shoulders. They slowly climbed the steps, and Mrs. Chitworth walked her inside. "Sit here."

Claire sat on the couch in the family room. Her stomach twisted on itself. She croaked, "I need Gatorade."

"I'll get it for you. Kleenex as well."

Still crying, she nodded.

Mrs. Chitworth placed a cold glass in her hands. "Drink this, dear. You must be all dehydrated. Now, now. Dry your eyes." She stuffed some tissues into her hand. "Tell this old woman what happened with your fellow."

Claire dabbed at her eyes. Slowly, she shared what had happened Labor Day weekend, then a couple of weeks later, ending with her utter humiliation at Mocha Joe's. "I can't stop crying. I worked Sunday. Then got a message from him saying he was sorry. I was fine until he called again on Tuesday. I skipped Bible study. Sonja came over, and I thought I was okay until he called Thursday and Saturday."

"What did he say?" Mrs. Chitworth asked. She took her hand.

"He wants to talk." Claire dabbed at her eyes. "I can't do it, can't let myself get hurt like that again. I mean, he made his position clear. I—I gave the pendant to Ben and Emma to give to him." More tears came. "I'm a mess."

"I'd be a mess too. I'm so sorry."

"I just don't know what to do. I don't!" Claire's chin began trembling. "It's just that when he called, he seemed remorseful. But I—I can't. I can't call him back. If I do, I'll cave and then I'll…"

Another sob escaped. She leaned over.

Mrs. Chitworth rubbed her back. "Oh, Claire."

She covered her face with her hands. "I trusted God, and now my heart is breaking."

"Do you still trust him?"

She lowered them. "What?"

Mrs. Chitworth sat on the edge of the couch, her blue eyes watery but radiating love. "Do you still trust God? It's okay to be honest. Only when you're honest with yourself will you allow him to work in your life."

"I—I don't know. I hurt Ziad so badly, all because I ran ahead of God. I hurt him so very badly. He's right. I was selfish. I used him." She flinched as the anguish on his face from that terrible Monday etched itself in her mind.

"I think you're being hard on yourself."

She pulled her hair band out and raked her hands through those sweaty strands. "I don't know what to do!"

Mrs. Chitworth gripped her hand. "Give it to God."

"What?"

"Give it to God. Your sadness. Your anguish. Your tears. Your concerns." Her neighbor squeezed her hands. "Take his hands, my dear."

Claire looked up.

Tears trickled down Mrs. Chitworth's cheeks. "You feel so barren. So alone. I know. I felt that way when Henry died. I cried for days. For months. Each day, and I mean each day, I had to take God's hands and walk with him. To say to myself aloud that he loved me and that he would never let me go." Her grip tightened to surprisingly strong for someone just turned eighty. "I had to seek out those promises. And when I finally believed them and stopped doubting so much, that's when I got my peace."

Still sniffling, Claire dabbed at her eyes again. "It's so hard!"

"I know, dear. I know." Mrs. Chitworth rubbed her back. "I'll pray for peace for you, that you'll reach out and run to him during this time. And I'll pray for Ziad as well, that he comes to see Jesus as his Savior and Lord. Let me pray."

Claire nodded. As her neighbor bowed her head, she gradually calmed until only her ragged breaths remained. For the first time in over a week, a faint light of hope glimmered in the darkness of her despair. She knew it might not last, but now, in that very moment, she was at peace.

Sunday afternoon, Ziad slouched on the couch in his living room and stared at a soccer match on the television. He lifted a cigarette to his lips. Sunlight seeped around the edges of the closed blinds. He should have been outside enjoying the first nice day in over a week.

Work, work and more work.

His one lousy excuse. He'd spent the past eight days avoiding his reality by working extra shifts at the Quick Fill or as a reserve officer. His daily workouts and extra hours studying for the GED assured he fell into bed too exhausted to dream.

He began flipping through channels.

Someone rang the doorbell.

"Ziad? You in there?"

Ben. Since the television blared, he couldn't ignore him.

With a sigh, he rose.

Ben leaned against the frame, this time dressed in sweats and a T-shirt. He tossed a careless grin in his direction. "Hey, my friend. What's up?"

Ziad retreated to the couch without a word.

If his rudeness put Ben off, he didn't show it. "You okay?"

"How okay should I be?"

"I don't know. You tell me. You mind if I open some blinds and windows? It kinda smells like cigarettes. And man stink and garbage. At least that's what Em would say." Without waiting for permission, Ben drew the blinds upward until sunlight poured in. He threw open the doors and windows, and as it blew into the room, a fresh breeze stirred up the smell.

Ziad winced. He hadn't showered in a couple of days, even with running. He'd resumed smoking and hadn't taken out the trash for a bit either.

Ben flopped onto one of the chairs. "We missed you at dinner."

"Claire did not." Why couldn't he stop with the low blows? He lit another cigarette and blew out a stream of smoke.

"You're right. She didn't because she wasn't there. We haven't seen her in a couple of weeks because she's been working so much." He shifted and carefully extracted something from his pocket. He held it up.

The diamond pendant on its delicate chain. In the sunlight, it splashed beams of color across the room. "I did see her in church, and she gave this to Em for you. I told her I'd bring it over."

He lowered it onto the glass coffee table.

Ziad stared at it as if it were a poisonous snake. He took a puff. His fingers trembled as he set his cigarette in the overflowing ashtray. With his elbows on his knees, he picked up the necklace and held it against his forehead. In Arabic, almost below his breath, he murmured, "What have I done? Forgive me, Claire."

He swallowed his emotions and with a deep breath, lowered his hands.

Ever the investigator, Ben studied him. He didn't call him on it, didn't say a word. Instead, he rose. "Let's go and kick the soccer ball around. It's too nice a day to be cooped up indoors watching it when you could be playing it."

He had him there. "Let me get my shoes."

"Well, come on then! Daylight's a'wasting."

A couple of hours later, the sun set as Ben picked up the soccer ball. He whistled the theme to the *Globetrotters* as he twirled it on the end of his finger. It spun off and bounced to the ground. He whirled around and neatly scooped it into the air with his foot before catching it. "Coffee?"

Oh, the joys of even a little exercise. Ziad felt better already. "Of course."

They rode in the Forester with the windows down. Ziad sniffed. He really needed a shower now. And ample deodorant. When was the last time he'd let himself get that unkempt? When he was in jail. The thought caught him up short.

"Ziad!"

He must have tuned out. "So sorry."

"I was saying we figured you and Claire broke up."

"How so?"

"You both went silent at the same time." Ben pulled into a parking lot.

Oh, no. Mocha Joe's. The scene of the crime. He couldn't go in there. Not now. Probably not ever again. Fortunately, a table at the end of the covered patio sat empty. "Perhaps I should wait here." He offered what he was sure was a sick smile. "Because of my man stink, you know." He fished some cash from his pocket. "Here. Arabian coffee."

"Be back in a jiff."

Ziad eased onto a chair. He lit another cigarette and took a puff. This time, its taste nauseated him. He set it in an ashtray and rested his elbows on the table.

"If you cannot accept me for who I am, then I want nothing to do with you." His arrogant words mocked him. "And that pendant? I would like it back. I will give it to a woman who is more deserving of my love than you."

She'd taken him at his word.

Now, he found himself in a tailspin with no idea of how to pull out of it before he crashed and burned.

Ben set a coffee cup on the table. "Here you go. One Arabian coffee. Black." He plopped down with his own cup and undid his sugar packet. As if to unnerve him, he took his time adding it and stirring in some cream. He looked him in the eye with a steely gaze. "Tell me something."

Fear unfurled inside of Ziad. He tried for casual by raising an eyebrow.

"Just what in the name of hushpuppies did you do to her?"

Oh, no. "I am not understanding."

"No, you're understanding perfectly, my friend." Ben leaned forward, his hands gripping the arms of the chair like claws. "You know what the barista said? She wished that cup of cold water Claire threw in your face had been boiling hot tea. Why on earth would she say something like that?"

Ziad's heart pounded. His friend reminded him of a coiled snake, ready to strike at the slightest provocation.

Ben had every right to pound him to a pulp.

Fingers trembling, he picked up his cigarette again. "I—we met here last Saturday. Claire had said she wanted to apologize."

"And that deserved your harshness?"

Guilty. "N—no. I…" What could he say? The truth. "I let my pride get in the way. I cut her down when I should not have, told her I wanted the pendant back, that I would give it to a woman more deserving of my love than she."

Ben leaned back, picked up his coffee, and whistled low. "Boy, when you go big, you go really big, don't you?"

Ziad lowered his head. To the metal of the table, he confessed, "If there are ever words I regret, those are the ones."

"Huh." Ben shook his head. "Wow. For once, I don't know what to say."

"Did you ever… did you ever tell her it was inappropriate for us to marry?"

"Uh, no. You're the one who mentioned it to me."

"She said it was our differences in faith. And I truly do not understand. She is a woman of the book—"

"Who has no intention of converting, and because of that, you would be unequally yoked. We talked about that, remember?" Ben sipped his coffee, then began shredding the cup holder. With a sigh, he shoved his drink aside. "Let me ask you something. What would you have desired for your sons in terms of a wife?"

"Her family being of good standing." Ziad paused. "Being educated. Attractiveness. Being a good Muslim or a willingness to convert—oh, I think I see where you are going with this."

"You and Sabirah had that great intimacy."

"It took years to learn."

"But didn't part of that stem from the fact you had a common faith?"

"I think I see what you mean. Sharing the same desires, goals, and values is crucial."

"And that usually springs out of culture, which comes out of faith, or at least it does in Saudi."

He had him there.

Ben fell silent for a moment. Then he looked up and met his friend's gaze. This time, his gaze glinted with earnestness. "Marriage is the only relationship where you truly share the deepest parts of your being. And if you don't share the same faith, I think that would be impossible. Say if Em were atheist and I were Christian. I think we'd have this huge hole that couldn't be filled because we'd have to agree to disagree on our deepest parts. We'd be missing that true intimacy. I think that's what worried Claire."

Ziad nodded. He shivered as the first chilly air of fall began filtering into the area. His heart ached, but it came clear to him in a flash. He hunched forward with his forearms on the table. In low Arabic, he confessed, "I still love Claire. No matter what, I still love her. No matter how much we hurt each other, that won't change. I think… I think hearing her say she loves her King more than she loves me hurt my pride. I don't understand it."

Ben leaned back and swung his feet onto the chair next to him. He gazed at his friend, this time with no anger. "I think she was trying to say she loves you very much, but she loves God even more because he is her Creator. And her King."

Ziad considered that one. "It intrigues me."

"What?"

"Her single-mindedness when it comes to doing Allah's will. That she would set aside her personal desires to do his will."

"Maybe the Allah you know and the God she knows are actually different."

Slowly, Ziad stubbed out his cigarette and leaned forward. "I would like to know more about the way she sees God. Perhaps you could tell me why this is so?"

"This requires more coffee. My treat. You can buy me some later on." Ben jumped up and headed inside. When he returned, he began speaking of a God Ziad hadn't known all his life, a God who was personal, who knew him inside and out, who'd cared so much that he'd sent his Son to die for him. Ziad found himself fascinated but on a more intellectual level.

Finally, Ben checked his watch and rose. "Look. I'm sorry, but I've got to go."

Ziad couldn't—no, wouldn't—let it go. "Can we meet more on this later? Perhaps with Bible and Koran in hand to discuss?"

"Absolutely. Tuesday's great for me."

As they returned to his apartment, a new peace Ziad didn't understand draped over him. Maybe their meeting the following week would help him sort things out.

They pulled into a parking slot.

Ben faced him. "Hey, before you go, my friend. I meant to tell you this earlier, but we obviously got sidetracked. I talked to Angie about the raid we're planning on that warehouse Thanksgiving night. She's approved you to be an observer."

Disappointment nipped at him. "Just an observer?"

"Yep." Then his friend winked. "Kind of like I was in Jeddah."

For the first time in almost two weeks, Ziad smiled. "I see what you mean. Thank you. I appreciate your request."

"I'll keep you posted. See you Tuesday."

Ziad headed inside. Yuck. It did smell, more than he'd realized when he'd holed up. Once again, he opened the windows and doors, then took out the trash, including the overflowing ashtray. The clothes he'd worn while smoking went into the wash, and he took a shower. Once clean, he scrounged up a supper of pita and peanut butter with the promise to make it to the store the next day.

Did the cool air ever feel so good. So did clean skin and hair. Ziad settled at his laptop. How could he discuss Scripture without a Bible? He called Ben. "If I were to order a Bible in Arabic, what translation should I get?"

Ben listed some.

Ziad found what he was looking for and ordered it. Good. It would arrive by the end of the week. Finally, he crashed instantly into sleep.

That dream came again.

Sabirah, this time with Basil.

Those scales.

Those stones he'd learned to fear.

And something new.

A pedestal.

Sabirah hugged their second youngest close. "Basil built it because he knows how much determining your fate means to you."

"It means nothing—"

"It means everything." Sharp words, especially for Sabirah. She glared at him as she ran her hands down her ebony hair. After dumping the gray stones onto the prayer rug in front of her, she placed a stone on the *Sayia'at* tray. "You hurt Claire."

"But she—"

"She loves you so much, Ziad. And you're good for her." A stone went onto the *Hasana'at* tray. "You've helped her heal."

Another stone went on that tray.

Protective anger flared in Sabirah's eyes. "Yet you nearly destroyed her with your words."

His pride flared. "She was the one who wanted to break up!"

"She has cried every day since then."

The accusations came.

His arrogance.

His rudeness.

His lack of compassion.

And his pride.

His stinking pride.

By the time, Sabirah fell silent, the *Sayia'at* tray nearly touched the pedestal. Anger replaced her sadness as she gazed at it. "I thought I knew you better."

Regret formed a hard knot in his stomach. "I thought I knew myself better. Please. I—I'm human!"

"Does that really matter in God's eyes?" With that, she rose and took Basil's hand.

"Sabirah, don't go! Basil. Sabirah, please! I'll apologize. I'll make it better. No!"

Ziad jerked upright. Sweat drenched him and dampened the sheets. He shook all over, and his chest heaved. He raked his hands through his hair. They came away damp. For a moment, he stared at the picture of him and Claire.

Just another reminder of his massive failure.

He placed it face down, then put his head in his hands as despair nearly drowned him. He'd failed. Utterly failed. And at that point, he saw no way to make things right.

# 35

Late Thanksgiving night, rain drummed on top of the FBI Ford Transit van. Only the sound of metal spoon on Pyrex penetrated the din as Ziad finished off the peach cobbler he and Ben had taken with them when leaving Thanksgiving dinner for the raid. Hmmm, mmmm. So good. "This is almost better than Claire's. I did not know your mother could make such a good dessert."

"Mom's the best. I'm glad she and Dad came to visit." Ben sipped from his thermos of coffee and shifted on a camp stool as he peered out the back windows at the rear of the warehouse.

"How is Claire?"

His friend shrugged. "Don't know. She's worked practically every day since the first of October. Good for the bank account but bad on the body. Em's worried she's going to work herself sick."

Ziad understood the need to keep busy, to avoid the tougher parts of life. He'd done the same until the flu had sidelined him at the beginning of November. Then he'd had no choice but to lie in bed and think—or read, including the Bible.

Interesting on an intellectual level, like those words had seeped into his head but not his heart. God could be personal? That's what Ben had said. Hard to believe, though. God wanted a relationship with him? Impossible. Yet when he looked around him at those who he realized had become his family by choice rather than origin, he found that hard to deny. Obviously, Ben had talked freely with him about his faith. Emma as well. And those he knew on the force who loved Isa? Sure, they didn't proselytize him, but the way they lived their lives, even dealt with criminals, reflected Isa just as surely as the sun on a mirror.

"Hey, earth to Ziad." Ben's teasing brought him back to where they sat.

"So sorry. I was thinking."

"I was saying Claire really does love you."

He swallowed hard. He had no answer.

"No, seriously. Like, she had all of us family over to her house last weekend and practically begged us to forgive you. That's how worried she was."

Would the regret ever go away? Probably not. "I love her. I know I said differently, that I would give that pendant to a woman more deserving of my love. She is the one. After Sabirah," he swallowed hard as he thought of her, "I never thought I could love someone again. Claire taught me differently. It will always be hers, even if we never get back together."

Ben nodded. He opened his mouth as if to say something, then closed it. "I know." He stilled. "Hey, check out our ten o'clock."

Ziad focused his binoculars. Through the pouring rain, he noted two suspects slinking into the area. They made their way down an alley formed by two warehouses.

Beside him, a camera clicked. Softly, Ben reported, "Angie, looks like two more potential dealers showed up."

The radio crackled before her voice came through loud and clear. "Taz and his crew noted eight. Add that to the four you've seen, and it sounds like all dealers are present but no product."

"Agree."

The van fell silent save for the incessant drumbeat of rain. Ziad began a scan of the surrounding area. Nothing moved. Even the stray dogs and cats had gotten wise and sought shelter from the Nor'easter as it blew inland from the Atlantic.

Then he saw it. At the other end of the alley, a truck with its head-lights off crept toward the warehouse. "Ben."

"I see 'em. Looks like our product's finally arrived. Show time."

Ziad smiled as he remembered those words from over a year and a half before. This time, he fulfilled the role Ben had taken previously.

A few minutes passed.

Ben tensed with his hand on the back door's handle.

His comrade reported, "Product has arrived. Repeat, product has arrived."

Angie murmured, "SWAT moving in. Stay put, you two."

Ziad ground his teeth. Did he ever want to be in the action!

An FBI SWAT team, battering ram poised, M-4s held at ready, slipped by them and worked their way down the alley. Another team approached the back door. The clang of metal on metal echoed above the rain. Then came a flash and crump of flash-bang grenades igniting inside. The SWAT team poured through the doorway. Shouting ensued.

Near the corner, a window popped open. Someone nearly fell onto the ground.

A runner.

Not this time. Not on his watch.

"We've got an escapee. Let's go!" Ben threw down his camera and pushed through the back doors.

Ziad followed through the downpour. He'd forgotten how fast his friend was as they charged along the fence. The suspect darted between two warehouses.

Ben accelerated and followed.

They rounded a corner.

Ziad skidded to a stop.

Nothing. Only rows of warehouses on either side of the street with pallets and shipping containers stacked here and there. Where was Ben?

His hearing and sight sharpened. Since he'd not been allowed to carry a gun as an observer, they were all he had to keep him safe.

His heart ticked up a few notches.

*Ben, where are you?*

He didn't dare call out and reveal his location.

He pressed himself flat against the metal of a container.

He was about to turn down another alley when Ben and the suspect sped past him like a falcon chasing a hare.

He took off in hot pursuit.

They skidded around another corner.

Ziad's lungs burned.

*Right. They went right.*

He turned in that direction, and they crossed another street, now far away from the center of the action.

Ziad slowed.

His lungs heaved.

He peered around him.

Over the pattering of rain that left him soaked, he listened.

*Whump. Crash.*

Someone grunted.

Ziad bolted in that direction.

Caught in the dead end of a warehouse and shipping containers, Ben grappled with their suspect like they were wrestling. He threw him to the ground.

The man tackled the FBI agent at his knees.

Ben hit the concrete hard.

The man drew back his fist for a killing blow.

Ben's arm shot out.

His fist glanced off Ben's face.

The agent stilled.

The man knelt beside him and felt along his side.

Ziad's heart shot to his throat.

*He's going for his gun.*

One chance and one chance only.

Like a feline predator, he charged without a sound.

He leapt into the air as the gun came free from its holster.

Ziad slammed into him.

The Glock flew off to parts unknown.

"Get off me!" Daoud al-Rashid shouted.

He lashed out with his foot and caught Ziad in the side.

He winced. "Not on your life."

Ziad's side hook connected with Daoud's head. Pain shot up his hand.

Daoud came after him with a forward kick.

Ziad dove out of the way and rolled to his feet. He ducked a side punch, then jabbed hard against Daoud's solar plexus.

Daoud moaned and collapsed to his knees.

Ziad needed cuffs.

Fast.

"Ben."

His friend groaned and pushed himself up on his elbows. "What hit me?"

"I need your cuffs. Now!"

That brought him to his senses. He tossed his pair to his friend.

Ziad slapped them on Daoud, then hauled him upright. "I will let you Mirandize him."

Ben did as Ziad searched for the Glock. He found it in a pile of rotting fruit and vegetables that made the stink of his apartment a few weeks earlier pale in comparison. "Eh, you might want to wash this."

Though blood poured from a cut above his eyes and a split lip, Ben grinned, "Thanks, my friend. You saved my life."

"But you bagged the suspect." Ziad winked.

"Ziad."

"Your case, your glory, my friend." A smile crossed his face. "I was just an observer, remember?"

Early the next evening, Ziad rubbed a towel through his hair as he wandered downstairs. Nearly a day later, his hand still hurt, as did his side. No harm done, the paramedic had told him. Just bruising that would heal.

"Em's going to freak when she sees this," Ben said after he'd gotten stitches for the cut above his eye. "Then she'll really freak when she sees the bruising over my ribs."

That brought a smile to Ziad's face. "Better you than I, my friend."

Now, Ziad turned the television to the local news station. He knew all about the leading story, had participated in it, albeit anonymously.

He sat on the couch with his elbows on his knees, his chin resting on his hands, as he watched the entire story, including the press conference. A smile fought its way loose as Angie and the Special Agent in Charge for South Carolina handled the press like pros. Ben stood in the background with the other task force members.

The Zap ring? Shut down, at least through Charleston. They'd arrested a dozen dealers who'd fanned out throughout the Carolinas, including Daoud al-Rashid and Mike Winthrop.

Ben's case, Ben's glory.

Like a faint twinge from a sore muscle, his pride twitched. That should have been him.

No. Ziad shut down that thought as well as the television. He rested his head against the soft cushion. Ben and the task force had done all of the hard work. He'd merely provided support where he could. Right then, he preferred the background.

What with his sweats on and the gas fireplace running to chase away the chill, he was warm. Comfortable. And tired after a hard workout at the gym. He dreamed.

Sabirah.

Those infernal scales of his life.

And Khalid. His youngest snuggled next to his mother. He giggled at something she said, and she kissed his downy hair.

Then came the stones.

One went on the *Hasana'at* tray.

"For your care about Claire and your love for her," Sabirah said.

Khalid leaned forward and added one to the *Sayia'at* tray.

Ziad stared. "What…"

"You envied Ben last night," his son said.

"I did not."

Sabirah added another stone onto the *Sayia'at* tray. Sadness reflected in her gaze. "And you lied about it."

Then went another. And another until once again, though he had several on the *Hasana'at* tray, the scales tipped in the other direction.

Ziad couldn't even remember his bad works.

He jerked awake. Despair tugged at him.

Hopeless. Totally hopeless.

No matter how many good deeds he did, he would never right those scales. Never.

No matter how hard he tried.

# 36

It happened. The second week of December, working nearly non-stop with barely a day off finally caught up to Claire in the form of a cold. As she crouched in the bay of the helicopter and counted quantities of the supplies they had, she couldn't focus.

Her nose twitched. A sneeze erupted, and she barely had time to aim it at her sleeve. She grimaced at the aftermath. "Gross."

Sniffling, she finished her work. With the bay doors shut, she headed inside to the helicopter crew's offices located in the ED clinic. The night shift flight nurse chatted with the two pilots who were on call.

"Meredith," Claire croaked.

Her coworker turned. "Boy, you sound terrible."

"I feel terrible." She coughed into her sleeve. "I'm headed home. Here's the list of supplies that need restocking."

She held out the note paper.

Meredith took it with the very tips of her fingers.

Claire cracked a smile. "Very funny. Have a great evening."

With that, she changed into a pair of jeans and a sweatshirt. Time to head home and get some rest. At least she had four days off, four days to sleep, read, and baby herself back to health.

"We can get some others to fill in when people call in sick," her boss had told her earlier that day. "You've worked entirely too much."

At least the work had soothed her soul.

And kept her from thinking too much about Ziad. Emma had told her he and Ben had begun meeting regularly to talk about the Bible. The week before, he even began attending their church.

Claire didn't hold out much hope. As she wandered down the hall to the parking garage, her mind flashed back to the meal she'd prepared for her family the weekend before Thanksgiving. And her speech. "I've realized one thing. I still love Ziad. Through it all, that's what I've concluded. I love him. He's not a Christian. I understand that. And I'll not marry him until he is. And if he never becomes one and I go to my grave single, so be it."

She stood by those words with her heart and soul. Unfortunately, she knew what that meant. She couldn't see him. If she did, she'd cave. *Lord, I wish there were another way. I truly do. But there isn't.*

She fished her unfamiliar fob from her purse, all thanks to the person who'd rammed into the side of her parked Mustang at a shopping center and run off without leaving any insurance information. The convertible now resided in the shop, and she was stuck with a crappy Chevy Cavalier for a rental. At least it had heat. And a radio. But not much else.

There! Claire found the teal vehicle toward the end. She shivered, more from the sudden feeling of being alone than the chilly air. Maybe she should return to the security desk and ask for an escort. No. She wanted to get home. Fast.

As she continuously surveyed the area, she made her way across the concrete. She slid inside and started the vehicle. It groaned to life. "For something to be so new, this is a piece of junk," she muttered. "Thanks for nothing, you jerk."

She pulled out of her spot and wound her way to the exit. The gate lifted. She turned right, then stopped at the stoplight to allow some passerby to cross. She turned on her right turn signal.

A shadow caught her eye.

It blazed toward her.

Her breath hitched, and she fumbled for the locks. "No!"

A man jumped inside.

Pain flashed across her cheek.

He pointed a gun at her heart. "Drive!"

Her hand snaked toward her purse.

"No, you don't!" He called her a foul name and tossed her purse into the back, then jammed the gun's muzzle against her temple so hard it hurt. "Onto Calhoun!"

Her tires squealed as she jerked into the turn. A pedestrian shouted at her.

She mouthed a silent plea. *Call for help!*

"Onto Lockwood!"

Claire skidded into the turn.

"Get onto US 17 North. Now." He called her another unflattering name.

Her voice trembling, she blurted, "If it's money you want, I don't have much, but it's—"

"It's not money, woman." His eyes narrowed, and he smirked. "It's you."

For a brief, insane second, she stared at him. He'd yanked the hood of his hoodie down, and in the dim flashes of streetlights, she noticed something like snakes tattooed onto his bald head. "Me? I—I—"

"Shut up. Onto I-26 West." Focused energy now, as if the carjacker knew precisely where to go.

Claire took several deep breaths. *Stay calm. Think. No one's going to help you. It's you and me, Lord. No one else.* She stomped on the accelerator and sped up. Maybe a cop would see them.

*I-526.*

Those words flew across her mind.

What?

*Take the exit.*

Again, those words as if someone had spoken aloud to her.

She cranked the wheel to the right, and they flew along the exit ramp.

The carjacker stared at her. "What are you doing? Who told you—"

"You want somewhere deserted?" She matched her volume to his. "That's where I'm going!"

He jabbed at her. "Get back onto 26!"

She jerked her head back, and his gun opened a cut above her eye. "Hit me again, and we both die."

She stomped on the accelerator. The Cavalier quivered as she passed seventy. She pressed toward eighty.

Maybe a cop would see them first and pull them for speeding.

*Ziad.*

It was as if the carjacker had spoken his name.

Of course he hadn't.

Maybe Ziad was on duty out on Clements Ferry Road. That was it! *Lord, let this work. Please!*

The exits for North Rhett and Virginia Avenues flew by in a blur.

"Turn around! What are you—"

"Shut up!" Her hands tightened on the wheel.

Blood oozed through her eyebrow. Oh, no. Not now. She couldn't pass out. Not while they practically flew across the Cooper River. Clements Ferry Road came up.

*God, please…* Her cry remained locked in her throat as the brake pedal vibrated. The carjacker's shouts faded as she focused on keeping them from flying off the exit ramp. Blue lights began flashing behind them.

The carjacker froze. "You stop, you die. Understand?"

He brandished the gun as if to emphasize his point.

He'd rather kill her than let her walk.

She had to end this. *God, please. I'm so scared.*

Peace descended as she realized what she had to do.

She stomped on the accelerator once more and blew by another two patrol cars, these coming toward her with their blue lights glittering in the cold air.

They whipped into a U-turn and became the closest pursuers.

Blood began trickling into her right eye.

Her pulse pounded in her ears.

Then came the lightheaded feeling.

Her vision began tunneling.

She refused to let up on the accelerator.

As they approached an industrial area, her vision shrank to a point.

"Lord, be with me!" she cried aloud as she jerked the steering wheel to the left.

She barely felt them go airborne, barely heard the screams—hers or the carjackers, she didn't know—as they clipped a pole.

Glass shattered.

Metal crunched.

Claire slipped into darkness.

"All units, a ten-twenty-six has occurred at the corner of Calhoun and Jonathan Lucas Street," the dispatcher called on the radio. "Hostage in the car. Car description: teal 2010 Chevy Cavalier, license plate South Carolina EEE 999. Subject westbound on I-26."

Where he sat in the early evening in his hide on Clements Ferry Road, Ziad jotted the plate number onto his notepad and straightened. A kidnapping? Not good. He listened as several of his comrades called that they were in pursuit. Then came another update. "Subject has taken I-526 East. Repeat. Subject has taken I-526 East."

"Ten-Four." The dispatcher repeated the information.

Time to move. He turned on his flashing blue lights but kept the siren off as he keyed his radio. "Dispatch, Unit Eight-Two-R moving into position to intercept if requested."

"Ten-Four, Unit Eight-Two-R."

"Unit Eight-Two with you." Eddie swung behind him.

Ziad squinted in the darkness and the evening traffic. He guided his cruiser around those who pulled over. Not much further, and he'd be ready to make the intercept.

"All units, suspect is northbound on Clements Ferry Road."

Ziad peered through the headlights.

Then he saw them.

Ahead, a mass of blue lights with a car in front hurtled toward him.

It blew by him and Eddie.

He hung a hard left in a U-turn and toggled his radio. "Unit Eight-Two-R in direct pursuit."

Ziad focused on his driving.

"Suspect is armed and dangerous," the dispatcher said. "Repeat, suspect is armed and dangerous."

They shot into a rural area.

The amber glow of streetlights from an industrial complex came up.

They left their jurisdiction.

The Cavalier jerked left!

Too fast to—

He gasped as it skidded off the road and sailed into the air.

It clipped a utility pole. Sparks flashed in the dark.

A body flew through the air.

The Chevy crashed onto the ground, rolled two more times, and came to rest on its roof.

Ziad slammed on the brakes. He jumped from his cruiser.

Eddie grabbed his arm. "Hold on, Big Z. We've got power lines down big time."

Ziad snatched up a flashlight and shone it across the area. Sparks crackled from the ends of some live wires. "We need to get to the car."

"Roger that. But without dying ourselves." Eddie raised his radio to his lips and made the call to the dispatcher for the power company to get out there, STAT. "Suspect down," he added as they stared at the moaning form of the carjacker. "Ziad, get to the car. Carefully."

They picked their way over the wires.

Ziad studied the Cavalier. It lay upside down, the roof partially caved in. Its wheels spun, meaning the car was in drive.

A sharp odor permeated the air. "Gas."

Not good at all. One spark… He shut down the commonsense part of his brain as he finished crossing the power lines and reached the Cavalier.

He fell to his knees and peered inside. A woman with long hair hung upside down from her seatbelt.

Ziad reached inside and turned off the ignition. The wheels began winding down. He fumbled at her neck for a pulse. Steady, thank goodness.

At his touch, she moaned.

"Help is coming," he murmured in an effort to assure her. *Keep calm.* She turned her head.

"Ziad?"

He froze at the thin, ethereal voice. Not...

"Claire?" He wormed his way inside and aimed the beam of his flashlight toward her.

His heart pounded. He couldn't think. *Breathe. You must breathe.* He examined her face. Scarlet with blood. It dripped onto the roof from a gash in her head.

She was bleeding to death simply by hanging upside down.

He yanked out his handkerchief and pressed it over her wound. "I am here. Where are you hurting?"

Her voice trembled as she replied, "Everywhere."

Fear uncurled within him. "Can you move your toes?"

"N—no."

He couldn't panic. It wouldn't do her any good. "Your fingers?"

"Y—yeah."

No comfort if she had no feeling in her toes.

"Paramedics are less than a minute out." Eddie now crouched beside him.

Ziad turned his head and squinted in the bright beam of his friend's light. "She cannot move her toes. We need to get her out."

"Not 'til they get here. Hang tight."

Claire's hand fumbled for his. "Ziad, I'm scared."

He gripped her fingers. "I know, *habibti.* I am here for you."

Eddie touched his back. "Ziad, man, the firemen and paramedics are here. Let them take over."

He hesitated.

"Sir, we've got to get in there," a paramedic said.

He had no choice. Ziad wormed free and climbed to his feet. Eddie took his arm and guided him across the wires. "The power company is ten minutes out. They'll cut the power when they get here."

"Claire cannot move her toes."

Eddie muttered something as he stared at a couple of paramedics lifting the carjacker onto a stretcher. "Our man's got a busted arm and is pretty banged up. Nothing that seems to be life threatening."

Ziad began shaking as adrenaline seeped from his system.

"Big Z, you need to sit down for a moment. Here." Eddie popped open the passenger door to his cruiser. He stared at the blood on Ziad's hands, then pulled a First Aid kit from the trunk. "Get cleaned up."

Using swaths of gauze, Ziad did just that. He shuddered at the red rapidly going to brown. Claire's blood—shed that night in ample quantities.

One of the paramedics ran over to them. "Hey, we need a landing site away from these power lines."

Ziad's breath caught. "Is she—"

"She's not going to make it without an airlift."

Panic tried to overtake him.

"Go down about two hundred yards," Eddie told him. "Block the road with me."

He stumbled to his patrol car. Moments later, they had the area cordoned off while some sheriff's deputies ran traffic control.

Above them, the ruby and emerald lights from a helicopter came closer. He flinched as the chopper, the hospital's logo lit up on the side, landed on the road between the crash site and their cruisers.

Keeping a wide berth around the swirling rotor blades, Ziad made his way toward the crash site. His breath caught.

Two firefighters had finally extricated Claire from the car and eased her onto a backboard. To be heard over the noise of the rotor blades, they shouted her vitals to the paramedics as they carried her across the wires to a waiting gurney.

Ziad didn't understand the terminology, but their tone revealed all.

Claire clung to life by a thread.

He followed them.

They secured her to the helicopter's gurney.

"Not you, Claire!" The flight nurse gasped.

Seeming to overcome her shock, she began demanding information.

They slid the gurney into the back and slammed the doors.

Without hesitation, the helicopter lifted off and sped toward the hospital only a few miles away.

Never in his life had Ziad felt so utterly powerless to do anything.

"Ziad al-Kazim," someone called. Detective Alan Rothschild, the detective he'd met that spring, strode toward him. "It's nice to see you again, though I wish under better circumstances. I got the call. Tell me what happened."

Eddie did most of the talking.

Ziad listened.

The beat of the rotor blades vanished, leaving behind the hum of firetrucks and chatter of the firefighters and other emergency personnel as they completely roped off the crime scene.

Detective Rothschild listened with narrowed eyes and furrowed brow. He sprang into action. "Let's bring the perimeter in tighter. Ziad, Eddie said you know her."

"I—I do."

"You mind calling her family?" the detective asked.

"I... I will." Ziad returned to his cruiser and pulled out his cell phone. He'd call Ben, let him tell the others. His stomach clenched. His knees began shaking as he dialed his friend's number. He leaned his back against the hood and pinched the bridge of his nose as his temples pounded from clenching his jaw.

"Ben Evans."

"Ben, it is Ziad."

"How's it going, my friend? Are you still on duty?"

"Still on duty, and no, it is not going well."

"What's up?"

Ziad leaned forward until his elbows rested on his knees. "Ben, it is Claire."

"What?"

"She—she has been in an accident. She was carjacked. I was first on the scene."

"Ziad—"

"I wanted to call you so you could tell the rest of the family."

"Where is she?"

"They airlifted her to Potter. I will be there as soon as I can be."

Silence. Ben had already hung up.

Detective Rothschild glanced up from his notepad. "Eddie told me about you and Claire. No wonder you're shaken. Go on."

"Sir?"

"Go on. We'll handle the investigation. See you later at the hospital."

Ziad didn't waste any time. He jumped into his cruiser and bolted toward the interstate and where his love clung to life by a thread.

# 37

"Where is she?" Twenty minutes later, Ziad burst through the doors of the Emergency Department.

The attendant stared at him, her eyes wide. "Who?"

"Claire Montgomery. She was airlifted here."

Minnie, the ED administrative assistant who'd taken a shine to Ziad, approached the desk. "Hey. She's in surgery. Second floor. Her family's already—"

"Thank you." He rushed toward the stairs.

His foot caught the top step, and he almost went down on his knees.

He righted himself and stumbled into the lobby.

"Ziad!" Emma ran into his arms.

He held onto her and caught Ben's eye. "How is she?"

He didn't answer.

Emma released him and returned to a chair. She curled up and stared at the doors leading to the operating rooms.

Delia sat down beside her and took her hand. Faith stared at the floor.

Claire's parents hunched nearby.

Ziad immediately knelt in front of Allison. He took her hands. "Please know I am sorry."

A tear slipped down her cheek. "She loves you, you know."

"I am privileged to have her love." His heart rejoiced before fear roared onto the scene.

David briefly gripped his shoulder. "Ben said you were the first there. Thank you."

His eyes filled, and he turned away.

Ben touched his shoulder, and Ziad joined him. "C'mon. Let's go to the café. I'm sure you need something to drink."

They wound up at a table in an isolated corner.

Ben's eyes hooded. He ran his hands through his hair, mussing it even further than it already was. He groaned as he scrubbed his hands across his face. "Sorry about that, but I didn't want to upset anyone any further. What'd you find?"

"Someone carjacked her. She was driving. I do not know what the carjacker told her, but she yanked the wheel hard to the left." Ziad shuddered as the grisly accident replayed itself. "They went airborne and clipped a utility pole."

Ben flinched.

"The car flipped three or four times before hitting and rolling onto its roof."

"And the carjacker?"

"He is injured. I am not sure how badly."

Ben jumped up and paced. He muttered something, then said, "And he's here."

"Probably. And in custody. Please, my friend. Sit. How is Claire?"

Ben resumed his seat. His brow knit as he stared at his hands. They'd begun shaking, and he wrapped them around his cup. "She's critical. Pretty bad internal injuries. The doc's addressing those right now. The next twenty-four hours…" He placed his hands flat on the table and hung his head. "She broke her back, Ziad."

"What?"

"Some vertebrae midway between her shoulders and hips—don't ask me which ones—were fractured during the crash. Bone is pressing on her spinal cord, so she's paralyzed from the waist down."

Ziad's heart plummeted. "I—"

"They're going to operate once all of the swelling goes down. Right now, they're using drugs to try and reduce it. Once she wakes up from the surgery, they should be able to tell pretty quickly if she'll be able to walk."

If she woke up.

Claire.

He flinched as if branded by a hot iron. He jumped up. "I need to be alone."

"Ziad—"

"Leave me be. Please." With that, he bolted to a small courtyard off the café.

He fled to a far corner and collapsed on a bench. Resting his elbows on his knees, he gripped his hair so hard his scalp burned. In Arabic, he whispered, "Why, Allah? Why? Why punish her? What do you want with me? I know I can't have her as my wife. Don't punish her for my bad works!"

He shuddered as he took a deep breath. "What do I need to do to get her back?"

No answer came. Not that he expected it. Not after everything tonight.

Ziad began shivering since he'd left his windbreaker in the car. His temples throbbed. He straightened and rotated his neck. That helped, if only a little. How much time had passed? His watch told him almost an hour. He needed to return to Claire's family.

An idea hit him. He detoured to the hospital's gift shop. A vending machine of artificial flowers sat outside its darkened windows.

He fished a five from his wallet and inserted it.

In return, he received a bouquet of silk flowers.

Arrangement in hand, he strode to the security desk in the main lobby. "Do you perhaps have a pair of scissors I could borrow?"

The guard shot him a look. "You want what?"

"Scissors."

She handed them over.

Ziad undid the tape holding the bouquet together and extricated a red silk rose. After trimming the stem, he offered the other flowers to the guard. "For your help."

She chuckled. "Gee, thanks, Officer."

When he arrived on the second floor, no one was there. Panic threatened his calm. He dashed to the nurse's desk. "Claire Montgomery—"

"Third floor," a nurse told him. "They moved her to ICU."

He dashed up another floor.

Everyone huddled together on couches and chairs in a corner. Ziad slouched beside Ben. "How is she?"

"They got her stabilized enough to move her up here. She's heavily sedated now to keep her from moving." Ben sighed. "Delia's taking Mom and Dad home. Faith's staying with them tonight. Em and I will be here. Grace is on her way from Clemson. Allie's got sick kids at home."

"We've got you on the list to see her," Emma said. She uncurled from her tuck. "C'mon. I'll show you where she is."

After announcing them, Emma led him down a hall with sliding glass doors on either side. She pointed to one on the left. "Come out when you're ready."

With that, she left him alone.

A nurse noted Claire's vitals. With a small smile, she slipped away.

His love lay stone still on the bed. A large bandage covered the cut above her eyebrow, and bruising had swollen her eye nearly closed and left a menagerie of black and blue behind. Her dark hair fanned out on the pillow. He sifted some through his fingers. "Claire, my *habibti*, my sweetheart."

He took her hand. In Arabic, he whispered, "I love you so much. I want you to live. I want to marry you. To be with you…"

Who was he kidding? That could never happen.

He pulled over a chair and sat down. "No matter what happens, you'll always be my sweetheart. My *habibti*. No one else on this earth will have my affection. No one."

He pressed her hand against his face.

The nurse touched him on the shoulder. "Officer al-Kazim, I'm Jeanie, her nurse."

"How is she doing?"

"She's holding her own." She made some more notations on a chart. "She's here with us, even if it doesn't seem that way. We have her heavily sedated so she won't move and injure her spine further. I'm sorry, but we're getting ready to bring in a new patient. We always ask everyone to leave while we do."

He nodded. He pushed to his feet, then slid the rose between Claire's fingers. "To know I love you, *habibti*. That you will be mine always."

Ziad bent and kissed her on the forehead just above the bandage. He deeply inhaled. Even in the hospital, she hadn't lost that fresh scent of soap and shampoo.

When he returned to the lobby, he dropped onto a nearby chair. Nausea joined the headache. "Where's Emma?"

"Bathroom." Ben leaned his head against the wall with a small thump. "She's scared."

"I am as well."

Emma returned.

He closed his eyes. An hour passed with hardly a word between him and Ben. Then another.

"Ziad, hi."

Detective Rothschild stood there.

Ziad rose. "Sir, have you finished?"

"We have. Is the family here?"

"I'm family," Ben said as he did the same. "FBI Special Agent Ben Evans. Claire's brother-in-law." Emma joined him. "This is my wife Emma. The others have gone home. What do you have?"

The detective led them down the hall to a conference room.

Funny how he didn't include Ziad. No, he wasn't family.

No matter. He knew what had happened, had witnessed it firsthand.

Rather than driving to District Headquarters, he headed to his apartment. By the time he unlocked the door, his stomach fairly heaved. He bolted into the downstairs bathroom and vomited into the toilet.

Moaning, he sat back with his head resting against the wall. Maybe he could sleep on the floor that night. No. He needed a bed. Somehow, he made it upstairs.

Forget his nightly ablutions. He slumped onto the mattress and closed his eyes. The events of that night twisted in his mind.

Claire screamed as she fell.

Glass shattered.

Blood streamed down her face. "Ziad, save me!"

"*Habibti*, reach for my hand. Reach!"

Their fingertips brushed before they both tumbled into the abyss.

He came to with the soft tinkling of a stream.

Claire sat in a white caftan with Sabirah across from her. A set of scales sat between them, a C etched in it this time instead of a Z.

Ziad sat up. "Claire, no. Not you."

Sabirah began placing stones one by one onto the scales. Many on the *Hasana'at* tray, but her *Sayia'at* tray sagged.

Claire bowed her head.

"No!" Ziad shouted.

His eyes flew open, and his chest heaved. This time, cold sweat drenched his uniform. He nearly ripped it off and slammed his hand onto the ceiling fan's switch.

The air cooled his body, but his mind churned. He flopped face first onto the bed as he tried to process the dream. His heart sank. Not even Claire—who believed in Isa as her Savior—was safe from the pits of hell.

Despair crashed over him.

Oh, he wished he could take her place!

*Claire will be all right.*

He raised his head. Had someone spoken?

Would she?

He doubted. And if she died, she'd suffer eternally.

Just like him.

# 38

The next day, Ziad stared at the information in a folder Detective Rothschild had left for him. He'd worked fast in the twenty or so hours since Claire's accident. To Ziad, it read like a crime novel, including the suspect's aliases.

John Brown.

Reginald Dalton.

Eric Johnson.

Floyd Wright.

Mustapa Amin.

Huffing out a breath, Ziad focused on the window. Muted sunlight struggled to break through gray clouds blanketing the area. Finally, he returned his attention to the folder. Detective Rothschild had worked backward from the scene of the crime. Someone had seen the carjacking and called the police. In the previous two weeks, hospital employees noticed Brown lurking around the intersection where Claire traveled. Ben told the detective about Claire's car being in the shop for body work because someone had rammed it in a parking lot. Surveillance footage from the shopping center showed it happening. Clearly, Brown had planned his crime well.

"There you are." Detective Rothschild tapped on the door frame. He joined him, as did Angie Rogers. "Angie, you know Ziad, right?"

"I do." Angie's dark curls bobbed. "How's Claire?"

Ziad recalled his earlier phone call to Ben. "Holding her own. They will operate first thing in the morning. Ben took Emma home for some rest."

The detective nodded to the folder. "I guess you saw the info I left for you. What are your thoughts?"

"I have my suspicions." Ziad took a deep breath. How much should he reveal? All. It might ensure that Brown remained in jail. He nodded toward Detective Rothschild's laptop. "May I use your computer for a minute?"

"Of course." The detective shoved the laptop in his direction.

Ziad located and printed a picture of Prince Yasin. He held it up. "I believe John Brown is linked to this man."

Detective Rothschild frowned. "How so?"

"That is what we need to ascertain." Ziad rose. "I would like to be in the interrogation room with you, if you do not mind."

"We can do that. But let me take the lead, all right?"

He nodded.

"Let's go." The detective led the way down the stairs to the second floor, where the interrogation rooms were housed. They paused in an observation room.

Ziad rubbed his chin as he studied their suspect.

Brown, his right arm encased in a cast, slouched on a chair. His left wrist was manacled to a three-foot chain attached to a bar on the table. He drummed his fingers on the roughened top. Snake tattoos coated the pale skin of his bald head. More snakes wrapped their ink bodies around his arms.

"Medusa," Angie muttered.

Ziad glanced at her. "So sorry?"

"A Greek goddess who had a head full of snakes. If you looked at her without a mirror, you'd turn to stone."

Interesting.

She shifted. "Alan, I'll observe from here since this is your case."

"This way." The detective nodded to Ziad, and they slipped into the room.

Ziad leaned against the wall next to the door.

Brown, his eyes hooded like the reptiles adorning his scalp, lifted his chin. "I ain't got nothing to say."

Detective Rothschild Mirandized him again, to which Brown replied, "I told that public defender I didn't want him in here."

"Your choice." The detective folded his arms and leaned his elbows on the table. "We pulled your prints. Sent them through our databases. Seems you either have a multiple personality disorder or a number of aliases." He listed them, then added, "You've got a rap sheet that could fill this room. Assault and battery. Robbery. Attempted murder. All in the DC area. You violated parole by leaving Virginia."

Brown shrugged. The corner of his mouth curled. "I'll get out."

"Don't count on it. Not after the judge revoked your bail today. Why did you, who has committed quite a bit of crime in the DC area, come down to Charleston for a simple carjacking?"

Brown snorted. "Maybe I needed a vacation."

"We haven't talked to the vic yet. We'll do that soon—provided she survives. She dies, you go down for Murder One, understand? We know you planned this well, and that's only with a few hours of work." Detective Rothschild tapped his folder. "You loitered at the hospital a lot. We're starting to see a pattern. You were following her. Learning her routines. Who knows what we'll find later?"

"Yeah? Maybe she and I have common interests."

Detective Rothschild's eyes narrowed. "What? Like crocheting or something?"

"Look, Detective." Brown nearly spat that word. "I never knew the woman before yesterday. I saw opportunity. I took it. But you ain't gonna pin anything on me that it was planned. Just as dusk can't touch dawn, you can't touch me!"

Ziad stilled. Oh, too well did he remember that remark coming from Prince Yasin's lips over a year and a half before. He opened his folder and glanced at the prince's picture. An idea came into his head. "Detective Rothschild, may I?"

Questions formed in the detective's eyes, but he rose. "Have at it."

With that, he exchanged places with Ziad.

"Who are you?" Brown asked. "You ain't no detective."

"First responder on the scene." Ziad fished a pack of cigarettes from his windbreaker. He lit one and blew the smoke toward the overhead lights.

Brown stared at the white cylinder. His eyes began gleaming. Was he salivating?

Ziad bit back his smile. "Would you like a smoke?"

"Yeah, man."

Ziad held out the pack.

The chain clinked along the table as Brown extended his left hand and took one.

The tail of a tattoo peeked between the knuckles of his ring and pinkie fingers. Score.  Ziad offered his lighter. "Better?"

Brown sighed, slouched, and blew out a stream.

Ziad opened his folder. "I am curious. Do you know this man?"

He placed Prince Yasin's photograph on the table, then studied the suspect's face.

Brown's eyes widened. His mouth slacked.

But only for a second.

He quickly smoothed his reaction into disinterest. His feet shifted as if he wanted to run.

Ziad waited a few moments. "I see you know him."

"Maybe."

"It… struck a chord with you. I believe that is how you say it. How so?"

Silence.

"Mr. Brown, we can sit here for the rest of the night if necessary. And the next day. And the next since your bail was revoked. Far better to discuss this now. You hand us a name, perhaps there can be a deal."

More silence.

Detective Rothschild stirred. "Mr. Brown, if our vic dies, chances are really good you'll get the death penalty. He's right. You talk, we talk to the Circuit Solicitor on your behalf. Maybe she'd let you continue your 'vacation' here in Charleston rather than let the Virginia authorities extradite you."

Brown puffed away as if considering his options. A minute ticked by. Then two.

Ziad let him. The uncomfortable silence would force him to talk.

Finally, Brown cleared his throat. "I don't know his name."

Ziad frowned. "Why not?"

"Look." Brown stabbed his cigarette on the scarred table top. "You know my Islamic name is Mustapa Amin. I went to services at my mosque the day after Thanksgiving."

Ziad nodded.

"So this dude." He tapped the printout. "He approached me. He had an accent like yours, said he'd heard I could be of service to him."

"How so?"

"To do a job for him." Brown clamped his jaw shut.

"We can help you, but first, you must help us."

"Look." Brown leaned forward. "You gotta believe me when I say I'd walked away from doing stuff like that. I knew I could get caught."

Ziad frowned. "Then why risk your freedom?"

"He offered me money."

"Like how much?"

"Try two million."

Ziad stilled. A slow burning began in his gut. The nerve of Prince Yasin! He threw around millions as if they were dollar bills. Suddenly, he realized Brown had started really talking. *Focus, Ziad. Now.*

"I had visions of going down to the Caribbean. You know," Brown smiled through the blue haze of cigarette smoke, "living there. Finding me a woman. I took it."

"Did he tell you his name?"

"Nope. And he didn't ask me mine, instead said he knew I was the one because of that tattoo you've been staring at. I figured he was someone important if he had that much money to spend. And he told me I wouldn't get caught. Just as dusk can't touch dawn, I wouldn't get caught.

'Course, he hadn't counted on that woman." Brown uttered an epithet about Claire.

Ziad's jaw tightened.

"He told me to kidnap her. Take her somewhere, rape her, and drop her off on the doorstep of this guy's apartment."

Something cold unfurled inside of Ziad. "Whose apartment?"

"A guy name Ziad al-Kazim. He gave me the…" His gaze drifted to Ziad's name badge. His eyes widened. He jerked back, and the chain holding him to the table snapped taut. "Dude, I—I—I didn't know. I…"

Ziad gripped the table so hard his hands hurt. Brown said more, but he didn't hear him through the noise in his head. He tensed, coiled energy ready to strike. No, he couldn't. Far better to leave now than to be charged with assault and battery, especially in the presence of the detective. He pushed to his feet. "You will get your punishment. I suggest you give a full confession. Perhaps then the judge will have mercy upon you. And perhaps Allah will have the same on your soul."

With that, he stepped into the hallway and leaned his head against the wall with a small thump. He glanced at his hands. They trembled. He clenched them into fists and stuffed them into the pockets of his windbreaker.

Detective Rothschild joined him, and they headed toward the stairs and his office. "Good job. Angie's working on getting us some info. Let's talk before I finish debriefing Mr. Brown."

Angie breezed into his office and set her laptop down on a small table. "Ziad, our analysts tapped into ICE databases and looked up your prince."

Detective Rothschild leaned against the edge of his desk. "How so?"

"Prince Yasin usually does his playing in Las Vegas. Twice a year, he goes there and spends a couple of weeks, probably gambling and doing whatever spoiled Saudi princes do when in Sin City." She tapped some keys. "That's been going on for years. A few weeks ago, right before Thanksgiving, he flew into the country, into Dulles, matter of fact."

"Right before the raid happened," Ziad muttered. "To oversee his operation from a little closer."

"Maybe." Angie tapped some more keys. "He left the Saturday after Thanksgiving. That's a mighty fast trip for one coming from so far, and it definitely breaks his MO. I think this warrants some checking out. I'll get my agents in Virginia to head to the mosque, see if someone can't place him there, especially if they saw him chatting with John Brown."

"Angie, thanks." Detective Rothschild straightened. "I've got a bad feeling this happened in retribution for the Zap raid."

Worry unfurled in Ziad's heart. "Claire could be in grave danger."

"You'll get no argument from me." He nodded. "I'll get some guards on her. Twenty-four-seven."

Angie lowered the lid on her laptop. "In the meantime, I'm calling up Ben's replacement in Jeddah. Now we officially need the SANG file on your Zap investigation, Ziad. Maybe he can demand it from General al-Talil. I'll keep you posted."

*Good luck on that.* Ziad wondered how many threats of an international incident it would take before the general agreed.

With a wave of her hand, Angie swished from the room.

Detective Rothschild picked up his notepad. "I think we're done here. I'll wrap things up downstairs. Go ahead to the hospital. I'm sure Claire will be glad to see you."

Ziad headed to his 4Runner. As he waited for the heater to begin working, he tapped his fingers on the wheel. His phone pinged.

A text from Ben.

He snatched it up.

*We're on go.* He nearly heard his friend's voice. *Pray that by this time tomorrow, Claire will be able to move her toes.*

Ziad carefully placed the phone in the cup holder. Claire had suffered because of him. Even if he couldn't fully connect the dots, he knew his actions almost two years before had culminated in the woman he loved nearly dying. Guilt sucked away his joy. He couldn't face her, not with knowing what he did.

With a heavy heart, he turned his wheels away from the hospital and toward Mount Pleasant.

# 39

"I hate this." Late afternoon on Christmas Eve, two weeks after surgery had restored movement to her legs, Claire sat in a wheelchair as Emma pushed her from the bathroom into her room at the rehabilitation center adjoining the hospital.

"I know." Her sister touched her hair. "Just one more week. Once you walk, you'll be free and clear of this."

"And the brace," she grumbled. Thanks to a rigid brace encasing her from just beneath her arms all the way to her hips, she couldn't bend or twist her torso a bit.

"All in good time." Emma parked the chair next to the bed and set the brakes. "Okay. You ready?"

Claire took her hands. "Ready."

Emma leveraged her off the seat. Together, they shifted, and Emma eased her into a reclining position on the bed. "How's the back?"

"Not complaining at the moment." Claire grimaced. "Not like it did earlier today. Your pal Mike's a taskmaster. I didn't know simply standing without the brace could be so difficult."

Emma smiled. "Mike works everyone hard."

The door to Claire's room opened, and Ben stepped through. "Hey, beautiful ladies. Santa's here."

Claire peered at the bags. "What did you bring me?"

"Gifts." He set a shopping bag on the foot of her bed. "I'll put these under the tree here." He shoved several gaily wrapped packages beneath a small tree Claire's mother had set up the day she moved into rehab. "Which one do you want to open tonight?"

"Oooh. That one." Claire pointed to a large box.

"Here ya go." He handed it to her. A grin twitched his lips.

"Okay. Now I'm suspicious." Claire ripped away the paper. She chuckled when she pulled out a stuffed turtle. "What on earth?"

Emma eased onto the foot of the bed. "When you first got the brace, you told the doc that if you were flopped on your back, you'd kick your arms and legs like a turtle because there was no way to right yourself. I couldn't resist."

"He's cute." Claire cradled him against her chest. "Thanks, Em." She glanced at the clock. "Hadn't you better get going since you're singing?"

"We've still got a bit."

Claire swallowed hard as the Christmas music playing on the radio shifted to one about home and family. Before she realized it, she blurted, "I miss Ziad." Her gaze slid to the red silk rose Emma had placed in a bud vase and set on a shelf next to her bed. "How is he?"

"He's okay." Ben settled on a recliner. "He's working hard, really hard. His manager at the Quick Fill upped his hours to three quarters time. And he's working twenty hours as a reserve officer."

Goodness gracious. He sounded like her—before the accident.

"Was he… was he there when…" She couldn't bring herself to finish.

Emma touched her foot beneath the blanket. "He was. He was there seconds after the accident."

Very vaguely, she remembered his voice. And his hand in hers when she lay deep in sedation. Then nothing. "I wish he were here."

"You know he left that rose for you. It was in your hand when you woke up from surgery."

Bless the kindness of nurses.

Ben cleared his throat. "He passed the GED with flying colors, says he's going to look for another job after the New Year."

Claire nodded. *Ziad, I wish you were telling me these things.*

"He's going to church," Emma murmured. "When he can, that is. He and Ben are really talking."

Hope ballooned.

No. She couldn't. It'd be too easy to get shot down in that regard.

Ben rose. "Babe, I hate to say it, but we really do need to go." He kissed his sister-in-law on the hair. "Hang tough, Claire. We'll see you tomorrow."

Emma took his hand. "Mama said something about bringing breakfast to you."

"Thanks, you two. I love you both."

With a small wave, they slipped through the door.

Claire sighed. Using her control pad, she cut off all of the lights so only the Christmas lights Emma had strung above her bed and those from the tree glowed. She picked up the silk rose and rolled it between her fingers. "Lord, I know you care about us all. You are so personal and care about the smallest sparrow. Help Ziad to see that you love him so much you sent Christ to die for him just as he died for me and for Emma and for Ben and a whole bunch of others. Help him to accept Jesus as his Savior and Lord. Please!"

Tears filled her eyes. Missing Ziad's arms around her became an almost physical ache.

"And Lord, I'm feeling really down. I miss having family here. Fill me with your presence." She swallowed hard and swiped at the tear sliding down her cheek. She sniffled and set the rose back in the bud vase before picking up her Bible and reading the Christmas story.

"Silent Night" played on the radio.

Midnight flashed up.

She whispered, "Happy Birthday, Baby Jesus."

After reclining the bed enough to sleep, she closed her eyes. As she drifted away, she prayed one last time for Ziad.

Shortly after nine on Christmas Eve night, Ziad dragged himself up the stairs to his apartment. He'd worked sixteen hours straight that day, all because no one wanted to work on Christmas Eve. Yassir, his manager, had shrugged. "They want off. You're Muslim like me. Why not take advantage of the day and earn some cash?"

Except earning money had only increased his loneliness as he watched families come and go.

No matter. He was done now. He could sleep.

After his last prayers.

Slipping into a white *thobe*, he knelt and began them.

His words echoed off the high ceilings into stillness. As he sat back on his heels, he peered around him.

Stark.

Black furniture. Not a magazine dared cross the coffee table.

And no signs of a woman's touch.

No curtains, plants, or even a cheerfully colored afghan like Claire had at her house.

*It doesn't have to be that way.*

Ziad frowned. He shook his head. "I am hearing things now."

Once more, the emptiness of the room gnawed at his soul.

He pushed down his loneliness and smothered a yawn. Time to head to bed so he could be at the Quick Fill by seven.

The dream came again.

This time, Claire and Sabirah sat across from each other. The golden scales had a C carved into the base.

Then came the stones.

One on the *Hasana'at* tray.

More there.

He nodded. Claire was a good person.

But then came one for the *Sayia'at* tray. A big one tipping the whole thing.

Why?

More stones on the *Hasana'at* tray failed to move the scales.

"No, Claire, not you!"

Neither woman heard him.

The *Sayia'at tray* tipped more.

They came to the last stone.

He jumped up. "No!"

A man joined them, this one dressed in a white *thobe* and with rugged features and olive tones that seemed familiar to him. He carried something covered in velvet

*Maybe I saw him on the streets of Jeddah.*

The man knelt and set his burden near Claire's scales. He pulled away the fabric.

Ziad gasped as he noted his own scales, its *Sayia'at* tray tipping more than Claire's.

With one swoop of his hand, the man toppled hers. It melted into a glowing pile of gold.

Claire and Sabirah hugged.

The man held out his hand for one last stone.

Ziad gasped as he stared at the hole in the man's wrist. Something red tinged his side, something that looked like…

Ziad's jaw dropped. "Blood."

The man took the stone and hurled it so hard it vanished over the horizon.

He touched Claire's hair, then Sabirah's.

He raised his gaze.

Ziad froze.

His insides quaked as the man locked him in his penetrating stare.

A kind smile crossed the man's face. He knocked over Ziad's scales, which melted into its own pile of gold. The man rose and held out his hand. "Come, follow me."

Ziad's eyes flew open as he released a hard breath. He stared into nothingness. Only the blue glow of the clock on the nightstand provided any relief. He pushed himself upright and sat there on the edge of the mattress for a moment.

Restlessness swelled within him until he could do nothing but pace. He jumped up, pulled on a pair of sweatpants and a SANG sweatshirt, and dashed downstairs. He scrubbed a hand through his hair as he muttered in Arabic, "I don't understand. I just don't understand."

Suddenly, it all came flying back to him, the dream he'd had a couple of weeks before and the most recent one. Though she was a good person, Claire, standing on her own merit, would still see her bad works outweigh her good. Allah would not view her in a good light. But now? And the fate of his own scales?

Recognition dawned. "Isa."

He'd seen Isa there with his former wife and Claire.

The way he'd looked at him…

Ziad shivered. Isa had seen into the furthest, dirtiest depths of his soul, into parts even Ziad refused to acknowledge. In a flash, it came clear to him. No matter how hard he tried under his own power, his good works never outweighed his bad. Isa had come, had died for him as only the marks could attest. Isa had done all of the work.

His heart began hammering as a passage of Scripture Ben had shared with him came to mind. *I will pour out my Spirit on all people. Your sons and daughters will prophesy, your old men will dream dreams, your young men will see visions.*

He whipped around and stared at the dormant fireplace. "God, is it true? Have you been speaking to me through these dreams?"

Ziad's knees began shaking so badly he had to kneel. As if someone pushed him toward the floor, he bowed. His voice shook as he confessed in Arabic, "God, forgive me. Forgive me for my stubbornness, my pride, my bad works." He collapsed onto his side. "Now I know I'll never be able to do enough good works to get to heaven. I can't do this on my own." He swallowed hard. "I need Isa." His fingers clenched the carpet. A small sob escaped him. A single tear slid over the bridge of his nose and dripped onto his hand. "Take this burden from me."

His breath eased from ragged gasps. He lay on the carpet for a few more minutes, then turned onto his back and stared at the still ceiling fan. Was that it? All he had to do? He thought about his conversation with Ben. Yes, it was. Joy filled him, and he rested in its afterglow for a while.

Claire. Suddenly, he wanted to rush to the rehabilitation center and tell her.

That weight fell back onto his shoulders, once more nearly crushing him.

She'd nearly died because of him. He wouldn't endanger her further. Not then. Not ever.

# 40

"Officer al-Kazim, thank you for your testimony." Sonja Williams smiled at Ziad, who sat on the witness stand of a courtroom. She turned to the judge. "Your Honor, I have no further questions."

The judge nodded at Ziad. "Officer al-Kazim, I appreciate your candor. You may step down."

Ziad stood. He ignored Shannon Radcliffe, the woman who'd hit him in June, as she glared at him. He returned to the gallery and seated himself behind the prosecutor's table.

"Good job, Big Z," Eddie murmured. "She doesn't have anywhere to go now."

The judge leaned forward. "Ms. Williams, Mr. Dunforth, approach the bench, please."

As the two attorneys joined him, Ziad listened. He caught snippets of the conversation.

"It's after lunch on New Year's Eve," the judge said. "I'm... no case... need a decision... or jail time... five minutes."

"What are they discussing?" Ziad whispered as the defense attorney returned to the table to consult with his client.

Eddie rubbed his chin. "Most likely, Judge Ayers wants to adjourn."

Ziad peered at Sonja, who leaned against the edge of the witness stand. She still wore her game face.

Brow furrowed and lips pressed together, the defense attorney approached the bench. "My client has decided to plead guilty."

The judge peered over his reading glasses. "Let the guilty plea be entered. Ms. Radcliffe, please rise. I hereby revoke your license for a year and require you to attend an outpatient treatment program. Upon completion of that, you will be required to do a hundred hours of community service followed by three years' probation. A DUI during your probation will result in permanent suspension of your license."

He faced the gallery. "I now declare today's court session adjourned until after the New Year."

Gavel tapped on wood.

Ziad rose and shrugged into his jacket. He followed Eddie into the hall and outside. "My first true court case beyond traffic court."

"And you did good." Eddie clapped him on the back. "See you next year."

Suddenly uncertain, Ziad paused at the base of the courthouse's marble steps. What did he want to do? Returning to his apartment promised nothing but loneliness. His friends on the force already had plans. He could go see Claire—

He stopped the thought. He couldn't. She'd ask about his role in her predicament.

"Ziad!"

He turned and found Sonja, her wool coat billowing behind her, hustling down the steps.

She stopped. "You did a great job back there. Thanks for your work on the case."

"It was my pleasure." He drew in a breath.

She peered at him. "Okay. What's going on?"

Maybe she could help. "May I interest you in a cup of coffee?"

A smile quirked her full lips. "Sure. I've got a little bit before I have to head home to get ready for tonight. Where to?"

They wound up at the Starbucks on King Street on the second floor and seated themselves at the very table where he and Ben had met the June before.

Sonja cocked a perfectly coiffed eyebrow. "Somehow, I don't think it's standard practice for you to ask a married woman to coffee. Especially the best friend of the woman you love."

That got a smile. "I know. A year ago, this would have never happened."

"What's up?"

"How is Claire?"

Sonja added some sugar to her coffee. "She misses you tons. She hasn't said as much, but every time I've been there, I've caught her looking either at your picture or that silly silk rose you gave her. She knows you're respecting the boundaries of your faith differences."

He swallowed hard and finally asked the question that had been bothering him for more than a week. "Does she know what happened?"

"During the carjacking?" Sonja sipped her drink. "When she was well enough, Alan Rothschild debriefed her."

Guilt pressed down on him.

"She doesn't blame you. Alan called you a hero, and you are. Look." She rested her elbows on the table and leaned forward. "I was on the Zap task force, remember? I know all about these guys we took down. They're vicious. I don't know another way to say it."

He couldn't disagree. "If Isa can forgive me, why can I not forgive myself?"

"There's no way—Wait." She peered at him. "Did I hear you right?"

"I…" He tried to reach for the English words to describe that night. "I saw Isa—Jesus. I now know he died for me."

Her eyes widened, and they began sparkling with unshed tears. "Wow!"

His cheeks heated. "It is not that big of a—"

"That big of a deal?" She wiped the corner of her eye. "It is. You don't know how many have been praying for you."

"What?"

"Ben for four years. Emma ever since she met you. Claire. And our Bible study. And others."

Stunned, he stared at her.

"Have you told Ben?"

"No. I—I worried he would blame me for what happened to Claire."

"Oh, no, no, no. Please don't beat yourself up over that. Wow." She shook her head. "I can't believe you could keep something like that under your hat for so long."

"What?"

Sonja smiled. "Look. You've got to let the cat out of the bag, okay? You need to tell someone. Not just to share, but because you need people there to guide you. We call that discipling."

"Oh, I see." Just then, his phone chirped with a text message.

Sonja's did too. She grinned. "Probably Dom. Hold on."

Ziad unclipped his phone and pulled up the text message from Emma. *Claire walked. Praise God!*

"Praise God indeed," he whispered as a lump formed in his throat.

Sonja lowered her phone. "Amen. I got the same thing. Ziad, go."

"What?"

"Go see her. Now."

Something he could only describe as joy burst open within him like a budding rose. "I am leaving now."

Sonja winked. "I'll be praying for you."

Ziad almost ran to the 4Runner, sped to his apartment, and jumped under a hot shower. He shaved and emerged squeaky clean. After adding the aftershave he knew Claire liked, he slicked back his hair.

What to wear? He laughed out loud as he caught himself thinking like a woman. Hangars scraped along their rod as he thumbed through his shirts. He selected the forest green one she loved along with a pair of khakis. He strapped on his silver watch, laced up his hiking boots, and headed downstairs.

Ziad reached for the knob of the front door, then hesitated. Christmas had come and gone without a present for Claire from him. No worries there. He opened the closet door to the study and retrieved the pendant from his safe. He held it up. It caught the late afternoon light and sent sparks of color across the room.

Time to go. He dropped the pendant into his shirt pocket and grabbed his Bible.

One more stop by the florist yielded a real red rose with a short stem.

Fifteen minutes later, Ziad strode down the linoleum of the hallway at the hospital's inpatient rehabilitation center. Room 208 with a guard outside. There! The door was cracked. After nodding to the guard, he pushed it open and smiled.

Curled up in the recliner, Emma worked on some sort of needlework by the glow of a lamp. Christmas lights provided the only other light.

Reclined, Claire slept in her bed with a comforter pulled all the way to her shoulders.

Emma glanced up. Delight lit her face. She hopped up and joined him in the hall. "Ziad!"

He accepted her hug. "How is she?"

Her smile could have lit up a cave. "Doing great. She walked five yards today. Five! It took it out of her, and she popped a Vicodin when she got back. Listen. Do you mind staying with her?"

Did he mind? Not at all. "As long as you need."

"Good. I'm famished. I'll bring Ben by afterward so we can ring in the New Year together."

Ziad settled onto the recliner and watched Emma gather her items and head out. Once they were alone, he shut off the lamp. In the warm glow of the Christmas lights, he examined Claire's face. Oh, how he'd missed her! He bent and kissed her forehead. Still that lovely scent of shampoo and soap. "I am here, *habibti*. I am here."

He reached across her and replaced the silk rose in its vase on the shelf with the real one.

Claire sighed deeply but didn't open her eyes.

He retreated to the chair and picked up his Bible. No worries about dim light. Right then, he thirsted for Scripture so much he'd read in the dark if needed. He turned to the Book of John. With one eye on Claire and the other on his task, he began reading.

Claire opened her eyes. Dusk had come, and now, Christmas lights cast a warm glow throughout the room. Beneath the comforter Emma had pulled over her, she felt warm, secure. She didn't want to move, not when the pain had eased to a dull ache. Who cared? She'd crossed a huge hurdle in her journey toward home. *T-minus seven days and counting.*

To her right, a delicate page turned.

Emma must have been reading her Bible.

She glanced that way.

Ziad.

Her eyes widened. Oh, did he ever cut a fine line in those khakis and his forest green shirt with the sleeves rolled up to just below his elbows. He rested his chin on one hand as he flipped through the book on his lap. Wait. Was that… She dared to hope. Through dry lips, she whispered, "Ziad?"

He raised his head. "M'Lady Claire."

His image blurred through the sheen of her tears. "You're not a dream."

"No dream at all." He knelt and took her hand, then kissed her palm and cradled it between his. "I heard you walked today."

"I just want to go home and sleep in my own bed."

"May I?" He gestured to the mattress.

She eased over. Without releasing her, he sat on the edge.

Her gaze once more slid to the black, leather-bound book he'd placed on an end table. Golden Arabic embossed the spine. A Koran? Or… "Is that a Bible?"

His dark eyes sparkled. "It is."

She blinked several times to keep her tears in check. "When—I—I don't believe it!"

"I am sorry I did not come over here sooner." His thumb caressed her palm. "I felt so ashamed."

"Why?"

"Your accident happened because of me."

"Ziad, no."

"But the investigation—"

"Detective Rothschild told me all about it." She curled her fingers around his. "I don't blame you, okay? I survived. That's all that matters." Her heart filled. "And if it took an accident to bring you to Christ, I'd do it all over again."

He shuddered. "No. Please, do not."

His fingers skittered down her arm.

Even with a long-sleeved T-shirt on, electricity shot upward. "When did you convert?"

Slowly, Ziad shared his experience that happened so close to midnight Christmas Eve.

Her eyes widened. "I prayed for you then."

"What?"

"Well, I've been praying for you a lot. I was all alone here and reading the Christmas story in Luke. Just as midnight came up, I prayed for you. God is good. He is so good."

"I was so worried you were angry with me. When I saw Sonja earlier today, we had coffee. She told me this news was too good to keep under my bag and that I had to keep the cat in the hat."

"What?"

"I said those phrases wrong, did I not?"

Joy filled her, and she began chuckling, which turned into full-blown laughter. "Maybe let the cat out of the bag and not keep it under your hat?" She groaned as her back protested. "I've missed you."

"I have missed you too, m'Lady Claire." He reached over to the shelf where she'd kept the silk rose. With a start, she realized someone had replaced it with a real red rose. He pulled it from the vase and handed it to her. "For you, beloved."

She held it up to her nose as she deeply inhaled the scent. Delicate, sweet. Beautiful. "Oh, Ziad."

Without breaking his gaze, he brought her hand up to his lips.

Was it possible to drown in the dark chocolate color of his eyes? And the feel of his lips on her fingers. She shivered.

"I would like to… well…" He looked away, then sifted some of her hair through his fingers. "I want to marry you—if you will have me, that is. I know," his Adam's apple bobbed as he swallowed hard, "we have a lot of ugliness in our past, but I cannot deny it. I love you, and I want to be with you for the rest of my life."

Joy once again filled her heart. "I love you too." A little bit of worry wormed its way inside. "I'd like that. Really. I would."

"But you have concerns."

"I want you to grow in Christ."

"You do not want—"

"Let me finish." She put a finger across his lips.

He nodded.

"I know where we're headed. Honestly. I do. But you said it. We have some rocky spots behind us."

He nodded.

"I want to wait a while before we marry. To get to know you even better and let you grow in your faith so you can be the spiritual leader of our household you need to be. Do you see where I'm coming from?"

He tucked a strand of hair behind her ear. "I do. Surprisingly, I understand. The old me—the prideful me—would have demanded we marry now. But yes, I do. I know I need to be—how do you say it?—discipled."

"Right." Claire smiled. "And Ben's the perfect guy for that."

"Enough serious talk." He skimmed his fingers across her cheek.

Oh, that touch. She'd forgotten the way she came alive near him. She shivered.

"Are you cold?" he asked.

*Just wanting you to kiss me.* "No."

"I was leaving my apartment when I realized I had no Christmas gift for you. Then I remembered." He reached into his shirt pocket and brought out a delicate silver chain. The diamond sparkled as it dangled from his fingers. "I would be honored if you would wear this again."

*Lord, you are so good. Thank you.* She nodded because of that infernal lump in her throat.

He leaned close as he fastened the chain around her neck.

Hmmmm, mmmm. That aftershave she loved. She wrapped her arms around him. He kissed her neck, then her cheek. *Oh, my goodness.* His kiss on her lips sent everything on high alert. When he finally released her, she trembled from head to toe.

He traced her lips with his finger.

She had to catch her breath. "I've missed that."

"Me too, *habibti.*"

"*Habibti?*"

"Sweetheart in Arabic."

"Seems like I have a lot to learn as well."

"And I will be glad to teach you." He swung his feet up and leaned against the mattress next to her. "Perhaps I should have asked permission."

"No need to ask." She rested her chin against his shoulder. The better to enjoy that spicy scent of aftershave. She slid her hand into his. Oh, how she'd missed that!

Comfortable silence ticked by before she asked, "Why do you call me Lady Claire?"

He chuckled.

"C'mon, Ziad. 'Fess up."

"In May, Eddie called you that."

"Oh?" She smiled. "Why?"

"He said you had class, even when in secondary school. I would say he is right."

A blush started. "I'm flattered."

That got an easy laugh from him.

She kissed him. "How about some television? The remote's on your side."

He turned on the television and located Animal Planet. "Better?"

"Much." She tugged up the comforter so it covered them both. She rested her head against his shoulder and closed her eyes.

Unexpected joy.

And peace.

She'd treasure it as long as she could.

# 41

"Mom, I'll be fine. I promise." Two weeks after she came home, Claire walked her mother to the French doors leading to the screened-in porch.

Mama studied her. "You're sure?"

"Ziad's going to be here at five. I promise I'll be okay for an hour."

"You know I can stay."

Claire relished the thought of a break from having someone in her house twenty-four hours a day. "My back's feeling good right now. I won't head upstairs. I'm just going to putter around the kitchen."

Finally, Mama nodded. She hugged her daughter in the same delicate way she had ever since Claire had come home from the rehab center. "You know I'm a phone call away."

"I know. Be gone with you." Claire watched as Mama headed down the steps. A cold, damp wind hit her in the face. What a nasty, gray January day. She shivered and shut the doors.

A gloom filled the family room even though it was just past four. Time for some light. And drawing. The doc had said to let pain be her guide and reduce activity rather than pop more painkillers. Oh, and go up and down stairs only once a day. At least she could lie on the soft couch now rather than the hard floor.

She grinned. Ziad had moved her coffee table into the den, and they'd both lain on the floor in front of the family room's fireplace. Her evening conversation, she'd joked, since he'd kept her company after his shifts as a reserve officer or at the Quick Fill. They'd talked about everything, from the Bible to teaching her Arabic. Then one evening, he'd put glow-in-the-dark stars on the ceiling in different constellations.

Also, she could sit up for longer periods of time. It certainly beat drawing while lying down or standing. With a steaming mug of tea in her hand, she stepped into her art studio and switched on the light over her drawing table. There, in a folder, sat her next project.

The emblem for Saudi Arabia. A palm tree and crossed daggers. Seemingly easy. Except she planned to cross-stitch it, which required first drawing it to scale on grid paper before even conceiving of stitching it. But a perfect wedding present. She began the drawing.

Half an hour later, her back twinged. Time to stop. She examined her work. Progress. She could probably begin stitching it before she returned to her job. Claire flipped the drawing over and stashed the printout in a folder.

Ziad would be here in fifteen minutes. She smiled. Maybe he'd rub her back. Over the past week, he'd taken to gently massaging the area where she'd broken her vertebrae. *Oh, my…* Even thinking about it, her cheeks warmed. A match made in all parts of their lives. She'd not deny that. And boy, during those fourteen weeks they they'd been apart, she'd missed his touch.

Mama had run the dishwasher after lunch, and she lowered the door to put them away. Just as she opened a cabinet door, the phone rang.

Ziad.

She smiled. "Hey!"

"How are you doing?"

"I'm fine. Just hurting a little. Mama left about forty-five minutes ago."

"I am on my way over and should be there in about five minutes or so. I am sorry I am late. I did not leave work until 4:15."

"No worries. Ben and Emma will be here by five as well. I'll see you soon."

"I love you, *habibti.*"

"I love you too." She smiled softly and hung up before resuming her work. Ouch! She flinched as her back barked at her. Time for a painkiller. Someone else could finish emptying the dishwasher. Now where was the orange juice? She opened the refrigerator and studied the inside. There. She pulled out the carton.

A rush of cold air greeted her. Ziad must have been closer than he'd realized. She picked up her glass. She began turning as she said, "You were—"

Pain across her cheek stole her words. She staggered as the glass flew out of her hand and shattered on the tile.

She whirled.

A masked man pushed her—hard.

She slammed into the cabinets. Her head cracked against the wood. Stars sparked in her vision. With a moan, she collapsed into darkness.

In the misty, chilly dusk, Ziad turned left into Claire's neighborhood. Time to spend the evening with her, something he'd begun treasuring. *God, thank you for her. Thank you for bringing us back together.* Now, they planned on spending that Friday evening together with Ben and Emma.

He slowed as he turned onto her street. Good. The squad car Detective Rothschild had promised remained at its post. Come Monday, the detective had told him, he'd pull the guards back since most likely, any threat of danger had dissipated.

Just as he pulled into the carport under the house, his phone rang. He grinned when he noted the caller. "Ben, my brother."

"How's it going?"

"I just arrived at Claire's house." Ziad slid from the SUV and winced as a cold wind bit into him. He shivered. "How are you?"

"Good. We're on our way right now." Subdued, as if maybe Ben had just argued with his wife. "We had our first appointment with our Realtor."

Ah, the source of why his friend sounded so quiet. "Did you have fun?"

"I'm not ready."

Ziad laughed. "It is like having children, my brother. Are you ever ready?" Before shutting the back door, he grabbed the three bags of groceries he'd collected for that evening's meal. "You will have to tell us about it tonight. So, are you ready to stand outside with me while we grill the meat?"

Ben groaned. "Maybe if Claire has some golf umbrellas we could use."

Ziad chuckled as he climbed the steps. "At least the ladies will be dry." He turned the knob. "Strange. It is unlocked."

"Maybe she forgot to lock it," Ben said.

"Possible." Warmth spilled over him as he stepped through the doors. "Claire?"

"She around?" Ben asked.

"I do not know." He frowned and surveyed the interior. Lights on in the studio but no Claire. The same with the den. He called, "Claire? *Habibti?*"

No answer.

"Should she be downstairs?" Ben again.

"The doctor told her to go upstairs and downstairs once a day. You know how stubborn she can be." Ziad set his burdens on the island and turned to open the refrigerator.

Something scraped on the tile beneath his foot.

He glanced down.

Broken glass, a puddle of orange juice. "That is strange."

"What?"

"Orange juice and a glass on the floor. And…" he knelt in front of one of the floor-to-ceiling cabinets and stared at some dark splatters. He touched them. His fingers came away red. "Ben, something is wrong. There is blood on the floor."

"On my way."

"Be care—"

"Get your hands up," someone ordered.

Ziad froze. Glancing over his shoulder, he noticed a shadowy form standing between the kitchen and the dining room.

"Ziad?" Ben asked, his voice now deadly calm.

Ziad slowly straightened. Grabbing the bag of vegetables, he hurled it at his ambusher's face.

His attacker cried out.

Ziad bolted toward the studio.

Someone slammed into him!

He tumbled to the floor and rolled toward the darkened foyer.

His phone went flying.

He kicked out.

Another yelp.

Ziad staggered toward the kitchen. He made it to the counter and reached for a knife from the lineup on their magnetic strip.

A gun muzzle rammed into his head. A third attacker growled, "I suggest you get onto your knees with your hands on your head."

No choice now. Ziad obeyed.

"Get him up!" the man snapped. A strange accent, one he didn't recognize.

His first attacker grabbed him by the jacket and hauled him upright.

Ziad kicked the man with the gun.

The Beretta flipped away to parts unknown.

He slammed the heel of his hiking boot onto his captor's foot.

The man's arch snapped, and he howled.

Suddenly free, Ziad dove after the gun.

There!

In front of the fireplace.

He lunged for it.

Something slammed into his head and shattered. Wet spilled across him. Claire's vase of flowers.

With a moan, Ziad collapsed onto the floor. *Ben, we need you. Come quickly!*

"Get him upstairs!"

Burning spread on his skull as one of his attackers grabbed his hair. Ziad stumbled upright to relieve the pain.

Something ran down his scalp. Water? Blood? Who knew?

Once upstairs, his captor jerked him left and shoved him through the double doors leading to the master suite.

Claire.

She huddled on the bed, blood on her chin from a split lip. Her face pinched in pain.

His heart dropped. No escape for either of them.

His captor kicked him behind the knees.

Ziad collapsed in front of the chair next to the French doors leading to the terrace.

A push between the shoulder blades sent him to the floor.

"Stay down!"

Another kick to his side sent a wave of agony along his spine.

He groaned.

Someone yanked him upright and twisted his arm behind him. He moaned as his shoulder burned.

The man with the Beretta paced in front of him. In that same strange accent, he said, "We must finish this. Now. Go get the knife."

His pal with the broken foot gaped. "What?"

"Get the knife, you idiot!"

Oh, no. Flashes of Sabirah's lifeless body formed. They weren't...

He stared at the monkey lamp he'd given Claire last spring. Someone had already unplugged it so it could be smashed on his head. Add that knife and gun, and...

No. He couldn't let that happen.

The leader sneered at Ziad. "We have orders that you are to watch, Ziad al-Kazim."

He thrashed, then cried out as another yank on his arm sent more ripples of pain down his spine.

The remaining man twisted Claire's arm behind her back.

She moaned, then whimpered.

# Exiled Heart

As his guard forced his arm up, Ziad sank to his knees. *Ben, come. Come fast!*

As Ben and Emma headed onto Ravenel Bridge toward Mount Pleasant after their first meeting on the peninsula with their Realtor, Ben flipped the radio to a country station. The windshield wipers of his Subaru Forester beat a monotonous rhythm against the rain that had moved in from the Atlantic.

Beside him, Emma remained uncharacteristically quiet.

He took her hand. "You feeling okay?"

"Yeah. I'm fine."

"What's up?"

Only the strains of "Alright" by Darius Rucker filled the air. Her grip tightened on his fingers. "We need to tell Ziad."

She didn't have to say anything else. He knew. "I've been praying about that a lot lately—ever since he converted."

"We shouldn't hold what we know back."

"I agree. You want me to call him?"

"Now?" she gasped. "Ben, we need—"

"No, to see if they need anything from the store."

She nodded and tucked further into her parka.

Ben dialed his friend's number.

"Ben, my brother."

Oh, what a joy to be called brother by him! "How's it going?"

"I just arrived at Claire's house. How are you?"

"Good. We're on our way right now." Ben cut a glance at Emma, who stared out the window. "We had our first appointment with our Realtor."

"Fun?"

"I'm not ready."

Ziad laughed. "It is like having children, my brother. Are you ever ready?" A car door shut. "You will have to tell us about it tonight. So, are you ready to stand outside with me while we grill the meat?"

Ben groaned. "Maybe if Claire has some golf umbrellas we could use."

Footsteps echoed on Ziad's side. "At least the ladies will be dry." A pause. "Strange. It's unlocked."

Ben frowned. "Maybe she forgot to lock it."

"Possible. Claire?"

"She around?" Ben asked.

"I do not know." More silence, as if Ziad searched for his love. "Claire? *Habibti?*"

No answer.

Ben's hand tightened on the phone. "Should she be downstairs?"

"The doctor told her to go upstairs and downstairs once a day. You know how stubborn she can be." Something clunked. Ziad drew in a sharp breath. "That is strange."

"What?"

"Orange juice and a glass on the floor. And," worry energized his voice, "Ben, something is wrong. There is blood on the floor."

Ben stomped on the accelerator. "On my way."

Emma glanced at him.

"Be care—"

"Get your hands up," someone ordered.

Oh, no. Immediately, Ben's mind switched into work mode. Quietly, over the pounding of his heart, he asked, "Ziad?"

The phone clattered as if falling somewhere. Then it cut off.

"Ben?" Emma whispered.

With one eye on the road, he punched in Angie's number. "Angie, we've got a situation at Claire's house." He rattled off the address. "I need an assist."

"Don't do anything until—"

"No time. Someone's there. A hit squad or what, I don't know. I'm going in." He guided them onto the exit for Coleman Boulevard, then blew through a red light. He cut around a couple of other cars. He hung a hard right into Claire's neighborhood and cut off the headlights as they skidded to a stop.

Ben cut the dome light off and hopped out before scurrying to the police cruiser parked in front of her house. He pulled out his key chain and turned on the Maglite hanging from it.

Two cops inside.

Both with holes in their heads.

He muttered under his breath and returned to the Forester.

Emma stood in the open passenger door. "Ben, you should wait for backup."

"No time for that."

"What?"

His heart pounded. "Get into the car and drive as far away from here as you can."

"Ben—"

"Claire and Ziad are in trouble. That's all I know."

"But—"

"Go!"

She shot him a white-hot look before running around to the driver's side.

He darted toward the house and stuffed his silenced phone into the inner pocket of his leather jacket before drawing his Glock.

Crouching, he dashed between Claire's Mustang and Ziad's 4Runner. Gun at ready, he stole upward.

No sound downstairs.

He peeked around the corner.

Someone limped into the dimly lit room and turned toward the kitchen. He reached for a knife on the magnetic strip.

Not on his watch.

Ben slipped inside. Softly, he called, "Hey, dude, drop it."

The man froze.

"Now." Ben nodded downward. "Put it down." He came closer. "On your knees. Hands on your head."

The knife clattered to the island, and the man sank to his knees. Ben wasted no time. He closed the gap and clonked him on the head. Once he cuffed him, he grabbed an apple from the fruit bowl on the counter and stuffed it in the man's mouth to keep him from crying out. "Here. You need some fiber."

He needed to tie his legs. Opening drawers, he came to a junk drawer. He pawed around until he located a charger cord. The box cutters he found would also come in handy.

Once he tied the man's ankles, he ran onto the porch.

*Forgive me, Claire.* He cut through the screen and hopped onto the railing before grabbing the supports of the terrace's railing. For a moment, he dangled two stories above the ground. If he fell…

He shut down that part of his brain. With superhuman effort, he swung his legs upward and snagged the cross piece. He pulled himself to a crouch on top of the railing, then dropped silently onto the terrace.

Claire screamed!

Without a second thought, Ben bolted forward.

Ziad's chest heaved. His head swam, and his shoulder burned. He tried to rise.

A jerk on his arm kept him on his knees.

His soft breaths sounded like roaring gasps in his head.

Ba-bump, ba-bump, ba-bump. The guard he'd injured hobbled down the stairs.

Then came a small noise from the other side of the French doors.

Had anyone else heard it?

Maybe Ben?

Ziad's heart thumped.

The leader must had heard something as well. He stepped to the door. Gun held at ready, he peered into the hall, then turned. "We do this now. Get her ready!"

Claire's guard slapped her hard across the face.

She cried out and tumbled onto the mattress next to the nightstand with the monkey lamp.

"Claire! Fight!" Ziad shouted. He somehow got a foot underneath himself so he took a knee.

# Exiled Heart

She struggled. The guard yanked her toward him.

Claire grabbed the lamp. She smashed it into his face.

He shrieked and tumbled backward off the bed.

She cried out as she brandished it in front of her.

The leader ripped it from her hands and threw it against the wall, where it shattered.

He pushed her onto the mattress.

She moaned and writhed against his hand around her throat.

A switchblade flashed in the light.

"No!" Ziad cried.

Glass shattered! Gunshots blasted as Ben blew through the doors.

Ziad's guard loosened his hold and reached for his gun.

Ziad ripped his arm free as he shot upright and knocked the man's arm upward.

The shot went wild.

He hurled a fist in Ziad's direction.

Ziad groaned as it connected with his cheek.

His guard leapt toward Claire.

Ben flew through the air.

He slammed into him.

The guard flipped and landed a hard right on Ben's nose.

Ben yelped and tumbled to the floor.

Ziad jumped the guard.

He looped his arm around his neck.

They fell backward onto the carpet, and he didn't loosen his hold.

The man thrashed.

Then nothing. He sagged to the floor.

Ziad shoved him aside and rolled to his feet. "I need something to tie him."

"Scarves." Claire crawled to her dresser and yanked several from her top drawer.

His guard began stirring.

Ziad tied him up.

Ben checked the leader's pulse. "This guy's gone." Then he collapsed against the bed. His nose sat at an odd angle. "Team Evans and al-Kazim does it again."

Ziad eased down beside him. "Your case, your glory."

Claire crawled over to him, and she laid her head on his leg.

Ben managed a grin. "No. *Our* case. *Our* glory." He picked up a piece of the shattered lamp. "O monkey lamp, you died saving our lives."

That got a weak laugh from Ziad.

Footsteps thundered on the stairs, and three SWAT team members burst into the room, followed by Angie. She stopped short and stared. "Looks like we arrived too late to the party."

Ben groaned as he touched his nose. "Uh, yeah. That was one party. Right, Ziad?"

Ziad's cheek had begun throbbing in time with his shoulder. "Of course. One big party."

He stroked Claire's hair.

She mouthed, "Thank you."

He took her hand.

Safe. Finally.

# 42

Five days later, Ziad sat on the couch in the suite above David and Allison's garage. He rubbed Claire's feet. "*Habibti*, you are doing well? Your back is not hurting? Or your lip?"

"I'm fair to middlin'." Her smile twisted thanks to the stitches running from her lip down her chin. "I hate this brace."

"The doc said your back will be okay, right?" Emma asked from where she curled up in a recliner.

"Fortunately. I'm glad they kept me in the hospital for observation. I really thought I'd re-injured it. I guess they did too if they put me back into the brace."

"Hey, Ziad, can you massage my feet like that?" Ben grinned from where he sat at the kitchen table and finished off the last slice of pizza. He rubbed Sherlock with his toes.

Ziad scowled. "I think not."

"How's your shoulder?" Emma asked.

He rotated it and winced. "It will heal with some physical therapy. I believe Claire's house is more of a mess than we are."

"Speak for yourself." Ben touched the tape holding his broken nose in place. "I look like I got into a bar fight."

Claire winked. "More for juicy office gossip." She cocked her head. "My carjacker's in jail, along with the remnants of the death squad. What about Prince Yasin?"

Ziad's mood darkened slightly. "He cannot be extradited for his crime."

"If there is any." Ben shook his head. "No definitive link means no convincing a US attorney."

She took Ziad's hand. "At least Mama and Daddy are putting me up until the cops are finished with the house and the cleaners and carpeting guys can get in there. And the porch guy. I thought the insurance guy would freak when he saw the scene."

Ben shut the lid to the pizza box. "Hey, Em, at least you don't have war wounds."

"I've got them mentally." She scowled at him. "You scared me to death, Ben Evans. I could have lost husband and sister—"

She clapped her hand over her mouth as her gaze shot to Ziad.

Ben rose and eased onto the floor so he leaned against the recliner. "That reminds me of something."

Claire struggled to sit up until Ziad helped her right herself. "What?"

Ben's gaze switched to Ziad. "Actually, it's about you. Or Sabirah."

Ziad frowned. "I am not understanding."

"I know." Ben looked down.

Emma touched him on the hair.

He raised his gaze. "Sabirah knew Christ."

Ziad stared. "How could she? She was Muslim the day she died."

"No, she wasn't." That came from Emma.

His heart sped up. "Please do not joke about this."

"No joke, Ziad." Ben's face remained solemn. "I promise on that one."

Emma rose and knelt before him. "One day last fall, I took a half day off from work and was at home. Sabirah invited me over for lunch in the *majlis hareem*. Do you remember?"

Ziad sifted through the memories, now so far and distant, like another lifetime ago. "No, I do not."

"I think you were hard at work on a case." Emma looked down, then met his gaze. "She'd begun having these dreams. She described them to me and wanted me to interpret them for her."

"What about?" He choked out those words.

"She sat across from a man with a set of scales between them."

Ziad reeled as if she'd slapped him. He jumped up and began pacing from one side of the room to the other. He raked his hands through his hair as the seven dreams he'd had over an almost two-year period flashed across his mind. He whipped around. "The man was Isa, yes?"

Emma stayed where she was. "At first, I didn't know. I told her I wasn't sure what it meant. But then, after I did some more reading on Islam while on vacation, I discovered the importance of scales and works. And in March of 2009, she told me that she'd seen nail scars and a wound on his side. I—I knew then. She'd seen Jesus."

A buzzing began in his head. Would he faint? He couldn't. He braced his hands on the kitchen counter and hung his head.

From far away came Emma's voice again. "I couldn't not tell her. I knew she'd seen Jesus, especially after she described him and the way he knocked over the scales."

He began shaking his head. Hope blossomed.

Someone touched his shoulder. "I promise I never meant to turn her from Islam. That was never my intention." Her blue eyes wide and pleading, Emma stood next to him. "I told her to weigh the consequences. She knew them. She was so scared to tell you. Terrified."

He straightened.

Emma backed away and returned to the recliner as if seeking protection. "That Friday afternoon when I visited her in the *majlis hareem* again right after your last bust. The day before she died." She lowered her head. "That was when she told me about the dream and that she trusted Christ as her Savior. She confessed she didn't have the courage to tell you. She was so afraid you would view it as a breach of trust."

Ziad wobbled to the couch. He sank onto the cushions as he tried to envision what would have happened. "I would have—how do you say it?—had it out with her. Perhaps disowned her. Cast her out, even."

"She's with Jesus," Ben murmured. He put his hand on his shoulder.

Claire wrapped her arms around him.

He leaned into her. "My boys. Muhammad Amir. Tariq. Basil. Little Khalid."

A trembling started deep within Ziad.

"When one comes to Christ, the household is blessed." Ben again.

His shoulders began quaking. "I—I do not see how."

Claire laid her chin on his shoulder. "Maybe you'll see them again. Sabirah accepted the good news. She may have been afraid to tell you, but perhaps she told them. And your parents as well."

A lump built in his throat.

Emma took his hands. She now knelt in front of him, and he met her gaze once more. Tears spilled down her cheeks. "Ziad, you'll see Sabirah again. Rest assured, you will."

The lump became painful. He didn't want to cry. Not in front of them.

A sob escaped him. And another. He leaned forward, put his head in his hands, and wept.

"We'll see you tomorrow." Ben's voice barely reached him. His friend touched his shoulder, then was gone.

Claire stayed near.

Watson whined and rested his chin on Ziad's knee.

His grief ebbed. Something filled him. Something strange. Something wonderful that he hadn't felt in a long time.

Peace. More than that.

Hope. And joy.

"Claire?"

She pulled back. Strands of dark hair stuck to the tear stains on her cheeks. A watery smile touched her lips. "I love you, my dear man."

He scrubbed his hands across his face and rested his elbows on his knees. "I… do not believe it."

"God blesses those who love him. Sabirah loved him. I know you lost her." She looked away and bit her lip. "I know you miss her. But what an incredible miracle—you coming to know him."

So much to take in. His own agony at losing Sabirah. Claire's at losing her Jackson.

And God for sending his own Son to the cross.

He gazed at the woman he loved. Something swirled in the jade green depths of her eyes.

She needed his reassurance.

He cupped her face in his hands and wiped at her tears. "I love you. Yes, I miss Sabirah just as you miss Jackson." He took a deep breath and fully steadied. "God brought us together for a reason. Through great pain has come great joy. Full circle, perhaps. Always remember that."

He helped her to her feet, then gathered her into his arms as that peace once more blanketed him.

An hour later, Ziad sat on the edge of the bed and watched as Claire slipped away into sleep. He kissed her on the forehead and murmured, "*Ana behibek, habibti.*" *I love you, sweetheart.*

He rose.

That night, he'd decided to sleep on the couch of the suite. Even though ten had passed, he found himself too stirred up, too awake to consider stretching out for rest.

He scratched Sherlock and Watson on their heads, then headed down the steps after ensuring he'd thrown the deadbolt.

A chilly breeze blew in from the creek.

No matter. His leather jacket protected him as he made his way through the live oaks. He stepped onto the dock. Images from when he'd discovered it ten months before crossed his mind.

That March, he'd thought he'd never fit in, never be happy again.

Now, he stood there brimming with joy.

In Arabic, he murmured, "I miss you, Sabirah. You and the boys and Mama and Papa. But I know you wouldn't want me to grieve for the rest of my life. Claire… You would like her just as much as you liked Emma. And yes, we will see each other one day."

The dry reeds in the marsh just below the dock rustled.

Somewhere in the distance, an owl hooted.

Peace settled over him.

Sabirah had heard him.

He smiled softly. Then he turned and headed toward the suite.

# Acknowledgements

Novels take the work of many hands to complete, and Exiled Heart was no exception. As I mentioned in the preface, I took an earlier work and updated it to reflect many things because I simply couldn't let Ziad's story go. I do want to thank my husband, Steve, for his encouragement related to redoing it.

I also want to thank my beta-reader team for this novel. Vicky Priest supplied good knowledge related to life in Saudi Arabia. Pam Vashaw offered good insight, as did Jenny Johnson. And of course, Steve provided his own keen engineer's eye to detail.

Finally, I want to thank my friends in the North Carolina Chapter of the American Christian Fiction Writers as well as other friends and family who have encouraged me throughout the years. Your support has meant the world to me.

www.ingramcontent.com/pod-product-compliance
Lightning Source LLC
Chambersburg PA
CBHW070356260626
47161CB00001B/161